Dear Reader,

Welcome to the wonderful world of *Scarlet*!

This month sees the launch of our exciting new romance series, offering you books I'm sure you'll enjoy reading as much as I've enjoyed selecting them for you. From June 1996 onwards, become a *Scarlet* woman and look out for four brand-new titles every month, written exclusively for you by specially selected authors we know you'll love.

At the back of this book you'll find a questionnaire and we'd be really happy if you'd complete and return it to us as soon as possible. Returning your questionnaire will earn you a surprise gift.

Scarlet is *your* list and we want *your* views on whether or not you like our selection of titles. So . . . feel free to drop me a line at any time, as I'd be delighted to hear from you.

Till next month,
Best wishes,

Sally Cooper

SALLY COOPER,
Editor-in-Chief – *Scarlet*

NATALIE FOX

DANGEROUS LADIES

Enquiries to:
Robinson Publishing Ltd
7 Kensington Church Court
London W8 4SP

First published in the UK by Scarlet, 1996

A copy of the British Library Cataloguing in
Publication data is available from the British Library

ISBN 1-85487-474-8

Printed and bound in the EC

10 9 8 7 6 5 4 3 2 1

CHAPTER 1

At seven thirty precisely Abigail Lambert began to seriously panic. Another half an hour and he would be here and *she* didn't want to be!

A thousand eastern curses on her sister for landing her in this hole; having to entertain an absolute stranger because Jess, no doubt through her own absentmindedness and inefficiency, had missed her Concorde flight back from New York and wouldn't be there to do the job of wining and dining William Webber herself.

Much as she adored her whacky sister, Abby could happily smother her with a wet pillow for this. She didn't know this guy, she didn't particularly want to know him and she certainly didn't want to entertain him when she should be calmly getting herself prepared for her Paris interview tomorrow, to say nothing of getting to the airport on time herself tonight!

Check-in at Heathrow airport was only two hours away and she should arrive in Paris in time for a good eight hours' sleep before her crack-of-dawn interview with the travel company that would hopefully ship her off to the Maldives on one of their luxury liners as chief entertainments person at the first opportune moment. No interview, no job. It was vital that she made it.

'Damn it!' Abby breathed impatiently as she gazed down at the table she had carefully set for two. The Waterford crystal sparkled, the silver cutlery shone and the white, gold–edged Royal Doulton china looked impressive, but the barley twist stemmed red candles in verdigris holders were a definite no–no. Did she have time to nip up to Kensington High Street to buy new candles? White or even natural beeswax would be far more tasteful. She glanced at her watch again. It was late–night shopping and she could whizz up there in a flash and be back in time.

Suddenly and sensibly she took a huge breath to calm herself. This was ridiculous, getting herself into a state over a couple of ill-matching candles. With any luck, he would not turn up. Jess's scheme of things rarely worked anyway and her sisters' friends and associates were as unreliable as Jess was. Nevertheless, the red candles were an appalling eyesore set amongst the crystal and silver on the cream damask tablecloth.

Having slung a cardigan over her best silk dress she was at the front door of the second floor flat in a prestigious block just off the high street when the phone rang, stopping her in her tracks. Ah, this could be the software tycoon friend of Jess's, ringing to cancel. Then she could breath again. Flinging off her cardigan she dived on the kitchen phone.

'Oh, Jess, what now?' she breathed with disappointment. 'It's all in hand. I was just nipping out for candles. I could only find the red ones left over from Christmas and I – '

Abby held the receiver away from her ear as a stream of expletives were hurled across the Atlantic.

'OK, OK! I've got the message. Leave the candles out. I just wanted to do it right for you, Jess. Where are you anyway?'

Earlier Jess had called from the airport in a panic when she had realized she'd missed the flight and wouldn't be home in time to entertain W. Webber and, hopefully, sell her software package to him. Her call then had been rushed and not at all forthcoming in exactly what was expected of her sister tonight. Just entertain him and give him the package was all she had hurriedly instructed. Hopefully, now Jess would fill her in in more detail.

'Holed up at the exclusive Corona State Hotel actually,' Jess laughed. 'You know senators stay here. It's gorgeous, dripping with chandeliers and French antiques. BA have been awfully decent about the whole mix up. I pleaded insanity, of course, said I found these time zones so confusing and that's why I'd missed the flight. You know it's just after lunchtime here . . .' She laughed again.

3

'I don't know whether I'm coming or going. Anyway, they are trying to get me on another flight back but unfortunately it won't be till tomorrow. So I've booked myself in here.'

'And I sincerely hope BA are footing the bill,' Abby ventured frostily and hopefully crossing her fingers around the phone.

'Nah, they're not that obliging. I'll have to square up on my Amex at some later date. Worth it though, the place is heaving with influential people. Who knows who I might bump into?'

Abby stifled a groan of despair and yanked open the fridge with her free hand to haul out a half-full bottle of Chardonnay. She could see the last Amex statement clearly in her mind's eye. Jess owed them thousands; but there again she might have missed a 0 or three and it was millions. Nothing would surprise her where her sister was concerned.

'Listen, Jess,' Abby started, shakily trying to pour herself a drink with one hand. Oh boy, did she need it. 'Considering our pretty grim financial status at the moment do you think it wise to be staying in a luxury hotel when a bench seat at JFK would suffice while you're waiting? Which brings me to Concorde itself. What's wrong with economy, for heaven's sake?'

'That's always been your trouble, Abby. You don't think big enough. You have to speculate to accumulate these days. You brush shoulders with the right people in places that the right people frequent. You get a better class of people on Concorde. The conference I came over for was a washout, the conference hotel dismal and I found out that anyone who was anyone wasn't staying there anyway. They are here at Corona State. So seeing as I missed the flight back I thought I'd switch hotels. I'm networking here as well as enjoying myself so don't get the hump over a paltry few thousand quid.'

Abby gulped her wine. What was the point of arguing with her? Jess had a will of her own. Trouble was, things just didn't work out for Jess most of the time. She flitted from one scheme to another, usually failing dismally but always picking herself up and dusting herself down, and with enviable optimism setting forth intrepidly once again, to yet more calamity. Their dire financial state had forced Abby onto the cruise ships, away from her acting career which, to be honest, hadn't exactly taken off and shot her to international stardom as planned. The cruise ships paid well and she could at least save money and bail them both out when things were going badly for Jess. It was what a younger, more sensible, down-to-earth, sister was for, Abby supposed.

'What about the caterers?' Jess was asking.

Abby gazed across the gleaming chrome kitchen and rested her eyes on the food the *Bon Appetit* outside caterers had just delivered. It had also cost an arm and a leg they could ill afford. The money their father had left them last year was nearly all gone, mostly on Jess's harebrained schemes, like this last trip to the States.

'Don't panic. It's all here. Poached salmon in lime sauce for starters, lamb noisettes that I can just pop in the micro, new potatoes tossed in some sort of creamy mayonnaise, Pavlova and – '

'Sounds safe enough,' Jess breathed in relief. 'Hope the guy isn't a vegetarian, or has an allergy to cream or something.'

Abby's insides twisted. 'Just a minute,' she wailed. 'Don't you know if he's a veggie or not?'

Jess's laughter down the line had Abby gripping her wine glass nervously.

'Darling, I've never met the guy. How an earth would I know his eating habits?'

'What!' Abby screamed, her head reeling. She thought she was going to faint. 'You've never met him?' she repeated idiotically. Strewth, she'd just presumed that Jess must know him well, certainly well enough to be entertaining him with a candlelit supper. 'You . . . you mean I'm supposed to entertain this guy, sell him your madcap idea for a new computer game, of which I know nothing incidentally, and even *you* have never met him before! Oh, Jess, you bitch! How can you do this to me? I'm alone here. He could be a raving maniac for all we know. I can't do it, Jess, I positively can't and besides – ' She was about to remind her sister of her Paris interview as further cause for the case against what her sister was expecting of her but she hadn't a chance with Jess in full tidal flow.

6

'Of course you can do it, darling,' she insisted down the phone. 'You *have* to do it for me, Abby. It's for us. My idea is worth a fortune. If I can get in with Webber's software company I'll be made. I need to sell that idea. If I don't, that luxury flat of ours you are standing in at this very minute will have to go – '

'Oh, Jessica!' Abby gasped, 'That's cruel! You're blackmailing me.'

Their adored father had spent his last ailing years in this lovely Victorian flat. The two sisters had nursed him through it all. He had leased it in better times for them all, before their mother had left him for a younger man. Over the years he had taught them not to be bitter over their mother's defection, taught them that sometimes marriages just didn't work out no matter how hard you tried. They had adored him for his strength, for his love and for just about everything he'd ever taught them. Abby wouldn't be able to bear it if this lovely home wasn't waiting for her when she came back from her trips. The place was so full of happy memories.

Abby raised her eyes heavenwards as she listened to Jess, twisting her heartstrings by bringing their late father into this. How he would expect her to do it for her sister, that's what families were for, and so on, and so on . . .

'All right, point taken,' Abby interrupted at last, thinking that this phone call was going to cost an arm and a leg too, and if Jess wasn't careful they would both be limbless before this William Webber ever arrived. 'Just one thing before you go, Jess. Trivial as this may sound to you,' she said rather tartly, 'how did all this come about? I mean, I'm dying of curiosity here, but how did you get this guy to agree to dining with you tonight if you've never met him before?'

'You don't want to know,' Jess sighed.

'I do, actually,' Abby insisted, nerve endings pulsing now because when Jess tried to evade an issue it was for sure for a reason. 'Give or else,' she threatened, trying to sound authoritative about it all but knowing she wasn't as skilled as her sister at it.

A deep sigh preceded Jess's words, which immediately put Abby on red alert and she gripped the receiver even tighter.

'I faxed him, actually. And before you start, Abby, let me explain about William Webber. He's the best, his software company is the biggest in the world and they just don't come any bigger. With a guy like that you can't go through the normal channels of communication, writing for an interview etc. You . . . well . . . you have to come on strong . . .'

Come on strong? Abby's heart was doing a million revs to the second now. 'Go on,' she croaked.

'Well, like I said I faxed him, briefly outlined my brilliant new idea, you know, just to whet his appetite and then . . . well, then I suggested we

8

discuss it further over a delicious meal and a crate of Dom Perignon, at . . . at the flat.'

'Oh, my God,' Abby breathed. The nerve of her sister.

'It worked, Abby,' Jess insisted. 'because he faxed me right back, said he thought the idea interesting, thank you very much and dinner would be quite charming. Abby, are you still there?'

'Just picking myself up from the floor,' Abby mumbled weakly. Oh, her sister was off the wall and this William Webber equally so. They would all end up in the funny farm before this was over.

'I've shocked you,' Jess said in a soft voice.

'No more than usual, Jess,' Abby bleated back.

'Sorry, darling, landing you in all this but honestly, Abby, I didn't think it was going to work out like this, you having to entertain him for me. I'll make it up to you, I promise. You know how I hate you travelling away so much. If this comes off you can say bye-bye to the cruise ships. It's for us, Abby. All you have to do is wine him and dine him, make my apologies for not being there myself and give him the package. It's in Daddy's study. Remember how it was his favourite retreat when he was so weak with illness and couldn't get out of the flat?'

Abby remembered and her heart riled at the emotional blackmail bit Jess was throwing at her. Jess and their father used to spend hours on the computers together. It was the one good thing Jess

9

had inherited from him, his wizardry at all things computerized. She'd inherited his eccentricity, too which most times was an endearing quality but at other times like now, very frustrating.

'So knock him dead for me, Abby,' Jess persuaded. 'He adores beautiful women, good food and luxury surroundings. I have absolute faith in you to pull this off for me, darling. You can do it,' she enthused.

'And how do you know so much about him if you've never met him?' Abby asked weakly, her head still reeling from all this.

'Gossip columns in the tabloids, of course,' Jess laughed. 'Playboy tycoons are always in the news. Listen, darling, I must go, I'm desperate for a frothy coffee. I'll probably have to pledge my kidneys for one here,' she chortled. 'Love you to bits, sweetie. Good luck.'

Abby squeezed shut her green eyes in ever more sufferance as she put down the receiver. And she was halfway to the funny farm already because here she was, dressed to kill in her best skimpy nut brown silk dress which complemented her nut brown hair which was far from skimpy. It tumbled around her golden brown shoulders in thick glossy waves that moved when she did. All this effort and expense for a man neither of them knew and a playboy tycoon to boot! The world *had* gone mad lately.

Ten minutes to go.

He wouldn't come, Abby thought with mixed

emotions. The man wouldn't come and she'd have to bin all this delicious food because she was in such a state of nerves she'd never be able to make any inroads into it on her own. She'd never eat again after tonight. But life had it's compensations, she told herself sensibly. If he didn't turn up she'd be off the hook, rotten for Jess though –

The security door buzzer went and Abby let out three small theatrical yelps of panic quickly followed by a deep shudder of dread. Damn him! The madman was here! He had actually turned up!

Plunging a finger into the creamy centre of the pink Pavlova dessert she scooped out a dollop of cream and crushed strawberries and sucked on it deeply, needing a sugar fix to get her to the door to answer the buzzer.

Oh, Lord, what had she got herself into, what had Jess landed her in? Quickly she consoled herself with the thought that to get to be a highly successful software tycoon you probably had to be a bit long in the tooth and she always got on well with older people. The senior citizens loved her on the cruise ships. Then she remembered what Jess had said: he adored beautiful women, well so had Aristotle Onassis! And anyway she wasn't beautiful . . . pretty perhaps . . . *Oh, God, she didn't want to be here*.

'William Webber for Jessica Lambert,' the resonant voice said efficiently after Abby had rather tremulously pressed the buzzer.

Abby drew on her acting abilities, not that she

11

had ever hit the big time on stage. One of life's ever-hopefuls she had travelled unsuccessfully from one audition to the next and finally opted for the varied, and much more secure, career of entertainments person on any liner she could charm her way onto. Cruise ships' entertainment swung from comedy sketches to poetry readings to bingo calling. Abby had done it all. It kept her and Jess out of a cardboard box on the streets, if nothing else.

'Come right up, Mr Webber,' she enthused brightly. 'Second floor – three A. The one with the potted . . . palm,' she added to herself as the intercom went dead.

Well, he was either hot footing up the road now or hot footing himself into the lift. Abby rather wished he was half way across Kensington Gardens by now.

She took a last look at herself in the hall mirror. She'd done her best and if it wasn't good enough, tough.

'I'll kill you for this,' she hissed at a framed photo of herself and Jess on the hall table below the mirror. She scooped it up and glared at her gorgeous zany sister. They were alike in a way though Jess's hair was redder and wilder. Only two years between them yet Jess *could* look far more sophisticated and mature than Abby ever could. She supposed Jess, in spite of the wild hair which very much reflected her wild nature, was more classically attractive – *when* she tried. Abby could see her now, hair scooped up on the top of her head, wearing her red Donna Karan suit which had cost another fortune they could ill afford, swanning confidently around that posh hotel in New York and turning every male head in sight.

'And you are going in the drawer, sis, because I don't want you glaring at me all night while I make an utter fool of myself.' She quickly planted a kiss on her sister's grinning face and shoved the picture in the hall table drawer, out of sight and out of mind.

Abby nervously opened the door on the second buzz and the first sight that hit her was a huge bouquet of sweetly scented white lilies and . . . and head-sized sunflowers, yellow and drenched with pollen. She started to sneeze immediately and by the time the paroxysm was over she was acutely aware of a very formal black uniform behind the rather humorous combination of flowers.

Her green eyes drifted up from highly polished black shoes to narrow knife edged trousers which seemed to highlight thigh muscles that might have looked more at home jogging on Malibu beach. The tailored jacket was resplendent with shiny brass buttons and there were braided epaulettes on the shoulders with a pair of white kid gloves rolled under one of them and . . . and was that a peaked cap tucked under the flower bearer's arm?

Abby was overwhelmingly disappointed for her sister and at the same time overwhelmingly relieved for herself. She wouldn't have to endure an awkward dinner with a stranger after all. The Webber tycoon had sent his apologies for not coming with the *chauffeur*!

A pair of remarkably penetrating blue eyes suddenly appeared around the side of the flowers and Abby nearly took a step back with surprise. This chauffeur was something else. Gorgeous with a capital G. He was incredibly good looking, with jet black hair, crinkle curly, that looked badly in need of a trim around the collar region. He had a marvellous even tan that said it all about his employer, William Webber. The computer tycoon obviously travelled a lot and gave his trusty chauffeur plenty of time off to cultivate that stunning bronze countenance.

After having visually absorbed the flowers, uniform, the eyes, the hair, Abby gave almost lurid attention to the features of the man. They were good and strong with a generous mouth that was set in more of a grim line than a grin. It seemed the giver of the flowers had more of a sense of humour than the deliverer.

Then suddenly a restrained smile teetered on the well-defined lips, showing the most perfect of teeth and forming tantalizing looking creases at the corners of the mouth. If Abby was at all that way inclined she would have swooned on the spot, but Abby wasn't the fainting kind. She'd met enough equally gorgeous men on her world travels and come to the conclusion that drop-dead, good-looking men usually lacked what lesser looking males possessed in abundance, heart. Nevertheless she gave him a smile in return. It seemed to relax him a little.

'Jessica Lambert? Mr Webber sends his profuse apologies for not being able to make your dinner date. A last-minute appointment came up, unfortunately,' he added, his rakish blue eyes giving her the once over of approval and obviously deciding on behalf of his boss that the last-minute appointment was indeed unfortunate.

Abby gave a small forgiving shrug of her narrow shoulders.

'Oh, well, that's life,' she stated obliquely.

And it was. Poor Jess, thwarted yet again. She imagined how Jess might feel if she were standing here as she should be. Desolate and disappointed that her little plan hadn't come off and she wasn't going to make the sale of the century and live in extravagant luxury for ever more. Abby, along with disappointment for Jess, couldn't help but be mightily relieved that she had escaped an ordeal that wasn't of her own making.

There was an uncomfortable silence then as if neither knew what to follow that with. Abby eyed the flowers, and oh, dear, was that a box of Bendick's exclusive chocolates peeking out from behind the bouquet? At least the Webber man knew how to make his amends.

The chauffeur's eyes dropped to the flowers and he shifted his feet uncomfortably as Abby stepped back from the doorway.

'You'd better bring those in. It was very kind of Mr Webber to make his apologies in such a generous way.'

She stepped further back as he came forward to pass her in the wide hallway and, without thinking, she emitted a small sigh of relief. He suddenly turned and looked at her.

'You are obviously very disappointed Mr Webber couldn't make it,' he said.

He'd misinterpreted the sigh. As she closed the door behind him she wondered how much this chauffeur knew; that Jess and William Webber had never actually met and all this had come about because her sister had rather zanily asked him to dinner to discuss something that, in Abby's thinking, he could probably live without. Surely the man had a whole team of staff working on new ideas for such a vast empire? Try telling Jess that though.

'Well, yes, I am rather,' she admitted and then it occurred to her that it was all a bit off really. Surely the tycoon could have phoned earlier? After all he had accepted the invitation in the first place, raised Jess's hopes and then, at the last minute, sent his chauffeur, bearing gifts and spouting apologies. Had he chickened out? Had he never intended coming in the first place? Abby supposed she'd never know. Oh, dear, she was being picky and unreasonable. He needn't have sent anyone or anything at all to apologize for not turning up.

'Come through to the kitchen,' she added. 'I'll put those flowers in water.'

He followed her in easy strides and shed the flowers and the chocolates into a heap on the stainless steel draining board, as though he was glad to be rid of them and not very happy at being asked to do William Webber's dirty work for him. In the manoeuvre, his peaked hat dropped to the floor as if he had forgotten that it was tucked under his arm and, as he bent to retrieve it, his epaulette caught and ripped on the nob of one of the kitchen drawers. The gloves tucked under it landed with a soft thud in the upturned peaked hat.

It was all Abby could do not to burst out laughing. 'Not your day is it?' she grinned.

To her complete surprise he didn't respond the way she thought he might, with a helpless grin in return. He frowned and glowered at her and looked so completely put out that Abby got the fleeting impression he hadn't had this job very long and wouldn't keep it very long if he continued in his clumsy ways. He picked the lot up with a grunt and slammed them impatiently into a pile on a nearby kitchen stool.

On impulse Abby offered him a cup of coffee, more to help cover his embarrassment than anything else. 'It's the least I can offer for your trouble. I'm sure delivering gifts to thwarted women isn't your usual occupation.'

'And what exactly do you mean by that?' he snapped.

In surprise at his abrupt tone Abby turned from filling the kettle. She shrugged. My, this man was touchy. 'I only meant that chauffeurs usually chauffeur, don't they? You know, sit behind the wheel and vroom, vroom, vroom round town to their heart's content all day.'

He stared at her so hard she thought perhaps a sense of humour wasn't in his make-up at all. Abby grinned in another attempt to put him at his ease, because she was beginning to see the problem here. He was new to the job, uncertain where she, or rather Jess, stood in the pecking order of his boss's life.

'You haven't been doing it long, have you? Chauffeuring that is?' she amended, her eyes sparkling with humour.

'Long enough,' he responded, relaxing slightly, leaning back against the work surface to watch her warming the coffee pot under the hot tap.

''Spect you get to meet interesting people,' Abby put forward, striving for a bit of easy conversation. He was hard-going and not making it easy for either of them.

'Very interesting,' he mused, gazing around the kitchen. His eyes settled on the chrome work surface on the other side of the kitchen which was laden with the food Abby should now have been feeding to his boss, William Webber.

'Did you do all that for Mr Webber?' he asked faintly.

Abby glanced at him and a frown was once more

18

marring his good looks. Again Abby wondered how much he knew and again decided nothing. Tycoons didn't tell their chauffeurs details of their private, or even working lives come to that, they just expected to be driven around with silent obedience.

'Yes. I went to a lot of trouble too,' she told him reproachfully. And why not let him believe she had slaved all day to prepare that little lot? Let him go back and tell his boss just what he had missed.

'It looks delicious. You are a very talented cook, Miss Lambert,' he complimented.

It was on the tip of Abby's tongue to now deny that she had made the food herself and to deny that she was the Miss Lambert he thought she was. He'd taken her for Jessica, the one his boss was supposed to be dining with. A sudden thought came to her, something small to cling onto and perhaps help Jess a bit. Why not let him believe it all? He would go back and report that Miss Lambert was rather a nice person, she was caringly brewing coffee for him after all, and that she had prepared a delicious meal and was very disappointed that his boss couldn't make it. And William Webber just might feel awfully sorry for putting her to so much trouble for nothing and contact Jess for a further meeting. There wouldn't be any confusion over identity because they had never met before and the chauffeur probably wouldn't be involved in the next meeting and thus give the game away.

Abby was rather proud of herself for her quick thinking Yes, all might not be lost this evening. It would soften the blow to Jess that he hadn't turned up if there was a possibility that he might at another time. So, it was swiftly decided. Tonight she was Jessica Lambert, not Abby. She was an actress, wasn't she?

'Seems a great pity to waste it all.' Abby heard through the mist of the deception plans forming in her head.

'I beg your pardon?' she said rather dazedly. She widened her eyes at the tall, dark chauffeur with the fascinating blue eyes.

'The food. It seems a great pity to waste it all,' he repeated.

Suddenly Abby got the message. He was smiling now, a lovely, lovely smile that caused her heart to squeeze. Abby decided he was very nice and probably very hungry. Poor love, at this time of the day he should be at home for his evening meal with his . . .

'Yes, it would be a terrible waste,' she said with a smile. 'I couldn't possibly eat it all on my own. Would you like to join me? Or perhaps your wife has your dinner waiting?'

He laughed. 'That wasn't a very subtle way of trying to find out if I'm married or not.'

Abby smiled with him, suddenly feeling the kitchen getting very warm which it wasn't. It was her inner self getting all hot and bothered. He really was a very attractive man and she found herself waiting with baited breath for him to enlarge on his marital status – or not. He put her out of her misery immediately as he spoke the words, 'No, Miss Lambert, I don't have a wife waiting or a live-in lover either.'

She was aware that *he* was aware she had been holding her breath waiting for his reply and thought it quite amusing. She turned away from him for fear of blushing like some drippy teenager.

'Well, that's all right then,' she breathed. Taking courage she turned back to him with a smile, abandoning the making of the coffee with a small shrug of her shoulders. The champagne was chilling in the fridge, so why not share it with him? Ah, but he was a driver, she reminded herself.

'Would you still like the coffee?' she asked. 'I mean, I have champagne but well, you have to drive and . . .'

'Yes, coffee would be better. Is there anything I can do? Open the wine for *you*, perhaps?'

The thought of quaffing Jess's champagne suddenly held great appeal. She'd earned it surely? But what an earth was she doing tonight? Offering William Webber's gorgeous unmarried chauffeur the meal she should have been eating with the computer tycoon himself? She silently cursed Jess all over again because she was getting far too deep into everything.

'It's in the fridge,' she told him, scrabbling in a kitchen drawer for a clean tea towel in case the wine spurted everywhere. When she went to hand it to him he wasn't there. He'd wandered across to the elegant dining-room which was off the kitchen, divided by floor-to-ceiling antique pine folding doors which were pulled back. He stood with his back to her and was obviously looking at the beautifully set dining table that she had taken great pains over for Jess's sake.

'You really have gone to great lengths for Mr Webber tonight,' he said darkly, as he turned back to her.

There was something in his tone Abby took exception to. It was almost as if he believed this was all to do with seduction and nothing to do with business. And then Abby realized that this man probably didn't know anything and was assuming that this *was* all about seduction. What had Jess said about WW – he adored beautiful women, good food, luxury surroundings? Well, Abby wasn't exactly beautiful, but she wasn't an old bag lady either and the food was good and the flat was luxurious, depending on your own personal standards. If Jess knew all that from the tabloids, his employee, this chauffeur, would definitely know it and was probably used to ferrying him from one exotic assignation to another.

And because she had anticipated his thoughts and felt quite miserable about them she suggested in a tight voice that they dine in the kitchen, buffet style.

'Why, is the dining-room not good enough for a

chauffeur?' he suggested frostily as he came to a stop in front of her, so close she could smell the quality of the good wool of his uniform and something else, the lemony balm of his aftershave which reminded her of luxury cruises in far away places. It jolted her into thinking that she was pretty dumb for asking this man to join her to eat when she could have been rid of him by now and winding herself down in preparation for her Paris interview first thing in the morning. Trouble was he was rather nice.

Abby lifted her chin defensively. She had made a mistake in suggesting the kitchen to eat in. For all she knew this man had hit hard times and chauffering wasn't his usual occupation. She hadn't meant to offend him.

'I'm sorry if that came out sounding class conscious, sorry you took it that way too, because it suggests you might have a chip on your shoulder as well as a torn epaulette.' She grinned to try and soften the suggestion and to try and warm him because he was still looking decidedly frosty. 'Look, no harm meant. I was thinking of myself actually. I have a flight to Paris to catch later and by the time we've eaten in the dining-room . . . well, what I mean is, it will be quicker and less trouble for me to clear away a couple of plates if we eat here in the kitchen, than to have to wash the crystal and strip the table of the linen and – '

'All right, all right. I get the message,' he interrupted, strong hands held up as a defence against her ramblings. 'Look, if it will suit you better, I'll just take the package you were going to offer my boss and get out of your way.'

'Th . . . the package?' Abby stuttered inanely.

He looked at her with those incredible penetrating blue eyes that seemed to bore into her very soul. 'You came up with an idea for a new computer game,' he prompted as if she had forgotten the purpose of the evening. 'You offered to discuss it with Mr Webber tonight over dinner and what was it, a crate of Dom Perignon?'

Abby nearly choked. *He knew.*

'Mr Webber instructed me to pick up the package anyway. He'll take a look at it and give you his opinion and if it's worth anything he'll be in touch. Yes, that was about all. Nothing else. Now if you *are* in a rush, I'll just take the package and be on my way.'

Abby allowed a warm flood of relief to ripple through her. At least this man now knew she wasn't one of WW's seductresses and for some peculiar reason Abby was glad of that. And perhaps Jess was still in with a chance if WW had instructed his chauffeur to pick up Jess's package. It was all a relief when she came to think of it. She hadn't been comfortable with the thought of entertaining a stranger and she knew nothing about computers or software and *that* would have come across to Webber as very unprofessional. She could have done Jess's chances more harm than good. Yes, this was turning out much better than she hoped. She was off the hook and the relief prompted her next words.

'No, I'm not in that much of a mad rush,' she found herself saying.

She smiled at him again and thought perhaps she might be overdoing the *bonhomie* a bit but, apart from the euphoria of relief, she found she couldn't help it with him. Apart from the few hiccups when she had thought she had offended him and he had thought her a seductress . . . well, what were a few misunderstandings? He really was very nice and very attractive and she hadn't dined with a man for yonks, had always been too busy cruising around the world for relationships. Whoa, she warned herself, this wasn't about to blossom into a relationship. Just take it for what it was, go with the flow as Jess would say. Yes, she would enjoy his company for a while.

'Please join me to eat,' she said sincerely. 'It would be a terrible shame to bin this lot and besides you never get much to eat on the Paris flights and I'm really quite hungry.' She was famished as it happened. Now that the pressure was off, her stomach was completely relaxed and raring to go.

He melted. Abby could see it in the sudden softness of his eyes and the way his mouth creased at the corners when he smiled.

'That would be very nice, Jessica,' he said warmly.

And Abby's heart did that funny little throb

again but it was tempered by a sudden dragging feeling that she wished she hadn't fooled him into thinking she was anyone other than Abby Lambert.

'I'm Oliver by the way. Pleased to meet you.' He held out a hand to her and Abby took it and it was as warm and strong as she had suspected it might be. She got a huge rush of adrenaline at the brief contact and as their eyes locked she suspected that he had experienced a rush of something too.

And it was then that Abby thought she might be in a bigger mess than she could have anticipated at the onset of this rather peculiar evening. She was old enough and wise enough to recognize the wow factor when it happened. It just had. But, for some peculiar reason, it was prickles of wariness that trickled her spine, instead of the delicious sensation of sexual chemistry. Why, she didn't know. Maybe it had to do with the fact that he thought her to be someone else and she hadn't put him right. But allegiance to her sister had crept in here somewhere. She had further cause to put a thousand curses on her sister tonight.

If only . . .

CHAPTER 2

It was with deep regret Abby decided not to come clean with Oliver for the moment and tell him who she really was. If . . . if later, when she could see how they were getting on . . . Oh, she didn't know, she really didn't.

She forced a smile and hoped it came across as genuine. 'Look, why don't you go and sit down and relax while I serve up the food?'

He smiled. 'Just one thing: could I possibly impose on your goodwill further and use the telephone?'

Abby's heart blipped this time. Phone the wife or the live-in lover he had denied, to say he was held up? Oh, Abigail Lambert, you of little faith.

'Feel free,' she told him. 'There's a phone in the hall, one in the sitting room and . . .' she nodded to the one on the kitchen wall, instantly hating herself for the thought that the one he chose would indicate that he might not have been wholly truthful in denying a partner. A depressing thought that came from past experience with

27

other tasty looking men she had met, the ones with no heart. And besides, why hadn't this gorgeous looking Oliver been snapped up? He must be about thirty five and was very eligible . . . Her heart plunged as he opted for the hall phone.

Abby busied herself with the food and at the same time strained her ears and said a silent prayer of thanks to herself for putting away that photo of her and Jess. He would have been gazing at it as he made his call and that would have complicated matters now that he thought she was her sister. 'And who is this gorgeous bird with you in the photo?' he would query with interest because all men were interested in Jess. And Abby would gulp and make some inane remark like, 'Oh, my great Aunt Florence. She lives in Katmandu, with her cats.'

Abby giggled to herself and concentrated on the calls he was making. There were two, she heard the dialling blips on the wall phone. The first call he made he didn't speak, the second call he made he spoke in such low tones it was impossible to make any assumption from the conversation. She hated herself even more for straining her ears so hard.

Five minutes later, when Oliver had discarded his uniform jacket and they were sitting at the kitchen table devouring the delicious salmon, he asked about Paris. And because of the champagne giving her added nerve and because she still didn't know him well enough to give him the benefit of the doubt over a partner in his life, Abby decided to take things one step further for Jess.

'Well, your boss isn't the only fish in the sea,' she started. 'I believe in speculating to accumulate,' she went on, parroting her sister. 'I have a Paris company interested in my proposition and I'm flying over this evening to see them first thing in the morning. It's a very good idea, you see. Very innovative and original.'

Abby felt quite safe in saying all this to Oliver. He was the chauffeur and probably knew as much about computer software as she did. If all this got back to WW though it would help Jess, perhaps prompt him to contact her sooner rather than later, if he thought another company was interested in her work. She imagined, where sales and marketing were concerned, it was all very competitive and cut throat.

'So, you are offering the same idea to all and sundry at the same time?' Oliver asked.

Abby gulped. Was that good or bad? Was that acceptable in the cut-throat world of computer software? Was there a code of honour in such dealings? She really didn't know. She shifted uncomfortably, because maybe all she said would get back to his boss and whether it would do Jess harm or good she really didn't know. Don't push your luck, Abby warned herself.

'More salmon?' she diverted.

She wasn't comfortable with this deception, not one bit. It was going way over her head. Back to the basics of life, such as food, was a far safer bet.

He accepted with a gracious nod of his head and then immediately said. 'What about New York? Have you put your idea across the Atlantic too?'

Crumbs, she could be digging her's and Jess's graves here. She studied her dinner plate intently. But why New York? Why on earth should he mention New York when she had only just been talking to her sister in New York? What a strange coincidence. She quickly put her suspicious thoughts to bed for the night. Only this very afternoon she had been putting together a murder mystery idea for the cruise ships and maybe she was still hungup on it. It was going to be a bit like an Agatha Christie party plan. A plan to get the cruisers involved in a mock mystery and find out who dunnit. Clues and red herrings and all things to be resolved in the end. She rather liked the idea of the Captain instead of the traditional butler having dunnit. That would go down well and . . .

'I mentioned New York, Jessica, didn't you hear me? And yes, I would like some more salmon.'

Abby's head came up with a jerk. She stared warily at him across the table, feeling a rush of colour creeping up her throat. Her voice came through a spurt of nervous giggling.

'I'm so sorry,' she laughed. 'I was miles away,' was the only feeble excuse she could come up with for not paying attention. 'I get carried away with my work at times, you know, thinking up new ideas.' No lies there.

He smiled back at her as she dished up the last of

the salmon for him. He held his plate out and she steadied it, brushing her fingers against his in the transaction. She felt the spark again, didn't like herself very much again for not admitting she wasn't Jess.

'Yes, I've heard you computer whizzes spend much of your time on another planet. Doesn't do much for my ego though, Jessica.' His eyes locked into hers and held them and Abby knew what he meant. He was obviously aware of his own good looks and his facility in holding women's attention unreservedly

'I'm sorry. It's not very gracious of me to be thinking about my work, when I asked you to stay for dinner. Let's start again, shall we?' Yes, good thinking Abby. A way out of this mess she was digging herself ever deeper into. 'Let's not talk about what I should have been discussing with your boss tonight. Have you seen the latest Tarantino film? So fascinating.'

And before she knew it Abby was beginning to unwind and enjoy herself. Later she made coffee and they made deep inroads into the Pavlova and Abby's heart skipped several vital heartbeats when he leaned across the table to delicately wipe a smidgeon of cream from the corner of her mouth with a very sensual fingertip.

'Thanks,' she laughed nervously. 'I'm a shockingly messy eater.'

'Well it wouldn't do for you to arrive in Paris with egg on your face, would it?'

Somehow the mocking tone and the substitute egg for cream grated on her nerve endings for a swift second and then the feeling was gone as she realized that she had been enjoying herself so much she had paid little heed to time. Crumbs, if she didn't get her skates on she'd not get to the airport on time.

Oliver was very quick to pick up on the sudden change of expression on her face and her quick glance at the clock on the cooker.

'Talking of Paris, I fear I might have taken up your precious packing time. I do apologize. Let me clear up for you while you get ready.' He stood up and started clearing the plates.

'Oh, no. I couldn't possibly let you do that,' Abby said quickly, getting to her feet and then blushing furiously because it had come out sounding as if she didn't want him around any longer. It was the very opposite but she was flummoxed for a few seconds by her own thoughts. The awful thing was she didn't want him to walk out of her life quite so abruptly.

They stared at each other across the table. A moment in time, when time itself seemed to stand still. The evening was over and both recognized it and regretted it. Abby's palms felt deliciously damp as she curled her napkin in her fists. What now? Would he ask to see her again? If he did, she would come clean with him right away, tell him who she was and apologize profusely for passing herself off as her sister. And she would think up a quick excuse for her behaviour too, though one didn't come instantly to mind, just in case he took offence. If he really liked her he would take it on that powerful chin though; forgive her completely, even have a good laugh over it as he took her into his arms and his lips came down on hers . . .

She felt quite faint with the explicitness of her fantasy. Oliver was still watching her as if he was struggling with some sort of decision himself. Or was it the end before it had begun? She waited expectantly for him to make the first move, to smile or say something. He did.

He broke the sizzling eye contact and lowered those fascinating eyes to the dishes again. 'I insist. It's the least I can do in exchange for a very interesting and entertaining evening.'

Was that it? Abby puzzled, disappointment wrapping its arms around her instead of his. Had she been mistaken in thinking that he was as equally smitten with her as she was with him. Smitten? Gosh, was that what had happened to her tonight. Cupid's darts and all that jazz?

'All right then,' she found herself saying weakly. 'If you insist.'

'Oh, I do, Jessica, I do,' he said mysteriously.

'Right then,' she murmured, backing away from the table. 'Right then. I'll get my stuff together.'

In the sanctity of her bedroom, she closed the door and leaned back on it. Phew, her heart was racing like a steam engine. Oliver was easily the most gorgeous man she had ever met but . . . but what? He disturbed her, in a funny way, like . . . well like what? She couldn't define it. Perhaps she felt this way because she was living a deception this night. The whole business of taking her sister's place and then Oliver turning up instead of his boss had all been too much for her. If only she had come clean with him earlier and told him exactly who she really was. Perhaps then she wouldn't feel so shaky about him.

Hurriedly Abby slid out of her silk dress and into blue jeans and a comfortable dark blue silk shirt for travelling. The interview in the morning took precedence over any other thoughts for the moment. She was cutting it fine as it was. She wanted that job, needed it badly if they were to get their finances sorted. This idea of Jess's obviously wasn't going to come to anything with William Webber, but maybe it would, she thought optimistically. She musn't forget to give Oliver the package before they parted. Perhaps then he might say, this can't be goodbye, I couldn't bear life without the thought of seeing you again!

'I'm ready,' she trilled as she stepped into the kitchen. Her overnight bag thumped to the tiled floor as she took in the grim state of the kitchen. That was men for you. He'd stacked the dishes in the sink but totally disregarded the waiting dishwasher. And she didn't have time to do the dishes before she left. Oh, well, Jess could tackle that when she got back; serve her sister right for putting her through this tonight.

And he had gone and hadn't said goodbye!

Abby was offended as well as hugely disappointed. Then she spotted Oliver's uniform jacket still draped over the back of the chair across the kitchen. Though her heart raced with excited relief that he hadn't left without saying goodbye, a frown nevertheless creased her brow. Where was he?

She went out into the hall. He might be using the bathroom. She chastised herself for not offering it earlier. He must have had to go looking for it.

Abby froze on the threshold of her father's book-lined study. Jess's computer was up, the silvery screen the only light in the heavily curtained room, shining as it was on the front of the chauffeur who had his back to the door. He was so intent on the screen he wasn't aware she was standing in the doorway behind him.

'Just what do you think you are doing?' she asked coldly.

Jess's computer was sacrosanct. Abby had been warned off it from the day it had been delivered and set up. It was the very latest equipment that had cost another arm and a leg. Not that Abby was remotely interested in something she had no head for, but nevertheless it had been drummed into her never, but never to interfere with it.

Oliver didn't even turn to acknowledge her panic-driven question. Suddenly the screen blipped and a game of Solitaire came up on the screen.

'These things fascinate me,' he said coolly. 'Amazing technology. Seventy years ago, Logie Baird introduced the first television and look how far we have come since.' He turned then and looked at her, his eyes narrowed. 'Incredible what people can do on these things now, isn't it?'

Why did Abby get the impression that the question came delivered with an arrow sharpened to a fine point? It seemed to pierce right through her, loaded with some paralysing poison that seemed to momentarily rob her of the power of speech. Was she overreacting because she had been so shocked that he had had the audacity to come into this room and tinker with Jess's precious computer? The hell she was, she thought, getting her equilibrium back. He shouldn't have done that. Nosed around the apartment and taken such a liberty in her father's study.

'Yes, quite incredible,' she acknowledged coolly, trying to forget her disquiet and yet with her mind racing ahead. This pushy chauffeur knew something she didn't, how to operate the wretched thing. She would have to ask him to switch it off for her because she didn't know how. If she made a vain attempt at it he would know she wasn't the whizz on the computer he thought her to be and possibly report back to his boss. Oh, how easily an innocent deception could evolve into a nightmare. Quite incredible!

'Look, could you put that thing . . . it off please. I really am in a terrible rush now.' She took great pains to look at her watch. Oh, Lord, she would have to run all the way to the underground. Would a taxi to the airport be quicker? Could she afford it, more to the point?

'Haven't you forgotten something?' he asked.

She'd watch him close down the computer, using that silly mouse thing Jess waxed lyrical over, and now he had come across the study and was standing in front of her, very close.

His nearness totally overwhelmed her. 'Passport, overnight bag, cuddly toy,' she tried to joke in a scratchy voice. 'No, I haven't forgotten anything.'

His eyes seemed to pierce right through her. In the dim light from the hallway she thought them now more grey than blue, not quite so fascinating.

'The package, Jessica. The point of all this. The all-important package.'

Her heart leaped all over the place. Jess's package, of course.

'Oh, yes.' She lunged into the room for it, brushing past him. 'Here, it's here . . . somewhere.' She found it, pushing aside papers and computer magazines to get to it. She handed it to him with a smile.

He took it but didn't offer her a smile in return which intrigued Abby. He turned the package over in his hands and then seemed satisfied and looked at her and said something which intrigued her even more.

'And of course you have a copy of this to take to Paris with you.'

A question or a statement she wasn't sure but what she was sure of was that Oliver took his chauffeuring duties far more seriously than just vroom, vrooming his boss around town.

'Why should that concern you?' she asked him racking her brain to recall just what she had said to him over dinner about her Paris trip. Oh, yes, all that speculating to accumulate, the bit she had copped out from, not knowing if she had been saying the right thing or not for Jess.

He looked angry for a fleeting second and Abby's brow came down in consternation. He noticed and smiled quickly.

'Didn't want you to forget anything,' he shrugged. 'I've already taken up too much of your time this evening.'

His smile widened and then he did something that completely threw Abby. His free hand snaked around her waist and he pulled her close to him. His voice was as smooth and as dusky as hot chocolate as he breathed, 'I've had a wonderful evening, Jessica. I don't want it to end so suddenly and because I want to put off our goodbyes, may I offer to drive you to the airport?'

Before she had a chance to answer or even give it serious thought her earlier fantasy became reality. His mouth came down on hers so softly and dreamily she felt her legs go weak at the knees. He held her strongly and yet incredibly sensitively, as if he didn't want to frighten her off with the unexpectedness of an intimate kiss so soon after meeting. Abby lost herself in the magic of the kiss. It was so divine she never wanted it to end. Her head emptied of everything but the sweet pressure on her soft lips.

And then it was over and he had stepped back slightly and she gazed up at him, soft and melting inside.

'I'll take that as a yes, then,' he smiled confidently down at her.

'Yes,' she murmured softly, recovered now. Already that feeling of disquiet was filtering from her thinking. He had been bored waiting for her to get ready. Just went looking for the bathroom and found himself in the study and couldn't resist a game of Solitaire on the screen. She'd made too much of it. He'd done no harm and he obviously knew what he was doing . . .

'Let's go then.'

And in a dream Abby went back to the kitchen to pick up her overnight bag and Oliver followed and gathered up his jacket and his cap and gloves. And still in a daze, she stared at the black stretch limousine parked outside the block of apartments. Somehow the gleaming dream machine jolted her out of her own bemused state, brought on by that delicious kiss and all it promised.

She looked at him with deep consternation puckering her brow. 'I know I'm late and all that and the lift to the airport would be most welcome but . . . but are you sure this is all right?' she asked with concern. 'I mean your boss might not like it,

you know, driving me to the airport in his . . . this
. . . this thing.'

'Oh, I'm sure he wouldn't mind, not under the
circumstances,' he told her.

'Circumstances?'

He grinned. 'Get in,' he ordered gently and
opened the rear passenger door for her.

'Oh, I'd much rather sit in the front with . . .
with you,' she murmured, hoping he didn't think
she was making a pass at him. The real purpose
behind the suggestion was powered by the
thought that she had never been driven in a car
such as this before, and by a uniformed chauffeur,
too. The thought was very unsettling, she might
get to like it!

She noticed his fingers tightening on the door
handle. 'Sorry, Jessica, insurance and all that.'

'Oh, yes, of course,' she burbled and then
grinned. 'I'll look on it as a treat then,' she
laughed and rather clumsily got into the back
seat and sank down into gorgeous springy leather
and let out a deep sigh of content. This was the life
all right. Jess would warm to this lifestyle, too.
Pity she wasn't here but if she were Abby wouldn't
be and wouldn't have met WW's gorgeous chauffeur who was now about to drive her to Heathrow
in a dream machine.

Oliver unceremoniously tossed her canvas holdall onto the back seat alongside her which rather
brought Abby's dreamy delusions of grandeur
down to earth with a jolt. She doubted he did

that to WW. Never mind, you couldn't have everything.

There was a sudden whirring sound and a very soft click on the doors as he started up the engine. Abby realized she was cut off from Oliver by plate glass. Oh, how the other half lived.

Abby gazed up at the block of flats, towards the first floor, knowing Baroness Marinka would be watching through the chink of her net curtains. She was. She gave her a grin and a royal wave as the limousine purred away from the kerb.

'Who's that?'

Abby jumped, realizing Oliver was speaking to her over an intercom. She didn't like the feeling of claustrophobia that was washing over her. She felt completely cut off from him and everything in the outside world. She wished she was sitting up front with him, it was a bit lonely back here.

'Um, er, the Baroness,' she replied, looking around her and wondering where to direct her voice.

She heard Oliver laugh and realized he could see her in the rear view mirror. 'Relax, Jessica. I can hear everything you say. Who is the Baroness?'

Abby obeyed and relaxed back in her seat. She gazed out of the windows as they cruised down Kensington High Street towards Kensington Gardens. It was getting dark already and the shops shone brightly and looked far more enticing from the windows of a plush limousine.

Abby laughed. 'She's not really a Baroness, well, I don't think she is anyway. She's sweet but a bit cranky. Lives on her own and watches everyone going in and out. I always wave to her. She's lonely.'

'She wouldn't have seen you wave. The windows are one way,' he told her. 'Does she know you are going to Paris?'

Abby gazed at the windows. One way, eh? Probably bullet proof too, her dramatic mind expanded.

'No, why should she? I mean I just wave to her now and then. She isn't a close friend or anything. Why do you ask?'

'Just conversation.' He tilted his head so she could see him in the mirror and because he was smiling that soft beguiling smile of his she tried to forget that sometimes he asked the most peculiar things.

Ten minutes later Abby looked anxiously at her watch. Oliver hadn't spoken since and because she felt so cut off with the glass partition between them she hadn't offered anymore conversation. She was going to be late, she realized. Check in was like *now*. Because she only had hand baggage that wasn't such a problem because she could whizz through quickly without the delay of checking in a suitcase, but nevertheless . . .

The traffic around Hyde Park Corner was almost at a standstill with the usual summer tourists not knowing where they were going and hesitantly vying for position with taxis who knew exactly where they were going, and at speed too.

Hyde Park Corner! What an earth were they doing here?

'Oliver, I don't mean to sound picky, but aren't we going the wrong way?' she asked worriedly.

'Trust me,' he said. 'I have direct radio contact with the RAC and there are some holdups at the beginning of the M4. I'm taking another route. Don't worry, Jessica. I'll do right by you.'

Abby tried to relax. She really did but it wasn't easy. She questioned the next direction he took, heading towards the City. She shouted again, realizing he hadn't heard her. Her palms were very sticky as she tried to lean forward and hammer on the partition. She misjudged the distance and nearly went down on her knees onto the thick carpet and in embarrassment in case he had noticed she sank back into her seat, clenching her damp palms tightly.

Hell, she was going to miss the flight.

'Oliver, this is ridiculous!' she screamed at last, frustration winning.

'Hey, don't shout, sweetheart. I can hear you perfectly well,' came his dulcet tones over the intercom.

Abby boiled inside. She knew he had only just switched on. How dare he cut her off like this and where had 'sweetheart' come from? She hated being called sweetheart in that way. All the *bonhomie* of the earlier part of the evening was now shimmering away from her and deep concern and anger taking its place. They were definitely going the wrong way.

'What sort of game do you think you're playing?' she accused bitingly. 'I'm going to miss my flight because of your ineptitude. Call yourself a bloody chauffeur, you couldn't find your way up a one way street without radar!'

He laughed. He actually laughed.

'This isn't funny,' she fumed. 'My future depends on that meeting tomorrow. If I miss my flight it will be all down to you!' Oh, this was awful. She shouldn't have allowed her heart to rule her head and agreed to him driving her to the airport.

'Cool it, Jessica,' he said softly now. 'I'll get you there in time. Just don't panic. Look, pour yourself a drink. In front of you. Relax, sweetheart.'

'And don't call me sweetheart!' Abby screamed but he was back in that silent world of his again.

Drink? How could she drink? She pressed a button in front of her and a drinks cabinet whirred out of the panelling. She stared at the contents. There was enough champagne in there to refloat the Titanic. Actually that was just how she felt, as if she were going down with the Titanic. The whole evening erupted like a silent iceberg inside her. Damn her sister, Jess, for starting all this and damn this ridiculously poor excuse for a chauffeur for messing up her plans. And she had actually liked him at first, more than liked as it happened, she'd fallen for his charms and had wanted to see him again. Never would be too soon now! Tears of fury and frustration

44

pricked at her eyes. She had so enjoyed his company tonight, had let him take her in his arms and kiss her. Was she out of her mind or what?

She breathed a ragged sigh of relief as at last she saw they were on the M4 now and going in the right direction. Her relief was short lived.

'Oh, for goodness sake, Oliver,' she cried. 'Wrong terminal! You've taken the wrong lane!'

'I beg your pardon.'

He was doing this on purpose, Abby fumed. He knew she was going to Paris. No one could be that dumb.

'I'm not going long haul. Wrong terminal!' she cried.

'Oh, sorry, force of habit, I'm afraid. Relax, Jessica. Have faith.'

He took the next exit off the motorway and lost more precious minutes. Abby couldn't bear to look at her watch again. This was a nightmare. There was only one interview for the cruise job, tomorrow morning, first thing. Damn him, she had to be there.

'Thanks for bloody nothing,' she breathed to herself as they purred into the kerbside outside the terminal. She scooped up her holdall and reached for the door and found it firmly locked. The other side, too.

Serious panic struck her for the second time this evening. She was locked in, for insurance purposes no doubt she thought furiously, punching at the door with her clenched fists.

'Oliver, let me out!'

Where was he? Oh, God, she inwardly groaned. He'd got out and was talking to an airport police officer on duty outside the terminal. They laughed and then Oliver turned back and walked nonchalantly, all-the-bloody-time-in-the-world, back to the parked limousine.

And because Abby was so anxious, so het up with frustration, she nearly fell out onto the pavement on her knees in her haste to make a dash for check-in when he opened the door for her.

Oliver scooped her up to steady her and reached for her holdall which was clutched tightly in one hand.

In a fury Abby lurched it out of his reach. 'I can manage thank you,' she huffed impatiently. 'And I won't thank you for the lift because it was a wretched nightmare. Take a tip,' she told him. 'If you want to keep your job get your bearings right and read a map now and then.'

'I got you here, didn't I?' he said.

But there was laughter in his tone which infuriated Abby so much she wondered how she could possibly have nurtured any romantic fantasies about such an inept idiot!

'Stuff you!' she screamed at him and flew like the wind, into the terminal building and as far away from him as was possible.

The smile dropped from Oliver Webber's lips as he slid his tall frame behind the wheel of the limo and snatched up the mobile phone.

'That number I gave you earlier, David, the number of the last incoming call to Jessica Lambert's flat. Did you trace it?' he asked his PA, deep concern furrowing his brow.

'Yes, sir. It's the Corona State Hotel in New York.'

Oliver's grip tightened around the receiver. 'The Corona State, eh?' he said grimly. 'The lady swims in affluent circles. Any chance of finding out who the call came from?'

'Could take time, sir. I could get on to it but have you forgotten your brother is staying there at the moment?'

'How the hell could I forget something I didn't know!' Oliver snapped. His brother infuriated him at times. Though he knew William had dashed off to the States at the last moment and landed him with the unsavoury job of dealing with the dangerous Jessica Lambert, Oliver didn't know exactly where Will was staying. At least he'd had the sense to notify their shared personal assistant where he was.

'As you know it was a snap decision on his part to attend the Hayton conference. Is it possible it was him that called Miss Lambert?' David suggested.

'No way,' he breathed impatiently. 'He was supposed to be dining with her and when I arrived she was very disappointed. She'd have known he wasn't going to make it if he had called her from New York.' Oliver worriedly raked fingers through his hair. 'Besides there has only been the one contact between them, the faxes, as far as I know,' he said ruefully. 'But this is even more worrying. Someone from the Corona State called her and that someone could well be a computer delegate at the same conference. If she's already approached other companies with the information she's got we are in dead trouble. Was Will meeting any serious competitors there? Anyone Miss Jessica Lambert could have approached before she got in touch with us?'

'Not as far as I know, sir. I gather the conference wasn't very high profile anyway. Perhaps your brother was simply liaising with a lady friend there,' the PA suggested knowingly.

'Yeah, that sounds more like it,' Oliver smiled ruefully. 'Look, call Will, tell him that I've got Jessica Lambert, well I will have when she comes haring out of here in a fury at missing her flight. I'm at Heathrow,' he explained. 'She was on her way to Paris to offer her priceless wares to Europe and I've managed to thwart her plans so far. She's not going to get away with this. Our whole future is at stake on this one and no sharp little hacker is going to make fools of us. I'm waiting for her now.'

'And is she worth waiting for, sir?' David asked.

Oliver could see David's tongue in his cheek as he made the suggestion. On a personal level as well as a professional level the lady was indeed worth waiting for. Both highly dangerous. She hadn't been what he had expected under the circumstances. She was stunning and that had thrown him. Young, beautiful, vibrant, he had had to keep reminding himself over dinner what a devious little bitch she was. Even when he had taken her in his arms he'd had to remind himself of the purpose behind it, lulling her into a false sense of security because he felt he had somehow aroused her suspicions. Under any other circumstances he would have swept her off her feet before that, as she had swept him off his feet with those amazing green eyes. But the lady was hazardous with the knowledge she held. She knew too much, far too much for her own good. Yes, she was too hot to handle in the intimate way he wanted to handle her and yet knowing all this about her his heart was nevertheless hammering as he waited.

'Yes, David,' he said tightly. 'She's worth waiting for.'

'And dare I ask what you are going to do with this dangerous lady, sir?'

'Bloody kidnap her, of course!' Oliver stated firmly as he snapped off the mobile.

CHAPTER 3

It was on a wild frivolous impulse that Jess
ordered a banana daiquiri at the cocktail bar
instead of her usual dry Martini. Booking herself
into this plush New York hotel didn't seem such a
good idea now and she needed the comfort of an
exotic drink. She'd found that now the conference
at the other hotel had closed most of the delegates
had moved on and there were only a few stragglers
left.

As usual she had got her timing all wrong. She
shouldn't be here. Though she knew Abby would
do her best for her with William Webber she really
should have been there herself. There had been no
reply earlier when she had called home again and
then she had remembered Abby's interview in
Paris. She was dying to know how she had got
on with Webber over dinner but she would have to
wait now and waiting wasn't one of her strong
points.

She felt so guilty now for putting her sister
through it. Sometimes she wished she had the

sensible stability of her sister. Abby wouldn't have missed her flight home. Abby wouldn't have been so extravagant and flown over to the States on Concorde in the first place and Abby wouldn't be sitting on a bar stool now waiting for an expensive cocktail she could ill afford and hoping to rub shoulders with someone influential in the computer world.

As the barman ostentatiously mixed her drink in a chrome cocktail shaker she glanced at herself in the mirrors behind the bar. She looked good in an amber coloured creation of silk with narrow shoulder straps in gold braid, and her dark Titian hair swept up in a crunchy pile on top of her head made her look highly successful. Pity she wasn't. Pity this was all turning out to be a waste of money and precious time.

She glanced beyond herself in the mirror and saw a crowd of conference delegates come into the bar. One she had spoken to before, a systems analyst from Chicago. Jess had crossed him off her mental list of people who might have influence but he had been a nice guy and his friends looked fun and perhaps she might join them for dinner this evening if they invited her.

'Thank you very much,' Jess smiled warmly at the barman as she signed for the drink. She dreaded to think how much her bill would be when she checked out. Taking the exotic long-stemmed glass she slid off the bar stool and turned to join the crowd from Chicago.

'Oh, my God!' she cried.

She hadn't seen the tall dark stranger standing behind her waiting to take her place at the bar. He was so close behind her she had jerked right into him. Jess stared at him in mortified horror. The frothy cocktail was dripping down the front of his expensive evening suit, down her hands and wrists, all over his shoes and hers. Oh, God, the wretched drink had just about hit everything. Her dress, his suit, ruined, ruined.

'Oh, I'm so terribly sorry,' Jess cried. In absolute embarrassment she stared up at him, not knowing what to do or say to make it any better. Why, oh, why hadn't she ordered a dry Martini!

Suddenly the barman was there, cheerfully trying to make a joke of it all and mopping them both down. They soon seemed to be surrounded by the entire hotel staff trying to clean up.

'Leave it,' the cool dark stranger said with a deep voice of authority which had everyone but a bemused, embarrassed Jess backing off. Grim-faced he gently but firmly prised the long-stemmed glass out of Jess's tightly clasped fingers, deposited it on the bar and then took her by one elbow and rather frog marched her to the exit door of the bar.

'I really am so terribly sorry,' Jess burbled as she teetered along beside him in her gold high-heeled sandals. 'Please let me make amends. I'll pay for the cleaning of course and – '

'Are you staying here or were you just hustling for business in the bar?' he interrupted brusquely.

In shock Jess pulled up sharply outside the cocktail lounge. No bones about what he meant. In a fury she wrenched her elbow free of his grip and then in a further fury she did something she had never done in her life before to any man. She lifted one hand and very smartly slapped him across the face.

'How *dare* you make such a suggestion!' she flamed at him, her whole shapely body poised to slap the other side of his face if he so much as hinted at adding more to that insult. 'Just you apologize for that,' Jess flamed on. 'Because if you don't I shall call management and have you removed from the premises and let me tell you . . .'

And she was still protesting furiously as with cool calm aplomb he reinstated his grip on her elbow and propelled her towards the lifts. He was mad, Jess could tell. His grip on her was ferocious. He almost flung her into the lift.

Mercifully they were the only occupants and as the doors slid silently shut behind them they stood at either side of the enclosed space and glared at each other. For the first time Jess looked at him properly and drew in her breath in silent admiration. He was easily the most impressive looking man she had ever seen in her life. Tall and dark haired with threads of silver at the temples, intensely dark grey eyes that might have been dark blue if he had been in a better frame of

53

mind. His mouth might have been generous too but at the moment was drawn into a thin line of contempt. His nose was perfectly straight, in fact the whole of his handsome features were as near perfect as could be. His bearing was sophisticatedly impressive too. Power packed were the two words that came readily to mind. So did stuffed shirt to add another couple!

For one very small instant Jess felt for him and the state he was in now. A man like him wouldn't take kindly to having a banana daiquiri plunged down the front of his expensive evening shirt. Nevertheless that insult was uncalled for, spilt cocktail or not.

'Well, are you going to apologize or not?' she threw at him before he threw another insult at her.

'I don't do apologies,' he told her coldly. 'Now before you throw another punch at me, are we going anywhere tonight?'

'Huh!' Jess squawked in astonishment at the suggestion. 'I wouldn't date you if you were the last man strutting the earth!' The nerve of him, accusing her of hustling and then suggesting taking her out!

'I wasn't asking for a date, sweetheart,' he said coolly. He glanced up at the floor indicator. 'I don't intend spending the rest of my evening in this lift. *If* you have a room here would you kindly proceed to it to clean yourself up and give me the pleasure of seeing the back of you.'

Jess felt colour rush to her face. This was all

getting worse. She'd thrown a cocktail down his front, slapped his face then jumped to the conclusion, very wrongly too, that he had just asked her for a date. In even deeper embarrassment she plunged an index finger at the control panel and depressed the button of her floor in complete and utter defeat. Best to keep her mouth shut from now on.

Seconds later the lift halted and she stepped out of it after giving him a careless look of abandon to show that his insulting words weren't worth insisting on an apology for. Almost immediately she realized she didn't have her evening bag with her. In the embarrassing scene in the cocktail lounge she must have left it on the bar. Her room card, her money, her credit cards, all were in the bag. Her heart started to thunder at the thought that she might not get down there in time to retrieve it. Someone else might pick it up.

'I've left my bag somewhere,' she muttered feebly and tried to turn back into the lift but he barred her way and with a deep sigh of irritation took her arm again and pushed her back out into the lift foyer of the floor.

Once again Jess found herself taken in hand and marched along the corridor.

'So you *were* hustling down there,' he seethed. 'You aren't staying here at all. I've been approached by many beautiful women in my time but you, lady, take the biscuit. Ten out of ten for your bloody nerve but nil for your methods. I don't take kindly to having an evening suit ruined by a drink that should be more at home on the dessert trolley.'

With that he stopped dead outside a door and opened it and pushed Jess inside the most lavish suite she had ever set eyes on. Pale blue and gold were the luxurious colours that hit her. If it wasn't for her racing heart she would have liked to have appreciated it all at leisure but fury spoiled it all. She swung on him defensively, green eyes blazing.

'Will you quit all this nonsense?' she cried angrily. 'I'm not a hooker but you are obviously well used to them. But this time you have made a grave mistake. I *do* have a room along this corridor and I *have* left my evening bag down in the bar and if I don't get down and retrieve it someone else will.'

He moved to the telephone on a glass topped onyx table across the sumptuous room. 'What colour is it?'

Jess gaped at him then understood what he was getting at. Still he didn't believe her. Heavens, if the bag wasn't there, if someone had already taken it . . . this man would think . . . She supressed a shudder. Somehow the loss of the contents weighed little against what he would think, that she was indeed a hooker. He might make her an offer. She'd die of embarrassment if he did.

'Same colour as my dress,' she offered tightly, 'with a gold shoulder strap to match the dress and my shoes too,' she added.

His cool, cool eyes raked her up and down before asking. 'Contents?'

Of her dress or the bag? she wondered as his eyes lingered on every shapely curve she possessed, starting with her banana-splattered toes and travelling up and up in insolent appraisal. Approval didn't get a look in.

'Dollars, room card, credit cards, lipstick, mascara, breath freshener in case arrogant bastards like you sour my mouth,' she retaliated furiously at him for that censorious look he was still raking over her.

He plunged an index finger down on the telephone and while he waited to be connected he looked at her lazily and arrogantly said, 'You want to be careful who you call a bastard in the States. You can only get away with it if the person is in fact a bastard. I'm not one. I have a full set of parents.'

'And I don't need a lesson in political correctness or your family tree, thank you,' she blurted back defiantly.

She thought she saw the beginnings of a tight smile at the corners of his mouth but he turned away from her before she was sure. He spoke softly into the phone while Jess miserably inspected the state of her lovely dress. It was ruined. More money down the drain she thought crossly. Story of her life these days.

At last he put the phone down after making another call and loosened his bow tie at his throat.

'Get your clothes off,' he ordered as he proceeded to loosen his shirt collar.

Jess backed off in a panic, took two steps back as she turned crimson with embarrassment. 'Now look here, I am not what you think I am,' she protested hotly. 'This isn't on, no definitely not!'

'As you say, definitely not,' he reiterated with a trace of impatience. He pushed his jacket back and took a stance with hands on narrow hips and leaned towards her. 'I don't pay for it, sweetheart – '

'You couldn't afford me!' Jess flashed back, quick as a whip.

'I could, darling, have no fear of that. I don't *choose* to, but thanks for the offer anyway,' he said smoothly. 'Now, will you get your clothes off. There's a valet on his way to take our clothes to the cleaners. It will take about an hour, so unless you want to stand naked in front of me for that time may I suggest the bathroom over there?' He nodded across the plush sitting-room of the suite. 'You'll find a robe on the back of the door and may I make another suggestion? Put it on after your shower because if you don't come out of the bathroom suitably clothed *I* just might take *you* to the cleaners and to hell with the expense!'

For one furious minute Jess gave him the blackest of looks she could muster and then turned on her heel and headed in the direction he had indicated with that arrogant damned head of his. She slammed the door after her with a hefty

wallop and leaned back on it with pure unadult-
erated frustration. How dare he? How dare that
arrogant, pompous creep make her feel smaller
and more insignificant than a flea!

Almost blind with fury she forced herself to
glance around the impressive marbled bathroom
with the gold fittings and dolphins heads in
profusion. There was everything here she needed
for a clean up and there was a lock on the door so to
hell with him. She clicked it quickly just in case he
thought of joining her. It was an interesting
thought, which she pondered for a mad minute
or two. Pompous and arrogant and a stuffed shirt
he might be but he sure came with power-packed
sexuality. Phew!

And English too, she mused, her temper cooling
as she stripped off and stood under the power
shower to rid herself of the unfortunate cocktail
which had landed her in this peculiar situation.
Hardly a typical English gentleman, though. Re-
served, yes, but certainly a man of the world to
take *her* for a cheap hustler! So he'd had the come
on from a multitude of beautiful women had he?
And just how many had he turned down as he had
so flatly turned her down?

She smiled a grim sort of smile at herself in the
mirror as she rubbed her wet hair after shampoo-
ing it for the second time this crazy evening. So,
he'd taken her for a hooker, that was bad enough
but on reflection who could blame him? Everything that had happened had been a complete and

utterly unfortunate accident but if she had intended picking him up for the night it wouldn't have been a bad ruse, throwing a cocktail down his front and anticipating him whisking her up to his suite to strip them both off. But, and it was a huge but, he had made it quite obvious he wouldn't take her if she came gift wrapped in krugerrands and Jessica Lambert suspected that deep down her fury was more about rejection than the initial insult. She couldn't remember a man ever looking at her with such distaste. Yes, a unique experience, but not very flattering.

'So, here we are,' she said cynically as she joined him in the sitting-room, suitable packaged in the bathrobe he had suggested and still rubbing at her mass of hair with a towel. She noted with a further snap of rejection that he had showered somewhere else and changed into fresh clothes and wasn't languidly waiting for her in a similar hotel robe to the one she was wearing.

He eyed her suspiciously from the hospitality bar where he was pouring himself a Scotch. Even in more casual clothes, linen trousers and a forest green silk shirt, his dark hair still damp and slightly tousled, he hadn't managed to shed the air of authority and power he wore so successfully. It occurred to Jess that she couldn't have chosen a better looking guy to fling her cocktail over if that had been her intention in the first place.

'Yes, here we are,' he repeated. 'Unfortunately your evening bag isn't.'

Before Jess could further protest her innocence, because it was quite evident he still thought her a liar and a hooker, there was a short rap on the suite door. She watched him as he strode across the room to answer it, already forming in her mind just what she was going to say to him in defence of herself.

'Your clothes,' he said, picking up his own evening suit and shirt from the back of a chair.

'Oh, yes, of course.' She hurried to the bathroom where she had left them and came back to hand them to the waiting valet who was taking all this in his stride from the look on his implacable face. When she turned back to the tall dark stranger he was pouring another drink at the bar. Brandy, she noticed. He came across the room to where she was standing like some gauche young thing, a bit like her sister might actually, not knowing where to put herself, and handed her the drink.

'You might need this. Your bag was last seen tucked under the arm of a young woman leaving the cocktail bar after us . . .'

Jess thought she was going to pass out. Her whole life seemed to flash before her eyes.

Suddenly she was slumped in a deep armchair clutching the brandy between white fingers and trying to get her paralysed lips to the rim. She gulped and choked.

'I'm sorry. These things happen,' she heard through a blanket of disbelief that was fogging her brain along with the burning sensation in the back of her throat. 'Hotel security are on to it. I'm sure – '

'You're sure what?' Jess suddenly wailed at him, the whole implication of what had happened hitting her with a force that erupted in fury. She leapt to her feet and glared at him angrily. 'You're sure it will turn up? Huh, some damn chance! My whole life is in that bag!' she screamed at him.

Her money, her credit cards, her room card key. Her room card key! Whoever took her bag could get into her room now and take the rest of her property! Oh, God, her software package too. She'd brought a copy with her just in case she ran into anyone of importance in New York. Though she was sure William Webber would flip over her brilliant idea she had learned from past experience that you should cover yourself for all eventualities. As it happened she hadn't yet met anyone of enough importance to show her wares too but if the package got stolen . . . it was worth a small fortune in the right hands.

'And this is all your fault,' she seethed on, slamming the brandy glass down on the coffee table with such force both nearly shattered. 'If you and your arrogance hadn't marched me out of that bar in such a fury I would have kept my head about me and not left my bag there in the first place!'

'Yes, I agree. This is all my fault,' he said quietly.

The soft agreement took Jess completely by surprise. Her lips parted in shock. The stranger stepped towards her and took her gently by the shoulders. His eyes looked truly regretful and Jess felt a huge rush of adrenalin at his touch which angered and confused her. Yes, it was all his damned wretched fault and here she was going weak at his obvious regret and actually enjoying his touch.

'I will make amends of course,' he said sincerely. 'The hotel will immediately change the code on your room key so it will be safe to return there but if you are of a nervous disposition you are most welcome to stay here the night and – '

And immediately Jess could see the implications of *that*. He might have made out he wouldn't pay for her services, at any price, but now he must know she wasn't what he accused her of. He was thinking he could get it for free! Vulnerability wasn't one of Jess's attributes. She was streetwise enough to know that a couple of good-looking, upwardly mobile people of the opposite sex sharing a suite with however many rooms spelled trouble. He hadn't shown any signs of being attracted to her, the contrary in fact, but Jess knew men. She knew herself too. He was gripping her shoulders just a little too intimately and she was . . . well . . . not exactly fighting him off.

'And I am certainly *not* of a nervous disposition,' she interrupted him forcefully, her eyes glittering with rage. 'But I might be if I stayed here a minute longer and as for spending the night here . . . You are off the wall, stranger.' Her chin jutted defiantly. 'I shall go down to reception now and sort all this out for myself.'

'I think not,' he said calmly, letting his hands drop from her shoulders. 'You are hardly dressed for a confrontation in the foyer of a very smart hotel and I don't think the management would take kindly to your appearance.'

Jess's whole body sagged as if weighed down with cement bricks. He was right. She'd made a big enough fool of herself tonight as it was. But what an earth was she to do? Her bag had been stolen and the repercussions of that didn't bear thinking about. She'd already run up hefty charges on her credit cards without a robber cashing in on them as well. No money, no room to go to till a new card was issued, nothing to wear but what she stood up in, his hotel bathrobe.

Her feelings of despair must have shown because he let out a small sigh and took her glass and refilled it at the bar. As he handed it back to her he spoke.

'I do apologize for this – '

'So you do do apologies after all,' she snapped back at him, reaching for the drink he offered and nearly taking his hand off in her eagerness to get at it. If ever in her life she needed a fiery boost of brandy it was like now.

'Rarely and only when I think it is fitting,' he came back cuttingly, glowering at her through

64

incredibly thick dark lashes. 'Now is one of those rare moments. It *is* my fault. I shouldn't have rushed you out of the bar quite so hastily and now you have lost your bag and I am sorry because it has obviously caused you some stress. But before you get any smart ideas that I might be humbling myself here I'm also sorry for myself. I had a dinner date that is now quite obviously off and you are the cause of that.'

Jess forced a thin smile after taking a deep sip of the revitalizing brandy. 'To be honest I care little about your dinner plans for the night. I'm sure the lady in question must be feeling pretty miffed,' she said sarcastically, 'but I'm not exactly over the moon at having had my bag stolen because of your fury, thank you very much. This could have been sorted in a civilized way. I did offer to pay for the cleaning and – '

'And you will,' he interjected darkly and turned away from her to sit down on a squashy blue silk covered sofa by the coffee table. 'Sit down,' he told her in an impatient tone that irritated Jess so much she felt like doing what she had intended and marching right down to reception, bathrobe and all and get this mess cleared up, her way not his.

'I said sit down,' he repeated, slightly more persuasive this time. 'I've ordered some food while we wait for your clothes and wait to hear if security have found your bag.'

Jess slumped down in the deep matching arm-chair across from him. He was right. She couldn't go storming around the hotel half-naked. He seemed to have everything in hand anyway. She was still mad as Hades though.

'Did the feathers fly with your lady friend when you put off your date?' she asked rather sarcastically.

'I didn't say I was dining with a lady friend.'

She'd bet he was though. She felt a curious pang of envy at the thought.

'And what about *your* dinner date?' he asked. 'Will your boyfriend be waiting downstairs for you? Would you like to call down and tell him what has happened?'

Jess glared into her brandy. To claim a boyfriend waiting would get her off the hook here. Trouble was there wasn't one and to claim one might be pushing her luck too far this evening, to say nothing of complicating matters more.

'I was alone,' she told him tightly and lifted her face to see a knowing look lighten his face.

'Can't say I'm surprised,' he said softly. 'Word must have got around New York that a beautiful mad woman was throwing yellow cocktails down the front of men's evening suits.' He followed that with a very small smile that had Jess's heart thudding just a little too rapidly for her liking. 'Before you did the cabaret with the cocktail, which made me wonder exactly who – or what – you were, I was about to ask you if you wanted a drink, actually,' he went on nonchalantly. 'I noticed you at the conference.'

Jess's eyes widened to huge green orbs of surprise. Now here was a turn around. Oh, be careful she warned herself. This was some tricky customer. Earlier he had been scathing in his put down, now he was coming on all charm and teeth. His date was a no-no after she had ruined his suit. She was available and half-dressed. She shifted in her chair, with her free hand tugged the robe over her knees and noticed guiltily that she had consumed all the brandy he had poured for her.

'So,' she responded, her voice a slight croak in her throat. 'You were at the Hayton conference, were you?'

Heavens, she hadn't seen him there. If she had she was sure she would have made a beeline for him because as well as being a stunner he had the look about him of great success.

'Yes, boring wasn't it? I bit too low key for my needs,' he added. 'I didn't learn anything I didn't already know and there were no useful contacts worth nurturing. My company is really too big but sometimes you can pick something up at these conferences that is useful. Not in this case though.'

Jess swallowed hard. He *was* someone big in computers. Her heart started to pound. She might have landed on her feet here. Maybe all this was down to fate. She had missed her flight back to the UK, had tipped her cocktail down him and possibly she couldn't have tipped it down a better person. She didn't feel so bad about landing her sister with entertaining William Webber and handing over the package now. Maybe this impressive stranger was someone bigger than Webber, though to her knowledge there wasn't anyone as mighty as he. But these days, who knew who was top dog. Here today and gone tomorrow.

She'd introduce herself in a minute, find out just who he was and possibly have him and the infamous William Webber bidding against each other for her idea. Suddenly she felt enormously hopeful for her future and it prompted her to lean forward in her seat and smile warmly at him.

'You were going to buy me a drink, eh? While waiting for your dinner date to turn up?' She softened the tone of her voice seductively. 'Now what would have happened if I had accepted and we fell madly in love over our dry Martinis? How would you have explained that away to your girlfriend?'

She was flirting now and enjoying the smile that was beginning to crease his mouth. Flirting came easily to her; the men were usually flattered to the hilt and it broke down innumerable barriers from the off. She had got off to a bad start with this stranger so it was about time she turned on the charm.

She waited expectantly for his response which wasn't as instant as she would have liked. Thoughtfully he twirled his glass of Scotch in his hands before speaking.

'I didn't say I was dining with a lady friend, did I?'

This was a cagey one, Jess thought. 'I can't believe a good-looking guy like yourself wasn't dining with a lady,' she went on, loading up the flattery.

One very dark brow rose quizzically and Jess wondered of she had taken on too much here. He wasn't responding, not in the way she had expected and hoped for. He was looking right through her as if he had already got her measure.

'Another drink?' he offered, unfolding himself from the sofa.

Resignedly Jess held her empty glass up to him. He took it and with a very small smile he said, 'Another brandy? Or how about one of those dry Martinis we are going to fall madly in love over?'

Jess's heart did a triple somersault. He *had* responded. 'Why not?' she whispered seductively and leaned back in her seat and ran her fingers through her damp hair, never taking her eyes off him for a second. He held the look for a mesmerizing second and then he turned away to the bar and Jess was able to breathe at last. He was gorgeous and someone in computers and if she played her cards right . . .

He handed her a very cool Martini and was about to sit across from her and fall madly in love with her when the telephone rang.

Jess said a silent prayer that it wasn't security calling to say they had found her bag, not yet anyway. She needed time with this man. She smiled to herself. Minutes ago she had been frantic at the loss of her evening bag and furious with him for his arrogance. And now? Now she was warming to him in more ways than one. Funny old world, she mused.

'Will you excuse me? This is business and I'd rather take this call in the privacy of my bedroom,' the stranger said as he strode across the room with the telephone dangling from one hand.

Jess settled comfortably in her chair after he clicked shut his bedroom door. Business, my foot. It was the girlfriend. She didn't mind though, not one bit. She was here in this lovely, sumptuous suite with him and the girlfriend wasn't. Shortly they would be sharing a meal together and a few more Martinis and they would talk and she would find out just who he was and then bang. She'd give him the outline of her idea, oh, boy would she sell it to him. If her evening bag did eventually turn up, hopefully intact, she'd be able to get into her room and show him her software, the hotel would surely have a computer terminal somewhere. And if her darling sister had done the same with William Webber, entertained him as planned, handed over her precious package, she could end up with two software tycoons bidding millions for her work.

This was turning out better than ever. Jess contentedly sipped her drink and rearranged the bathrobe to show a glimpse of her lovely legs while she waited for him to come back and thought it would be easy to fall in love with him over a few more of these. She grinned to herself. Actually the drinks didn't come into it. He was someone successful in computers and easily the most gorgeous looking man she had ever met and perhaps she was halfway to being in love with him already.

William Webber sat on the edge of the bed and spoke softly into the phone. 'No, Oliver, you haven't caught me at an inopportune moment. Yes, I am entertaining but not between the sheets. It's a long story that involves a lady and a banana daiquiri and one day I might tell you about it but for the present we've got more serious things on our minds. David said you were planning to kidnap this Jessica Lambert. I sincerely hope this is one of his dry jokes.'

Oliver laughed down the phone. 'He was deadly serious, Will. I have her here at Brooklands, the package too. She has another copy in her possession. She was on her way to Paris with it but as yet I haven't got my hands on it. She's spitting feathers and refusing to talk but I'll calm her down. I persuaded her it was a good idea to stay the night and see you personally when you got back. Funny thing is, she seems completely unaware of what she is doing.'

William kneaded his brow and wished his brother could have handled it more sensitively. Kidnapping was bizarre to say the least.

'How do you mean?'

'At first I thought she must be some sharp

71

operator. I mean she's already had the nerve to offer us our own work. She stole that idea from us, whether she did it with inside information or through her own hacking skills, I don't know but she seems so innocent I think she must be working with someone. You know, putting her upfront to lull us into a false sense of security, she really is strikingly lovely, and then her accomplice slamming in with the blackmail theory we talked about after she sent that fax. I think you are right, what was the point of her offering us our own work and hoping to get away with it? She can't think us stupid enough not to know what is going on.'

'It's not the new game I'm so worried about,' William said, 'though it's worth a fortune to us. It's the rest of the top secret information she could have got hold of at the same time. We have other new ideas on the go that our competitors would give their eye teeth for. If she has been infiltrating our system from home then she is some smart lady.'

'Dangerous, too. By the way, I've seen the equipment at her flat and it's capable of doing it, but of course it's the operator that matters, she must be hot stuff at it. As you know it isn't easy. Anyway, she still thinks I'm your chaffeur,' Oliver went on ruefully, 'and I'm not enjoying the deception very much. I'd much rather work my magic on her in my true persona.'

'Millionaire playboy,' William sighed. 'Take it

easy, Oliver, this is too serious for your little seduction games. We're talking a serious breach of security here. Handle her with care. Where is she now?'

'In the drawing-room. We'll stay the night but I'm damned if I'm going to put on that uniform again tomorrow, danger woman or not. How did the conference go?' Oliver asked, changing the subject.

'Waste of time. No talent to pick up on.'

'Business talent or female talent?'

'Neither, though a few more dry Martinis and I might find myself in trouble,' William said ruefully.

'So you *are* entertaining?' Oliver teased.

'You have a one-track mind, brother. Look, I'll be back tomorrow to sort all this Lambert business out. Now is there anything else you have to tell me?'

'Nothing. Don't worry about a thing. What's she like by the way?'

'Stunning,' was all William said as he put the phone down.

He sat for a few minutes kneading his brow and trying to get everything into perspective. It would go against all his principles to pay a blackmail demand if that was indeed the intention behind all this. Pay up or I'll offer all this information to other computer companies, he could hear the Lambert woman saying. Already she had copies ready to bargain with. Oliver had done well to keep her from going to Paris. Was she working on her own and was Oliver misjudging her innocence? If she was sharp enough to have done what she had done she was probably sharp enough to fool his brother who had a weakness for beautiful women. Well, he'd make that judgement for himself when he met that dangerous lady.

He sighed heavily as he stood up and raked fingers through his hair. And there was another dangerous lady only feet from him at this very minute. Dangerous to the heart. He'd never met anyone quite like her. Wild and tempestuous she aroused every basic male instinct he possessed. But for some unearthly reason he was holding back from her. Not like him at all. She intrigued him, he supposed, and he wanted to get to know her, her mind and her body, and that was a first for him.

Before going back to join her he pulled open the drawer of his bedside table and took out her evening bag. While she was showering the security manager had returned it. It had been found on the floor under the bar stool she had been sitting on. A large tip and the assurance that the young lady was his date had ensured that the security man had handed the bag over with a knowing wink. And then because she fascinated him so and he wanted to keep her close he had lied to *her* telling her it had been stolen.

William Webber flung the bag back in the drawer and turned the key in the lock, impatient with himself for pulling such a shabby trick. It wasn't like him at all. Normally women didn't have such an enormous impact on him, but this one was different. Yes, she could be a danger to his heart but at least she wasn't a danger to his life's work. His brother Oliver was dealing with that dangerous lady. His troubles were minuscule in comparison.

Pulling himself together stoically he took a deep breath and pulled open his bedroom door to rejoin the lady who had had such an impact on him this curious night. Maybe by the end of it he would know whether or not he was going mad.

CHAPTER 4

'I've told you, Jessica, there is nothing to worry about. The boss is away and once he knows what has happened he will agree with me that this is the only solution,' Oliver told Abby persuasively. 'On his behalf I'm offering you the hospitality of his home for the night. We'll try the Paris shuttle again first thing in the morning.'

Abby broke her vow of silence and shot to her feet in the very elegant drawing-room of William Webber's country mansion somewhere in Kent. Where, she didn't exactly know. The last few hours had been the very worst of her life. She still couldn't believe all that had happened tonight. Here she was in William Webber's home of all places when she should have been in Paris. It was a nightmare.

'First thing in the morning will be too late,' she stormed. 'There is absolutely no chance I'll make my appointment now but if you hadn't been so stupidly incompetent I would be in Paris at this very minute!'

'Ah, so you are condescending to talk to me now,' he said with a tight smile. 'I wouldn't have put you down as a sulker.'

'I had good reason to sulk,' she protested vehemently. 'You were waiting outside the terminal at Heathrow with such a smug expression on your face that I was beginning to think you had purposely taken those wrong turnings and made me miss my flight.'

'I wouldn't call it smug,' he told her. 'I thought it was caring. I was worried about you. I thought I'd wait in case you had indeed missed your flight.'

'And then you offered to drive me down to Dover to board Le Shuttle and – '

'And I would have driven you all the way to Paris if things had worked out as planned,' he finished for her.

'You got lost again!' Abby practically screamed at him, her eyes wide with anger. 'Is it any wonder I refused to speak to you after that? I'm only speaking to you now because I can't believe you had the audacity to bring me here and actually suggest I stay the night in your boss's home!'

She had nearly died of shock when after what seemed hours of driving down leafy lanes he had pulled the limousine into security gates and up a mile long driveway to this impressive mansion. Before that, when she had realized he was hopelessly lost yet again she had tried to protest over the intercom but he had switched it off, as he was wont to do when it didn't suit him to hear her rantings on his driving skills. Several times she had actually tried to get out of the limousine when he had pulled up at traffic lights but it had been hopeless. The damned car was like Fort Knox, all avenues of escape impenetrable. If she hadn't known him better she would have seriously thought she was being kidnapped. She didn't know him at all when it came down to it, she thought ruefully, but he had no reason to kidnap her so she had quashed that dramatic theory.

Then when they had arrived here, Oliver saying that as they were in the area of William Webber's home why not overnight there, he had taken her bag, brought her into his boss's house and told her to make herself at home, just like that! She couldn't get over his nerve. His boss would have a fit if he knew his chauffeur was acting so familiarly in his home while he was away.

'I should never have agreed to let you drive me to Paris in the first place,' she cried, suddenly so weak and exhausted she wanted to lie down somewhere and sleep for a week. She sank back into the chair she had been sulking in for the last fifteen minutes while he had gone off to make a phone call or put the kettle on or whatever.

Oliver crossed the room and sat on the edge of the chair and started to gently massage her shoulders. 'You were looking so desperate when you came flying out of the terminal,' he said softly. 'It was all my fault and I realized that and the very least I could do was to offer to drive you all the way. I'm truly sorry we got lost on the way to Dover. I'll get a map out later and find out exactly where I went wrong and we'll set off first thing in the morning. You'll feel better for getting a good night's sleep.'

Though the pressure he was exerting on her shoulders was very soothing she wasn't about to be so easily placated. This was all his fault. The interview was off, she wouldn't be going to the Maldives and now she felt like a trespasser in someone else's home. *His fault*.

'Don't do that,' she said impatiently and shot to her feet like a jack in the box. 'You are far too familiar by half,' she reproved.

'Oh, come on, Jessica. I'm only trying to relax you. I thought we were getting on so well,' he laughed. 'I have kissed you or have you forgotten?'

'Would that I *could* forget,' she snapped, also wishing he would take this seriously. He seemed to think it a huge joke that he was incapable of driving from A to B without losing himself. She leaned towards him as he still sat perched on the arm of the chair she had just furiously vacated. 'This whole evening has turned into a farce. I should never have invited you to dinner in the first place. You,' her finger came up and pointed at him, 'are a walking disaster, or should I say a driving disaster. If I didn't think we would end up on the Pennine Pass I would insist on you driving me home this very minute. How you ever got a job as a chauffeur I can't imagine. Not only that but don't you think you are pushing your luck just a mite too far?' she finished sarcastically.

'In what way?' he asked with a small smile on his lips and playfully snatched at her pointed finger. 'It's rude to point,' he teased.

Abby retrieved her finger with a sharp jerk and ignored the teasing reprimand.

'I thought that was quite apparent. You have brought me to your boss's home and he isn't here. You have told me to make *myself* at home. This isn't *your* home to be so free with.'

'It's my home too. It's a live-in position,' he told her lightly.

'Not for long, if William Webber has any sense,' she retorted. 'Anyway, chauffeurs usually live over the garage block or the stables or somewhere out of sight till they are needed. They do *not* entertain women in the drawing room of the master's home.'

He had the audacity to laugh. 'Oh, Jessica, you are so quaintly old fashioned. Times have changed, the lord and master bit doesn't happen these days. Mr Webber believes that his home is his staff's home too. I have my own rooms upstairs. We get on well.'

'Look, you aren't getting the point. Mr Webber isn't here and you had no right to bring me to his home and offer to put me up for the night even if we were in the area.' She straightened herself up but still glared at him. 'This is embarrassing for me. I don't want to be here. I don't feel comfortable. I shall ring for a taxi and – '

'It's very late, Jessica. There are no local taxis that would come out at this time of night,' he paused to look at his watch, 'this time of the morning actually and besides we are setting off for Paris first thing. I do insist on taking you, it's the least I can do.'

'Tomorrow is too late. I told you my appointment was first thing,' she huffed at him, folding her arms across her chest and starting to pace the thick blue Axminster carpet. Oh, it was hopeless. She'd never make the interview now and it was the only one the cruise line was giving. They worked to a very tight schedule. The Maldives was definitely off and it was as much her own fault as his, she thought objectively. She shouldn't have fallen for his good looks and his lovely eyes and his smile and invited him to share the meal with her. It had all gone so well at first and then disaster.

'Can't you reschedule your appointment?' Oliver suddenly suggested.

Abby turned on him, amazed to see he had slid down into his boss's lovely velvet armchair and was sprawled in it with one leg flung over the arm. Talk about taking advantage while the lord and master was away.

'No, I can't,' Abby murmured, remembering she had implied that she was seeing a computer company to offer her sister's software package to. If only she had never started this deception. He still thought her to be Jessica, funny how she was used to being called by her sister's name by him now. Still, she was in too deep now to wriggle out of it and admit that she had been going to Paris for an interview for a job and she wasn't Jessica Lambert at all but Abby, the sister who knew precious little about anything that came up on a computer screen.

She offered no further explanation for why she couldn't reschedule because she couldn't think of one and she just prayed he would drop it. She *would* ring for a taxi and hope that one would come out for her. Heavens the cost from here back to London, but to hell with the cost, for sure she couldn't stay here the night.

'I will try for a cab,' she stated determindely, looking around for a telephone.

'No, you won't, Jessica,' he said softly as he uncoiled himself from the chair and came to stand in front of her, so close she could smell his lemony balm again and it made her tingle with awareness. He took her two small hands in his and held them gently at her side. 'Now listen to me. You are very tired and stressed out, you need some sleep and frankly so do I. We'll talk about this in the morning.'

'I can't stay!' Abby wailed, wishing he wouldn't caress the palms of her hands this way because it made her feel more vulnerable than ever. In spite of the catastrophe tonight he had at least waited for her outside the terminal, worried about her and was now trying to make the best of things for her. She supposed he was very nice, a rotten chauffeur, but still very nice. 'You *can* stay, Jessica. You've missed your appointment in Paris so why not make the best of a misfortune? This could all work to your advantage anyway.'

'And how do you make that out?' she implored, her eyes wide and pleading. She could see no advantage whatsoever in missing out on an important career opportunity and having to stay the night in a house she shouldn't be in with an employee of the mighty Webber who might not take kindly to having his chauffeur bring her here. Besides the chauffeur in question was very charismatic and as he had said he had kissed her and . . . he might kiss her again and she really didn't know how she would react if he did.

'Mr Webber will be back shortly and then you can put your proposal to him personally, as originally planned,' he added persuasively.

She'd never thought of that. Her heart started to pulse nervously because she had given scant thought in the last hour or so to how all this had started. It was one thing to wine and dine this William Webber and hand over Jess's package in the safety of her own home, but to meet him on *his* home ground? Being the whizz he was he probably had a computer set up here in his own home and he might want to go over her sister's work with her and talk about it further and then . . . then the game would be up. She'd have to admit she wasn't who his chauffeur thought she was and a tycoon as big as him wouldn't cheerfully take to having his time wasted by a small time actress and cruise ship's entertainments person and a chauffeur who had messed up on his mission. Poor Oliver, he wouldn't come out of this very well either. WW might sack him, sooner rather than later!

Oh, what a mess her sister had landed her in. Damn her, she was in some luxury hotel in New York, no doubt having a good time and expecting her to do the business with William Webber.

And what would Oliver, the incompetent chauffeur, think of her deception, especially if he got the sack over it? She really did like him and it appeared he liked her too. He might have ruined her chances of the cruise job but he was trying to make amends. And that kiss too and the way he looked at her, like now, eyes smouldering, waiting for her to agree with him and relax once the decision was taken to stay.

'I don't know,' was all she could murmur weakly.

'Well, I do know,' he said softly and then he did what she didn't want him to do. He bent his dark head towards her and their lips met in another sizzling, knee-weakening kiss that sent her senses spinning till she couldn't think straight. All thoughts that when WW returned everything would hit the fan fled from her reasoning. His arms came around her and held her firmly against him in case she thought of escape. But there was no escape, only complete and utter submission on Abby's part as the kiss deepened to one so sensually emotional she thought she might burst into tears if he stopped.

Minutes or possibly hours later Oliver moved slightly back from her. Abby opened her soft languid eyes and stared up at him, not knowing what to say or do. She felt bewitched, as if he had cast a spell over her and made her his slave for life.

'That was beautiful,' he murmured throatily, 'and *you* are beautiful,' he said, tenderly tipping her chin so he could look deeper into her lovely eyes. 'I'm going to be very strong tonight, Jessica,' he went on smoothly, inching back from her, 'because I don't want to frighten you away. I'd like to take things further tonight but I mustn't. I've never met anyone quite like you before. I'm truly sorry for what I've put you through this evening. But now I'm going to make you a night-cap and then I'm going to tuck you up in bed and I have a feeling tomorrow will be the beginning of something big between us.'

Weak and half-senseless with fatigue Abby couldn't utter a word. What was he saying, that he respected her and liked her enough not to try anything on with her this evening? He was different, she thought dreamily. Most men she had met had been out for the main chance. Here they were, alone and miles from the outside world and yet all he wanted to do was make her a nightcap and tuck her up for the night and tomorrow . . . tomorrow held so much delicious promise she thought she might not sleep a wink tonight after all.

'Come,' he said, 'let me show you the guest suite.' And he took her hand and squeezed it reassuringly and led her out of the drawing-room into the spacious hallway with many doors leading off it.

Abby got her senses together as Oliver led her up the curving stairway with the highly polished mahogany bannisters. It was a sumptuous mansion furnished with priceless antiques and lovely silk drapes at the huge mullioned windows. It showed William Webber's wealth, but didn't shout it out. Her sister had said he liked beautiful women and luxurious surroundings and in any other situation she would look forward to meeting such a fascinating man. Playboy he might be but he had taste and style. She was glad Oliver was with her now though. Oliver was the real world, not a playboy at all but a very nice, caring chauffeur.

And because she already had some sort of feelings for him she knew she owed it to him and of course her darling sister to go through with this deception. She didn't want to think more deeply about it now because she was so terribly tired. Troubles slept on usually resolved themselves by morning. A bright new day might bring some bright new ideas on how to handle all this.

'Oh, Oliver,' Abby breathed, panic resurfacing as he opened the door of a small suite of rooms at the end of a wide corridor. The sitting-room was

86

beautiful, decorated in her favourite colours, soft peach and off white and washy green. The drapes were traditional chintz, slightly faded and all the better for holding history in their folds. There was a small chintz covered sofa and chair and a small Georgian desk under the window. Beyond the room Abby could see a bedroom decorated in the same colours with a lovely antique four-poster bed taking pride of place against one wall. It was so lovely and tasteful and so peaceful she knew she would sleep like a log, if only . . .

'Oh, Oliver,' she repeated, worriedly turning to him. 'Are you sure this is all right? I mean he might hit the roof when he comes home and finds me here. And he might take great exception to his chauffeur being so forward. I mean you haven't been doing the job long and you can't know him very well.' She bit her lip with anxiety.

'I feel I've known him a lifetime,' Oliver told her with a reassuring smile. He put her overnight bag down at her feet and she thought he was going to take her in his arms again but he didn't and she was a little bit disappointed because she needed some comfort. 'Now you unpack like a good girl and I'll go down and make you a drink. Any preference?'

She thought a stiff alcoholic drink might make her feel less guilty for putting him to so much trouble tonight, might make her sleep better too, but somehow she thought a warm milky drink might suit this warm glow inside her better. He was being so nice and he had said such lovely things and as he had said, tomorrow . . .

'Perhaps a hot chocolate would be nice,' she said demurely.

'Your wish is my command,' he grinned and gave her a mock bow.

'Oliver,' she said softly as he was about to close the door behind him. He stopped and popped his head round the door. She smiled at him shyly. 'I'm sorry for shouting at you in the car and being such a nuisance to you tonight. I suppose anyone can get lost. I was just frustrated,' she admitted with a helpless shrug of her shoulders. 'I'd missed my appointment and . . .' she shrugged again. 'Now you are doing your best for me and I want to thank you for that. It's very sweet of you, thank you.'

For a second she saw his eyes glint suspiciously, as if he didn't feel very happy about her humbling herself to him with an apology or maybe his conscience was pricking him for being such an idiot in getting lost so many times. Her heart went out to him. He might be on good terms with William Webber now but tomorrow might be something else. She suppressed a deep shudder at the thought and then resolved once again to make the very best of it when she faced WW, for everyone's sake.

'You didn't have to apologize, Jessica, or thank me,' he said gruffly. He shut the door behind him and Abby bit her lip wondering if she had upset him by trying to make amends. Men didn't usually like their frailties pointed out to them and she had told him more than once his driving skills were naff.

She was caught on the hop, looking and feeling gloomy about herself when he pushed open the door again.

'By the way, that copy of the software package you were taking to Paris. I think it might be better in the safe overnight.' He stood in the doorway and held his hand out for it.

Abby was so taken aback she had to dredge her mind again to recall all the lies she had told him. No, not lies exactly. She hated that word. Just a mild deception that now seemed to be getting totally out of hand. She didn't have the copy he was talking about in her possession because it didn't exist, but to deny it now . . .

'Oh, no, that isn't necessary,' she said hesitantly. She tried to force a smile while thinking on her feet. The smile turned into a giggle. 'There is so much security here . . . the gates and the alarm system you switched off when we came in . . . I mean, I'm sure a burglar just wouldn't dare,' she laughed. 'It's . . . it's quite safe with me and . . . and well thank you for offering. I've put you to enough trouble tonight.'

Her heart twisted as she saw what looked like a flash of anger in his eyes and then suddenly he was smiling that ravishing smile of his and her heart settled. They were both very tired and perhaps she had misinterpreted him.

'I'll get your drink,' he said and clicked the door

shut again and Abby squeezed her eyes shut with relief.

Tomorrow she would tell him the truth. She would *have* to tell him the truth because this was getting unbearable.

Wearily she picked up her bag and took it into the bedroom and put it on the bed. There was an *en suite* bathroom and she longed for a soak in the deep Victorian bath but perhaps she might benefit more from it first thing in the morning, to wake her up and get her head sorted out as to what she was going to say to Oliver, and William Webber when he arrived home.

She pulled her old cotton nightie out of the bag and shed her jeans and shirt and underwear to put it on. She rather wished she had brought something more glamorous. She smiled to herself. Jess would have done. If Jess was here now with the gorgeous Oliver she would be dressed for the kill in silk and lace. No bones about it Jess would be putting this situation to her full advantage. Though perhaps not with a chauffeur, Abby thought ruefully, as she brushed her teeth in the bathroom. As Jess had always said, she hadn't yet met a man to match her in brain and guile, to say nothing of wealth and kudos. Was there more to this ruse of Jess's perhaps, more than just selling him her idea? she puzzled. Jess was so beautiful that men fell at her feet in adoration but she usually cast them aside with indifference. But William Webber was obviously a man of great means. Apart from all Jess had read about him Abby could now vouch for that because she was here in his luxurious mansion which reflected his wear and status.

It was an amusing thought to go to bed on, Abby thought as she slid between the pure cotton sheets of the four-poster, that Jess might be after William Webber's heart as well as selling her software package to him. Trouble was Jess was so accident prone she'd have made more of a mess of things than she herself was doing. Oh, well, Jess wasn't here anyway. And tomorrow she would be facing WW and not Jess and if she really put her mind to it she might do better than Jess herself in selling the idea.

She wished she'd taken more interest in her sister's and her father's preocupation with all things computer. But perhaps when she came face to face with WW she could make a swift exit and leave him to look over the work in peace and quiet and then if he was really interested . . . then it would all have to come out but by then he might be sold on the idea and not care that she wasn't Jessica Lambert in person.

Oh, she was too tired to worry about it now.

Minutes later she blinked open her eyes and Oliver was standing by the bed holding a silver tray with a steaming mug of chocolate on it, biscuits too. How thoughtful of him, she thought dreamily. She wriggled up from the sheets and smiled at him as he sat down on the edge of the bed.

'You look beautiful in sleep,' he said softly and

then shattered the warm feeling with the follow up, 'Pity about the nightie.' Then he grinned so widely she knew he was only teasing her and she wasn't at all offended.

She tucked the sheet up under her chin and grinned back at him. 'Well, I didn't think I'd be spending the night in a romantic four-poster,' she laughed taking the mug of chocolate from him.

Oliver looked up at the framework of the bed. 'I never thought of this bed as being romantic,' he muttered thoughtfully.

Abby now wished she hadn't mentioned it. He might think she was a bit brazen and pushing for something more than he had already given tonight. It was enough that he had shown such respect and caring for her. Enough to show her that he really had feelings for her. She sipped her chocolate appreciatively and he caught her eyes as he directed his back to her. Abby felt a *frisson* down her spine as their eyes locked for what seemed like forever. She was sure they had something going but sometimes he looked at her so strangely she couldn't make him out. She was the first to break the lingering eye contact. She lowered her thick lashes and gazed down intently at her mug of chocolate.

He got up suddenly and then bent and kissed her brow swiftly and bade her goodnight and before Abby could catch her breath to say goodnight back he was gone.

With a sigh she drank the chocolate and then

settled down in the romantic four-poster and one of Jess's much used phrases came to mind; funny old world. It sure was. She was falling in love with a gorgeous chauffeur whom she had only just met this evening. She should be in a hotel in Paris, not a rich man's home in Kent. She wasn't herself anymore, Abby Lambert, she was her sister, Jess. Tomorrow held a lot of promise after all the nice things Oliver had said, but it could also turn out to be another disaster when William Webber turned up. Yeah, funny old world, she mused and then fell soundly asleep.

Oliver Webber poured himself a triple Scotch in the drawing room and gulped it down in one. What the hell was happening to him? Making warm milky drinks for a dangerous lady who totally confused him, to say nothing of the pull on his heart in her direction. Bloody *romantic* four-poster. It was a bed, for heaven's sake, a bed he would have cheerfully leapt into with any of his previous girlfriends. Women in his life had never been a problem before, take them or leave them had been his philosophy of life.

And here he was holding back from Miss *Femme Fatale* who was more of a threat to his heart because of her complexity. He couldn't make her out. She knew enough to bargain her way around the world and make a killing for herself and completely and utterly destroy Webber Software in the process. And yet she was so completely and utterly adorable.

Sassy yes, but with an underlying innocence and sweetness that fascinated him.

Was she an innocent victim, being used by someone much cleverer than herself? Or was she the smartest, trickiest lady it had been his misfortune to meet? And hell it was a misfortune to meet her. He hated what he was doing, fooling her into thinking he was the chauffeur of William Webber, his very own brother and business partner. Nevertheless, he hated what she was doing, trying to defraud them and taking them for fools. And most of all he despised himself for feeling this way about her. Wanting her.

He poured himself another drink and went to the window to gaze out over the family estate. There was a full moon and as far as he could see was Webber's land. He wanted to keep it that way. He wasn't about to let Jessica Lambert strip them of a lifetime's work. He should have come down on her hard tonight, forced it all out of her, found out if she had a contact in their network, if she was working alone, what she intended doing with the priceless information she had, how much was the blackmail demand.

Instead his heart for once in his life had overruled his head. Warm milky drinks, romantic four-posters, kisses he should have avoided instead of succumbing to. He slammed his unfinished drink down on a side table and muttered grimly as he barged out of the drawing-room, 'You, Jessica Lambert are sending me insane!'

94

CHAPTER 5

'So where were we?' William said thoughtfully as he went back to join the daiquiri lady in the sitting-room of the suite.

'I think we were about to fall in love,' Jess reminded him with a meaningful smile.

William sat across from her and Jess noticed his eyes gaze with approval over the length of leg she was showing.

'It's that easy, is it?' he asked wryly when at last his eyes came up to meet hers full on.

'You tell me,' Jess bantered, her green eyes sparkling in response.

He shook his dark head slightly. 'No, you tell me,' he said with a small smile. 'Women are the authority on affairs of the heart, so they say.'

'Is your wife such an authority?' Jessica asked astutely.

Best to get that out of the way sooner rather than later. He had successfully evaded answering her about a dinner date with a lady tonight, so perhaps it *had* been a business dinner and perhaps wifey was back in the UK, tucked up with a golden labrador at the foot of the bed. She wondered if he would be truthful, if there was a family back home and thought perhaps he would be. He didn't appear to be the two-timing sort. She held her breath waiting for an answer.

He smiled secretly, which put Jess on alert.

'Why don't you just come out with it and ask me if I am married or not?'

'I thought I just did,' she grinned at him.

He laughed. 'Yes, I suppose you did and of course you did ask about a lady friend too. Well, let me put your mind at rest before we do this falling in love business. There is no dutiful wife at home with two point four children but there *are* a dozen or so lady friends scattered around the world, however none that I couldn't live without. Does that satisfy your curiosity?'

'Hum, only a dozen. You surprise me,' she teased slightly, so as not to show her relief. Brilliant, nothing she couldn't handle. He liked women and there was no wife so it should be plain sailing once she got to know who he was and where and how he operated in his business life.

'And you? Is there a husband, a lover, someone in the pipeline?' he asked, his grey eyes sparkling with humour.

'Free as the proverbial bird,' she came back with, feeling exactly that, now that they had revealed their single status to each other. Green light, road ahead clear and unobstructed, so it was go, go, go.

'Now, that does surprise me,' he said sincerely, somehow switching the conversation around so that he was flattering her now. 'Any reason for your single status?'

'Many,' she told him truthfully. 'In spite of what my adorable late father taught me after his marriage to my mother collapsed I can't help but feel cynical about marriage. He said that sometimes no matter how hard you tried failure was sometimes unavoidable. Generally I'm a risk taker in life but where marriage is concerned I'll need to be one hundred per cent sure. The affairs of the heart I have indulged in in the past haven't fully met my criteria, all have fallen short of my expectations. Perhaps I expect too much, a melding of the minds combined with sexual chemistry does seem to be too much to ask for these days.'

'Oh, I don't know. You just haven't met the right person yet and perhaps one hundred per cent is a bit ambitious to aim for.'

Jess laughed. 'Well I'm not going to lower my standards by even one per cent just to come down off the bachelor girl shelf. I'm happy as I am and to be honest, these days I get more of a buzz from my computer work than I do from some of the wimps I've met lately.'

'And this work of yours, what does it entail and who do you work for?' he asked and Jess wished he hadn't diverted the conversation away from affairs of the heart. She'd rather have liked to have delved into his philosophy of life and why he was still single. Later maybe, the night was young.

So, to admit to being out of work and heading for bankruptcy in the not too distant future if she didn't sell her latest idea would hardly inspire confidence in him if he was indeed someone very big in computers.

'I'm freelance,' she told him confidently. Not exactly a lie or the truth but freelance was loose enough and sounded good enough to appear successful. This man wouldn't deal with anyone other than successful, she felt sure. He had already admitted the conference had been too low key for him.

'And what does freelance cover exactly?'

Jess wished he hadn't asked. She had been concentrating so hard on her new project these past months that outside work had been of no consequence.

'Oh, just about everything. Consultation on proposed systems, expansion and improvement of existing set ups, installation of software, networks and operating systems,' she scrolled confidently.

Perhaps if she had indeed concentrated on these things she might not be here now. But the mundane had never really appealed to her, the big time did. As she had told him, she was a risk taker, and a certain risk had got WW to accept her dinner invitation. She briefly wondered how Abby had got on with him.

'I'm very impressed,' he responded with genuine interest.

She smiled at him. 'And do I get the chance to be impressed by your list of attributes?' she said meaningfully and picked up on her initial flirting streak by casting her eyes suggestively over his body.

'Now what could you possibly mean by that?' he asked innocently and Jess knew he knew exactly.

Before she could reply with something witty and snappy there was a light tap at the door which he got up to answer, sighing lightly as if the interruption wasn't welcome at the moment.

Jess prayed it wasn't her evening bag back yet. Not yet, just a little while longer with this fascinating man. She turned to see her prayers answered. No security manager clutching her precious evening bag but a waiter. He wheeled an impressive chromium food trolley over to the circular dining table across the room and in silence proceeded to place silver salvers onto it.

The stranger came across to her when he had left and Jess stood up as he held his hand up to indicate the waiting table.

'I wish I had some clothes on,' she said ruefully. 'The food looks delicious and deserves better than a bulky towelling bathrobe.'

'I think you look lovely as you are,' he said with a smile.

'In a bathrobe? You're just being kind because this is all your fault,' she reproved lightly. She stopped at the table as he held the chair back for her. 'Just one thing before we sit down to eat. Don't you think we ought to introduce ourselves?' she suggested with a small laugh.

He smiled at her, a smile to die for. He was really relaxing now and what a gentleman, Jess thought as he waited for her to seat herself. His cloak of arrogance had definitely slipped and underneath was an even more shockingly attractive man

'Lady's first,' he insisted.

'Jessica Lambert. *Miss*,' she added brightly, just to remind him that there were no holds barred this evening. She held her hand out towards him to complete the introduction.

He didn't take it immediately and as his eyes widened in what could only be described as surprise she wondered if he ever would. Had she been too forward in flirting with him? Was he one of those rare breed of men who didn't take to having a woman come on to him, wanting to stay in command and do all the running himself?

His hand finally came up to grasp hers but it didn't come with the warmth and perhaps the *frisson* of awareness she expected. And his eyes, they had narrowed to suspicion now and that was a mystery.

'The ubiquitous Jessica Lamber, eh?' he murmured mysteriously as he let her hand go.

He adjusted her chair behind her and as he came round the table to seat himself across from her she noticed a dark frown marring his brow. He appeared puzzled, which equally puzzled Jess. He knew another of the same name, she thought quickly, a former lover perhaps, one he didn't perhaps wish to remember.

'I've never been referred to as ubiquitous before. Would I be right in thinking that perhaps one of the dozen or so lady friends you can live without carried the same name?' she daringly suggested.

He smiled at last, a little uncertainly though, Jess thought. 'Exactly,' he said. 'An uncommon name, but, yes, indeed I do know another. I don't know what sort of food appeals to you but I ordered something bland. Caesar salad to start with and turbot in wine sauce.'

'Haven't you forgotten something?' Jess asked as he placed a bowl of salad in front of her.

Without looking at her he murmured, 'I asked for them to omit the anchovies. I can't stand them. Hardly a Caesar salad without them but – '

'I didn't mean the anchovies,' Jess interrupted, wondering why he was suddenly rambling on about them. He seemed miles away all of a sudden, as if he was having second thoughts on this intimate dinner in his suite with a lady who had messed up his evening and his suit. 'I meant you have forgotten to introduce yourself.' She smiled encouragingly, not wanting to lose his interest at this early stage. 'Now fair's fair. You know just about everything about me now and I know very little about you.' She leaned forward in her seat and gave him her very best flirtatious charm. 'If I am to fall madly in love with you tonight I'd like to put a name to you.'

'Yes, of course, a name,' he muttered obliquely as he fiddled with the serving spoons. 'It's . . . it's Oliver. I . . . um . . . I head a computer corporation in the UK.'

'Oh, which one?' Jess asked enthusiastically. 'I know them all, in fact I'm a very good friend of William Webber, you know Webber's Computers. Don't tell me you are in direct competition with them,' she laughed, forking her salad keenly. She looked up to see him staring at her blankly, his features now tight with tension.

Jess gulped down a mouthful of lettuce with a shaving of parmesan and her heart went quite cold. Her and her big mouth again, claiming a friendship with a tycoon he undoubtedly must have heard of, or worse might actually know and be on his Christmas card list.

'Well, not . . . not an intimate friend, so to speak . . .' she started mumbling.

Oliver cleared his throat and interrupted her. 'I've heard of them, of course, but I wouldn't claim to be in direct competition,' he assured her tightly. He reached across the table and filled her wine glass to the brim with Californian Chardonnay. He smiled suddenly. 'Now let's put business behind us this evening, shall we?' he suggested warmly. 'Let's just concentrate on us. Don't you think fate took a hand for us this evening?'

Jess carefully lifted the brimming glass to her lips and gulped at it before putting it down. Thanks for small mercies that he had got off the subject of William Webber. She concentrated her thoughts on Oliver. With such a fascinating man it was easy to put business out of sight and mind. He had responded to her, was openly showing his personal interest in her now and this wine was going down exceedingly well.

'How do you mean?' she whispered breathlessly.

'Fate in the form of a very wilful banana cocktail. Very novel,' he said seductively. 'If we do fall in love and this turns out to be the night of the century, who knows, we could end up telling our grandchildren how we met and share the joke with them. It is a rather bizarre way of meeting, don't you think?'

Jess's heart flapped like fledglings' wings on their first flight out of the nest. Already he had raised the evening to the wild blue yonder of a future together *and* grandchildren. For a mystical moment she projected herself forward in time. Marriage to this man could well be a merging of the minds to say nothing of the sexual chemistry she was responding to. The full one hundred per cent and more. But was it the brandy and the Martini and the wine, a lethal cocktail of drinks, that might be sensually misting her vision? Ah, *in vino veritas*, in wine the truth.

And when he reached across the table and took her hand and gently placed his warm, seductive lips on the back of it Jess knew that she was falling from a great height and enjoying the sensation immensely.

'I find you fascinating, Jessica Lambert,' he murmured as he let her hand go. 'You are the one good thing that has come out of this trip to New York. When do you plan to return to England?'

'I . . . well I . . .' She didn't want to go back, not yet. She didn't want to admit to being a fool for missing her flight and waiting around for BA to inform her of the next one either. Concorde would impress him but somehow that didn't matter anymore. If he suggested she stay on with him for a few wild reckless days of passion in New York she jolly well would.

'When are you due back?' she countered softly, giving him the chance to take this enigmatic evening another step further.

He held her limpid wide eyes forever and then he gave a very small shrug of his broad shoulders. 'At this very moment I care little,' he said throatily. 'I think I'd rather like destiny to guide me from now on. How do you feel about destiny, Jessica?'

There was a yawning silence as Jess dreamily considered it. She was reading him all right and the chemistry between them was positively rebounding off the walls. As she pondered her answer, not usually slow in coming forward, but for once wanting to come up with the right reply, he rose to his feet and without changing the slumberous look in his lovely grey eyes he came around the table and took her hand to urge her to her feet. Tenderly he drew her into his arms and as their lips came together Jessica experienced the most delicious rush of female hormones. Her head swam in the glorious feeling of abandon. She didn't like to think that this was rushing it a bit. Somehow it felt just right. Warm and sensual and just perfect.

At last they drew apart and smiling softly Oliver drew back a wisp of hair from her face. 'You didn't answer my question,' he murmured.

For the life of her Jess couldn't remember it now. She gazed up at him, feeling very much moonstruck at this moment. Heavens, Jessica Lambert, moonstruck. She might be her very own sister standing here, all innocence and vulnerability instead of the streetwise one she had always imagined herself to be.

He laughed softly. 'You look slightly dazed. I'm flattered,' he said smoothly. His hands slid down from her shoulders and crept round to grasp her bottom and draw her hard against him. 'I'll repeat the question,' he went on seductively. 'How do you feel about destiny, Miss Jessica Lambert?'

She knew the question was breathed with innuendo. He was really asking more, was she willing to make love to him, did she *want* to? It was indeed destiny, one small, unexpected slip of her cocktail glass had drawn her into this man's charismatic world. They hardly knew each other but it felt as if they had known each other for ever, and that was destiny for you. To follow your instincts was one of Jess's strengths but sometimes weaknesses Abby would warn her. Well, Abby wasn't here now to preach to her the rights and wrongs of following your heart. Jess knew in her own that this was right and it was enough to guide her.

She raised her arms and smoothed the sides of his wonderful face. To hell with networking for business. Pleasures were few and far between in this hard world and this man was the pleasure palace to end all.

'I'm not often lost for words, Oliver,' she breathed sensuously, 'but perhaps this answers your very complex question.' She raised her lips to his in utter submission and he took up the challenge with a sudden surge of erotic passion that nearly melted her bones.

He parted her lips with a skill that made Jess's nerve endings race and as a hand crept sensuously inside the top of her robe to smooth over the mound of her breasts she knew there was no going back. Her heart and her senses were in control. She wanted him and he obviously wanted her and the banana daiquiri seemed like a lifetime away.

Her warm breast swelled with erotic pleasure and he drew back from her lips, lightly nipping her lower lip before nuzzling his way down to her swollen nipple.

Jess gasped in wonderment as he drew lightly on her flesh – his tongue causing the nub to pulse – then more fiercely as he registered her sigh of pleasure and became intensely aroused by it. Jess was already spinning out of control, wanting him more than she had ever desired anyone in her life before and that was further confirmation that he was someone special.

'I think bed is the place for us at the moment,' he whispered hoarsely at her throat and before Jess could get her muzzy head together he had literally swept her off her feet, up into his strong arms and carried her over to the bedroom.

Jess clung to him, nuzzling kisses into his hair and neck as he kicked open the door. In the next instant they were on the bed and Oliver was raining kisses over her throat as she arched passionately against him.

Her bathrobe fall open as he touched every part of her silky body till she was almost drugged with need and then she opened her languid eyes to see him move away from her to peel off his clothes.

Soft table lamps glowed at the side of the bed and Jess watched in fascination as gradually his clothes were shed to reveal the most perfect male body she had ever seen. He was bronzed from some exotic holiday, smooth skinned except for a mass of dark springy hair down his chest which went on and on to the most delicious . . .

Jess moaned and closed her eyes in disbelief. Magnificent was the word that pulsed through her weakened mind. And then she was gathering him into her arms and there was not a slither of air between them as their mouths hungrily sought each other's and their breath quickened dangerously.

But a rapid lover Oliver wasn't. Jess lay beneath him hardly able to believe how perfect he was. He touched her in just the right places, kissed her passionately till she lost all her senses and writhed her aching body helplessly under him till she thought she couldn't hold back one second more. She clung to him, parted her lips for him as he ravaged her with deeply passionate kisses.

She gasped with shock and pleasure when they could hold on no longer and he entered her deeply. His own moan of pleasure excited her and her hands grasped his hips and held him deep inside her as the first wave of erotic delight shook them.

And when he started to move rhythmically inside her Jess knew she had never experienced anyone like him. Her body was in some place she had never been before, and was way out of control. She was lost in a sea of heavenly turmoil, thrashing wildly and moving with him and murmuring his name till he covered her mouth and seemed to hold them suspended in time.

Their climax came with the force of a hurricane, the turbulence of a typhoon and such a rush of molten fire Jess thought her last moment had come.

She heard the soft murmur of his voice as they

trembled against each other. 'Beautiful, beautiful, Jessica,' he moaned and then he lay across her, softly kissing her face and smoothing down her wild hair with tender strokes of comfort.

Soft and languid they lay in each other's arms and Jess fought to stay awake. She was limp and sated and wanted to stay this way forever, in the security of his arms, feeling his hot body hard against hers and his lovely mouth brushing across her heated skin, cooling and soothing her, winding her down and down.

At last Jess opened her eyes to see him lying next to her, supported on one elbow and gazing down at her with a very small smile creasing his mouth.

'One hour and fifty five minutes,' he murmured softly. 'I call that a record by anyone's standards.'

She smiled weakly. 'It felt like three seconds.'

He lowered his lips to hers and kissed her lightly. 'I like your sense of humour.'

'Who was joking? We sure haven't been making love for one hour and fifty five minutes.'

He laughed and slid his hand under her bottom and gathered her harder against him. 'We have *known* each other just one hour and fifty five minutes, fifty six or seven by now,' he teased, 'and I take great exception to the three seconds bit too, it was all of five.'

She laughed. 'I was teasing *you*,' she admitted.

'I like your teasing, in fact I like every part of you, even your mind.'

'Hey, watch it buster,' she whispered and slid

her arms around his neck to kiss his lips. 'Two can play at that game,' she told him when she finally released his mouth. 'I rather like your mind too, apart from other things,' she added meaningfully.

'And you do play games, don't you?' he responded and leaned up to gaze down into her lovely face again.

'Meaning?' she uttered softly, hoping he wasn't about to spoil it all by bringing up the cocktail again, as if she had done it on purpose, the sort of games she might play to get her man.

'Computer games.'

Jess wrinkled her nose provocatively to mask her disquiet at having the real world encroach on something that had just happened so sensuously. Funny he should mention computer games when it was the last thing on her mind at the moment. Had she mentioned her new project to him this evening? She had intended to, but then something rather wonderful had happened and now she couldn't remember if she had or not.

Thinking about it now though she felt a prickle of unease at the thought of her evening bag being delved into, her room key found, her room being ravaged and her precious software whisked off into the wild blue yonder where she had been minutes ago. But robbers weren't usually bright enough to know anything about such things as computer software . . . she hoped.

'Hey, where are you?' he whispered in her ear as he nuzzled his lips against her.

She grinned to hide her sudden concern and lack of attention. Perhaps this wasn't the right time to share her worries with him. 'I thought the usual thing to do at moments like this was to light up a cigarette and blow smoke rings into the air, not talk about work,' she teased.

'You're right,' he breathed. 'How insensitive of me. Do you want a cigarette? I don't smoke myself but I'll ring down for some if you want them.'

He went to roll off the bed as if her wish was his very command. She caught his wrist before he could escape. 'I don't smoke but thanks for the offer and don't run away. It's supposed to be the women that do that.'

He looked puzzled for a moment and then he smiled and sank down to the bed again. 'You're different,' was all he said and lowered his mouth to kiss her lightly on the lips. 'I've just picked you up in a bar, made love to you and . . .'

'Lost my evening bag,' she interjected with humour sparkling her eyes. 'Talking of which,' she paused to let out a regretful sigh. 'I think I'd better ring down to hotel security and see if anything has turned up.' She didn't want to get up, far from it, she wanted to be here in this bed with him forever but concern was seriously nagging at her now. What had happened between them had been ecstatically beautiful and she had tried to forget all else but the all else just wouldn't go away.

Oliver suddenly pinned her back on the bed and

rolled across her. 'It's all in hand,' he whispered in her ear reassuringly. 'If there is any news they know where to find you. I don't want to lose you. I want to forget there is a world out there,' he murmured throatily. 'Now, why don't we just shut it all out and lie here and contemplate a repeat performance of what is indeed turning out to be the night of the century. How does that grab you?'

Mischievously she took his hand and guided it towards her femininity. 'Hereabouts,' she uttered helplessly, knowing he was right and the world could wait. 'Sometimes actions speak louder than words.'

She flowered under his seductive touch, cast everything but him and his tender exploration of her willing body from her mind. Her future was on hold. She didn't want to think about robbers or the next flight back to the UK which she suspected she might miss – *again*. She'd met a wonderful guy called Oliver and she was crazy for him and he for her and that was all that mattered.

And as the intensity of his lovemaking deepened, soaring her back to the delicious wild blue yonder of abandon, she didn't care if the morning never came.

Sometime in the early hours of the morning William Webber eased himself out from the warm, loving arms of Miss Jessica Lambert and sat on the edge of the bed with his head in his hands.

She slept soundly and beautifully next to him but sleep was beyond him. After a while he turned and gazed down at her, his eyes deeply troubled and guilt thrumming through his head.

She was lovely, a bit on the wild side but adorable and irresistible nonetheless. He felt like the king of the rats for what he had done. He had made love to a woman who had puzzled him deeply enough to want to keep her close to him in the only way that had come to mind at the time. He wasn't proud of his actions. But what had started out as a ploy to seduce her into his life more intimately and so ensnare her heart and guarantee that she wouldn't slip out of it as easily as she had slipped into it, had ricocheted back on to him. He'd scored an own goal. As soon as he had taken her in his arms he knew the initial intention had been way off course. He wanted her for her, not who he suspected she might be, but nevertheless he felt burdened with guilt over his first intention, loving her with intent.

Was she the *real* Jessica Lambert, the one who had faxed him in the UK with her bizarre proposal? The infamous Jessica Lambert who held his company secrets in her deceptive palms? If so what was she doing here in New York? Hadn't the *real* Jessica Lambert been kidnapped by his brother!

Slowly he got up and slipped on the robe he had slowly slid from her lovely body only hours ago. Silently he went out to the sitting room and poured himself a large Scotch.

113

Would it stretch the imagination too far to believe that there was more than one Miss Jessica Lambert? So many coincidences though. Both were in the same business and, God damn it, she had confessed to being a friend of William Webber. He was William Webber, for heaven's sake! What the hell was going on?

He started to pace the floor, his mind racing so hard he thought he might explode before anything was resolved. He had very nearly blown it all after they had made love and he had unwisely mentioned computer games. If she was who she claimed to be, surely that would have raised her suspicions? Apparently not.

He should phone his brother Oliver . . . He rubbed his brow with the hand that held the glass. She had shocked him so deeply when she had introduced herself she had forced him into a lie. His brother's name was the first to come to hand. What was happening to him? He was turning into a liar and a deceiver, all because of a damned cocktail and a pair of gorgeous green eyes that had melted his heart.

He sighed deeply and drained the Scotch from the glass. He would keep her close to him because he wanted her close to him and tomorrow, no today, he would find out more. Her evening bag, that would confirm her identity, he hadn't even opened it. Later he would. Later he would get David his PA to run some checks for him, later he would call Oliver too. Now he wanted to go back to her and hold her in his arms and make love to her because she was the most exciting woman he had ever come across. Dangerous lady or not, he didn't know. For the time being he didn't want to know.

CHAPTER 6

The next morning, dressed in what she had arrived in the night before, jeans and silk shirt, Abby stood at the first floor window and gazed out over the estate of William Webber. Watery sun drizzled over woodland and emerald green lawns. To the right there was a topiary garden with yews cut into the shape of peacocks and cockerels. There were real peacocks too, strutting their stuff along the cobbled pathways that linked the topiary garden to the rose garden below the window.

Abby could breathe the scent of them from here and it didn't help. A night in that lovely romantic bed hadn't helped much, either. Though she had slept well enough, through sheer exhaustion, her troubles had not been resolved by morning as she had hopefully anticipated. A long languishing soak in the bath hadn't cleared her head, either.

She desperately wanted to clear her conscience with Oliver this morning but had got herself in too deep and lacked the courage for the moment. But it was going to take more courage to face William

Webber some time today and she couldn't fathom out which would be worse.

She turned bleakly away from the window and saw a phone by the bed and looked at her watch. Jess couldn't be home yet, could she? She dialled her own number anyway and was greeted by her own cheery voice on the answer phone, saying no one was home and leave a number. She hesitated for a few seconds. Should she leave a message for her sister, saying she had missed her Paris trip and giving this number? She glared at the phone. There wasn't a number on it to give. She slammed the receiver down impatiently. And what else could she say? I'm staying at . . . where? She didn't know, only that it was William Webber's home *somewhere* in Kent, and his chauffeur had brought her here, via every known road logged in the AA roadbook!

Crumbs, she'd always accused her sister of being whacky and irresponsible, so what would Jess think of her now?

'Were you making a phone call?'

Abby jumped as if she had been shot. He must have heard her slam down the receiver. She turned to see Oliver standing in the doorway, mercifully out of his bulky uniform and dressed in black chinos and a black polo shirt and looking doubly gorgeous this bright morning. 'Er . . . yes . . . I'll pay for it of course.'

She went to reach for her bag but he stopped her with. 'Absolutely no need. Who were you calling?' he asked, coming towards her with a nice smile on his face, his hands plunged into the pockets of his chinos, stretching the fabric to its limits across his narrow hips.

'Um . . . er . . . just . . . just my sister.' She felt she must be blushing guiltily. But she was the only one who knew her sister was the real Jessica. She took a silent breath to calm herself.

'And where does she live?'

Abby wondered why he needed to know and then she smiled hesitantly. Perhaps he thought she lived in Hong Kong or somewhere else faraway and how was he going to explain that to his boss when the phone bill came in?

'Don't panic, only London.' She didn't say Kensington, sharing the same flat, because that might complicate things even further. Though perhaps now might be the time to come clean.

'And what did you tell her? That you were being held hostage in deepest darkest Kent?'

Abby's eyes grew wide. At one point last night she had been convinced she was being kidnapped but for the life of her she couldn't remember voicing her opinion to him. Had she been so enraged she had?

'That was a joke,' he smiled at her as he stepped closer. 'You're obviously not a jokey sort of person first thing in the morning.'

Abby smiled weakly, but that was all.

'So, what did you tell her?' he repeated, stopping in front of her and lifting her chin to look down into her eyes.

Abby wondered why she was getting the Spanish Inquisition this morning. Heavens she'd only made a phone call.

'She's not in yet.'

'Bit of a night clubber, is she?'

Abby frowned now. He was suddenly very interested in her sister. Again she calmed herself. Oliver knew nothing and it was her own guilty conscience giving her hassle.

'No, she isn't really but well . . . she's been away and I thought she might be home and well . . . well she wasn't.'

'Did you leave a message for her, telling her you weren't in Paris after all?'

Abby glared up at him suddenly. 'Look what is this? I'll pay for the miserable call if you like. I got the answering machine and didn't leave a message but it must have cost all of ten pence. I'll pay you now and be done with it.' She spun away from him. 'Honestly all this fuss about a trivial phone call. I mean I understand you don't want to fall any further out of line with your boss and your job is probably already at risk anyway but this is ridiculous!'

He let her blether on and then he burst out laughing. 'You're such a grouch in the morning. Are you always like this? I hope not. I don't want to wake up to that every day.'

Abby dropped her handbag back on the bed and turned round to him. Had she just heard right, that he was already anticipating waking up with her *every* morning? Her heart raced perilously.

119

'Oh, Jessica,' he breathed, trying not to laugh anymore. He came and took hold of her shoulders. 'I'm only trying to break the ice with you this morning. The phone call doesn't matter one bit. You're not still worried about being here, are you?' He didn't give her time to answer but caressed her shoulders reassuringly. 'It's all right I've spoken to Mr Webber and told him everything. He's looking forward to meeting you. He said to make you feel at home till he gets back.'

In a way Abby was relieved WW knew she was here and had welcomed her to stay but . . . 'And . . . and when will he be back?' Abby asked tentatively. She had very mixed feelings in that direction. Best to get their meeting over and done with before she cracked up altogether but a few more hours alone with Oliver would be nice, she thought selfishly. It would give her a chance to come clean with him.

'Oh, who knows, he'll call when he's on his way.'

'Where is he exactly?'

'New York.'

Abby only just stopped herself blurting that that was where her sister was, too. But it made sense to keep Jess out of all this for a while longer, at least till she told Oliver the full story. She directed her thoughts to WW and hoped he wasn't as scatty as her sister and missed his flight too, because she could be waiting for him forever.

'You must know what time you have to pick him up from the airport?' Abby queried.

'He'll call en route but there again he might not and just arrive in a taxi,' he said casually.

Abby tried to relax. 'Yes, well, he might get here quicker by cab,' she teased.

He looked puzzled then got the message and grinned at her. 'That's more like the Jessica I have grown to love and adore. Now what would you like for breakfast? I haven't eaten yet so we'll breakfast together and then plan our day.'

She hoped not a round trip of Kent because they might end up in Norfolk. It was better to think lightly when Oliver was around. She had bypassed the love and adore bit because he was only teasing to make her feel at ease. Wasn't he?

As she went down the stairs with him she thought she wasn't at ease at all and wished she was. He obviously had a very trusting relationship with his boss for him to agree so readily to his chauffeur taking her under his wing till he got back. But still she didn't feel right here. If only she was indeed her sister. Jess would be having a ball with all this stately home business.

'No staff?' Abby asked as she gazed around the magnificent kitchen. It was hugely countrified with a green Aga and masses of scrubbed pine cupboards and other kitchen equipment. There was a chunky refectory table by the window which overlooked a walled vegetable garden where a weather-beaten gardener was working at the cabbage patch with a trowel.

The homely sight of him was welcome, but the

sight of a homely housekeeper would have been more welcome. Surely there was one or two around for such a vast mansion?

'Mr Webber gave them time off while he is away,' Oliver told her, pulling open drawers and shutting them again, looking for whatever and not finding it.

Abby supposed his chauffeuring duties didn't stretch to all things culinary. She hovered by the big table, watching him frowning with impatience as he clattered around in the drawers.

'Um, what are you looking for? Can I help?'

He turned and grinned at her sheepishly. 'I'm not very au fait with this kitchen,' he admitted. 'Mary's usually here to cook and look after our needs. Mary, the housekeeper,' he added.

With a sigh Abby stepped towards the fridge which was set back in an alcove. 'I've got the message,' she resigned. 'You want me to cook the breakfast.' Any delusions of grandeur fled from her. It would have been nice to have been waited on by a cheery housekeeper in this lovely old mansion. Not only that but a sight of one of WW's staff would have given her a measure of the man himself. Her father had always said you could tell the true character of a person of means by the attitude of their staff. Oliver himself, incompetent as he was, didn't give away anything about the wealthy tycoon's character. Tolerance perhaps: William Webber sure had a lot to put up with with a driver who couldn't find his way around a roundabout.

'Would you?' he said with relief, turning to her

and beaming. 'I've some calls to make and you know, things to do.'

Abby smiled at him. 'I'll give you a shout when it's ready.' Though she suspected a dinner gong was the way to do it here.

'You don't mind do you?' he asked, coming to her and pushing a wisp of hair back from her face. 'The food you prepared last night was so delicious I'm sure you can do wonders with a side of bacon and a basket of eggs.'

Abby laughed, though it had a hollow ring to it. Her conscience snapped at her for the millionth time since he had come into her life. Chef of the year she wasn't but he thought her to be.

'Yes, well being the grouch I am first thing in the morning don't expect a banquet,' she told him warningly.

He bent and kissed the tip of her nose before striding out of the kitchen, stopping at the doorway to say. 'I'm sure whatever you prepare will be better than I could do.' He was about to close the door behind him, Abby watching with a small helpless smile of resignation on her lips, when his head came round it again. His eyes were directed beyond her to the kitchen window. 'Just thought I'd tell you that the gardener is Spanish and doesn't speak a word of English and he's deaf, too, so don't bother trying to strike up a conversation with him, it will only give him stress.' With that he closed the door behind him.

Abby stared at the back of the door in silent

astonishment. What an earth was that about, warning her off speaking to the gardener? Sometimes Oliver did and said the most peculiar things. And how come suddenly he had calls to make? What calls could a mere chauffeur have to make? The man was a mystery but obviously a trusted member of WW's staff.

She sighed in resignation. She was here and apparently welcome so why not make the most of it and try to enjoy herself. Jess would. Jess would throw caution to the wind and revel in every minute of this rather odd situation. So would she then, Abby vowed.

Looking around for a kettle she found one and filled it at the deep Belfast sink and plugged it in, eyeing the Aga suspiciously. Was she expected to cook the breakfast on that? She shuddered and then was relieved to see a back-up electric cooker in the corner.

Coffee first though. She found all she needed and when the kettle boiled she went to the kitchen door and opened it. To hell with Oliver, that poor gardener toiling away in the morning sun looked in need of sustenance.

At the top of her voice she shouted out to the gardener in her schoolgirl Spanish. '*Buenas dias, señor. Quiere café*?'

The gardener looked up, his face flushed with the effort of bending over the cabbages, his eyes twin pools of bewilderment. So, he wasn't all that deaf, Abby was relieved to find.

Abby shouted louder. '*Quiere café, señor?*' This time she mimed it, lifting her hand to her lips with an imaginary cup in it and going through the motions of sipping it.

The gardener's eyes widened. Abby wondered if she had got her Spanish right and if he was deafer than she thought. Then to her surprise he uttered something which to Abby's sensitive ears sounded very much like, 'bloody 'ell' and he threw down his trowel and shuffled off.

Suddenly Abby felt a fierce grip on her elbow and she was yanked back into the kitchen and the door was slammed behind her.

'I thought I told you not to embarrass the gardener!'

The sharpness of Oliver's tone shocked her immensely. He held her shoulders rigidly and Abby gazed up at him, her green eyes wide and innocent. Then he softened his grip on her and smiled benignly. 'Sorry for shouting but he is a funny old boy and according to Mr Webber gardening staff are hard to find. Don't want to cause any ructions, do we?'

'I was only asking if he wanted a cup of coffee,' Abby pleaded her innocence.

'I told you, he doesn't speak English.'

'I asked him in Spanish.'

'He's deaf.'

'He swore at me in English,' Abby insisted.

Oliver seemed to grit his teeth. 'Profanities are the first words foreigners pick up.' He let her go.

125

'I'll have a word with him. He shouldn't go around swearing at the house guests.' He went out the back door before Abby could protest on behalf of the gardener. Poor old soul hadn't exactly sworn *at* her, more a mutterance under his breath. And wasn't Oliver taking too much on his shoulders in reprimanding one of the staff, when he was also one of William Webber's employees?

She watched as Oliver strode through the vegetable garden to have a word with the gardener who had taken refuge in the greenhouse. She bit her lip. This sort of life with staff to deal with wouldn't suit her at all. It was a different world. If she were mistress of the house she'd be sipping coffee with them in the kitchen and gossiping and no one would get any work done. But she wasn't and never would be a mistress of any house such as this, she thought. More Jess's style. She turned away from the spectacle of the innocent, deaf, Spanish gardener getting a dressing down and got on with the breakfast, wishing she had never stepped out of line and offered him a drink in the first place.

'I couldn't be doing with all this,' Abby said as they sat drinking more coffee after eating a huge breakfast of bacon, eggs, tomatoes and oyster mushrooms. The tomatoes Oliver had brought in from the greenhouse, obviously back on good terms with the gardener now.

'Doing with what?'

'Staff and running a place like this. I don't know the pecking order. I mean you and the gardener, for instance, you telling him off. But then I suppose your position is higher ranking. You shouldn't have done, you know, ticked him off. I'm sure he didn't mean it. I expect I just frightened him, him being foreign and deaf and all that. Funny you being a chauffeur and speaking fluent Spanish, too. I suppose it's expected now with all this Euro stuff.' She giggled suddenly. 'I don't expect you get lost over there. Was that your last position, working for some Madrid businessman?'

He was staring at her so hard Abby wondered if she was rambling on too much. She tended to do that when she was ill at ease. She asked herself why she was still ill at ease with him. They had just shared a lovely breakfast and it was a glorious day and the prospect of sharing it with him till WW came home should be a pocket of pleasure to cherish for a while because once the tycoon came back then she would have to think fast and furious.

'You have the most wonderful eyes,' he murmured.

Abby lowered them. He hadn't heard a word she had said.

'Tell me, have you always worked with computers? Somehow I can't imagine you in a darkened room for days on end, booting in and sweating over bytes and icons.'

Abby gulped down her coffee. He did know something about computers. Jess used words like that. Trust her to come up against a chauffeur with the knowledge she so sadly lacked.

127

'I always wanted to be an actress,' she diverted quickly. 'But so do thousands of other women I suppose. It's hard out there. I did a few auditions but gave up in the end and started working on the cruise ships.'

'Cruise ships, eh. Where does computing come into that?'

Abby shifted uncomfortably in her seat. She shouldn't have mentioned cruise ships. She was supposed to be her sister, the computer whizz. 'Oh, well, it's just a sideline. A hobby really. I just muck around with the old computer, you know, between cruises.'

'The package you prepared for my boss, I wouldn't call that just mucking around. It's very professional indeed. Did you work with someone else on it?'

'You . . . you've looked at it?' Abby broached in surprise. He really did have a very good relationship with his boss to go snooping in the package that was nothing to do with him.

'Er, well, Mr Webber wanted me to take a look just in case there was some mix up. I dabble myself a bit, remember, you caught me in your study. So, do you work with anyone else?' he persisted.

Why did he ask such things? Abby pondered. 'No, all my own work,' she told him in protection of Jess.

He grinned suddenly. 'So, beautiful, what shall we do with the rest of the day?' he murmured, changing the subject suddenly.

Again Abby shifted uncomfortably. The change of subject, though a relief, brought another set of worries. Nothing would give her greater pleasure than to wander around this glorious estate with Oliver . . . but her courage was beginning to flag. She couldn't even answer Oliver's questions coherently let alone come face to face with WW and try and somehow sell her sister's package to him. Oh, Jess, she groaned inwardly, it's such a mess and I do want to do my very best for you but I'm hopeless.

'I do rather think I'd like to go home,' Abby whispered plaintively.

'What for?' Oliver laughed. 'Most girls would give a limb to spend some time here,' he said rather condescendingly. 'There's an indoor health complex, swimming pool and sauna and jacuzzi, to say nothing of a stable full of very rideable horses. Mr Webber said to make you comfortable and I would be failing in my duties if I let you go.' He stood up and started to clear the dishes.

He stopped when he gazed down at her and saw her troubled features. He smiled and sat down again, leaving the dishes in a haphazard pile on the edge of the table. He took her small hand in his and squeezed it tenderly. 'Now, listen, Jessica. There is no need for you to rush away. Paris is out and I gather you must be between jobs at the moment. If all goes well with Mr Webber you might never need to work again. Why don't you relax and have some fun with me.' His voice softened considerably. 'To be honest, Jessica, I can't bear the thought of taking you home. I think I'm beginning to fall in love with you, if I'm not already,' he laughed teasingly. 'Stay with me and I promise you you won't be sorry.'

And then he raised her hand to his lips and kissed the back of her fingers and Abby closed her eyes. Oh, how persuausive he was. How nice and considerate and warm and sexy. She wanted to stay, so very much, but did she have the strength to keep up this pretence? And then because he was drawing her up from the table to gather her into his arms, she knew she couldn't.

Just before his lips came to claim hers she tried to utter that she needed to tell him something. But it was hopeless. The kiss was already there, working it's magic on her sensitive lips, melting her bones, sweeping her away on a magic carpet to the heavens.

His arms slid around her to tenderly caress her back and she felt the need for him to hold her like this forever. She was lost, hopelessly lost, as the kiss deepened.

Slowly and helplessly she lifted her arms and linked them around his neck. His evocative cologne, fresh and lemony, spun her senses till she knew she had met a man she wanted to be with, and yes, more than just a day too.

'You were about to say something,' he murmured when he grazed his mouth from her lips to sensuously brush them over her throat.

'It . . . it doesn't matter,' she breathed and then bit her lower lip as his mouth moved down to where her silk shirt gaped slightly. He kissed her soft warm silky flesh and she thought she heard him sigh, clearly as helplessly spellbound as she felt in his arms. Was he serious about falling in love with her? Was she already in love with him? Were they heading for some sort of an affair? Was she as irresistible to him as he was to her?

At last he drew back from her and when she looked at him his eyes were so deeply hooded with controlled passion she felt her heart squeeze with happiness. And what he did next, easing the gaping silk back into place to cover the scented skin he had just kissed, told her he was a real gentleman and would do nothing to hurt her.

'You are such a sweet temptation, beautiful Jessica,' he murmured throatily. 'I can barely be in the same room with you without wanting you in my arms.' He lifted her chin and looked deeply into her dreamy wide eyes. 'You are easily the most wonderful thing that has happened to me recently.'

Shy and embarrassed and her heart thudding with happiness Abby parted her lips and the first thing that came out was a teasing reprimand. 'Only recently,' she tempted.

He grinned widely. 'No, sweetheart, forever. Nothing like you before.'

'Oliver! Ollie, darling! Anyone at home!'

The cry came from somewhere outside. Abby

shot back from Oliver's arms and she could have sworn he did the very same thing for suddenly they were feet apart and a rush of colour had darkened his cheekbones.

'Excuse me a moment, that sounds like the . . . the stable girl,' Oliver said quickly.

Before she could come back with some remark about the darling bit, he was gone.

Curiosity propelled Abby to the kitchen window. She saw a lovely girl astride a magnificent black stallion and Oliver was at the horse's head, leading him aound the side of the house by the bit, hurriedly too. Abby felt a giveaway tug of jealousy at her heart because by no stretch of the imagination could that lady be described as a stable girl. She was dressed in full riding gear, jacket and jodhpurs and hard hat. Abby was knowledgeable enough to know good cut and quality when she saw it. She was lovely too, beauty that came with good breeding, like her damned horse, Abby thought miserably, gathering up the dirty breakfast dishes and slamming them into the dishwasher.

So Oliver did have a girlfriend. Maybe not a live-in lover but someone special in his life because she had called out darling to him. Abby sat down with a bump in the chair at the table by the window. And she was jealous. It was a horrible feeling inside, one she had little experience of because she had never felt like this with any man before. She recognised it as jealousy all the same. She bit her bottom lip hard. It wasn't a nice feeling. Oliver wasn't nice after all, he had lied to her and he had led her to believe . . .

'That's that sorted,' Oliver said breezily as he swept back into the kitchen a few minutes later. 'That was Melanie – '

'The stable girl,' Abby finished for him tightly, not prepared to believe a word of his glib explanation. Somehow her disbelief must have shown because Oliver immediately shot to her side and squatted down on his haunches to speak to her.

'No, she isn't the stable girl,' he told her. 'She's Melanie from Park Hall across the way. The daughter of friends of Mr Webber's. She comes here to ride with the girl grooms when she is down from London. They are away too and old Bert is tending to the horses. She found no one at the stables to ride with and came to the house and – '

'And called you darling,' Abby put in miserably, regretting it immediately. She was showing she cared and if she was going to be hurt she didn't want it known.

'Society girls like Melanie call everyone darling, even their horses. She calls me Ollie to, which I loathe but I have to put up with it because I am, after all, only the chauffeur.'

And it was because he was the chauffeur Abby let the jealousy go from her heart. If he was William Webber and she had fallen in love with *him* she wouldn't have believed that there *wasn't* anything between him and a society beauty. *Lady*

133

Chatterley's Lover came briefly to mind though, the lady of the house falling in love with the gamekeeper, but that was fiction.

She smiled hesitantly and Oliver tipped up her chin. 'I'm glad you were jealous because – '

'I was *not* jealous!' Abby responded defensively and shot to her feet.

Oliver caught her wrist before she tried to flee from the room. He swung her back into his arms and held her tightly. There was a small gleam of triumph in his eyes and a very small knowing smile hovering at the corners of his mouth.

Sophisticated in the ways of love and emotions Abby wasn't. She knew she had left herself wide open with that hot denial and now he was going to tease her over it and she wouldn't be able to bear it.

'I'm flattered,' he breathed, 'and to put your embarrassment to rest let me tell you that if any man had called you darling I would be feeling very much the same.'

She stared up at him, her bones melting again. 'Would you?' she croaked weakly.

'You bet, *darling*,' he murmured and nuzzled her hair. 'Now let's forget girls like Melanie,' he whispered in her ear. 'You are worth ten of her. It's just you and me and the beautiful day ahead of us. Let's enjoy.'

And enjoy Abby did, after making a very firm resolution in her mind. Two actually. Firstly, she was going to be honest with WW when he returned, tell him outright why she had deceived his chauffeur into believing she was Jessica Lambert and why she had done it, for her sister's sake. Secondly, she was going to pick the right moment to tell Oliver the truth. He was being so wonderfully caring and it wasn't right to carry on this deception. But the right moment was all important. She would bide her time and until then, yes, she would relax and enjoy herself.

They toured the estate on foot which was stunningly lovely on such a day, Oliver showing her the gardens and lingering in the rose garden to pluck her a thornless deep red rose which she carried with her, clutched in her warm hand and inhaling it's wonderful scent whenever she thought he wasn't looking. She was a romantic at heart and thought he might be too, but clutching the rose dreamily to her nose all the time would give too much of her feelings away.

He asked her if she wanted to ride and though she was tempted she refused on the grounds she wasn't competent enough to take on one of the superb thoroughbreds in the stables. But the health complex tempted her sorely. The swimming pool looked gloriously inviting. It was covered in a glass dome, the azure blue water was surrounded by tropical plants and the temperature was hot and sultry. At one end of the pool there was a sitting area with a bar and deeply padded loungers and more exotic plants. Abby was completely and utterly in awe of the luxurious surroundings William Webber lived in.

Oliver directed Abby towards the changing rooms, ignoring her protests that she hadn't a bathing suit with her. She found everything she wanted in the room, a selection of bathing suits and bikinis, all designer wear, as were the robes and the pile of springy soft towels. So William Webber was indeed a bit of a playboy Abby thought as she stepped into a slinky aquamarine blue one piece with a Sunseeker designer wear label in it. She wondered what society beauty had worn this before her, or how many come to that.

They swam lazily together and then Abby pulled herself out and sat on the edge of the pool and watched Oliver. He swam magnificently and effortlessly, his body honed to such fine tanned perfection she wondered about his past life. If she didn't know who and what he was she would think he was born to all this luxury.

'The sauna is on,' he told her swimming up to her and grasping her ankles playfully.

'I've never had one before,' she admitted.

'Not on the cruise ships?' he laughed, letting her go to tread water and push his wet curly hair from his brow.

'I was always too busy,' she grinned.

'Surfing the Internet, no doubt,' he said cryptically.

'I haven't surfed either,' she laughed. 'I'd probably fall off a surf board and get water up my nose and I hate that.'

For a second he looked completely taken aback

and Abby thought he must think her so childish
for admitting such a thing. He grasped the side of
the pool and looked up at her sitting on the edge.
He frowned darkly.

'I said surfing the Internet, it's computer jargon.'

Oh, my God! Abby felt a deep flush course her
body, starting from the tips of her wet toes and
spreading up and outwards like a bush fire. Jess
said things like that. What it meant she hadn't a
clue. Oh, she should have paid more attention to
her sister's world.

Abby kicked out at the water to splash Oliver.
She laughed to cover herself, she *lied* to cover
herself. 'I know that!' she told him. 'I was . . . I
was trying to be witty and amusing. You know, a
play on words, surfing. Honestly, Oliver, where's
you're sense of humour?'

'Oh, I get it,' he laughed at last but by then
Abby had scrambled to her feet, cross with herself
for missing a golden opportunity to be honest with
him and admit the whole, wretched deception.

She was in the changing room about to peel off
her swimsuit when he came up behind her and slid
a soft towel around her shoulders.

'Here, let me do that for you.'

And to Abby's astonishment he stripped the
swimsuit from her, mercifully under cover of
the towel. Then he turned her into his arms and
lightly kissed her wet nose.

'Are you enjoying yourself?' he asked tenderly.

'Of course,' she smiled up at him bravely.

'I wondered. I thought you seemed a bit cross with me for not getting your little joke.'

It was on the tip of her tongue to tell him she was cross with herself for not being truthful with him. But it was getting worse. No time seemed the right time to tell him.

'I . . . well . . . I was thinking about the sauna, you know, not having had one before and well . . .' She floundered to an embarrassing stop.

'So what are you worried about? It's perfectly safe.'

But how safe? Didn't you use a sauna naked and she was already naked under this towel and . . . and . . .

Suddenly he laughed lightly and kissed her nose again. 'Come on. You need educating in what most people take to be perfectly natural.' He let her go and she grasped at the towel for propriety and he laughed again and took her hand so she was forced to cling onto the towel with only one.

'You really are the sweetest, most adorable creature I have ever met,' he uttered as he led her to the sauna cabin.

Once inside the hot, hot pine cabin Oliver took her in his arms and tenderly and sensitively pulled the towel from her slim body.

'Oliver no,' she almost whimpered as her bare skin was exposed to the delicious waves of heat.

'It's better with nothing to restrict you,' he whispered. 'There, wonderful, isn't it?'

Naked and shy she stood in front of him as he kicked off his swimming trunks and turned to her. 'You are so lovely, Jessica,' he breathed and kissed her lips softly and then he lifted her and lay her on a towel on a slatted pine bench.

'You're not going to beat me with half an oak tree, are you?' she murmured teasingly. Surprisingly, *amazingly*, now that they were both naked, it seemed the most natural thing in the world. Being naked in a sauna wasn't like being naked anywhere else.

'Birch twigs, not oak trees,' he said softly with a smile as he took up his position on a bench across from her. He lay back and threw one bronzed arm over his face and appeared to go off to sleep.

Abby lay on her side, an arm supporting her head and gazed at him. He was beautiful, so completely relaxed and at ease with her that it made her feel as if they were meant for each other. She cast her eyes everywhere over him, knowing he couldn't know she was looking at him, but she knew. Knew that she was falling hopelessly in love with him. He was different. He had kissed her, passionately and tenderly and now they lay naked together and it all seemed so right.

She lay back and closed her eyes and the heat was deliciously relaxing and sleep inducing but she couldn't let go. The heat was having another curious effect on her. It made her feel as if every nerve ending was pulsing in some uninhibited way. She realized it was a sexual feeling, one of need, wanting to feel Oliver's wonderful body closing over hers. She wanted him to kiss her and love her and touch her body, to claim it forever as his own.

He was kissing her now, deeply, sensuously, his lips parting hers and probing her secret self. Dreamily she opened her eyes and it was deliciously true. Not a dream or fantasy but wonderously real. Oliver was leaning across her, hot and damp, kissing her mouth and running his hands across her breasts. With a small gasp of pleasure she lifted her arms and linked them around his neck and clung to him, her body on fire with need.

And then her conscience stole up on her and like a cold compress it clamped around her heart. She couldn't let Oliver love her this way, not yet, with him believing what he did about her. Her whole body tensed in his arms.

'I . . . I can't,' she whispered throatily as she struggled out of his embrace. Hot and deeply flushed she wriggled off the bench and pushed blindly at the door of the sauna.

Oliver caught up with her in the changing room again. He gently wrapped a towel around her hot naked body and pulled her into his arms and held her tightly, the length of his hard body as tense as hers in restraint.

'And I shouldn't have done what I did,' he whispered. 'Forgive me, Jessica, darling. I find you so tempting. I want you so very much. I want you in my life forever.'

And with that heart-rending admission Abby
buried her face in his neck and bit hard on her
lower lip. She had let everything go too far. It was
all different now. Her need and his need were
powering them into something very scary. They
were falling in love and they wanted each other
and instead of feeling euphoric with happiness she
felt wretched. She needed more time and yet that
more time she craved would be unbearable.

She pushed away from him, took tentative steps
back from him to put distance between them for
safety.

'I . . . it's too soon,' she murmured, hardly able
to meet his eyes. She studied a point above his
head. 'I . . . I want to but . . .

'I know, darling,' he breathed. 'You're right, we
need time.'

And with relief at his understanding she allowed
her eyes to meet his.

'And we have that time, Jessica,' he told her
softly. He smiled, a soft, understanding smile that
filled Abby's heart with a surge of guilt instead of
joy.

He left her alone to shower and as Abby stood
under the cooling pulse of water she closed her
eyes and wished with her treacherous heart that it
was all different. Love shouldn't be a tangled web
of deceit. It should be as honest and pure and
wonderful as Oliver was making it. He was patient
and caring and so uncomplicated he made her feel
like some Mata Hari. She must tell him the truth

and some time very soon before it became impossible.

Oliver dived naked into the swimming pool and swam a punishing length before allowing his head and his heart to right itself. He had come so close to making love to her in the sauna and thank God she had had the sense to put a stop to it.

He was now convinced that she was working with someone else. There was no way she had put that software package together. She knew nothing about computers. All that nonsense about surfing. She had left herself wide open and in a way he regretted putting it to her that way. But he'd had to know.

Not that the knowledge in anyway eased the situation. He could give her the benefit of the doubt and believe that she didn't know what she had got herself into but when she admitted that she had ambitions to be an actress, well, she could be acting her socks off now.

And he wasn't such a bad actor himself. She still believed him to be the chauffeur. Christ, what a mess. He would have to carry on the deception for a while longer in the hope she might confess who she was working for. If she found out he was a Webber now it would be the end of it all. Though her intention was to sell them back their own work and slam in with a blackmail demand for the rest of the knowledge they must have lifted at the same time as the game, she would know the game was up when she realized he had fooled her. It would be the one thing guaranteed to send her flying off to another computer company and trading her wares. There were enough unscrupulous dealers around who would snap up her offer and try to put Webbers out of business.

But putting business aside she posed another threat. He wanted her more than ever now. He found himself thinking of marriage, which was crazy. Married to her he could save her from herself. He had this overwhelming need to protect her suddenly. He cared about her so deeply he didn't want her to get herself into any more trouble than she was in already.

Marriage? It wasn't even funny though his brother would find it so. Will would have him certified. And perhaps rightly so. He hadn't been in his right mind since she had opened her apartment door and started sneezing fitfully. It had been downhill all the way after that. Oliver Webber, eternal bachelor playboy, had finally met his match.

Hauling himself out of the pool he raked his fingers through his hair and grinned widely. Bloody funny, putting all else aside, it felt damned good, bloody damned good!

CHAPTER 7

'And who might you be?' Jess was challenged icily.

The voice cut through a dreamy haze. Jess tried to blink open her eyes, not quite sure where she was for the moment. She stretched lazily. Now she remembered. It had indeed been the night of the century. She could still feel Oliver's arms tightly wrapped around her, his mouth on hers, his long hard body pressed into her. As she struggled to rouse herself she remembered his last sensual kiss on her brow as he whispered something about getting up and having to go out and to stay right where she was so they could begin the day of the century to follow the night.

She smiled and pulled the pillow under her neck and curled herself into a comfortable ball. She was in love and the feeling was delicious, light and frothy and . . . delicious.

'I said who are you?' the voice persisted.

Jess groaned into the pillow, eyes tightly closed on her sweet dreams. Why did the real world have to encroach?

'Can you come back later?' she mumbled slee-pily. Chambermaids were a pain. 'I'm sure there must be other rooms you can be getting on with.'

Suddenly the sheet was whipped back from her coiled form and as she blinked open her eyes in shock she looked up to see that the body that went with the shrill voice couldn't possibly belong to a chambermaid. She was tall, statuesque, impecca-bly tailored in a stunning red power suit and looked every inch a very successful lady.

'Get out of that bed you little tramp,' the blonde shrieked furiously.

Fully awake now Jess shot up in the bed as if the foot of it were on fire. She snatched at the sheet for protection but the blonde was quicker. She yanked it way out of her reach.

'No you don't, honey. Modesty doesn't go with the hooker persona. Now just you get out of that bed before I call security and have you thrown out. Hustlers are frowned on in this hotel. Your damned feet won't touch the ground by the time I've finished with you.'

Jess's temper was quick to rise. This was the second time she had been accused of hustling. The first time excusable as things had turned out but she wasn't taking it from this fast bitch. Who the hell was *she*?

'Be careful who you call names, sweetheart,' she bitched back at her, swinging her shapely legs over the edge of the bed to get gracefully to her feet. Defiantly not defensively she stood naked in front of the now wide-eyed blonde. That was the way to do it. Brazen it out.

'Just who are you?' the blonde asked for the umpteenth time.

'I could ask you the same thing, *honey*,' Jess said sarcastically, looking her up and down as equally as disparagingly as the other woman was giving her the once over.

The blonde was easily six inches taller than Jess, with no curves where Jess's were. The blonde was the archetypal, anorexic model type with the added power of success. Soft, warm and curvaceous, Jess felt like a Reubens model in comparison to her. But it didn't make her feel less than perfect. On the contrary. Icy and abrasive the woman might be but Jess was no slouch in handling people.

'I think *you* had better come up with a very convincing reason for hauling me out of my dreams before *I* call for security,' Jess went on.

The blonde threw daggers at her before whipping a bathrobe up from the floor and flinging it at Jess. She stood watching her putting it on, her arms folded across her skinny breasts and her pale eyes narrowed angrily as Jess defiantly took her time with the job.

'I'm Venetia Crossland, journalist on the *State News*,' she snapped icily. '*And* long-time lover of the man whose bed you have just crawled out of. Now if you are wise, honey, you'll get your butt out of here pronto because I have influence in this town. Rub *me* up the wrong way and you will wish your mamma had never conceived you.'

Jess stared at the other woman, astonished at the vicious outburst and then her face broke into a grin of mischief. She wasn't easily put down, and this Yankee broad didn't fill her with fear. Claiming to be Oliver's lover, was she? Was this a woman scorned scenario? Was she the dinner date Oliver had put off last night? One of the numerous women around the world he could live without? Very possibly. No problem. After the night of the century Jess was in no doubt that she and Oliver had something going, something worth battling for with this pushy blonde.

'Yes, he has admitted he has a girl in every port. Is New York a port?' she asked lightly and purposely vaguely. 'No matter,' she said with a dismissive shrug of her shoulders. 'Ports, cities, capitols, who cares? The truth of the matter is that I was in his bed last night and not you.'

'How dare you! How dare you!' the blonde screamed, almost apoplectic with rage.

'Well I do dare,' Jess told her insolently. 'I don't take kindly to be woken by a screaming banshee so I suggest you get out of here pronto if you know what is good for you. Oh, and on your way out, leave the key card of this suite on the table. You won't be needing it anymore,' Jess added triumphantly.

Venetia whoever, flushed and wide-eyed and obviously very shaken, only aroused a smidgeon

147

of sympathy within Jess's heart. She looked the sort who could handle life and it's let downs well enough. In any other situation Jess's heart would have bled for her and herself at this embarrassing confrontation but Jess was still warmed by her night with Oliver, a very special night. His tenderness coupled with his passion had convinced Jess that it was special.

'How . . . how did you know I had my own key?' the blonde asked, suddenly rallying.

'You don't look smart enough to have broken in,' Jess retaliated, her chin held high and inwardly fighting the reasoning that she had got into the suite with a key that Oliver must have given her so therefore she must be someone close to him. She didn't want to think of that yet. 'On second thoughts,' she held her hand out, palm upturned, 'give it to me now, journalists aren't exactly known for their trustworthiness.'

'You bitch,' the blonde huffed as she fumbled in her red matching Gucci bag. 'You've not heard the last of this. I came to do a story on the richest, most eligible guy in the computer world and this will sure as hell make the headlines. "Tycoon entertains tart in his suite."'

So she wasn't a long-time lover, perhaps only in her dreams. Whatever, Jess was desperate to hear the last of it too, so to be rid of Venetia's presence she impulsively opened her mouth in defence of herself and Oliver.

'You do that, honey,' she drawled sarcastically,

remembering what Oliver had said about political correctness in the States. She stepped closer to the blonde and narrowed her own green eyes at her. 'But you take legal advice before you print a word,' she told her warningly. 'I'm not the tart you think I am and I'm sure the richest, most eligible guy in the computer world won't take kindly to being associated with one, so you watch it, sister.'

Eyes blazing Venetia slammed the key card into Jess's waiting palm. Her lips thinned cruelly as she hissed. 'You could have fooled me, *sister*.'

And because of that last sarcastic stab Jess's hackles rose once again. She rammed the key card into the pocket of her bathrobe robe and clenched her fist around it to try and curb her temper, but not with a lot of success.

'I obviously did, which says a lot for the sort of journalist you are! Pulp fiction, are two words that come readily to my lips,' Jess couldn't resist.

Jess thought she had overstepped the line then, if that was possible with a pushy journalist who must have had worse thrown at her during her invasive career. Venetia seemed to swell with indignation like some defensive cat. Jess only just stopped herself stepping back and out of reach of the physical and verbal punch line which she felt the woman was about to throw at her.

'How dare you!' she flamed again which made Jess think she wasn't a very versatile journalist. She appeared lost for new words to show her anger.

Jess held her ground and lifted her chin primly. 'Thank you for calling, Miss Venetian Cross-patch . . .'

'Crossland, Venetia Crossland,' she corrected forcefully. 'Remember that name. You haven't heard the last of it.'

'I sincerely hope I have,' Jess muttered under her breath as the blonde twirled on her high heels and headed for the door. Jess followed just to make sure she left.

The short walk through the suite seemed to have the effect of giving the journalist time to think and breath, Jess supposed, because when Venetia turned to confront Jess at the door her features were perfectly in control again.

She smiled sweetly at Jess. 'You won't last long, Miss UK, circa nineteen seventy nine. Move with the times is my last tip to you, out of his life. You might have shared his bed last night but someone else will be warming it tonight. *Me*, because we go back a long way.' She paused to look Jess up and down with obvious distaste. 'You're not his type, honey. You'll run to fat in a couple of years, if not before. He likes sophistication and you girl, ain't it!'

Jess wanted the last word, she wanted it so badly as a retaliation against the bitch's insults that she didn't give those last words much thought. Anger and defiance made them surge to her lips.

'Men rarely marry the type of women they are expected to marry,' she told her tightly. 'I might not have bones sticking out of my hips like yours but few wives have. If you ever come near my fiancé again it will be my greatest pleasure to kick your skinny butt down Fifth Avenue. Now get out!'

Stupified the blonde journalist glared at Jess as if she had gone mad. Her classic features took on a paler shade of white and her mouth started to pucker.

'You . . . you are his fiancée?' she wheezed at last.

Oh, God, she'd gone too far, Jess thought in panic. She shouldn't have made such a dangerous claim. But it was out, shot out in anger and defiance of this abrasive woman's insults. Tightening the belt of the robe around her Jess swung open the door of the suite. No use denying it now, she would make a bigger fool of herself if she did and she didn't want the woman to think *she* had won.

'No comment,' she muttered as she gripped the door handle tightly ready to slam it shut after Venetia.

The journalist had an admirable talent for recovery, Jess had to admit. The sneer was back on her face in a flash. 'I won't offer my congratulations Miss . . . er . . . what did you say your name was?' she asked craftily.

Jess hadn't and Venetia Crossland knew she hadn't. But Jess wasn't to be outsmarted on the last leg of this awful confrontation.

'No comment,' she repeated and those were her very last words because Venetia just nodded knowingly with a smirk on her face and then turned and walked tightly out into the wide corridor without a backward glance at Jess.

Jess didn't slam the door after her. She shut it very quietly so the other woman wouldn't know how deeply she had upset her. Jess stood by the door and covered her face with her hands and took deep breaths to calm herself. Her head was spinning. That awful, awful row had been worse than waking up in the morning to face a bowl of out-of-date muesli!

And that determined, wretched journalist wouldn't have any trouble finding out just who she was. That was her job. She probably knew the manager here and what with all that palaver last night with the spilled cocktail and her evening bag going missing the whole world must know that Jessica Lambert had spent the night in this suite. Oliver's suite. She didn't even know his surname. She was in love with and had spent a night with a man she hardly knew!

The whole world seemed to close in on Jess then. Hesitantly she moved across the sitting-room of the suite and stood by the window looking down into the street where life teemed in its thousands, people milling everywhere in the hot, hazy sunshine.

She hugged her arms around herself and rather wished she was down there, anonymous and going about her business or just shopping till she dropped like those elegant women were doing. Had she really just claimed she was going to marry a man she had only just met, and made the claim to a one-time lover of his, *allegedly*? The woman was a journalist, had a key to his suite and was obviously very miffed at finding Jess in his bed and that didn't bode well for a good honest clean bit of journalism. Oh, strewth, what had she done?

But Venetia had no story, Jess tried to convince herself, rubbing her upper arms worriedly. Oliver might be rich and eligible but his engagement would hardly warrant mentioning if that indeed was Venetia Crossland's intention.

Yes, she was panicking over nothing. She was barely awake yet. Jess poured herself an orange juice at the courtesy bar and sipped it thoughtfully. But the very worst thing of all this morning was coming face to face with one of Oliver's lovers, if what the journalist had said was true. Somehow she felt wounded and bruised and supposed that was because of her feelings for him. So soon and yet so deeply affected by him. For once in her life she had met a man she felt was her equal and wanted to be with and that blonde had come part way to spoiling it all.

Shakily she put down the glass and went through to the bedroom. She slipped the bathrobe off her shoulders and held it open to look at herself in the full-length mirror on the wall. For all her gall in holding her own with the journalist woman her insults had cut deep. Jess wasn't fat at all! A size fourteen wasn't fat. The night of love with Oliver had brought a flush to her whole body. True, her hair looked wild and unkempt this morning but . . . surely she didn't look the sort of loose woman the journalist had accused her of being?

Jess lowered her head and bit her lip. Oliver had adored her body. His lovemaking had been so perfect that she couldn't feel guilty about it. These things happened. Never, never would she have given herself so easily if it hadn't been just right and completely natural. It *had* been right. It hadn't just been sex, they had made love. Oliver had said wonderful things to her and he had meant them. She lifted her head and scooped her hair back from her face and held it on the top of her head. When she tried she *could* look sophisticated . . .

In exasperation she let it fall. To hell with boney hips. Why let a skinny bitch like that put her down? She let the robe drop to the floor and went through to the bathroom to take a shower. She had nothing with her, no clothes or her personal toiletries and as she stood under the power shower concern crawled through her. Her wonderful night of love with Oliver had swept away the harsh fact that her bag and its precious contents had gone missing.

A frown of worry creased her brow as she dried herself. Last night she had been floating on cloud nine because of Oliver's charisma and she'd done nothing to cancel her credit cards as she should have done.

So deeply concerned with her problems now Jess jumped in alarm as she stepped back into the bedroom to see Oliver at the bedside table. Hearing her he snapped shut the drawer he was leaning over and turned to her to give her a beautiful, welcoming smile.

It was all Jess needed to ignite her worries, and that dreadful row with the journalist, into a sudden and very out-of-character flood of tears. Slumping down to the edge of the bed she covered her face and wished that awful Venetia hadn't started her day so badly with her bitchy cruelty, and that her bag hadn't gone missing and that she hadn't given it serious thought till just now, *and* that Oliver hadn't given her that beautiful smile because it had tipped her over the edge.

'Hey, what's all this?' he asked with concern as he plumped down beside her and drew her into his comforting arms. He held her tightly as she whimpered like some dizzy teenager against his silk-clad shoulder. 'Now vulnerability isn't one of the characteristics I had you down for,' he tried to joke to cheer her. 'Having regrets about our night of love, are you?' he added softly.

Jess's head jerked up from the shoulder she had been drawing comfort from. 'Oh, gosh, no,' she blurted and lifted her hands to rub at her face and didn't succumb to the undignified temptation of asking him if he had regrets this morning. 'I . . . I don't know,' she sniffed. 'It's all just hit me, last night and everything – '

'I have no regrets,' he said and hugged her to him. 'And you shouldn't have either. We are after all, consenting adults.'

Jess pushed him away, stood up and snatched at a box of tissues on the bedside table. She blew her nose loudly before going on. Consenting adults, she thought painfully, that sounded as if it hadn't been special at all to him

'I'm not crying over us,' she told him shortly, in control again after her silly outburst of sobbing. 'As you said, we are adults. I expect you do it all the time, pick up women and bed them . . .' Oh, what was she saying? She was sliding down the typically female slippery slope of accusations on the morning after the night before, expecting the dawn to be all rosy and praying he would be feeling the same and finding it was just a fling to him. Some of that awful journalist's wicked insults must have rubbed off on her, putting doubts into her mind.

'Oh, Oliver,' she moaned and slumped down next to him, screwing the tissue in her fingers. 'I didn't mean that. I take it back. The gypsies crept in overnight and put a curse on me,' she rambled.

'Jessica,' Oliver breathed with a laugh. 'What on earth is the matter with you?'

'Oh, everything,' she moaned. 'Look at me, I haven't anything of my own. For all I know my room has been plundered overnight, my credit rating will be nilch after those robbers have cleaned me out with my credit cards. I expect they have taken all my clothes as well and then to be woken by that bloody, bloody Valkyrie!'

'Who an earth are you talking about?' Oliver asked, mystified.

'That woman, Venetia – '

'She's been here?' His tone was incredulous.

Oliver got up from the bed and took a stance away from her, by the window gazing down below as she had only just done. It was the sort of thing you did when you couldn't face someone. Jess's heart plummeted. The blonde *was* someone valued in his life.

Suddenly he turned to Jess. 'What did she say to you?' he asked levelly.

What was more to the point she supposed, was what she, Jess, had said to Venetia. She couldn't admit it though, that in a rush of temper she had claimed they were going to be married. He would never understand the female logic of defence in such a situation. He would just think her some pushy female who was obviously idiotic enough to take a night of love seriously. Sadly, miserably, and yes, idiotically, she had but perhaps not seriously enough to think that he might feel the same way as her. It was a very sobering thought. Back on line Jess stood up from the bed and pulled the robe she had practically lived in lately, tightly and protectively around her.

'She said a lot actually,' Jess said stoically. 'It wasn't very pleasant for her letting herself into your suite with her own key and finding me in your bed.'

Oliver turned to her, his face gravely tense. It was a look that said it all to Jess. The blonde *was* someone special to him.

'So what exactly did she say?' he persisted.

Jess could only summon a shrug in her misery.

'Look, Jessica. I want to know. I wouldn't have had that happen for the world. It's cheap and tacky and I don't want you to think – '

'Cheap and tacky,' Jess cried back at him, indignant now. 'Yes, it damned well was, for her and me and you don't come out of this an officer and a gentleman. Was she your date for last night?'

'Is that what she claimed?'

'Does it matter?' Jess cut back bitterly.

Oliver stepped towards her, angry now and Jess thought, just typical of a man, back him into a corner and he'll turn on the anger and make *you* feel in the wrong.

'Yes, it does matter,' he said insistently, coming to a halt in front of her. His eyes were darkly serious as he glared down at her and Jess expected the full rejection now. She prepared herself by lifting her chin and clenching her fists tightly at her side in anticipation of the pain that was to come.

'Venetia is one of the women in my life I can live

without,' he started to explain. 'I'm thirty eight years old and single and it would be ridiculous to assume that I haven't got a past with women. Venetia is one of the more persistent sort. I take her out when I'm in New York and I sometimes take her to bed too. I'm not a monk and she sure isn't a nun. She wasn't my date for last night because I don't operate that way. I would not have simply cast her aside for a better option, you. I had a business dinner arranged last night which I cancelled for you. I've no regrets. I do have regrets that you met her that way and with hindsight I regret giving her a key to the suite. She's a journalist and she wanted to do a profile on me and I have a busy schedule and told her to catch me when she could. Now,' he lifted his hands and gently took her shoulders and his eyes suddenly softened and Jess felt her heart melting. 'Now you tell me exactly what she said to you?'

Oh, he was right. It was silly to think he'd never had women in his life. It hadn't been an issue before but when one had dragged her out of bed and called her names and made claims of being the next in his bed it soured the whole beautiful night they had just shared.

'Nothing really,' Jess mumbled, her head lowered so their eyes wouldn't meet. 'She . . . she was just shocked to see me and me her. I told her to push off.' She plunged her hand into the robe pocket and came up with his key card. 'I . . . I rather took the liberty of saying she wouldn't be needing this anymore.' She offered it to him and when she looked up to see why he wasn't taking it she saw that his eyes were glistening with humour.

'Oh, Jessica Lambert,' he breathed softly. 'I can't imagine any other woman but you seeing off Venetia Crossland.' He brought his hands up to cup her face and looked deeply into her misty green eyes. 'Forget her. I had, completely. I'm sorry you had to suffer her.' He bent and kissed her full on the mouth, a stunning kiss that brought the night flooding back like a warm tropical tidal wave. Jess let it soothe her and then arouse her and before she knew what she was doing she was forgiving him in her heart and lifting her arms to link around his neck.

And then when he moved himself erotically against her body the feeling of something very special strengthened inside her. Venetia was the past in his life, and very wonderfully, Jess felt she was the future.

'I should never have left you this morning,' he broke away from her mouth to whisper in her ear. 'You're far too precious to be left alone but there were things that needed to be done. I've taken rather a liberty this morning.'

Jess frowned and looked up into his face, wondering what sort of liberty he had taken. By the strange look on his face it didn't appear to be a nice one. She tried to analyse his expression, almost guilty was the nearest she could come to explain it. As if he had something to tell her that he didn't feel comfortable about.

160

Jess's heart tightened. It was bad news.

'I . . . I took the liberty of shopping for you this morning. As you said, you haven't anything and I've bought you toiletries and some new clothes and – '

'My . . . my things have gone from my room,' Jess gasped, her eyes wide with distress. 'Oh, no,' she moaned, lifting her hands to her face and swaying with the shock. It had actually happened, she had been robbed and he had gone out and bought her new clothes.

Oliver grasped her upper arms to steady her. 'Jessica, it's all right,' he told her gently. 'Clothes are replaceable – '

She jerked her hands from her face. 'So my room *was* ransacked?' she cried, hoping for a last minute reprieve.

Oliver nodded grimly. 'I'm sorry, Jessica. They were professionals and apparently it happened almost immediately after we came upstairs to this suite. Security seem to think it was partly an inside job. Several staff knew we were here together – '

'It happened that soon,' Jess interrupted. 'But they must have known last night so why didn't they tell us?' she wailed.

'Probably because they thought they could sort it out before panicking us,' Oliver reasoned kindly. 'No hotel likes to think they have failed with their security measures. I spoke with the manager early this morning – '

'But this is ridiculous!' Jess suddenly stormed

and swung away from his steadying hands. Fearfully she started to pace the bedroom floor. 'I should have been informed. There are things to be done, my credit cards to be cancelled . . . Stupid, I should have done that last night,' she cried, thumping her head with the heel of her hand. But she hadn't because Oliver had literally swept her off her feet and into his bed. Why, oh, why hadn't she had her wits about her last night?

'It's all done. I did it first thing.'

Jess stopped dead. Her mind racing. 'But first thing would have been too late if my bag was stolen last night! Oh, I should have thought and – '

'Jessica, please stop panicking. Everything is going to be all right. This is all my fault anyway and if your cards have been used overnight then I will make it up to you. After breakfast I'll take you out and I'll buy you anything you wish – '

'I don't want you buying me anything I wish!' Jess stormed raking her hair from her face with tremulous fingers. The package, her precious software package. That would have gone too. Months of work lost. It was a copy but that wasn't the point . . .

'Oliver, you don't understand. This isn't just a question of clothes and some damned toiletries. Oh, God,' she suddenly moaned, doing a mental check list of her belongings. 'My passport too. It was too big to go into my evening purse. I left it in my unlocked suitcase.'

She collapsed onto the edge of the bed again and held her head in her hands. How was she expected to get back to the UK without a passport? BA had been very good about her missing her flight but they were hardly going to let her on Concorde without a passport. Oh, why couldn't she be more like her sister, sensible and not so prone to making idiotic decisions all the time? Why had she come over here in the first place *and* missed her flight back?

'Here,' she heard Oliver murmur, and then her passport was pushed into her hand. Jess jerked her head up to look at him. He smiled. 'It was the one thing they left behind, your passport.'

Wide-eyed, Jess gazed at it, clutched in her hands, relieved of course but . . . She looked up at him with a frown on her brow. 'Was there anything else left, Oliver?' she pleaded desperate to know.

'Like what?' he asked and even in her bemused state of despair she thought he had said it rather bitingly, as if she was the sort of woman to scream and throw a fit over losing clothes or her favourite lipstick.

'I don't mean . . .' She lowered her head and shook it and then she stood up and faced him. 'Did . . . did they leave a package?' she asked unable to mask her concern.

He frowned darkly. 'What sort of a package?'

Obviously not, Jess thought miserably. A package was a package whatever sort.

'I . . . I brought a package to the States with me,' she began. 'Something I've been working on recently. I've devised a new computer game and . . . and well, you being in the business yourself will understand the secrecy that it entails, how competitive it all is.'

'Indeed I do. So why bring it here?' Oliver asked tightly.

'To sell it of course,' she told him, starting to pace up and down again. 'It's why I came to the conference, hoping to meet someone big enough to offer it to. It's priceless, Oliver,' she breathed worriedly, stopping to face him. 'It's gone missing and if those robbers have any sense they could offer it to the right person and it would be snapped up and I'll lose out.' Jess lifted her hands and pushed her hair nervously back from her hot brow. 'That package was my future. I could have made a killing with it.'

Oliver said nothing, made no comment whatsoever and Jess looked at him in surprise. So much caring from him and yet now he was looking at her as if she had just crawled out from under a slimy stone.

'What's wrong?' she asked.

He seemed to give himself a mental shake and forced a thin smile to his mouth. 'But you have other copies and the original disk, no doubt, so why the anxiety?'

'Because the original's back in the UK,' she told him forcefully, 'and I'm here and the copy was too till it got stolen. Now it could be anywhere and by

164

the time I get home it will all be too late and I would have lost out on something that would have made me a fortune.' And something else crossed her mind. If Abby had done the business with William Webber and he was interested enough to buy it and then her new game cropped up here in the States . . . Oh, Lord, it didn't bear thinking about. She'd be out before she was in. He would probably sue her and no one would ever take her work seriously again.

'Last night you mentioned William Webber,' Oliver suddenly said coldly.

Jess jerked her head up to gaze at him in alarm. It appeared he had the capability of channeling into her thoughts. She was so stunned she couldn't make a comment.

'You said you were a friend of his,' he went on. 'Well, Webber is the biggest so how come you haven't offered it to him?'

'I . . . er . . . I . . .' Jess was lost for words. Wanting to sound big she had admitted a friendship with someone she didn't know, someone Oliver did. So what now, deny she knew him, mumble something about trying to impress him with a big name? She couldn't, it would sound childish and immature. 'Well . . . it's simply because we are friends that I haven't offered it to him,' she blurted. 'You know how it is, never mix business with pleasure.'

'So you wouldn't have offered it to me?' he asked.

'What do you mean?' she asked in surprise.

'Mixing business with pleasure. I'm in the business too, remember, and we had a helluva night of pleasure. Or perhaps that was what last night was all about,' he suggested darkly. 'Perhaps you do mix the two. Perhaps you thought by spending the night with me you might be able to ingratiate yourself into my confidence and sell me this precious package of yours.'

Jess's heart squeezed painfully. So that was what he thought. The rat. But not without a smidgeon of foundation. At first last night she had thought to flirt a bit and promote herself. But then things had taken off on their own and the last thing on her mind when he had swept her off to his bed had been any thought of selling him her idea. Her eyes narrowed warningly. Her index finger came up and she waved it at him. 'Out of order, Oliver Twist, that was horribly out of order! I did not spend the night with you for any other reason than I wanted to.'

'It was only a suggestion,' he muttered.

'Well, you know what you can do with your suggestions, shove them where the sun don't shine!' she blazed furiously. 'I'm out of here.' She strode purposely to the door.

'Where exactly?'

She turned at the door and glared at him. Where indeed? She wasn't credit worthy in this hotel anymore but they owed her. Oh, boy did they owe her.

'To get myself a suite as smart as this because if not I'll sue this hotel for allowing my room to be ransacked. And I'm going down to reception like this,' she huffed and pulled at her robe, 'and to hell with the consequences, so there!'

She turned and wrenched open the bedroom door and was halfway across the sitting-room before she saw the pile of parcels heaped on the sofa and the chair beside it. She stopped dead and her eyes widened. There were boxes and glossy bags with names to turn a girl's head. Chanel, Armani, and . . . and Christian Dior. Jess swung round and Oliver was right behind her. He caught her in his arms before she could make another break for it.

'Oh, no you don't,' he warned, grasping her so tightly there was no escape. 'You have a suite, this one, with me. You have clothes enough now, not that you are going to get a chance to wear any of them, not yet anyway. So all your troubles are over, Jessica Lambert. Or perhaps they are just beginning,' he added meaningfully as he closed his mouth over hers and slid his hand inside her robe and seductively ran his fingers over her breasts.

Dazed, Jess felt herself sliding down to the floor, with Oliver sliding down with her. Dazed, Jess felt the sweet pleasure of his sex pressing against her and the hunger of his kisses on her mouth. But she wasn't dazed enough not to wonder why he had suddenly made such an awful suggestion that she had slept with him for gain.

Later she would thrash it out with him but now she just wanted to thrash *around* with him. She had missed him, while he had been out shopping for her, she had been bearing insults from one of his former mistresses and claiming she was going to marry him and missing him like hell.

Now as Oliver's magic worked on every sense she possessed, as he entered her she knew she wanted her boast to come true. She loved him and wanted to be his wife and if that was being ambitious so be it.

Then all else was forgiven and forgotten as he moved passionately inside her and she coiled her legs and arms and heart around him.

William stood by the window and stared down at the flow of traffic in the avenue below. He smiled a very small smile at the squeals of delight coming from his bedroom as she unpacked the boxes and bags he had bought her. Women, designer clothes and a full-length mirror were a mystery to him. She, in particular, was a mystery to him. She was Jessica Lambert all right. The one he should have dined with in Kensington. He'd started by rifling through her evening bag as she slept in the early hours of the morning, then it had just been a matter of calling David his PA and feeding him the revelant information and waiting for him to run the usual checks, right down to her colossal overdraft.

She was a hungry lady, in debt and living

beyond her means in a fashionable flat in fashionable Kensington. Hungry ladies did dangerous things. He needed to think that to redeem himself. He'd lied to her from the start, about the evening bag, about her room being ransacked. It was all intact, just along the corridor, everything untouched, everything but the package he'd found when he had gone through the room. Before shopping for her he had run it through a computer network in the conference facilities of the hotel. No doubt that she had infiltrated their network. The game was identical to the one they had devised. No other information on her work though, just the game but it was enough to convince him she knew more.

Yes, a tricky lady. She would risk carrying the game around with her but not the rest she knew, that was indeed priceless. No, she'd bring that in when she had hooked her buyer. Tricky and a mystery because there were times when he could hardly believe her capable of such deviousness. Like now, squealing with delight over a few clothes, like earlier and last night, her lovemaking so completely and utterly natural. A woman who gave herself with such unbridled passion couldn't be all bad.

And he was in love with her.

No use denying it. William Webber was crazy for her, crazy for a dangerous lady. He sighed deeply. And what to do about it? Pace it was all he could do. In time she might give herself away, in time he might too. She didn't know who he was, though that had been a close shave with Venetia letting herself into the suite this morning. Obviously neither of them had mentioned names. He was sure Jessica would have said something if she now knew he was William Webber, especially after making claim to know William Webber last night. No, that bit of temptation he had pushed onto to her to confess had passed without incident. Jessica Lambert did not know she was having an affair with William Webber.

William moved to the phone and his hand hovered over the receiver. He should call his brother and ask who the hell he thought he had kidnapped because it sure wasn't Jessica Lambert. But David would have done that by now and making calls while Jessica was around was dangerous. He would bide his time, let his brother sort out his own messes. For now he wanted to be with his own dangerous lady, see her delight at his purchases, just bloody be with her.

CHAPTER 8

Abby stared glumly down at the mess she had made over what would never, never pass for a spaghetti Bolognese in an Italian restaurant. The pasta was way beyond *al dente*. It had overcooked while her back was turned and massed into a congealing blob that was stuck to the bottom of the pan. And the sauce. Oh, Lord she had got it all wrong, there was too much wishy washy tomato sauce, not enough herbs and the meat she had found in the freezer should have been minced. She'd used frozen fillet steaks, hacked them into small pieces and nearly caused frostbite on her fingers because she had been too terrified to experiment with the catering sized food processor she'd found in the larder.

And Oliver had been no help whatsoever. An hour ago he had left her to it, suggesting she cook spaghetti because he loved it, claimed he had paperwork to do in his room for a while and would come down later when it was ready. Paperwork? What paperwork could a chauffeur have to do? Perhaps he was sorting out a mound of parking tickets!

Abby uncorked a bottle of red Rioja and poured herself a much needed glassful. She'd probably got the wine and the country of its origin wrong too. She and Jess always drank red with pasta, right or wrong she didn't know but they preferred it. Jess always did the cooking at home simply because Abby was away quite a lot but mainly because Abby was so bad at it.

Wearily Abby sat at the kitchen table and stared out at the silvery night. It had been the most wonderful day of her life. Oliver had been so attentive and caring. After their swim and sauna they had lazed around the house and gardens some more. Lunch hadn't been a problem, Abby had made sandwiches, easy peasy, and they had eaten them outside on the terrace with a delicious bottle of Sauvignon. Then when the afternoon had clouded over they had wandered inside to watch a video, *Romancing the Stone*, which she loved but had seen before and so had Oliver, but watching it together had been as if for the first time. At the end of the film he had taken her in his arms and kissed her, saying he would kill a crocodile for her, too.

Now it appeared the perfect day was about to turn sour because she was such a dreadful cook and the game was up. She would have to confess that she hadn't cooked that delicious meal for his boss and outside caterers had been responsible. But her culinary disaster could be a blessing in disguise, she convinced herself. It would pave the way for the rest of her confessions, that she wasn't Jessica Lambert, but Abigail, Jess was her sister and the whizz on the computer not she, and she was genuinely sorry for taking so long in coming clean with him but . . .

'But what?' Abby groaned under her breath before taking a huge slurp of fortifying wine. There really wasn't any excuse for her behaviour, other than wanting to help her sister. Things had gone so far and deep with Oliver that using allegiance to her sister as an excuse sounded feeble now that she was running it through her mind. It was the truth though. She had done it all for Jess, as her sister would do for her if she was in a spot. Sisters did that for each other, she would tell him. But she could hear his hurt protestations already. How could you? I thought I was someone special in your life. Am I nothing? Is your sister more important than me? What sort of a girl are you to make a fool of me this way? I'm deeply hurt. Get out of William Webber's house this very minute and never darken his doorstep again!

'Hmn, smells delicious. I'm starving.'

Abby shot to her feet, nearly spilling the glass of wine in her eagerness to get between Oliver and the culinary disaster. She stood in front of the cooker where the mess languished in stainless steel pans on the top of the cooker. She spread her arms widely so he couldn't see it all. Her green eyes were orbs of panic.

'Oh, please don't look, Oliver, I beg you. It's not a pretty sight.'

'Jessica, darling,' he laughed hesitantly 'What's wrong?'

'Everything,' she blurted. 'I've just made a terrible hash – '

'I love hash, it's my second favourite after spaghetti.'

'Oh, listen, Oliver!' Abby cried in frustration. She let her arms drop weakly to her sides. 'I'm an awful cook. I tried but it was hopeless and it all went wrong.' She took a deep breath to urge the rest of the confession into her mouth but he didn't give her space to deliver it. He laughed lightly and took her in his arms and hugged her.

'Strange kitchen,' he offered. 'And I just left you to it. I'm sorry. I should have helped you but I'm a bit hopeless in the kitchen too. Let's have a look and see what we can salvage.'

He tried to ease her aside but Abby was too ashamed to let him. He was so kind and thoughtful in making excuses for her she felt doubly guilty. She firmly stood her ground and clenched her fists.

'I've something to tell you, Oliver,' she said breathlessly. 'And I want you to listen carefully and not interrupt me. I can't cook. I never have been able to. Some people can but I can't. It's just one of those things you can do or you can't do. I can't. So now you know. I'm a rotten cook and I don't like doing it anyway. If I did like doing it

I would probably be better at it than I am, you know, practice makes perfect they say, but the fact is . . . the fact is I can't cook,' she finished lamely.

Oliver was gazing down at her in astonishment at her outburst and then he simply shrugged and murmured, 'So?'

'So . . . so what?' she stuttered inanely, wondering why he wasn't jumping up and down in rage.

'Exactly. So what?'

He was looking puzzled now. Sometimes he was a bit slow on the uptake she had noticed, as if he couldn't make her out at times, but why now when she thought she had made it all so clear?

'You . . . you don't understand, do you?' she bleated.

'What is there to understand, Jessica, darling?' he asked softly now, as if she were a child to be handled with TLC.

Well, tender loving care wouldn't come into it anymore when she spelled it out to him. She took a huge breath and blurted it out in a rush. 'I didn't cook that meal for William Webber the other night . . .' Last night as it happened, her mind flashed. Only last night, twenty-four hours ago! She had lived a lifetime in a mere twenty-four hours. Fallen in love, lived through several nightmares and soared dreamily to heights she'd never thought possible and . . . and now it was all going to fall around her ears. 'I didn't cook that meal,' she repeated fretfully. 'Outside caterers did it all. They suggested the menu and cooked it all and then delivered it with instructions on what to do with it, how to warm the lamb through and what to serve with what.'

Oliver looked at her so gravely she felt her stomach knot painfully. He folded his arms across his chest to glare at her *more* gravely. He hated her for her deception, he'd never forgive her, she had lost him forever now. Then she saw a glimmer of humour in his eyes and a crinkly smile at the corners of his mouth and then he couldn't hold back any longer, he burst out laughing.

And it wasn't funny, Abby thought with a sinking heart. He just wasn't making it any easier for her.

'It isn't funny, Oliver,' she tried to reprimand him sternly but it all came out in a breathy sigh. 'Don't you see? I claimed I did cook that lovely meal and . . . and you said it was wonderful and said what a good cook I was and . . . and it was all a lie, you see. I *lied* to you Oliver.'

'Oh, Jessica, darling.' He gathered her into his arms and held her warmly. 'I do adore you. You are so funny and sweet. I don't care a damn that you didn't cook that meal.' He drew back from her and lifted her trembling chin and gazed down into her lovely eyes. 'Honestly I don't and if you led me to believe you did it doesn't matter one iota.'

'But I lied,' Abby protested.

'So what? The world revolves around untruths. Besides it wasn't a serious lie, just a mild deception and I can take that on the chin.'

But could he take the rest on that wonderful

chin of his? Abby thought in despair, her courage sliding out from under her feet. The rest was a serious lie, though she had never actually *lied* about her true identity, just gone along with his belief that she was Jessica. And let it go on and on and on till now when it was becoming near impossible to confess.

'Hey, cheer up,' he smiled encouragingly. 'We've had a wonderful day so don't let's spoil it over a silly little white lie. Now let me take a look at this disaster and see what we can do about it.'

He lightly brushed a kiss across her brow before shifting her aside and in abject misery Abby watched him step closer and peer down into the pans. She didn't care about the spoiled meal but she did care very deeply for him and his feelings. She should have told him everything but her courage had failed her yet again. She was so afraid he would hate her and yet she knew in her heart she was making it worse by putting it off. When she did finally tell all he might . . . might what? She asked herself sensibly. He cared for her, didn't he? He was always saying wonderful things to her and leading her to believe they had a rosy future together. So what difference if he found her to be Abby not Jessica? What was in a name?

'I think this can be rescued,' Oliver was saying, prodding at the now congealing sauce to go with the already congealed spaghetti.

Abby reached for her wine glass and gulped at it and had a brainwave.

'Let's go out to eat,' she suggested brightly thinking that in a busy restaurant she might find it easier to confess and with people around he might not explode with the indignation she might otherwise get.

'No, Will . . . Mr Webber might come home,' Oliver said quickly as he continued to probe the food with suspicion. 'You were right, Delia Smith you ain't,' he joked, albeit disappointedly.

'All the more reason to go out,' Abby pushed, also suddenly feeling the need to get out and see people. She'd had a similar feeling earlier on and had supposed it was because the lovely mansion was so isolated and there were no staff around. She was used to London with people teeming everywhere and though the country was lovely she was a town girl at heart. Of course, Oliver was wonderful company but they had rather lived in a vacuum and . . .

'No!' Oliver snapped, jerking Abby out of her reverie about the town versus the country. 'No, Jessica,' he added more softly. 'I need to be here in case Mr Webber calls.'

He turned to her and smiled and Abby tried to forget that he had snapped at her rather abruptly. Yes, of course, he might call and want Oliver to pick him up at the airport and he was on tenterhooks waiting for that call because when it came it would mean that their intimate time together here at his boss's home would come to a close. Her thoughts prompted all sorts of questions, to say nothing of the awful ache in the pit of her stomach which was all to do with the thought of at last coming face to face with William Webber himself.

'Have you any idea when he'll be back?' she ventured with first.

'He's a law unto himself. Do you reckon if we ran this spaghetti in hot water it would help?'

Abby took the pan off him and went to the sink with it to run it under the hot tap as he suggested. So he didn't know when his boss was coming home. She hoped sooner rather than later. She wanted it all over with. 'What's he like?' she asked.

'Good looking, rich, clever. It runs in the family,' he told her riskily.

'Oh, he has a family. I thought he was single.'

'He is. But . . . but he has a brother and parents. The parents live in the South of France, retired.'

'What's his brother like?' she asked the back of his neck as he stirred the sauce over a hotplate.

'Good looking, rich, clever,' he told her without turning.

'And where does he live and what does he do?'

'He lives close by, in the same business.'

'Married?'

He turned then and looked at her darkly, which rather surprised Abby. 'What is this, twenty questions?'

'No,' Abby breathed and shrugged. 'I was just curious. It's natural, after all I'm a guest in his house and when he comes back I . . . well . . . it would be nice to know a bit about him and . . .'

179

She faltered to a stop, suddenly realizing that she probably knew more about William Webber than she knew about Oliver. Had Oliver recognized that and was offended that she wasn't asking about him? When she came to think about it, neither of them knew very much about each other. Though they had only known each other a short while, that short while had been intense, every minute spent together and yet she didn't know if he had a family or not. Somehow they seemed to have hedged around it.

'And what?' he prompted.

Abby smiled. 'And nothing. I'll meet him soon enough. But what about you, Oliver, any brothers and sisters? What about your parents?'

He turned abruptly back to the pan of sauce which was bubbling and spitting now. 'I have a brother too, and parents of course. Tell me about your sister?' He lowered the hotplate and turned to her and this time he was smiling at her.

And now Abby wished she hadn't started all this. It had been easier living in a vacuum with him, no one else encroaching into the little world they had settled in while waiting for WW to return.

'Er, what do you want to know?' She slopped the spaghetti around in the pan of hot water and didn't make eye contact with him for fear of giving anything away.

'Let's start with what she does for a living.'

He would start with that wouldn't he? 'Um, not

a lot at the moment, she's between jobs. You're right, I think we can salvage this,' she said, coming off the subject of her sister which was highly dangerous. It made her wonder about Jess though. Was she home yet? She really ought to phone again. If she wasn't home yet she should leave a message because Jess expected her to be in Paris and she wasn't. It would be wonderful if Jess was home though because she might know what to do and come up with a plan to get her out of this mess. *A plan like, why didn't she come down to Kent and take over!*

What a brilliant idea! Abby suddenly thought. If Jess was home she could come down here! There would be some explaining to do but with Jess beside her, a trouble shared was a trouble halved.

'Do you mind if I make a phone call?' she asked, taking him completely by surprise.

He seemed to stiffen over the pan he was still stirring worriedly. 'Who do you want to call?'

'Er . . . I . . . I just want to cancel a dentist appointment for tomorrow. I won't be able to make it. It doesn't look as if Mr Webber will be back tonight.'

She held her breath hoping he would accept it because she didn't want to say she was going to call her sister again. If Jess was home and they arranged for her to come down she would tell him the truth. Yes, she definitely would. Over dinner, she would tell him everything and tomorrow she and Jess would face William Webber together. If

Jess wasn't home . . . nerves hit her again. Did she have the courage to come clean with him anyway?

'Isn't it rather late to be phoning your dentist to cancel an appointment?'

Abby bit her lip. Stupid, of course it was, she finished her clinic at six and it was eight now.

'I've got her home number. She . . . she has several surgeries and keeps an appointment book at home and doesn't mind evening calls at all,' Abby poured out, making it up as she went along.

'Go ahead,' Oliver smiled warmly. 'And then we'll eat.'

Abby was halfway across the spacious kitchen before he stopped her with, 'There's a phone here.' Abby swung round and Oliver was nodding to the wall phone.

'Um . . . my . . . my address book is upstairs. I can't remember her number off hand.' She was off before he could say another word, off and belting upstairs taking them two at a time in her eagerness to get away. On the landing she stopped and drew breath. She slumped down into a Queen Anne chair and held her head in her hands.

This was ridiculous! She'd had enough of all this. Lying, lying through her teeth when there was absolutely no need. Oliver cared about her enough not to take umbrage that she had fooled him. She was making such a song and dance of it all and she shouldn't be. She should be open and truthful but the trouble was it was just getting worse to admit it all to him.

Right. She was going to phone Jess and tell her all, she decided firmly as she got up and went to her bedroom, tell her sister she'd had enough of this deception, she loved Oliver and hated fooling him and this was all her fault and if she didn't get down here to Kent . . . Where, for God's sake, where on earth was she anyway?

Determinedly Abby sat on the edge of the bed, lifted the phone and stabbed out her number. If Jess was home she would jump at the chance to come to William Webbers home, then she would dash downstairs and ask Oliver exactly where they were and tell him the whole sorry story from beginning to end and call Jess back and . . .

The answer phone clicked on. 'Oh, pick up the phone if you're there, Jess,' Abby pleaded and waited. Nothing. Abby's heart sank. 'Oh, Jess,' Abby bleated into the recording machine. 'You have put me in some mess here. I'm not in Paris as planned. I'm at William Webber's home in Kent with his chauffeur, Oliver. I'm crazy about him and hate what I'm doing to him. He thinks I'm you and it's awful and I'm terrified of coming face to face with WW. I wish you hadn't started all this, it's wrong. I feel like a criminal and no money in the world can compensate for what I'm going through and – '

A hand came out and slammed over the telephone, cutting her off, another shot out and snatched the receiver from her hand. In terror Abby gazed up into the implacable face of Oliver. His eyes were narrowed to shards of steel as he glared down at her seated nervously on the edge of the four-poster bed.

'Just what the hell do you think you are doing?' he grated furiously at her.

Abby tried to pull back from him but he hauled her to her feet.

'I heard every word of that,' he bit out, 'every damned word. If that was your dentist, I'm James Bond. Who the hell are you and what sort of game do you thinking you are playing?'

Oh, God, Abby thought in panic, not like this, she didn't want to make her confessions to him under a cloud of anger and fear.

'I . . . I meant to tell you,' she croaked fearfully, 'but it just got out of hand. Oh, Oliver, I'm so terribly sorry for deceiving you. It's not like me at all. I'm so honest and I've never done anything like this before. I just got caught up in it all and . . . and you thought I was Jessica and . . .' She couldn't finish. He was glaring at her as if he hated her.

And then suddenly he pulled her into his arms and held her tightly and she felt the anger and tension drain from his body and she thought she heard him murmur, 'Thank God,' against her hair but she wasn't sure.

She was crying now, deep sobs against his shoulder, saying she was sorry, sorry, sorry. The relief that at last he knew washed out of her with her tears.

'So if you aren't Jessica Lambert, who are you?' he asked between her plaintive cries for forgiveness.

Abby tried to lift her face to look at him but he held her firmly against him, stroking her hair soothingly and gently rocking her, not angry anymore but obviously still very confused.

'I'm Abby,' she croaked weakly against him. 'And I'm so sorry, Oliver, because you think of me as Jessica and I don't expect you'll ever want to see me again and that's why I kept the pretence up so long. I didn't want to lose you and it just got worse and worse and more difficult and – '

'Shush, darling,' he soothed. 'It's all right. You've got yourself into a terrible mess and it's not your fault. I can't be angry with you, my darling. You are still you and . . . and . . .'

He lifted her chin and looked down into her tear-filled eyes. All the anger and shock was gone from his beautiful face and Abby knew it was going to be all right and the feeling was so good she wondered why she'd thought it would have been different. What a fool she had been to let this dreadful deception go on so long. He had shown such deep feelings for her she should have known he wouldn't be cross with her.

'And did I hear right?' he breathed softly, 'Did I hear you say you were crazy about me?'

Happily Abby gazed up at him through her tears. 'Y . . . yes,' she murmured hesitantly. 'It's why I made the call,' she confessed. 'I couldn't bear it any longer, you calling me Jessica and believing that I – '

'Oh, my poor love,' Oliver breathed before closing his mouth over hers. The kiss was deep and forgiving and Abby's heart swelled with love. She clung to him, loving him more for his understanding. He was such a good man, such a wonderful man and she had hated deceiving him and now it was all right.

And because she was so happy and her heart was relieved of all the bound-up tension she had caused herself she was now free to love him unreservedly with nothing to mar the beauty of it all.

'Oh, Abby,' he breathed passionately against her flushed cheeks. 'I should have known you were an Abby and not a Jessica. I love your name, it suits you and I'm as crazy about you as you are about me. Abby, Abby,' he repeated softly, murmuring it within small kisses he played across her throat. 'I'm going to make love to you now because the time is right.'

Suddenly the bed seemed to float up and draw them into its downy depths. Oliver sprawled across her and he looked down into her face and smiled as he moved wisps of hair from her fevered brow. 'It's going to be all right, my wonderful Abby. I'm going to look after you and I won't let anything happen to you. We'll face this together so you need have no fear. I'm sure none of it was your doing. You're just so sweet and vulnerable that you got sucked in. I'll always look after you, I promise you.'

He bent his head and kissed her deeply and sensuously and Abby wrapped her arms around him and clung to him. How wonderful to have his love and support and forgiveness. She had nothing more to fear and the feeling was ecstatic, the lifting of her heart and soul and the weight of responsibility shimmering away leaving her free, free to love the man who had come so unexpectedly into her life such a short while ago.

And then all thoughts left her dizzy head as his kisses took on a new depth of passion till she was helpless under his caresses. He ran his hands down over her breasts and the need for him was so intense and deep she wanted nothing between them. No restrictions, nothing but his warm naked body to close over hers and possess her for evermore.

He unbuttoned her blouse, feathering kisses across her throat and then lowering his mouth to her warm scented cleavage. Abby writhed under his touch, lost herself in a world of sensuality she had never experienced so deeply before. He loosened her clothes and she ran her fingers through his dark silky hair and gasped with pleasure as his mouth closed over her engorged breast, drawing deeply and erotically on her sensitive nub.

There were no inhibitions for Abby. Her love and need for him and her love and need to please him gave her courage to be as free and adventurous as he. Oliver removed their clothes with a lightness of touch that did nothing to hinder the progressive passion of their feelings. And when at last they were naked together there was a delicious rush of desire as their bodies melded and flamed with a depth that had them both gasping against each other. So intense were the feelings as Abby returned every exploratory caress, every moist intimate touch till they were both in such a fever of need it was impossible to hold back.

With a groan of submission Oliver entered her at last, magnificent in arousal, strong and powerful and yet tender and erotic as he pressed into her. Abby flowered for him, clung to him, breathed his name in ecstasy as he moved inside her. He mouthed deeply passionate kisses across her willing mouth as they clung to each other, moving against each other, wanting each other for ever.

They moved as one, they drove their passion hard to heights of pleasure Abby had never known existed. She cried out his name as she teetered on the brink of hedonistic pleasure and cried out again when the release came, a fire and an explosion of wondrous feeling that shook her tremulous body. And then Oliver kissed her ever more deeply, parting her lips hungrily as his own climax drove him harder and harder. Then he moaned out her name, her very own name, collapsing across her to hold her more fiercely. Then a delicious silence except for their breath steadying and their two hearts pounding as one.

With her head still slightly muzzy from their depth of love she lay in his arms, so sublimely happy and content she never wanted the feeling to end. And when Oliver grazed comforting kisses over her brow as she lay in his arms she knew that it never would end. He was the only man she ever wanted in her life.

'I love you, Abby,' he murmured. 'I fell in love with you over a bunch of lilies and sunflowers. We'll be married, of course, immediately. I want you to be my wife and then I can look after you properly. You can leave your life of crime behind you and never look back.'

Abby blinked open her dreamy eyes and gently manoeuvred her face to look at him. His lovely features were at rest, as if he too was suddenly free of anguish, his eyes closed with exhaustion after their lovemaking. His lashes were so dark and long, he was beautiful and wondrous and so . . . so funny. She smiled lovingly at him. She remembered what he had overheard when she had been leaving a message for her sister on the answerphone. She'd said she'd felt like a criminal. How sweet and funny of him to take it so seriously.

She lay back against her pillow in sweet contentment. Darling Oliver. He did say the most peculiar things at times. But she was getting used to them now. She suppressed a small sigh of contentment so as not to awaken him. So this was what a whirlwind romance felt like, deliciously right. It was of no matter that they had only known each other a short while. It was perfectly right. And he wanted to marry her, he loved her so deeply already, he wanted to marry her. But that was his way, she mused happily. Impetuous, darling Oliver. No talk of an engagement, just the simple statement that they would marry of course.

She kissed him lightly on the cheek before snuggling against him. Tomorrow she wouldn't need Jess to be with her to face William Webber. She had Oliver with her now. She had no fears anymore, not a single one. Life was too perfect. Wait till she told Jess.

Oliver lay with his arms possessively around Abby and listened to her soft, contented breathing. No sleep for him, though he ought to be exhausted enough to sleep for a week. In a mere twenty-four hours he had switched from his playboy image, not unfounded either, to a man about to marry an adorable Abby who needed protecting from herself.

He should have known she wasn't an unscrupulous dangerous lady from the start. Poor darling, what had driven her to get involved so deeply in this mess? She was being used and didn't know it. Tomorrow he would find out who and where this Jessica Lambert was and he wouldn't handle her with the same gentle care he had used on

Abby. He'd make her pay for what she had done.

The marriage bit though. Oliver stirred restlessly. Had he gone over the top there? Had that proposal been born from weakness after the most exciting and satisfying lovemaking he had ever performed? He did love her, he felt sure, but had he had his head turned by her innocence and vulnerability and this compulsion to protect all he and his brother had worked for over the years? Once his wife she couldn't go through with what that Jessica Lambert had put her up to. Once his wife there was no going back, it would be for life.

Christ, what had he done and said? He'd never thought about marriage before. Had never met a woman to fill that need. Abby filled his needs in so many ways, though. She was a terrible cook but that wasn't a problem, he had a cook, and so many staff she wouldn't ever have to do anything but love and adore him as she so obviously did.

But how would she feel when he admitted to her that he wasn't the chauffeur but the rich clever brother of that other rich clever brother, William Webber? She would be delighted of course, as any other woman would be to find she had landed one of life's most eligible bachelors. It was a good feeling knowing she loved him for himself and not for his money. With the others he had never known. Probably why he and Will were such confirmed bachelors, you never really knew what women thought.

Abby was different though and yes, he was going to marry her. He moved to kiss her lovely brow. Tomorrow, before his brother got home, he'd tell her who he really was. He could almost hear her cries of delight already.

She murmured softly next to him and he moved against her and she smiled sleepily and as he started to make love to her again his head emptied of all else but giving this lovely creature his very best.

CHAPTER 9

Jess straddled Oliver and worked at him and thought she must be the luckiest girl alive. He was a lover par excellence. Insatiable too. He made her feel so good. He lavished her with attention and she had hardly drawn breath all day. Venetia was forgotten, her lost package was a thing of the past to be worried about in the future and definitely not now, and now she couldn't do enough for him. She worked harder to relieve him.

'Jessica, honey,' he groaned under her, 'are you sure you know what you are doing? It's getting damned worse rather than better.'

Jess laughed and pummelled her hands into his back all the more. He lay face down under her on the bed and she was astride his buttocks and working her way up every vertebra of his spine with aromatherapy oil, working it into his muscles and trying to ease the pain in his back.

'You have to reach the pain barrier before you reap the benefits,' she told him. 'Your own fault anyway, dragging me around every New York art gallery this afternoon, playing the hero and not admitting to a dodgy back.'

'It wasn't dodgy till I met you,' he groaned into the pillow.

'Aha, blaming me for your insatiable sexual appetite, eh?'

'No, blaming your's. You can't keep your hands off me.'

She gave him one last viscious pressure plunge on the base of his spine as punishment for that remark but before she knew it she was jerked off his buttocks and he had rolled her under him.

'Now look what you've done,' he groaned at her and thrust himself hard against her.

'That was the intention,' she giggled as she took his erection in her hands and stroked him seductively. 'Sex is the best therapy for an aching back.'

'So why the massage?' he asked as he grazed his lips heatedly over her mouth.

'Double indemnity,' she told him. 'I wanted to arouse you in case you couldn't arouse yourself.'

'Hardly a problem with us,' he murmured as he parted her thighs and stroked her temptingly. 'I could do this all day,' he added.

'You do,' she whispered, aroused to breaking point already. 'I nearly died of embarrassment when you took me in your arms in front of that Botticelli.'

'Botticelli wouldn't have minded. He would have loved to have painted you.'

'Are you saying I'm fat?' she uttered weakly as he thrust into her so expertly

'I'm saying I adore your curves as Botticelli would have and Reubens and the other guys who painted fat ladies.'

'So I am fat,' Jess said morosely, putting it on because he'd just said he adored every curve. She wriggled under him, knowing it drove him wild.

'Perfect for me but then I'm a greedy bastard. I want it all and you, sweetheart, have it all, in triplicate,' he teased. As he moved inside her, he bent and took her lips possessively and then murmured. 'You talk too much.'

'Huh, that's good coming from you,' she rejoined and then gasped with pleasure as he moved so erotically against her she thought she might never speak again.

'Sex machine,' he groaned when at last they collapsed together, hot and moist and drawing deep breaths.

Jess laughed and leaned up on one elbow to look down into his face. She tweaked at the silver grey hair at his temples. 'You know for an old man you're a bit of a sex machine yourself.'

'I'm only thirty eight going on seventy five at this present moment,' he told her gruffly. He opened his eyes and smiled at her, reached up and cupped the back of her head to pull her down to him to part her lips once again. His eyes were serious when he let her go after plundering her mouth till she thought he was ready to start all over again.

'You, Jessica Lambert are some lady, you know. I like a lady with a head, yours fascinates me. Tell me about this computer game you've thought up. I'll tell you if it's any good and – '

Jess laughed and pushed him away. 'Where's the romance in your soul, buster,' she teased, swinging her legs off the bed and reaching for the pure silk oyster-coloured robe he had bought her. 'Who wants to talk of such things at a time like this?'

He grinned at her as she sat at the dressing table and pushed at her hair and peered at her flushed face in the mirror.

'Now come on, don't be picky. I've loaded up the compliments, comparing you to a priceless oil painting, now I'm bored and want to talk computers and – '

Jess turned and with a mock cry of disgust hurled a hairbrush at him. He ducked and it clattered against the carved headboard and he laughed and sat up in the bed and topped up both their glasses of champagne.

Jess turned back to the mirror and looked at him through the reflection and her heart squeezed with feeling for him. They were so good together that it was like her best romantic fantasy in life coming true and then winning the national lottery the same week. *Your cup runneth over*. She'd by pass the win on the national lottery though if she had to make a choice between it and him. She watched him in the mirror, sipping his champagne and watching her watching him. Oh, boy, was this affair special. It had it all, laughter and fun and sex and the man had a brilliant brain and knew it all. Art and culture, how they had argued over Picasso, him against that particular style of modernism, Jess all for it. But she had seen his point and he had seen hers and though neither had been swayed either way the argument had been sizzlingly stimulating. *And* he was the one man in the world who could hint jokingly at her abundance of curves and get away with it.

'Venetia said I would run to fat soon,' she uttered as she got up and slid the silky robe off her shoulders to look at the body he adored so much. Self-obsessed she normally wasn't, but that crosspatch journalist had got to her.

'So what if you do,' he told her. 'It matters not to me. I lo . . . I like you the way you are,' he corrected quickly.

Slowly Jess turned to him, her heart on hold. He had nearly said he *loved* her the way she was. The fact that he had corrected love to like she saw as a defensive action, as if he didn't want to commit himself so soon. She was already committed, body and soul and because of the incredible way they were together she thought he must surely feel the same. But he didn't seem the sort to be rushed. He could be cool and calculating as well as being a lot of fun to be with. She had watched the way he'd negotiated the asking price of an oil painting, secured it at several thousand dollars below what they were asking. All done with cool calm integrity and grace and infinite patience which had left Jessica in awe.

'I have a confession to make,' she said at last.

'Ah, I don't think I'm going to like the sound of this,' he mused.

Jess shrugged. 'You're going to get it anyway.' She took a deep breath and noticed that Oliver seemed to be holding his own in expectation. He looked rather grave too. She wondered what he was expecting.

'The reason I'm still here, in New York that is, well, I did a silly thing . . .' She lowered her lashes. He already thought her a little crazy anyway, and enjoyed it, so perhaps he wouldn't think her completely scatty when she told him.

'I missed my flight back to the UK. What with the time difference and all that it's easily done,' she said with a dismissive shrug. 'BA promised to get me on another flight home and well . . . they did, they called this morning when you had popped downstairs for a paper. Anyway . . . it went . . . sort of two hours ago . . . and well, obviously without me . . . and . . . and I should have told you.'

'You're telling me now,' he said quietly.

Jess looked up at him and he was smiling. 'Yes, but you're not reading me,' she said in a small voice, uncomfortable because he might think her excessively pushy.

'I read you very well, Jessica.' He patted the bed

beside him. 'Come here and let me put your mind at rest. You didn't take up the flight because of me and you might find this hard to believe but my flight left two hours ago as well. As you see, I'm not on it.'

Jessica flew across the room and flung herself into his arms. She was flattered beyond measure.

'I couldn't bear to leave you,' she uttered helplessly, covering his face in kisses.

'And I couldn't bear to leave you,' he laughed.

'So what are we going to do about it?'

'Fool around here a while longer and worry about the future some other time,' he told her.

So, he didn't want to think about it now, too soon for him maybe. They had a future together though, surely? An affair like this couldn't just fizzle out.

Jess settled down next to him and sipped her champagne contentedly. When she was with him nothing else mattered, now was of the essence.

'Now tell me about this package of yours,' he murmured persuasively. 'I could make love to you for ever but let's take a break and talk about the other thing that is close to both our hearts, eh?'

And because Jess knew him well enough to know that he was certainly not tiring of her and certainly not bored as he had jokingly said she didn't take the suggestion to heart. So she told him all about her computer game, refusing to let the worry of its loss curb her enthusiasm. Best to look on the bright side and think positively, that whoever had taken it didn't realize its worth and had tossed it in some trash bin.

Oliver seemed genuinely interested after she had outlined her idea, he asked several pertinent questions and they talked about it, him asking her how the idea had come to her and how she had developed it to such a stage. Jess found herself going beyond the game and telling how she and her father used to spend hours on the computers together and how she had found their shared interest had filled a void for her after his death.

Later, a surprisingly subdued Oliver rolled off the bed they had stayed snuggled on finishing off the champagne and talking shop and suggested they dine out that evening.

Jess happily showered while he made some phone calls and then dressed in a gorgeous black and cream Dior creation Oliver had bought her, eager to make herself look particularly ravishing for him. During the afternoon she had noticed how he turned heads wherever they went and when she had jokingly pointed it out to him he had insisted the head-turning had been due to her. She was used to male interest but American women gazing at her was something new. But then she supposed he was the main point of interest being so good looking and obviously successful and she, just through being at his side, was a natural curiosity.

'You look wonderful,' he told her when she finally emerged from the bedroom in a cloud of

Dioressence, her Titian hair coiled up onto the top of her head, her make-up perfect.

'Your evening suit didn't suffer any damage,' she teased, looking him up and down and remembering their first encounter, him dripping in banana daiquiri in the cocktail lounge.

'My heart did, though,' he teased, kissing the tip of her nose lightly.

Jess smiled up at him and thought her heart was in a pretty sorry state too. Everytime she looked at him it raced deliciously. This was love all right and it was terrific.

'Where are we eating?' she asked as she tucked her new evening bag under her arm.

'I usually dine at Sardi's but I thought the hotel's French restaurant was a safer bet. I just might feel like dragging you up here between courses and ravishing you to death,' he teased as he put his arm around her shoulder to lead her to the door.

'Sort of intercourse,' she laughed happily.

They were still laughing when they entered the elegant restaurant downstairs. The maitre d' showed them to their table in an intimate, softly lit alcove and after seating Jess he moved Oliver away from the table and spoke quietly to him. Jess watched, madly curious but unable to hear what was being said. Suddenly she saw Oliver's face take on an expression as equally worried as the other man's.

Before Jess knew what was happening Oliver

had turned to her and signalled for her to get up. Apparently they were leaving and fast. Hesitantly Jess got to her feet and then suddenly there was confusion.

Jess felt Oliver's firm grip on her elbow just as the restaurant's double doors flew open and what looked like a small army of paparazzi swarmed in like bees, carrying cameras and with recorders slung over their shoulders and round their necks. Hotel security guards followed swiftly and there was a brief skirmish when one of the vacant tables keeled over but some of the photographers got through and headed straight across the restaurant's floor towards them. Everyone seated at the tables froze into a tableau watching in shocked surprise.

'Move, Jessica, move,' Oliver urged furiously.

There was a binding flash of lights and Jess's first thought was that it was some sort of raid on prohibition like the old black-and-white movies. They were suddenly surrounded and Oliver, still gripping her firmly, tried to push his way through the mêlée of photographers snapping away at them.

'When's the wedding, sir? How did you meet? Is this a whirlwind . . .'

It came to Jess in a crippling, mind-searing, heart-stopping second of realization. These were the press. Venetia was press. She had lied to Venetia in defence, claimed she was going to marry Oliver, simply to be rid of the woman and her biting cruelty. Oh, God, this was the pay off time for her lie. How stupid of her to rub a treacherous journalist up the wrong way. Now everyone knew, damn Venetia had tipped them all off and they were hungry for a story. Oliver was just going to hate all this and hate her for being so stupid and indiscreet with Venetia.

'Miss Lambert, tell us about the affray in the cocktail bar,' a greasy journalist directed at Jess. He pushed a portable microphone into her face and Jess recoiled in terror. 'Is it true you were rowing and threw your drink at your fiancé?'

'Mind your own damned business!' Oliver grated furiously, knocking the microphone away from Jess. And with Jess hanging grimly onto his arm he pushed through them, his free hand swatting at the cameras that were held up to their faces.

The security staff managed to get them to the foyer and into the lift and just as the elevator doors were closing a paparazzo put his foot in the door to halt it. 'Sir, you're the richest guy in town, you owe us a story. Is your affair with Venetia Crossland definitely over and . . .'

The man was hauled backwards out of the lift by security; not without help from Oliver who lunged forward and gave him a hefty shove along with a stream of expletives. His face was as black as thunder.

Jess flattened herself against the back of the lift and closed her eyes in despair. It was awful, awful, awful and she daren't open her eyes and look at Oliver's face. He would hate her for this. It would ruin everything. He'd never understand why she had done it.

There was only the sound of Oliver's deep breathing, trying to control his temper, and the pounding of Jess's heart in the confines of the lift. Could he hear it? Did he know and could he ever understand what she was feeling at this moment? Utter despair and regret for what had happened.

Slowly Jess opened her eyes to see the back of Oliver as he stood waiting in front of the doors for the lift to stop. The set of his shoulders was hard, as he fought to keep control of his temper. In confusion Jess's mind started to race again. He was furious, not only with the press but with her, too. If he wasn't he would have gathered her into his arms to comfort her after their terrifying ordeal. True, he had reason to be mad with her, she conceded charitably. He was probably thinking there was no smoke without fire because the paparazzi didn't go hell bent for a story when there was no hint of one. He would be thinking that Venetia would have something to do with it because he had determindely asked her what she had said to Venetia and vice versa when she had told him of her visit.

But why had those press people rushed at them so dramatically and so determindely? Jessica Lambert was a nobody and . . .

And Oliver was.

The thought crept all over her, tingling her skin as if someone were rubbing her down with a sour lemon. She had never given it any thought before, that with Oliver so rich and successful he must be a celebrity. The press didn't hound anyone who wasn't. Jess clenched her fists tightly and bit her lower lip as the lift shushed to a halt. Was she dumb or what? So damned love smitten she didn't even know who she had been making love with!

'I . . . I expect they got that . . . that story about the cocktail from the staff,' she offered weakly as she followed him to the suite.

Oliver said nothing. Tight-lipped, face as grave *as* a grave, he let them into the suite, almost pushing her over the threshold and slamming the door after them. From then on he completely ignored her and it truly frightened Jess. Twisting off his tie and flinging off his dinner jacket he tossed both down on the sofa on his way to the phone. He picked it up and in a low, low voice spoke to whoever, so low and secretively she couldn't hear.

In a daze Jess kicked off her high heels and went to the courtesy bar. She needed a drink and he would too in a minute because when he came off that phone she would have some explaining to do. She poured two Scotches with trembling hands, her mind already forming an explanation. Venetia had wound her up so tightly she had just blurted out the news of their so called engagement in defence of her own bruised feelings. She hadn't been able to help herself. She was stinging after

Venetia claimed a long-standing relationship with Oliver and had just verbally lashed out. She had done it because she loved him. Would he understand and forgive her?

She offered him the drink and he practically snatched it from her fingers.

'Oliver . . .' she breathed faintly.

'Don't say a word,' he clipped. 'Not yet.'

Jess gulped at her own drink and watched him pace the room, eyes down, so deep in thought it was as if she didn't exist.

'Oliver. I can explain and it isn't what it seems. . .'

She gulped again. He couldn't even look at her. What an earth was going through his head? Fury with her, fury with Venetia because surely he could put two and two together and come up with the same equation she had. Venetia, the woman scorned and acting out her revenge. Unless of course the affair wasn't finished and that was why he was so angry. The journalist who had pushed the microphone into her face had known they had once been an item. Did the whole world know? Oh, God, it got ever worse. She, Jessica Lambert, was but a fling, Venetia was the real thing for him.

Weakly she sat on the edge of the sofa and waited and waited for him to say something. So what was he waiting for, the right words to get her out of his life? She'd die of a broken heart if he did.

Minutes later, though it felt like hours to Jess's fragile heart, there was a light tap at the door which made Jess jump with fright. Oliver strode across the room and wrenched it open, snatched at the papers a valet held out to him and slammed the door on him.

He strode back into the room, scouring the front page of . . . Jess inwardly groaned . . . the *State News*. Venetia had indeed done her very worst, the bitch. Oliver stopped dead in the middle of the room and let out a moan and uttered angrily. 'Jesus Christ!' He balled the paper in his fist and threw it across the room then he turned on Jess, his eyes narrowed dangerously, every facial muscles tense with anger.

'Stay where you are,' he ordered thickly. 'Don't move an inch.' His finger came up. 'You, lady, have some serious explaining to do. Get thinking and quickly, too. You've gone too bloody far this time!'

He stormed into the bedroom, slamming the door behind him and Jess held her head in her hands in despair. If he truly cared for he wouldn't be so mad. Obviously the thought of being engaged to be married to her was as repugnant to him as Venetia's confession to being his lover was repugnant to her.

Oh, why had she been so stupid, why hadn't she thought before speaking to that stupid, skinny, journalist? She had ruined it all now. Oliver hated her, she had pushed him too far. He'd never believe her explanation, he would see her as some gold digger, trying to coerce him into marriage by speaking to the press about their relationship. He was a good honourable man and this was all so damned tacky.

Slowly and hesitantly Jess got up from the sofa to pour herself another drink. She wondered what he was doing in the bedroom. Packing her clothes for her, getting ready to boot her out of his life? She wouldn't be able to bear it. Tears filled her eyes and she fiercely clutched the glass of Scotch in her fingers, and through the blur of her despair she saw the crumpled newspaper lying on the floor.

Shakily Jess put down the glass and bent down for the paper. Tremulously she smoothed out the creases. She curbed her tears to be able to read the damning headlines.

WILLIAM WEBBER, BACHELOR *EXTRA-ORDINAIRE*, SUCCUMBS AT LAST

Jess read it again and again, her heart on hold, the whole of her body paralysed with shock. This was a mistake. This couldn't be true. The walls seemed to be closing in around her. Suddenly she felt terribly sick. She had to sit down before she fell down. She slumped on the nearest chair and read the whole of the article, every word, mouthing the words in disbelief as if by speaking them it would sink in. There was a long protracted deliverance of his previous form with women, his background, his wealth, his status. Jessica Lambert only warranted a small bitchy paragraph, no one had ever heard of her, she was a nobody, a surprising choice for the wealthy tycoon and then her own feeble quote, that men rarely married the type of women they were expected to.

William Webber. Oliver was William Webber! Jess couldn't believe it but there was a photograph of him and Venetia at a charity ball, right here in this very hotel, to confirm who he was. Though she had read about him before she had never seen a picture of him. Oh, God, she had made love to William Webber, she was in love with William Webber!

Stupified Jess leaned back in the chair and stared at the wall. He had lied to her. Fretfully she thought back to when they had introduced themselves to each other. He must have known she was the Jessica Lambert he was supposed to be dining with in the UK and for some very strange reason chosen not to admit who he really was. And she had admitted knowing him too, claimed William Webber was a personal friend, and still he hadn't said anything. Why, oh why, had he done that?

Guilt, maybe, for being in New York when he had accepted her dinner invitation in the UK? Oh, poor Abby, going to all that trouble to entertain him and getting herself stressed out over it and no one had even turned up.

But surely not reason enough to fool her, to make love to her so passionately, knowing he was living a lie?

And now that lie was out. Though he had tossed

the paper across the room before storming off to the bedroom he might have known she'd pick it up and read it and find out just who he was.

Why the deception? There was no earthly reason to fool her, unless of course he loved Venetia and Jess was indeed a fling.

Anger flowered then, not in a heated rush but all the more dangerous for building up slowly. The bastard. Whatever his reasons for fooling her he had the audacity to be mad with her when she should be mad as Bedlam with him. There was no time for hurt, just this slow burn inside her against him for lying to her, making a damned fool of her.

She flung the paper aside and got up and crossed the room and pushed open the door to the bedroom. She was going to have it out with him.

Jess froze in the doorway, her heart seizing. Oliver sat on the edge of the bed, holding the phone to his head and by the sound of the conversation he was booking a flight. But it wasn't that that shocked Jess so, knowing he couldn't wait to get out of her sight was bad enough but there was something worse.

Painfully her eyes locked on what was lying next to him on the bed. Her evening bag. The one that had supposedly walked out of the cocktail bar tucked under the arm of a strange woman.

Jess's mouth dropped open as wide as the bag was open. She saw her room key, her bits of make-up, her credit cards. It was there, before her very eyes, everything.

Realization crawled through her venomously. He had lied to her, more lies. He'd told her the room had been robbed, told her everything was gone. He had bought her new clothes, promised to honour her credit cards . . . Oh, God, why, why, why?

And then she knew. More evidence smacked her right between the eyes as curiosity shifted her gaze to take in what else was on the bed alongside him.

Before booking his flight back to the UK he had started to pack. There were clothes strewn everywhere, bags half-filled, a briefcase open. Sticking out from that open leather briefcase was . . .

Jess swayed, recognizing her software package instantly. In an instant she had the answer to everything and it shook her deeply and painfully. The bastard, the absolute bastard. He, damned William Webber, was stealing her idea! He was the one who had ransacked her room and found the package. He had pumped her for information on it and wasn't even prepared to trade for it honestly. He had stolen it and now he was preparing to make his getaway. The paparazzi had given him the perfect out and now he was booking his flight to freedom.

'You bastard!' she screamed and flew at him blindly, wanting to hurt, hurt, hurt him for his treachery.

He caught her right wrist and deflected the blow before it made contact. So quick were his reactions it took her by surprise and she was thrown off balance and fell across the bed. In the fuzz of her

211

fury she heard him say down the phone he would call back and then he had her pinned down on the bed, forcing her arms above her head and out of harm's way. His eyes were black with fury.

'You bastard!' she seethed again through clenched teeth, hating him for the accusing look he was giving *her*. How unjust! 'You've lied to me. I've just read that newspaper and found out you are William bloody Webber and you lied to me and called yourself Oliver. You stinker. Just you wait till the world hears what a devious rat you really are.'

'Don't make threats to me, Jessica Lambert,' he ground out. 'You've crossed the wrong man. I'll drag you through every court this side of the Atlantic and the other before I've finished with you.'

'*You* . . . you'll drag me through every court!' Jess protested furiously. 'No chance, sunshine,' she spat out. 'It'll be me dragging you by your fingernails through every court!'

'You want to make a bet on that?' he warned dangerously. 'Don't even think about it, you devious little bitch. This whole episode was planned by you from the beginning. The damned cocktail, the seduction, the bloody lot, even down to telling the world we are going to be married. Don't take me for a mug, Jessica, and don't come on with the innocence. You knew I was William Webber from the start because that is what you planned. Just one thing before we get out of here, who is the other little hooker working her wiles on my brother back home?'

'Your brother?' Jess squealed, squirming under him, desperate to be free. 'What the hell has your brother got to do with anything? I don't know what you are talking about. I haven't planned anything. You are the thief and – '

His eyes were needle sharp slits of fury as he positively shook her as he held her. 'Christ, you think you are so smart, don't you? Wrong, Jessica. You're not smart at all, just dumb. You and your accomplice are in for the shock of your lives.'

'My accomplice?' Jess croaked in amazement. What the hell was going on here? He *had* gone mad.

'Yes, your accomplice, you working this side of the Atlantic, her working the other. Two dangerous ladies with one thing in mind, to see Webber's ruined and make yourselves a fortune. No chance, sweetheart, no chance in hell.'

Suddenly he released her and for a second Jess was too stunned to move. Then the adrenalin shot her to her feet and she glared at him furiously, shaking with it.

'I don't know what the hell you're going on about but it sounds as if some madness syndrome has got to you!' she screamed at him. 'I've just picked up that newspaper and found I've been making love to William damned Webber and I didn't know. You said you were Oliver, you bastard and now you're trying to make out I'm in the wrong. All to cover what you are really up to, you thieving bastard. How dare you, how bloody dare you do this to me!'

'Get changed,' he ordered abruptly, his fists tightly clenched at his side. 'Get out of that dress and – '

'Oh, rowing turns you on does it?' she said scathingly, hands on her hips now. 'Huh! I wouldn't make love with you if you metamorphosed into . . . into my favourite actor!'

'Making love to you is the last thing on my mind,' he rapped back. 'Your comeuppance is first on the agenda. Now do as you are told, get out of that sexy dress and get your stuff packed ready for moving out of here tomorrow. All your belongings are in the other bedroom and you sleep in there tonight because I don't want you in my bed again. Move because we have a flight to catch first thing in the morning.'

Jess stared at him in complete and utter disbelief, thinking things were getting worse. 'I'm going nowhere with you,' she retorted as if he was crazy. 'I'll get my own flight back to the UK.'

She reached across the bed and snatched up her evening bag and then snatched up her package too and waved it at him. 'How could you, Oliver, or William, or whatever your damn name is? How could you steal my bag, steal my property, lie to me, cheat me, bloody ruin me?'

He ignored her evening bag but wrenched the package from her hand, so powerfully and determindely he threw her off balance and she had to grasp the headboard to steady herself. He held the package behind him so she couldn't reach it.

He laughed then, a dry cynical laugh without humour. 'You have the damned nerve to accuse me! You're the cheat and the liar. Well, the game's up, sweetheart. I've suffered you up to now, knowing what you were up to but the paparazzi were the last straw. How dare you claim to be my fiancée? You don't con me any further. The buck stops here. Now do as you're told and get changed and packed. We're getting out of here in the morning because the press don't give up. We'll be hounded into the ground.'

'Good!' Jess yelled at him, waving her bag at him, threatening to hit him with it if he stepped an inch closer to her. 'I'll give a bloody press conference now, a kiss and tell story and boy will I tell what you have done to me, stealing from me, stealing my ideas. Then you'll be in the mire, right up to your neck in it!'

She went to turn towards the door but he spun her back to him, gripping her so fiercely she feared for her life.

'You are the one up to your neck in it, sweetheart. Now listen good. When we leave this suite together in the morning you will not utter one word. Do you hear me, not one single word to anyone,' he ground out unmercifully. 'We are the engaged couple, remember? You will cling onto my arm as if we are indeed a loving couple. You'll cling onto my arm as if your worthless little life depended on it and let me tell you, it does. You utter one word out of line

215

and you are going to be in serious trouble.'

'Huh, don't try and scare me, buster,' she seethed defiantly. 'I'm not flying back to the UK with you and if you think – '

'Who said anything about flying home! No, Jessica Lambert, it isn't going to be as easy as that. You'll find out where we are going when we get there. Till then keep your pretty little mouth tightly shut.'

And then Jess laughed. She couldn't hold it back a second longer. 'You really are mad,' she laughed, shrugging herself forcefully out of his grip. 'I'm going nowhere with you,' she told him for the second time.

'You are, Jessica,' he told her firmly and decisively. 'You jump when I shout from now on because you are in big trouble. My brother and your accomplice will be on their way to the same destination shortly and when we rendezvous the pair of you will be held till our lawyer arrives.'

'Held, lawyer, accomplice,' Jess croaked out, parrot fashion. 'You are out of your mind! What accomplice? I haven't got one. I don't know what you are talking about!'

He glowered at her as if she were the one pleading insanity.

'The little bitch passing herself off as you, wining and dining my brother in your Kensington apartment and trying to work the same scam as yourself. Ring any bells, does it?' he mocked cruelly. 'He's been holding her hostage in the

216

UK while you've been working your charms on me. Well, crunch time is approaching and you two are in for a few shocks because we don't take kindly to blackmail attempts.'

Numbness crept all over Jess. Oh, he was mad, her head was spinning with his madness. Blackmail, scams, hostage. What had he said, Abby, her darling sister, was being held hostage in the UK? Oh, my God, what was happening, what an earth had gone wrong?

'I mean it, Jessica,' William Webber told her darkly, his eyes so deadly cold and serious she knew he did.

But she couldn't move. Her body was cold and paralysed with shock. And then her head started to clear, though she still didn't understand him. All she did understand was that her sister was in danger and somehow she was to blame, it was her that had put darling Abby at risk.

Like an automatum she eventually moved to the door. She had to do as he said or she might never see Abby again. They were both in the hands of madmen, him and his brother, whoever he might be. But what had she and Abby done to deserve this? What on earth had they done?

She didn't know but very soon she would, *if* she did as she was told. She had to, of course, there wasn't a choice. They were both at risk. Both in the hands of dangerous men. The Webber brothers. Both madman.

CHAPTER 10

Happily, ecstatically, Abby whirled around the kitchen of Brooklands, hugging herself. It was the most beautiful summer's day, the sun shining hazily and it was warm and humid. She flung open the back door and closing her eyes tightly she breathed in the heady scents from the garden, roses and honeysuckle, their perfume more potent for having her eyes shut. She loved Kent, she decided. It was so English, such a lovely peaceful place. She hoped they would carry on living here once they were married. Not here in the mansion, though. Perhaps William Webber would give Oliver an estate cottage. He sounded a nice, considerate boss to work for. And once they explained to him about the mix up he would consider Jess's project and probably give her a job and all in their lives would be perfect.

And she was going to learn to cook, she decided, excited at the prospect. She'd never had reason to before but now she was in love and going to be married to the most wonderful man in the world and that was reason enough.

Breakfast first though. She'd mastered the art of bacon and eggs so perhaps some kedgeree this morning. She started pulling open drawers and cupboards in the kitchen looking for a cookbook. She found one and sat at the refectory table by the window to browse through it.

'How are you coping without Mary?'

Abby looked up in surprise and saw, what was her name? Melanie, standing in the kitchen doorway, in full riding gear again, thrumming a crop against a long firm thigh.

'Mary?' Abby repeated.

'The housekeeper,' Melanie snapped impatiently and then loosened up. 'You obviously don't know her. She's fine, a bit of an old harridan but then being a temp you'll probably never meet her. Where's Ollie?'

Abby stared at her, puzzled. Temp, did she think she was a replacement housekeeper while the staff were on leave? It was quite funny really, considering she couldn't cook for the life of her.

'Oliver has gone out for a while,' Abby told her, emphasizing his full name. She hoped Melanie wasn't going to continue calling Oliver Ollie, she didn't like it either.

'Where?' the girl asked, gazing around the kitchen as if Abby were lying and he was lurking in the larder.

Abby didn't know. Oliver had kissed her earlier

and said he was going out and she hadn't questioned where because she hadn't thought to. She'd still been dreamy and perhaps not fully awake after their wonderful night.

'Just out,' Abby told her, fiddling with the corner of the cookbook which was open on the kedgeree and devilled kidneys page.

To Abby's surprise the elegant girl stepped into the kitchen and peered over her shoulder at the book and let out a braying laugh that sounded remarkably similar to a horse whinnying.

'Don't bother cooking those, he hates stuff like that. Stick to bacon and eggs. I'll just go and see if he's around.'

'I said he's out,' Abby repeated, on her feet now as Melanie stomped across the quarry tiled kitchen towards the rest of the house. Honestly, the nerve of her, just barging in and not taking Abby's word for it that Oliver wasn't here.

'I know you did,' the girl said haughtily, stopping to glare back at her with bright blue eyes. 'But I'd rather check for myself.'

'There is absolutely no need,' Abby told her firmly. 'I'm not a liar.'

'I didn't say you were,' Melanie said, looking quite affronted. Her beautiful eyes narrowed. 'But being a temp and probably a bit nervous working in a grand house like this, you *could* have made a mistake.'

Abby grinned helplessly. She couldn't go on letting the other woman think she was a member of the staff and a pretty dim one too.

'I'm not a temp,' she told her lightly because she didn't want to embarrass her by sounding offended by the mistake. 'I'm a . . . a friend of Oliver's, staying for a while until Mr Webber returns. We have some business to discuss and – '

'A friend of Ollie's, eh? Business, eh?' Melanie stepped towards her, as she did so her lovely eyes raked Abby from head to toe, obviously not convinced that Abby, dressed in jeans and one of Oliver's shirts bunched into the waistband, could possible be a friend of the chauffeur's, and have business with William Webber as well.

'What sort of business?' she asked haughtily.

Her tone of disbelief rankled with Abby. What business was it of hers? She kept her cool though, because she didn't want the daughter of a friend of William Webber to accuse her of rudeness. That wouldn't do Oliver's position any good.

'Oh, computer business,' she said offhand, as if she knew it all.

'That's not what Ollie told me,' the other girl protested. 'He said you were filling in while Mary was away.'

Abby blinked and it was a while till that sank in. Oliver had said she was a temp? Melanie must have seen her in the kitchen when she had last called, when Oliver had rushed out and led her and her horse away. He must have made up that story to get rid of her. But why would he do that? Ah, perhaps he felt it his duty to his boss not to discuss

221

any business arrangements with friends of the family. Abby rather wished she had stuck to Melanie believing she was temporary staff now. She didn't want to get Oliver into trouble.

'Yes, well, I can't speak for him, suffice to say that he isn't here and I am.' She flicked the cookbook closed and smiled at Melanie, thinking her the sort you'd rather have as a friend than an enemy. 'Thanks for the tip about the bacon and eggs. Perhaps kedgeree was a bit ambitious for a first attempt.'

Melanie remained on the spot, a couple of feet from Abby, still thrumming her crop, and looking at her curiously. It embarrassed Abby to be stared at so. She cleared her throat.

'If you'd like to leave a message for Oliver I'll be glad to pass it on. Of course you could wait or go for a . . . a trot or something. He shouldn't be long.'

Melanie seemed to pull herself together.

'Okey, dokey. No, I won't wait. He's probably on his way over to me anyway. If not would you remind him of the party Saturday night? Tarts and vicars. I know it sounds terribly low class but it's a charity do and we all like to make the effort. Tell Ollie to pick me up around nine. The usual, drinks first at Park Hall and then chocks away.'

Abby's mouth dropped open. Oliver was taking Melanie to a party?

'What are you staring at?' Melanie asked tightly.

It was Abby's turn to pull herself together. 'Er,

well, Oliver didn't mention it . . . the party and well . . . ' Her voice gave out.

'Well, he wouldn't have done, would he?' Melanie simpered. 'It has absolutely nothing to do with you.' With that she went to the back door and turned before stepping out into bright sunlight. 'Make sure you give him the message and you can tell him to call me as well. We usually ride together every day when he's home, and the rest of course,' she added meaningfully and syrupy. 'He'll be suffering withdrawal symptoms if I know Ollie.'

Abby's heart froze as she watched Melanie stride past the kitchen window without giving her a backward glance. Bad vibes juddered through her, flushing her heart into action. Melanie had definitely given the impression of knowing Oliver rather too well for her liking. Riding every day, parties, withdrawal symptoms, what sort of withdrawal symptoms? Not difficult to imagine, she thought despondently as she realized what Melanie had meant. They were lovers!

Abby sat down at the kitchen table and stared bleakly at the cookbook. Oliver had explained that Melanie came to ride with the grooms and it was a lie. She came to ride with him. They had a past together and obviously still a present.

The thought was appalling and pulled Abby up sharp. She bit her lip and stared out of the window. It wasn't such a wonderful day after all. Kent wasn't the garden of England as she had thought earlier, when her love and happiness had made her float around the kitchen.

The more she thought about it the more she was convinced her assumptions were not ill-founded. Apart from Melanie practically ramming it down her throat, the fact that Oliver had told her she was a temp was devious. Had he fobbed Melanie off so as not to arouse her suspicions that she, Abby, was someone in his life?

To give him a huge benefit of the doubt he could have said it out of loyalty to his boss. Abby was here waiting for WW with a business proposition which was highly confidential and was nothing to do with anyone else. But the seeds of doubt were bedded in and she wasn't convincing herself.

The chauffeur and the rich, spoilt society daughter, she pondered miserably, her heart so dull inside her she wondered if it would ever pump properly again. It happened all the time, Lady Chatterley and her lover lived, in fiction and in life.

Oh, she was rambling. Oliver had been so sincere but their affair had been spectacularly whirlwind. And that was the trouble she realized. It had been *too* whirlwind. Love rarely hit you that way, it was more a growing process, surely? But she did love him, Abby's heart told her, because if she didn't she wouldn't be feeling so dreadfully hurt and doubtful about Oliver's feelings for her now.

She was desperately trying to cope with that

hurt when Oliver returned, breezing into the kitchen, looking so handsome and happy and carefree. She wanted to rush to him and fling herself in his arms and forget Melanie's visit and think only of their wonderful night of love. But she couldn't.

'Have you been to Park Hall?' she challenged, beating eggs in a bowl to within an inch of their lives. 'Because if you have you had better start explaining and quickly too. I know our affair has been swift and intense but you said you wanted to marry me and I believed you but I'm beginning to have my doubts. I'm not a temp and you shouldn't have said I was and you didn't mention any tarts and vicars party and I know we've only known each other a short while . . . but what I'm really trying to say is . . .' She slowed her pace, with the eggs too. 'I think we've taken things too far and too soon. We hardly know each other and it's stupid, really stupid but – '

He had drawn her into his arms before she could regain her breath. He was laughing too, again not taking her seriously. *And* there was a huge bunch of red roses trapped between them.

Abby pushed him away and stared at them clasped in one hand and then stared at him, still laughing at her.

'You are a funny little thing first thing in the morning,' he said.

'It isn't first thing. It's gone ten and . . . and . . . what are those?'

225

'Roses, of course. It's what men in love buy for the women they love, romantic red roses.'

Oh, no, gullible Abby was not going to be fobbed off and placated with a bunch of red roses.

'And it is what men with guilty consciences buy for their ladies and don't you think the plural, women as opposed to woman, is a dead giveaway, Ollie, darling,' she breathed sarcastically.

Oliver looked astounded and then he got the message. He tossed the roses down on the table and placed his hands arrogantly on his hips and leaned towards her.

'We've had a visitor this morning, have we?' he mocked.

'And don't use the royal we with me,' Abby flamed, 'and don't patronize me in that tone of voice. Yes, I've had a visitor but she came looking for you and it was Ollie this and Ollie that and you told her I was a temp, filling in for Mary. How dare you do that? You've been having an affair with her behind Mr Webber's back, haven't you? And you still are. Well let me tell you one thing, you're just a game to her. Women like her don't marry chauffeurs. She's using you. Her father and Mr Webber would have a fit if they knew what was going on between you behind their backs.'

There, it was all out. Abby took a deep breath to calm herself. Oliver stood watching her, not saying a word but at least he wasn't laughing anymore. In fact she thought he looked rather relieved for a fleeting second and she wondered what that was about, but who knew with him.

'And another thing,' she blurted. No, it wasn't quite finished yet. 'There is a rose garden out there teeming with beautiful red roses, why drive off to buy any? Unless of course you went via Park Hall to see Melanie and confirm your party arrangements. Tarts and vicars and chocks away and all for charity and all that.'

He folded his arms across his chest and leaned back against the table. 'Ah, I'm beginning to see things more clearly now. Do you want to hear some explanations or are you determined not to give me the benefit of the doubt?'

Abby lifted her chin. 'There is no doubt about it. Melanie came looking for you as she does every morning apparently. You ride together and *apparently* do other things together and you are taking her to a party Saturday, drinks first, *as usual*, at Park Hall. And though she didn't exactly say you were bedding each other, being the lady that she is, withdrawal symptoms *were* mentioned and I'm not daft enough to think either of you has a drink problem!'

'End of story then,' Oliver said dully after a long pause in which Abby wondered what he might be dreaming up to say in his defence after her outburst. He turned away from her to gather up the bouquet of roses from the table. He gave her a very hostile look as he dramatically binned the lot before leaving the kitchen.

So that was it, was it? Abby thought miserably as she stood alone in the kitchen, the silence suffocating her till she thought she would choke. Just like that he had shrugged it off, and shrugged her off too. With damp palms and a heart as tight as a wound spring she stepped out into the sunlight and sat at a rustic bench just outside the kitchen door and stared despondently at the cabbage patch.

She had ruined it all now. Flown at him like a jealous idiot and not given him a chance to explain. But he hadn't even tried to, hadn't looked as if he wanted to bother fighting for her. He'd not denied it so it must be true. He and Melanie were having an affair. And she was some prize idiot for falling in love with him so quickly and so miserably deeply.

She didn't want to be here anymore, she decided fretfully. She wanted to be home, with Jess, to cry on her shoulder and blame her for all this. But it wasn't Jess's fault, she reasoned. Her sister had started all this but she wasn't responsible for the outcome, that was down to gullible Abigail. And how gullible could you get? Why wait for William Webber to return now? It was all hopeless. Oliver had fooled her, he had made love to her but he had someone else in his life. And now because it was all over she couldn't face WW, even for Jess. She just couldn't.

She would leave of course, pack her things and get a taxi and leave because it was impossible to stay now. Depression swamped her as slowly she went upstairs.

'So, our first row and you are leaving,' Oliver said from the doorway of the bedroom.

'You don't expect me to stay, do you?' Abby didn't even lift her head from packing her bag on the bed. 'I thought we had something special but I was wrong.'

'We do have something special,' Oliver told her. 'Whirlwind or not it is still something worth fighting for.'

'You didn't put up much of a fight. End of story sounded just that to me. *Fin.*'

'You were in too much of a temper,' he reasoned calmly. 'You were hurt and stinging from whatever Melanie said to you and whatever I said would come out sounding like a poor excuse to your ears.'

'Well, I'm still hurt and stinging so don't bother with the excuses now!' Abby snapped, pushing her silk shirt down the side of the bag.

'I wasn't going to. True we have fallen in love rather rapidly but that isn't reason enough to believe the worst of me.'

Abby lifted her head and looked at him then, her heart aching because he wasn't making any sort of denial. 'No, it isn't. It's true though, isn't it? There is something between you and Melanie.'

'Yes, there is but I'll correct that to yes, there was. Up until forty-eight hours ago I was a free agent, single and playing the field like any other red-blooded male.'

Abby stared at him, her lips slightly parted in surprise. Where were the denials she had anticipated?

'You didn't expect that, did you?' he said smoothly, reading her accurately. 'You expected a denial. Some sort of explanation that would exonerate me and please you.'

Slowly he came towards and very determindely he picked up her bag and upended it on the bed. Her belongings tumbled out in as much disarray as she had packed them.

He spoke very assertively to her. 'You're not running away; cowards do that. If you have true feelings for me you'll trust me. Yes, Melanie and I are close but we won't be in the future because I have you now. If I told her you were temporary staff it was to protect you. I didn't want a scene. As far as I am concerned Melanie and I aren't an item anymore. I shall get around to telling her in my own good time and I can assure you there won't be any broken hearts involved. She knows the score – '

'That . . . that an affair with a chauffeur in her position is going nowhere,' Abby managed to get out hopefully. Yes, she was still clinging on, praying that what he was saying was true, though she had absolutely no reason to disbelieve him. She did trust him, but couldn't he see that her doubt was born out of hurt? Melanie had been so convincing and it had stung so much to hear that she and Oliver were close.

He glared at her coldly. 'You know I'm getting a bit fed up with this, putting my position as a chauffeur down all the time. It's a good, honest, decent job and you make it sound as if I'm the lowest form of service life.'

'Oh, no, I didn't mean . . . Oh . . .' Abby dragged her fingers through her hair. It was all going wrong again. 'I'm sorry, Oliver, I didn't mean it to come out sounding like that.' She tried to force a small smile, hating herself now for saying and thinking all the wrong things. 'I'm not used to this sort of life, staff and chauffeurs. I mean, you're the first one I've met and I thought they lived over garages and well, you are different and your relationship with your boss is different. And then I find that you have been having an affair or something with a wealthy socialite and I find that confusing and . . . and Melanie is . . . is so awful and I'm not like that and – '

'And that's why I love you,' Oliver said quietly and reached for her hand and squeezed it. 'You're different and sweet and you make me feel a rat for being cross with you. Come here.' He pulled her towards him and she fell into his arms.

'Oh, Oliver. I hated it, thinking you were so close to Melanie.'

'Melanie is nothing. Forget her, Abby. She's my past and you're my future. I shall call her and tell her to forget me and she will because that's the sort of life she revolves in. You're right, I was just a game to her.'

'Oh, I don't understand this funny world you live in,' Abby moaned.

'You had better get used to it, darling, because you are going to be a part of it when we are married.'

She lifted her face to look into his charismatic blue eyes. 'Oh, Oliver, do you mean that? You still feel the same way about me after my awful accusations? I am truly sorry. It's being here this way, waiting for Mr Webber to return and having to tell him I'm not Jessica. It's been such a strain and the deception has worn me down. I wish I had never got involved and I just wish we had met under different circumstances because then it would have been all right.'

'Oh, darling,' Oliver breathed and hugged her to him. 'It is going to be all right. I promised you I would look after you and I will.' He nuzzled her hair and then he drew back from her and looked deeply into her eyes. 'Nothing is going to be right till we clear the air between us. I'm glad you know about Melanie now, though I would have told you anyway because I don't want us to have secrets from each other. But it happening like this has brought me up sharp and made me think. There shouldn't be anything between us.'

'Abby, darling,' he went on seriously, his eyes suddenly hooded with concern. 'I want you to tell me everything and then I have a few things to tell you myself. Nice things and I know you will be delighted but first you must tell me how you got into this mess. Tell me everything.'

Abby gazed up at him in puzzlement, her eyes wide. 'Tell you everything about what?' she murmured.

'Jessica Lambert, of course. All I know is that the scheming bitch put you up to this and – '

Abby shot out of his arms in an instant. Her sister a scheming bitch? What an earth was he talking about?

Oliver took her shoulders to steady her and he smiled and spoke softly to her. 'Don't be afraid, Abby. Just tell me how you got involved with her and how she talked you into all this. I know in my heart you wouldn't have dreamt of doing anything dishonest. She sounds like some female Svengali who has bewitched you. Did you meet her on the cruise ships or perhaps you worked for her and – '

This time Abby shot back a yard from him in confusion. Hadn't she told him Jess was her sister? Her head spun. She hadn't. She had just assumed he knew. And why had he called her sister a scheming bitch, a Svengali who had bewitched her, talked of dishonesty so bitterly, as if Jess had done him some sort of personal disservice? She felt sick and her head felt peculiar and then suddenly it all cleared and she was angry with him for talking of her sister in such a nasty way. He didn't know Jess was her sister but that was no excuse. And anyway, whatever this was about it wasn't anything to do with him. If there were any more confessions to be made it was to William Webber and not Oliver.

'Darling, what's wrong?'

He went to reach for her again but she side-stepped him and lifted her hands to warn him off.

'Don't touch me, Oliver. I don't know what is going through your head but there seems to be a bit of confusion here, on my part and yours. I think you are taking on too much here and I strongly object to you even thinking that there is dishonesty involved. It was a very mild deception, me leading you to believe I was Jessica, and Jessica is far from being a scheming bitch and really all it boils down to is this has nothing to do with you anyway. I shall explain everything to William Webber when he gets here. This to to do with Jessica and him and nothing to do with us.'

Oliver's eyes hardened. 'It has everything to do with us. I don't want you to get yourself into any more trouble than you already are.'

And because of the anger in his eyes and further accusations that she was in some sort of trouble for a silly little deception, she let rip.

'The only trouble I'm in is wondering why you are doing this to me. You're interrogating me as if I've committed a crime. It was only a little deception that was very easy to slip into under the circumstances. You believed I was Jessica and I let you believe it. You are making a mountain out of a molehill and to be frank now, it has nothing to do with you.'

'It has everything to do with me – '

'Nothing, Oliver,' Abby seethed. 'You are William Webber's chauffeur and nothing more and nothing less. While he's a way you might like to think you are the boss around here but the fact is you aren't. I'm not liking the sound of you at the moment. Hoping for promotion or something, are you? Ingratiating yourself into his good books and hoping for a pay rise?'

He was about to reach out for her again, in anger too, but he stopped dead and Abby heard a phone ringing in the distance. She let out a breath of relief because Oliver looked so angry, angry enough to have struck out at her, but he hadn't. He had controlled himself on hearing the phone. Now with clenched fists and drawn features he strode to the door of her bedroom and without turning he barked at her, to stay where she was because 'the truth will out!'

And what did he mean by that, Abby wondered, still angry herself. Angry at him for *his* anger. What in heaven's name had she done or said to have turned him into such a madman, making accusations, insulting her sister that way?

Oh, to hell with him. She couldn't work him out. She'd always thought he said and did some odd things but when you were in love you could make excuses.

Abby slumped on the edge of the bed, thinking

she had done a lot of slumping into chairs and on beds since meeting him. Most of the time it was exquisite being with him but at times, like now, he filled her with trepidation. Such a huge row over something so petty. They were only just in love and yet everything was going so badly wrong. First Melanie, how she wished that awful woman hadn't called this morning. So, once he'd had something going with her but she believed him that now it was over. And then had she offended him again with her accusation that he was only the chauffeur? Why did she say such things? He seemed to bring this out in her, her worst behaviour. But he did seem to take a lot on board, going on about Jessica as if she were some criminal, and the way he had gone through Jessica's software package like that. He did take a lot on himself. He was strange at times.

She waited and waited for him to come back. An absolute age, in which time she calmed herself down. The truth of it all was she still loved him. He puzzled her, though. She tried to convince herself that she must have deeply confused him with her behaviour, pretending to be her sister, but there really was no excuse for him to say the things he had.

She ran the relevant words he had used through her mind again. Dishonesty, Svengali, mess, trouble, scheming bitch. What an earth did they mean? She felt as if she had stepped into an act of a play that didn't belong to the main plot, as if two very different scenarios had been muddled together.

And the way he had latched on to criminal, just because he had overheard her joke about it rather dramatically over the phone. Had he really taken her seriously? And why?

She rubbed her forehead and started to pace up and down by the side of the bed, the lovely bed they had made love in. She stopped and stared at the bed. Last night had been so perfect, loving him, him loving her, so perfect. But it had all gone so wrong this morning, all because of Melanie. She seemed to have opened a hornets' nest of emotions.

But Melanie had nothing to do with what Oliver had just brought up. And another thing, he had said he had things to tell her too, nice things, things that would delight her. She doubted she could ever feel delight again after all the awful things he had said about her sister.

But he didn't know Jessica was her sister, she reminded herself. Perhaps he thought it was Jess's idea to fool William Webber with a personality deception. She would tell him that it wasn't so. As soon as he came back to her she would tell him who Jess was. Her sister who had missed her flight back from New York and asked her to entertain WW on her behalf. Not posing as her, that had been her own idea, to better her position for the sake of her sister.

She should have told him all this before. Last night, for instance, when she had blurted out her confession, not able to live with it any longer. But

237

actually he hadn't given her much of a chance. Somehow they had been making love before anything more could be said. Maybe this was all her own fault, Oliver's confusion. She hadn't explained clearly enough.

Well, she would when he came back. They would sit down and start all over again. She didn't want to lose him, she decided. Their love was too precious to allow it to be lost in confusion.

Half an hour later she was still waiting. She picked up her clothes and shook them out and placed them back in the drawers and then she heard him and turned.

'Oliver, I – '

'Put those clothes back in your bag,' he clipped from the doorway.

Her eyes widened at the grave expression on his face. He wanted her to leave after all. She really had offended him.

'I . . . I've decided to stay,' she told him softly. 'We must talk, Oliver. I'm sorry for all the things I said and there are more things I have to tell you and – '

'You'll get your chance,' he told her stiffly. 'But not now. Get your stuff together, we're leaving.'

'But I don't want to go home now. I – '

'You're not going home.' He stepped towards her, white-faced, all bound up with tension. 'You're coming with me,' he added flintily.

'But where?' Abby asked in bewilderment.

Oliver didn't say anything immediately. He

raked a hand through his dark curly hair and turned away from her to gaze out of the window.

Abby was suddenly afraid. He looked as if something serious had happened and he had bad news to convey to her. But no one knew she was here so it couldn't concern her.

'Oliver, what is it?' She stepped towards him and touched his arm.

He turned to her and then a smile creased his mouth and Abby got the feeling he had just made a decision.

'That was Mr Webber on the phone. He has been further delayed and to make amends he wishes me to bring you to him.'

'Us, go to him? In New York?' she uttered in amazement. 'But . . . but didn't you explain about me, that I'm not Jessica?'

'He already knows that,' Oliver said on a sigh and raked his hair again.

'He does?' Abby breathed worriedly.

Suddenly, Oliver was smiling again and he reached up and softly stroked her cheek with the back of his hand. 'This is an ideal opportunity to clear the air once and for all, Abby. We have to go, he was adamant.'

Abby held his hand against her cheek. Perhaps he was right. A lot of air needed to be cleared. But New York? She could pass Jess winging her way back over the Atlantic.

'No,' Abby murmured suddenly and let go of his hand. She shook her head to add emphasis to her decision. 'I don't want anything more to do with this. I'm not going to New York to meet Mr Webber. This is Jessica's problem, not mine. I've carried out my part of the bargain, handing over the package and – '

Suddenly Oliver snatched at her, gripping her upper arms strongly. 'And got yourself in a terrible mess,' Oliver insisted. 'And now is the time to prove your innocence, or at least to admit you didn't know what you were getting yourself into. I won't let Webber be too harsh on you. He wants this meeting, he insists on it. There will be lawyers present and – '

Abby recoiled back from him in shock. 'Lawyers!' she croaked.

Oliver held his palms up to her and his eyes were suddenly deadly serious as were the harshness of his next words. 'Right, enough is enough. Your playacting has gone way out of bounds, Abby. You and Jessica are in serious trouble and if the pair of you know what is good for you you'll drop the whole sordid business. That's why we are flying down to the Caribbean now. William Webber already has Jessica Lambert in his custody. She has caused mayhem in New York and they have to get out fast. We are joining them. Now I want no more arguments or plaintive cries of shock and surprise. You knew what you were doing, though perhaps you didn't know just how serious the offences you were committing were. Now get your few belongings packed. We leave in fifteen minutes.'

In shocked disbelief Abby spent five of those fifteen minutes rooted to the spot where he had left her.

William Webber had her sister in custody? They were joining them in the Caribbean? This was way beyond anything she could have imagined.

This was all down to Jess, Abby came to the conclusion, rubbing her forehead with worry. What had her crazy sister done now? Whatever, it sounded serious.

And Abby had to go because, if Jess was in trouble she needed to be with her.

With shaking hands she quickly packed her things. Oliver would explain *en route*. He seemed to know everything about everything, which was five hundred per cent more than she knew. Yes, he would explain on the way to the airport, if he ever found his way there without getting hopelessly lost.

No, that wasn't funny, Abby remonstrated herself as she wiped a tear of concern from under her lashes. Not funny at all. Her sister was in big trouble and Oliver seemed to believe she was, too.

Suddenly she was very afraid.

CHAPTER 11

Jess was in no mood to appreciate they were flying down to the Caribbean first thing the next morning, how could she when she was being kidnapped and forced to take this journey under duress? She sat, mentally and physically exhausted, next to William Webber in the first class section of their flight to Grenada, resting her head against the porthole window.

She hadn't slept a wink all night and had only known their destination by glancing at the flight board as William hustled her through check in at the airport. He was refusing to speak to her, refusing to answer her fevered questions on why he was doing this. At one point she had nearly admitted that her so called accomplice was in fact her younger sister and if anything happened to her he would wish he had never been born. But she held back, fearing that if he did know they were so close, the torture, or whatever he had planned for the pair of them, would be intensified.

Jess moved her head slightly to glance at him as

he studied an in-flight magazine, flicking the pages impatiently, so strung up she thought he might snap any minute. This was the man she had loved so passionately and she didn't even know him. He was a stranger, and yet only hours ago he had been her life.

She turned her face back to the window and relived the last few hours. They had been pursued by the press from the minute they had left the Corona State Hotel that morning and in fear for her sister Jess had obeyed his strict instructions before they set off, not to speak to anyone. If it hadn't been for deep concern for Abby, Jess would have broken away from William's fierce grip on her elbow and run for her life, straight to the police, to accuse him of theft and abduction. But she couldn't take any risks till she made sure Abby was safe.

She blamed herself entirely for this fearful predicament they were both in. All because she had absentmindedly missed her flight back home. She shouldn't have pushed Abby into going on with the dinner party on her behalf. It must have been a terrible shock for her coming face to face with William Webber's brother. And him holding her hostage in the apartment. So Abby wouldn't have made it to Paris for her interview. If only Jess had phoned home, she might have got an inkling of what was going on. Somehow Abby's voice answering the phone, if she had been allowed to, would have given something away and Jess could have summoned help.

But all that was conjecture because Jess had been so wrapped up in her love, having such a damned good time, she had selfishly not given a lot of thought to her sister. The feeling wasn't good.

'You are taking all this not speaking too far, Oliver, William, whoever you bloody are,' Jess hissed at him through tight lips, not able to stand the interminable silence any longer. 'You are childish – '

He turned and his mouth clamped over hers but it wasn't a true kiss, though to outward appearances it would look like one. It was a gesture to silence her, brutal too. A harsh warning to shut up or else.

His voice was a husky whisper which he grated in her ear. 'There is a newspaper reporter in the corner who probably has a highly sensitive recording device secreted about his person. Shut up!'

He went back to reading his in-flight magazine. Jess scrabbled in her bag for a pen and a small pad she always carried with her. She scribbled furiously.

With your devious, scheming, mafia type actions to date I'm surprised you haven't had him ejected from the plane without a parachute at thirty thousand feet. PS I hate you.

She shoved it under his nose. He read it. He took her pen and the pad and wrote.

With your devious, scheming, mafia type actions to date I'm surprised you are taking all this so amiably. Why don't you eject yourself out of here without a

*parachute and save us all a lot of trouble? PS The
feeling is mutual.*

Jess wrote back.

Why don't you?

William scribbled.

Now who's being childish?

Jess gave him a filthy look and shoved her
thumb in her mouth and started sucking it.

William smiled sardonically and concentrated
on his magazine.

They were met at the airport by two large West
Indians in tropical whites who boarded the plane
before anyone got off. One each side of the
spluttering reporter they lifted him under his
arms and effortlessly removed him from the cabin, his feet not touching the ground.

White-lipped, Jess watched through the window as they frogmarched him over to a small white
building set apart from the others and disappeared
inside. The reporter's feet still not having touched
the ground once.

'That's what you get for fare dodging,' William
whispered to her with satisfaction and a smug
expression on his face.

'You *are* the bloody Godfather,' she breathed
back, realizing the unfortunate reporter's rapid
exit was his doing.

He simply smiled at her enigmatically, which
made Jess think she might have hit the nail on the
head. It was a terrifying thought.

All thought of calling on that poor unfortunate reporter for help was now gone. She had considered it during the flight, somehow getting a message to him that she was in trouble and so was her sister and the man she was travelling with was a pyschopath and if he wanted the coup of a lifetime, stick around. Trouble was everytime she had made a move, to go to the toilet or just to stretch her legs in the cabin area William Webber had been there, stuck to her like a recalcitrant toffee paper.

Well, at least with the exit of the determined reporter William would ease up on her, she supposed.

'Can we speak now?' she ventured as they emerged from the plane, Jess nearly choking with the heat and humidity that hit her after the air conditioning of the plane.

'You speak when you are spoken too, Jessica, and not before. I'm still as mad as hell so don't think you can get round me with some feeble excuse you've had time to think up while travelling down here. The journey isn't over yet.'

And it wasn't. In a daze of exhaustion Jess was hustled into a white taxi by William, their luggage following in another cab. She tried to speak again but the black look William gave her shut her up immediately.

The driver appeared to have been given the same instructions, open his mouth on pain of death. He sat stiff and unyielding in the driver's seat and made no conversation whatsoever as he hurtled the cab away from the airport.

Jess didn't even consider asking him for help, she'd seen enough already to know William would stop at nothing to keep her quiet.

The lush green island was stunningly beautiful and Jess wished she was here under different circumstances. But she supposed being held hostage in a tropical paradise was better than being held in some squalid cellar somewhere. She shivered, thinking that they weren't there yet and with mad William Webber anything was possible.

'You can't possibly be cold,' William murmured under his breath, and fanned himself with the magazine from the plane.

'I was shivering with dread,' she hissed, 'wondering where we are going to finish up.'

'You, afraid?' he sneered. 'Drop the vulnerable act, Jessica. You have nerves of steel and you are going to need them.'

'I'd like to know what I've done,' she breathed drily, 'because all this is verging on paranoia. I didn't write that newspaper report, your lover did. I have no marriage pretensions where you are concerned and all I can say is that my computer game must be pretty hot stuff for you to go to such lengths to get it for nothing and – '

'Be quiet,' he warned lethally.

And Jess clamped her teeth together and gazed out of the open window in misery. It was hopeless. But she'd find out what all this was about when they arrived, wherever they were going. It appeared they were driving deeper and deeper into jungle and if she hadn't been worried before it would have crashed around her now. Where on earth would she end up, and would Abby be waiting and what state would she be in, trussed up, gagged? And for why?

Ten minutes later they took a bumpy track that led ever deeper into jungle and then suddenly, over a hump, Jess saw a small marina below. It was tiny and exclusive with only a few pristine luxury yachts moored at a jetty which projected into sea that was so blue it was unreal. As they drove down the dusty track to the secret, palm-fringed cove it struck Jess that she had spent the last couple of days making love to probably one of the richest men in the world.

She knew one of the yachts would be his. He had power, the heavies back at the airport were proof of that, only very rich, powerful, important men had that sort of security back up on call. So why, why oh, why was this mega man doing all this?

As Jess hung on to her seat as they hurtled down to the shore she no longer needed to be told by William Webber to keep her mouth shut. Her silence was grimly self-instilled. Somehow the reality of all this was becoming evermore unreal. She had devised a new computer game, nothing more, nothing less. It was worth a lot, yes, quite a lot but not enough for this man to risk his status to get it for nothing. He'd spoken of scams and her accomplice, all as if they had committed a great crime and –

'Out, Jessica,' she was ordered.

Jess blinked and slowly slid out of the back of the taxi, her clothes sticking to her, a trickle of perspiration furrowing down the small of her back.

'Where now?' she managed to murmur, blinking her eyes in the glare from the shining white seaworthy dream machine moored seductively at the jetty where the taxi had screeched to a halt in a cloud of dust and sand. The name on the side of the yacht read, Webbers' Wonder.

'Crumbs,' Jess muttered. 'What a naff name. Sounds like a wet lettuce!'

For the first time since setting off on the trip from hell William Webber afforded her a very small smile. 'For once I agree. My brother named it.'

'He's naff then, is he?' Her heart went out to Abby, held hostage by a Webber with as much imagination as . . . as a wet lettuce.

'He's rich and can afford to be naff at times,' William told her as once again he seized her elbow and guided her along the jetty.

'Madness runs in the family too, I suppose.'

He made no comment back as a crew member appeared and Jess was shown downstairs to a cabin.

Jess gulped. The luxury was beyond her. Chrome gleamed everywhere, white leather fitted sofas lining the rosewood panelled walls of the sumptuous lounge area. It was all deliciously air conditioned and cool. William, who had followed her down the few steps from the upper deck, stepped across the thick white carpeted cabin to a bar and started pouring drinks. He spoke softly to one of the crew members, who then left them alone.

Jess had strained her ears to hear what was being said but all she could catch was the name Oliver Webber. 'Is Oliver your brother?' she asked.

'Yes,' he told her, handing her a tall glass of fresh lemon and lime juice laced with vodka. 'The crew will return for him when they have dropped us off. He and his – companion are on their way from Heathrow.'

'Your brother and my accomplice?' she questioned sarcastically, sipping the drink and eyeing him thoughtfully over the frosted rim of the glass. He looked as exhausted as she felt. His cream linen suit was designer crumpled, his hair, slightly damp with the humidity, curled at the edge of his collar and her whole heart dragged at the sight of him. Exhausted but still so ravishing, still so sexually power packed and she was still stupid enough to be drawn to him. But it would be an ephemeral feeling, she resolved. After what he was putting her through, how could she ever feel for him anything deeper than a passing sexual chemistry?

'At last you admit to one, now,' he drawled knowingly.

'No, I don't. You were the one that mentioned

an accomplice, not me. I'm just going along with it for a quiet life,' she told him offhandedly.

'I doubt your life will ever be quiet again, Jessica. They say the echo of prison life can drive you insane in the end.'

'You've obviously done time then,' she drawled sarcastically.

His eyes narrowed, not amused, obviously thinking her the mad one.

'You can't even take this seriously, can you? It's all just one huge joke to you.'

'Huh, some warped sense of humour you have if you think *I* think this is a joke. None of this is faintly amusing, Oliver – '

'William,' he corrected.

Jess couldn't help it, her eyes suddenly filled with tears. She gulped more of her drink to quell them before he noticed. 'You took your brother's name to fool me, how low can you get, *William*,' she uttered mournfully.

'Never as low and as calculating as you, Jessica,' he said solemnly, his eyes cold and accusing. He drained his drink and then nodded across the lounge. 'There's a bathroom through there. Perhaps you'd like to freshen up. The last leg of our journey will be over in an hour.'

Jess lifted her chin. 'And then where will we be?'

'On my island, where privacy and isolation will enable us to get down to the root of all this.'

Jess gave him a sardonic smile. 'Along with the

251

lawyers and your brother and my accomplice eh?' she drawled sarcastically. 'What's the name of this place, Fantasy Island? If it isn't it should be because all this is beyond belief.'

He shrugged. 'I agree. And it all started with a banana daiquiri. You are some fantastic lady, Jessica Lambert. With your talent for deception I rather wish we were on the same side instead of the deadliest of enemies.'

Jess was chilled to the bone by that. Her eyes flickered hurtfully. 'And yet you made love to me,' she said faintly. 'According to you, I engineered it all and still you made love to me, knowing who I was.'

His eyes narrowed darkly. 'It takes two, Jessica. Your motivation doesn't go without question either, but mine was to save what I've worked for all my life, decently and honestly. You are powered by nothing but greed, a huge difference in my book.'

'You cold bastard,' she breathed, hating him down to her heels, hurt beyond measure that he could bring their passion down to such a miserable, unfeeling level. Every time he had touched her, caressed her, made love to her, he had been doing it with intent. And he believed her to be similarly motivated. It hurt terribly. It angered her maddeningly. She wanted revenge for all this, but what could she say or do to get back at him?

He said nothing, simply nodded his head across the room, reminding her of the bathroom. Then he turned away from her.

The oily throb of the engines started up and jolted Jess out of her dreamlike state. Never had she felt so weak and ineffectual. Always she had been able to pick herself up and give herself a mental shakedown and get her life on line again. This time she felt as if there was nothing more to draw on. No strength, no flush of adrenalin, no will. She was bone weary, sick with worry over Abby, and desolate that her heart had fooled her into falling in love with a cruel monster.

Shakily Jess found the luxury bathroom and locked herself in it. Where and when had it started to go wrong? What was he accusing her of? What had happened to Abby at the hands of his awful brother? Abby was innocent of all this and she had involved her and it was all her fault and where was it going to end?

There was so much she didn't understand, so much confusion and all over that stupid software package that William now had in his possession. The other copy was no doubt in the possession of his ghastly mad brother, because Abby in her innocence would have handed it over. So, putting aside all this performance of kidnapping and holding them hostage, those devious twisters had her over a barrel. She wouldn't be able to sell it elsewhere. Webbers would produce it and with the power they had she had as much chance of taking them to court and suing as she would have of winning the Grand National on the back of a Vietnamese pot-bellied pig!

Jess slid out of the clothes she had travelled in, a cream silk Versace dress William had bought her. Why had he done all those things when he thought her to be some sort of criminal? None of it made sense. It was Venetia's newspaper report that had sparked all this, a sort of last straw that had tipped him over the edge. Supposing she hadn't made that stupid marriage statement to Venetia, what then? Would he have carried on loving her, spoiling her, lulling her into a false sense of security? The end result would have been the same though, she thought miserably. He had only ever wanted her software package. What a liar and a cheat and a rat . . . and the best lover she had ever had or ever wanted in the future. Damn him to hell and back.

Jess showered and wrapped a towel around herself and came out of the bathroom to find a bedroom across the passageway. She gazed at the bed, a huge bed draped with floaty white chiffon. It looked like a wedding bed, virginal and inviting. Her eyes filled up again as she stepped towards it. She would have married him if he had asked her. He'd talked of the night of the century and what he would tell their grandchildren and she had swallowed it all and fantasized about a future with him. And how dumb could you get!

Slowly Jess let the towel drop and slowly she stepped towards the bed. She lay down on it, naked she coiled herself up for protection and let her mind wander. She wanted revenge for what he had done to her, bitter sweet revenge.

But nothing was possible because he was untouchable. He was too successful, too high-powered, too damned smart. Except for . . .

Jess blinked open her eyes and smiled and then uncoiled out of the negative foetal position and stretched her lovely body lazily. He might have her software package but she had a certain package that was irrestible to him. She was it, she was the package that might be his undoing. You couldn't fake passion. You felt it or you didn't. He might have loved her with intent but she had for sure turned him on. And she could do it again.

Sometime soon they would be arriving at this fanstasy island of his and he would come and get her and she would be waiting. Warm and sexy and inviting she would be lying naked on this bed waiting for him. He wouldn't be able to resist her but she would be able to resist him, quite easily after what he had done to her.

Jess smiled and closed her eyes. She'd drive him wild and then . . . and then she would laugh in his face. Just like that, ha, ha. It would be but a small sweet revenge but it would give her great satisfaction to do it. She couldn't wait to see his face as she pushed him away, just at the moment when he would be at his weakest and most vulnerable, just at the moment when . . .

Jess moaned softly and her body writhed under the divine pressure that was pulsing heat through her languid limbs. His mouth was hot and seductive, his touch on her breasts tantalizingly teasing.

His lips moved to one swollen nub and drew deeply on her. She was unfolding like a flower in the heat of the morning sun, limbs uncoiling, skin tingling with fire and ice, wanting and needing and he was giving. Kisses and small licks of passion, his tongue probing the inner secrets of her mouth, his fingers brushing between her thighs. She moaned again and again, soft, hungry little moans of wanting. She moved against him, thrusting herself at his powerful body. Her arms enfolded him, raking through his thick hair, drawing him down and down.

She gasped and arched her back, on the very brink of that exquisite explosion of white fire inside her as his fingers caressed her, the heat unescapable, burning, burning . . .

'Nice try, Jessica,' she heard through the vapours of hellfire.

The pressure was suddenly lifted and she snapped open her eyes with shock, as if someone had just tipped a bucket of chipped ice all over her.

William stood by the bed looking down on her. Fully clothed in tropical whites his smile was knowing, his eyes coldy unemotional. Her cooling body wasn't cooling quickly enough for her not to realize just how inflamed she had been only seconds before. She had been on the verge of . . .

'You bastard!' she panted furiously, too weak to sit up from the bed and lash out at him.

'So you keep telling me,' he gloated. 'But then women are turned on by bastards, aren't they?'

'You!'

'You dirty rat,' he mimicked like some movie gangster. He flung the towel at her contemptuously and it fell across her body, effectively covering her aroused body but not covering her fury and embarrassment. 'I wonder what the female equivalent of that is,' he mused sarcastically. He leaned towards her, eyes glittering now. 'Consider it said whatever it is, Jessica. And don't ever again use the lowest trick in the world to try to get your own back on me. This sucker doesn't bite!'

'How dare you!' Jess blustered, on her knees suddenly. 'I was asleep and you, you, you touched me and – '

'In your dreams, sweetheart. Now get up from there and dress and remember one thing before you try that again. I put business before pleasure and I always have done,' he added lethally.

With a cry of fury and exasperation she lunged at him, but he was quicker. He moved slightly and she missed and fell across the bed, her face coming up against his thigh.

He laughed and caught her chin and lifted it slightly. 'Your persistence astounds me, darling, but you are a few inches off course.'

She snapped at him then, closed her small white teeth around the side of his hand and bit him sharply.

Success. She heard his grunt of pain and then the world tipped. She felt herself rolled over and then she felt three or was it four or five resounding slaps on her backside.

Humiliated beyond anything she had ever experienced in her life Jess buried her face in the bed cover and screamed as hard as she could. She screamed and pummelled the bed for what seemed like hours and when eventually she rolled onto her back, exhausted with spent fury, her face flushed and tear-streaked, her throat hoarse, he wasn't even there.

'I hate you! I hate you!' she screamed but no one heard her.

Later, a subdued Jess emerged on to the sweltering upper deck. The engines had stopped ages ago but humiliation still stinging had kept her below deck till she was composed enough to make an appearance. Only two crew members were still aboard. Neither could look her in the eye, though one couldn't hide the smirk on his face as he grappled with a coil of rope on the deck.

They had heard, Jess thought miserably. They must have heard her deep humiliation, the world must have heard.

Jess blinked her eyes against the dazzling sunlight. The yacht was moored at a jetty and was still. The island was totally bereft of any sign of life. Her eyes scoured the beach, so white and pristine as if no one had ever set foot here before. Beyond, leaning palm tress fringed what looked like more jungle. The squawk of parakeets were the only noisy invasion to complete an utter privacy and silence.

'So, you have emerged at last,' she heard behind her and swung round to face her tormentor, William Webber. 'And not before time. Sulking doesn't suit you, Jessica.'

'I wouldn't have thought sexual harassment, grievious bodily harm and pyschopathic tendencies would have sat happily on your shoulders either, but there you go. You learn something new everyday,' she sniped back at him.

'Very true. Let that be a lesson to you, several in fact. Never let your guard down, don't judge a book by it's cover, never count your chickens – '

'Dry up, William, you are beginning to sound like the complete volume of words and phrases. Here's one for you drop dead!'

Jess stormed off along the deck of the yacht.

'Where are you going?' William called after her.

'To walk the plank, better get it over with now rather than wait for you to slow torture me to death!'

'Yes, well don't go empty handed. There's an ice box or three here to be taken ashore. Make yourself useful,' he snapped at her.

Jess turned and stared at him in amazement. 'I'm not your damned skivvy,' she blurted.

'You are now, Jessica, and I am serious. There are no staff here to jump at your beck and call. You pull your weight or starve!'

'Anorexia beckons,' she bit out sarcastically and, ignoring the ice boxes heaped on the deck, strode towards the gang plank.

'And you could do with it,' he snapped back.

'Not funny!' she cried without turning to look at him.

Her high heels sank into inches of powdery sand as she stepped onto the beach and she thought how ridiculous all this was. She wasn't dressed for being a castaway. Impatiently she kicked off the shoes and threw them as far as she could up the beach because he had bought them for her. Then she winced as the hot sand burned her feet. Grimly she walked on, to where she didn't know but all she did know was the need to put distance between her and the monster from the deep.

A rough stone pathway started at the edge of the sand and led up through thick lush greenery and Jess wished she hadn't carelessly thrown of her shoes because the stones were hot and rough under her soles. She hated him ever more for this indignity. Bringing her here to this farce of a place and what would she find at the end of the yellow brick road, a hellish mud hut?

'Oh, my God,' she breathed in amazement. It was paradise on earth.

The path had led to a lush tropical garden that was a riot of colour and perfume. Purple and carmine red hibiscus, pink and white oleander and creamy jasmine grew in sweetly scented profusion. Jess, enthralled, stepped into a tunnel of heady jasmine growing over rustic poles.

'It's the garden of Eden, isn't it?' she heard behind her.

Jess swung round and William was behind her, loaded up with ice boxes and cartons of provisions.

'Yeah, and we all know what happened there!' she grated and stepped out of his way so he could pass.

'Well, it's not going to happen here, sweetheart,' he said as he carried on up the path.

Jess followed, tight-lipped.

There was no mud hut at the end of the tunnel of jasmine. Bright green savanna grass spread out before the most glorious wooden villa Jess had ever seen in her life. The roof pitched up like a church, elegantly piercing a clear azure sky, and a wide shady verandah ran the length of the building. There were huge open windows with wooden shutters each side and several wide glass patio doors onto the verandah. Cane peacock chairs adorned the wooden deck and parrots and parakeets sat in flamboyant poinciana trees watching them curiously.

In awe Jess stepped up onto the verandah and peered through one of the open windows. A spacious sitting-room was exquisitely furnished with blue-cushioned cane sofas, and blue and white Ming style urns with whispery ferns growing from them were dotted around the cool looking room. There were ethnic rugs in shades of terracotta and cream scattered on the dark polished wood floors and high up in the pitched roof Singapore fans whirled lazily.

It was the most glorious place on earth to be

held hostage in, Jess thought wildly. If William thought he was punishing her with this he'd thought wrongly. She threw herself onto a wide padded cane lounger on the verandah and closed her eyes. There was nothing for it but to milk it for all it's worth, she thought dreamily.

'Get in the kitchen and unpack the groceries,' he ordered as he came outside. 'Then mix us some drinks and start preparing a meal for us both.'

Jess opened her eyes and smiled coquetishly. 'No way, buster. If I'm to be a prisoner here I shall not raise a finger to help you.'

He came and stood over her, hands on narrow hips, his eyes gleamed dangerously. 'Let's get one thing straight, Jessica, you are the one in the wrong, not me. Now I could make things hell on earth for you while we wait for the others to arrive but it's up to you. Round the back of this villa there is a generator room. It's hot and dusty and dark and all sorts of ghastly creatures live in there. It has narrow windows and a dirt floor and definitely no running water. It also has a heavy wooden door with a padlock on it. I could chain you up in there and leave you without food and water. You could scream to your heart's content but no one would hear you because when the crew leave with the yacht there is just going to be the two of us here. Inside this villa there is available every luxury. The choice is yours. Make it easy on yourself or not. Personally I don't give a damn!'

Jess hitched herself up to lean on her elbows and

glared at him furiously. 'Rhett Butler you ain't, William, so fiddle de dee, to you. I'd rather share a dirt floor with an army of man-eating spiders than raise one little finger to provide a meal for you. Got it?'

Sometimes Jess wondered at her own stupidity as William reached down and hauled her unceremoniously to her feet. Like the poor unfortunate reporter on the flight she found herself frog-marched along the verandah, her feet barely grazing the wooden floor.

He dragged her down the steps around the back of the villa to the generator hut. The door was already wide open and even with sunlight dappling in the doorway she could see it was a place of torture.

Jess shivered and recoiled back. 'OK, OK, I've got the message.' She tore herself out of his grip and spun to face him, her eyes wide with determination, her whole body stiff and poised with rage. 'I'll do whatever you say. I'll cook for you, I'll slave for you and I'll even lick the verandah clean every morning if you so wish but remember one thing, William Webber, you won't break my spirit and you won't get away with this. You can't keep me here forever. One day we will have to return to civilization and when we do I will tell the world what a devious, thieving schemer you and your naff brother are. You might be able to hire heavies and smart lawyers but the truth will out. I have done nothing wrong, but you have broken every rule in the book and I'll bring Webbers down. You have my word of honour on that!'

He stood in front of her, arms folded across his wide chest. 'Have you quite finished?' he drawled as if all she had said was merely water off a duck's back to him.

'Yes,' she said determindely. 'And so are you, William, because when your greed took over your sensibilites you took on the wrong cookie. You won't win, not ever!'

'I already have won, Jessica Lambert. Hackers as dangerous as you get put away and you and your accomplice are going down and – '

'Hackers!' Jess exploded, her heart chilling. He *was* crazy.

He smiled thinly. 'Christ, you've come this far and still you are trying to turn on the innocence. Well, not another word, Jessica, not till the lawyers get here and take your statement and mine and that of your lying little accomplice. And no doubt my brother will have his own version to add. You haven't a hell's teeth of a chance of getting away with this.'

Shocked Jess stepped back from him. He was crazy, totally and completely out of his mind. She'd never hacked in her life, so what an earth was he talking about? Her own computer mind scrolled through everything he had said, before and now and she came to the ghastly conclusion that this had gone beyond just the theft of her software package. Accusing her of hacking, gain-ing unauthorized access to computers, infiltrating his organization's network?

Jess licked her dry lips. This was serious. She well knew the penalties of doing such a thing and getting caught. It was a criminal offence. Suddenly she was frightened. What chance would she stand if this man was determined to put her and Abby down? But she was innocent and he wouldn't believe her if she tried to explain. But explain what? Where and how had all this come about? If someone was tapped into their system, it wasn't her.

She didn't know what to do or say now. She was completely and utterly at a loss for words. Play for time was all she could do. And if he kept up this mental pressure . . . an idea was beginning to form in her head. If he persisted with this charade she knew just how to put the frighteners on him. And she would. She would terrify him into releasing her and Abby, she would use the most terrifying ploy to the world's top computer company that would throw them all into a panic. And it would cost them, more than him and his brother could ever imagine.

Stepping further back from him Jess licked her lips again. She held her palms up to him in total submission. 'No, I won't say another word,' she whispered hoarsely. 'I . . . I'll go and make us a . . . a drink.'

'Good girl,' he coaxed softly. 'You do just that while I see to the crew before they leave. And no funny business, dangerous lady. It's all over bar the shouting.'

And then he stepped towards her and lifted her chin. He looked deeply into her eyes before saying softly, 'If it's any consolation to you, you were the best, you know.' He lowered his mouth to hers and shocked her deeply by claiming her lips in a kiss that confirmed he had been the best for her, too. And it hurt so much that he believed her to be so wicked and had loved her with such deadly intent. And she did want revenge for that.

She drew back from him at last and scoured her mouth with the back of her hand.

'I don't think you know just how dangerous a lady I really am, William.' She smiled seductively. 'It isn't over bar the shouting. It hasn't even begun yet.' With that she turned away from him and headed back to the villa.

And there was silence behind her as she left him. He hadn't even given her the satisfaction of laughing at her. So, perhaps she had frightened him and the thought wasn't satisfactory at all. That kiss had told her that in spite of everything he could still arouse her and that was because he had been the very best. There would never be anyone like him again. And wasn't that just sod's law in her life?

CHAPTER 12

'But why can't you tell me what is going on, Oliver?' Abby pleaded as she sat on the edge of the bed in a pink and white Miami hotel suite. 'You make me feel like a criminal and I haven't done anything. I really haven't.'

She couldn't believe she was here, overnighting before their flight down to Grenada the next morning. She was totally exhausted, dizzy with fatigue in fact and totally confused. Everything had happened so fast she didn't know if she was on her head or her heels.

Oliver had ordered a taxi to take them to the airport, obviously the urgency of the matter had put him off driving the limousine, they might never have got there. Because of the taxi driver Oliver had sworn her to silence and she had sat tight-lipped and worrying herself sick. At the airport they had been ushered into the VIP lounge to await their flight, via Miami because it had been too short notice to go direct, and still Oliver assured her everything was going to be OK and not to fret and he wasn't at liberty to say more. They had travelled first class and the only consolation Abby could find was that William Webber thought the matter urgent enough to allow his chauffeur and herself to travel this way, exceedingly comfortably.

And though Oliver had shown care and consideration for her so far she felt that most of the time he wasn't with her at all. He'd lapsed into long silences and rubbed his forehead a lot and several times he had nearly lost his temper when she had been particularly persistent with her queries and proclaiming her innocence. She didn't know what she had done anyway, only passed herself off as her sister and that wasn't a crime to warrant lawyers. Then she had given up because Oliver had slept most of the flight anyway.

What sort of mayhem had Jess caused in New York? Oliver had said William Webber had her in his custody. It sounded as if she had been arrested but Webber was a software tycoon not the FBI. How come Jess was in America with him when she should have been at home? What an earth was her whacky sister up to now? And because Abby was so afraid for her she hadn't pushed Oliver for too much information. He was in a difficult position being an employee anyway. He was looking so washed out now as he paced up and down in the suite her heart went out to him. It couldn't be easy working for a man like William Webber.

'I've told you, darling, Mr Webber won't allow

me to say a word about all this. I can't break a confidence,' Oliver reiterated bleakly.

'You've said all that before,' Abby almost whined and sat on her hands and stared gloomily at the pink and white carpet at her feet. 'I don't know what is going on. You mentioned lawyers and that frightens me. I know this is all to do with my . . . with Jessica Lambert but I know her and she wouldn't do anything wrong and I just think there must be a huge misunderstanding somewhere. Is it to do with this computer game of hers? Oh, I do wish I knew what was going on. I don't know what we have done.'

Oliver came to her and held his hands out to her. She took them and he drew her to her feet and hugged her tightly. 'My poor darling little innocent. I do believe you. I realize I must have frightened you back at Brooklands but I've promised you I'll look after you and I will. We'll sort this out when we get there – '

'Where though, Oliver?' Abby pleaded mournfully against his shoulder. 'You said the Caribbean and – '

'We . . . William Webber has an island, a place we . . . he goes when he wants peace and seclusion.' He drew back from her rather abruptly. 'Look, Abby, I really shouldn't be talking about this – '

'I know, darling,' Abby interrupted and she forced a small smile for him. 'I think it's awful the pressure he is putting you under. It's not fair on you. I don't like him already. The sooner we get this sorted out the better.' She looked up at him, her eyes pools of distress. 'Oh, Oliver, I wish I could fully appreciate all this, the lovely flight here and this lovely hotel, but I can't. I'm so worried.'

Oliver smiled. 'I don't want you to be worried, Abby.' His smile spread to a grin. 'Yes, we should be appreciating all this and not pacing up and down. We'll go out for a lovely meal and first thing in the morning before our flight we'd better get you some new clothes, you've nothing suitable for a hot climate. Yes, we'll shop for you tomorrow, we'll run up a few bills on Webber's credit card and – '

Abby laughed hesitantly. 'Oh, no, Oliver, don't be silly.'

'No, I insist,' Oliver said determinedly. 'Come on, let's get ready and hit the restaurant for a meal and Abby,' he cupped her face and looked deeply into her eyes, 'remember, darling, I won't let anything happen to you. This Jessica has got a lot to answer for but I will speak up for you because I know you are innocent, though I did have my suspicions at first. But knowing you and loving you now I realize how that woman has hoodwinked you. She tried it on Webber but he saw right through her so she isn't as smart as she makes out. She'll pay for all this and I'll make sure you walk away from it unblemished.' He kissed the tip of her nose. 'I'll go and take a shower while you rest and then we'll eat. You'll feel better for some decent food inside you.'

And Abby did her usual slump onto the bed when he left for the bathroom. What did all this mean? And why had he had suspicions about her from the start? Why was he saying all these bad things about Jess? If she told Oliver they were sisters would he be able to tell her more?

She felt trapped again, caught in another deception. How could she now admit they were sisters after all the insults Oliver had directed at Jess? She felt a pang of guilt for not sticking up for Jess from the first, but it had all come as such a shock. But soon the confusion would be sorted out. It may well have been sorted out already. Jess wasn't a scheming bitch and William Webber couldn't believe that she was, whatever all this was about.

And Oliver, what a strange relationship he had with his boss. He knew an awful lot about William Webber's business life, more than an ordinary chauffeur should. And all this, the hotel suite which was sumptuous but the pink and white decor not to her taste.

She'd noticed Oliver using a Webber company credit card to pay for everything, so even though only a chauffeur he was obviously a trusted one. And he was quite ready to run up the bills on it, offering to buy her clothes. She wouldn't accept of course. She'd manage somehow.

With a mournful sigh Abby lay back on the bed and closed her eyes. There was so much she didn't understand and it was so worrying, but at least she had Oliver by her side. She trusted him and he was going to protect her and once they all got together this mess would be resolved and everyone would live happily ever after.

Later Abby awoke to Oliver's kisses and she murmured softly and wrapped her arms around him. He smelt deliciously lemony from his shower and she needed his comfort and his lovemaking. He made her feel as if there wasn't a nasty world out there to be tackled. He made her feel so good.

He moved inside her and kissed her so deeply and passionately that all her worries were alleviated. She wrapped herself around him and drew him down into oblivion. He was a wonderful lover, so keen to please her, so expert at all the things that made her happy. As his passion grew, driving her to that luscious place of sweet pleasure she knew everything was going to be all right because he loved her and she loved him.

'Oh, Oliver,' Abby gasped. 'I don't think I realized until now just how wealthy William Webber was.'

She stood gazing at the stunningly beautiful yacht moored at the marina. It was going to take them on the last leg of the journey to William Webber's private island and Abby was shaken by its streamlined opulence. The lovely mansion in Kent had been testimony of his success and status but this, and a private Caribbean island as well, phew!

Though she was nearly on her knees with heat

and exhaustion, and the effects of a few rum punches on the flight, she was making an effort for Oliver's sake. She was quite worried about him. He'd grown more tense during the flight down to Grenada, she had drunk his rum punches too, because he said he needed to keep a clear head, and the taxi ride to the marina had been a roller coaster nightmare and now he was looking quite pale and drawn.

Again she was angry with William Webber for putting so much on Oliver but she had to admit he had handled the travelling arrangements with aplomb. She'd commented that he obviously knew his way around the world and he had admitted it wasn't his first visit down here. It accounted for his wonderful tan, though now it looked as if it was waning.

'It's a lovely yacht. Naff name though, Webbers' Wonder. Sounds like a limp lettuce,' she giggled, hoping to cheer him up.

He scowled at her before saying, 'Yes, well he's so rich he can afford to name his yacht whatever he damned well pleases!'

'Sorry I spoke,' Abby muttered under her breath.

She sighed and curbed a hiccup. Oliver wasn't to be cheered. It rather put a damper on her own feelings which had been surprisingly uplifted at the sight of the lovely island of Grenada. Oliver might think they were approaching the end of the world but Abby thought it all beautiful and because it was so glorious, hot and sunny and amazingly green and lush she had felt happier about everything. Nothing horrid and nasty could happen in such an exotic place.

This was all a horrible misunderstanding and if Jeremy Beadle popped out from behind a palm tree she wouldn't be at all surprised. Of course Jess hadn't been taken into custody, more than likely William Webber had fallen madly in love with her and whisked her down here for a Caribbean wedding and . . . Oh, dear, Abby thought she *had* drunk too much. She was beginning to fantasize . . . and hallucinate . . . Oliver was on board the yacht now and appeared to be handling the waiting crew with a heavyweight authority.

For a while Abby held back from going aboard to join him. There seemed to be an argument going on with a lot of waving of hands. Oliver's in particular were working hard as if he couldn't get through to the men and they might respond to sign language.

Abby swayed slightly on the jetty, the sun beating down on her bare head. She wished she'd bought a straw hat in Miami, in fact she wished she had let Oliver kit her out in tropical gear as he had wished. But she'd been adamant. There was no way she could run up William Webber's credit card bill when he was a complete stranger to her. She had her pride after all.

Her pride wasn't helping her much now though, she thought ruefully, her blue jeans were stifling her and the silk on her back was clinging uncomfortably and what was the hold-up on board?

'What's going on?' Abby asked when Oliver, grey-faced, returned to the jetty to pick up their bags.

'Apparently there is a storm warning and the crew advise staying here till tomorrow.'

'Sounds wise judgement to me,' Abby commented.

'Look at the sky, Abby,' Oliver grated, 'not a cloud in sight. There's obviously a carnival on the island tonight and the crew don't want to miss it. Come on, let's get aboard.'

Abby knew about the unpredictability of tropical weather and she worriedly held back. 'Hold on a minute, Oliver. If the crew don't want to go out it will be for a good reason.'

He swung on her. 'Suddenly an authority on seamanship, are you? As expert as you are on the computer?' he drawled sarcastically.

'Huh, you can talk,' she bit back, riled at that jab. 'You claim to be a chauffeur but you can hardly call yourself an expert on anything else but getting lost. Don't forget I've worked the cruise ships and know how quickly the weather can change, especially in the tropics. 'Spect they have typhoons round here,' she finished with a shrug.

Oliver raked a hand through his already dishevelled hair. 'Getting cold feet, are you?'

'Cold feet about what?' she asked in amazement,

hands on her hips now, partly to steady herself.

'Coming face to face with William Webber and your accomplice and having your whole deception blown wide open!' he suggested darkly.

Abby's eyes widened. Suddenly the rum punch euphoria was slipping out of her grasp. 'I . . . I don't know what you mean,' she whispered plaintively.

Oliver let out a low groan, dropped her holdall and gathered her into his arms. But Abby wasn't having any of it. She pushed him away.

'You're always doing that, Oliver, hugging me to make it all go away,' she protested. 'I know you are tired and stressed out with doing all this running about for your boss but I'm tired too. Sick up to my chin with you making wild accusations all the time. Jessica isn't my accomplice and – '

'Oh, no you don't!' Oliver suddenly roared and Abby was relieved to see he wasn't directing that roar at her.

The crew were leaving the yacht.

'Get back on board!' Oliver ordered thickly and ran towards the yacht.

'No sir,' said the one who looked as if he was in charge. 'I value my job too highly to take any risks and there's a storm brewing. Mr Webber wouldn't take no chances and – '

'I'm giving the orders now and I'm telling you if – '

'And I'm telling you, sir,' the burly West Indian

stated empathatically, 'no insurance company in the world will pay up if we don't heed weather warnings. That boat ain't the QE2 and it will go over if we hit a squall. No, sir, I'm taking my crew off.'

'*My* crew!' Oliver shouted. 'If you leave now you're all fired!'

'Oliver!' Abby breathed in amazement. Honestly, he really was taking too much on himself.

'Consider us fired then, sir.' The big man said quietly and strolled along the jetty with the crew going after him.

'Damn them!' Oliver muttered furiously under his breath.

'Oh, Oliver,' Abby breathed worriedly. 'You shouldn't have done that. Mr Webber will go mad when he finds out what you've done, fired his crew.'

He turned to her, his eyes wide as if he couldn't believe what she had said and then his anger quickly drained and he smiled thinly as if he couldn't believe what *he* had just said to the crew. He shrugged and picked up her holdall again.

'He'll understand. The urgency of this matter demands that I have *carte blanche* to do – ' He suddenly stopped and gazed at her bleakly. 'Oh, Abby darling. I can't go on with this any longer. I didn't want to say anything till we were all together. I've been driving myself insane on this journey down here. I should have told you before.

There are things I have to tell you, important things. I know you'll be delighted at the . . . Abby, darling, are you all right?'

She wasn't at all all right. Her head was suddenly spinning and the glare of the sun on the top of her bare head was . . .

'Oh, dear, you've gone quite green,' she heard Oliver say.

He grasped her around the shoulders and guided her towards the yacht. 'You need to lie down. Don't worry, darling, I'll look after you.'

'I'm all right, Oliver,' she murmured, rallying slightly as she allowed herself to be helped aboard. 'It's the heat I think.'

'More like the drink.'

She tried to giggle but it didn't quite happen. 'What . . . what were you just saying? Something about telling me something. Oh, Oliver,' Abby gasped, swaying against him as he helped her down a few steps.

She focused her eyes on the gorgeous cabin below deck. 'Oh, this is lovely and so . . . tasteful.' She couldn't believe the opulence.

He hardly gave her a chance to fully appreciate the sumptuous leather and the splendid decor as he helped her through to a passageway and through a panelled door to a bedroom.

'Oh, it's heaven,' Abby whispered, just wanting to lie down on that luscious bridal bed and sleep forever. Her head felt so heavy.

'Come on, let me get your clothes off,' Oliver

said caringly. 'I shouldn't have let you drink all my rum punches and what with the heat, it's all too much for you.'

'Oliver, we can't make love here, I mean it's not right and . . .' She giggled and fell across the bed and giggled again as Oliver pulled off her jeans and loosened her blouse. And then there was sweet oblivion of another sort as her whole naked body sank into a downy delight of cool comfort. She was asleep almost immediately.

Oliver stood by the bed and gazed down at her. He leaned down and smoothed a wisp of hair from her brow and then he kissed her sweet lips lightly. She was so adorable, so innocent and lovely. She didn't deserve what was coming to her, but then perhaps ignorance was bliss. How he had held back from telling her just who he was on the trip down he didn't know. It had been a colossal strain. But Will had been adamant. What she didn't suspect she couldn't act on. She might have tried to make her escape if she had known of his deception and just what was waiting for her at the end of this journey.

She had been a little fool to get involved with Jessica Lambert, but he was still sure she didn't know what she was doing. Will was convinced she was as guilty as the other was. He was convinced the pair of them were too dangerous for their own good. True, Jessica Lambert was highly danger-ous but not his Abby. She was only an unfortunate victim.

He had promised to protect her and he would, even if it meant turning against his own brother. Though he wasn't happy with that prospect. He and Will had worked so successfully together that to break the bond of brotherhood and a business partnership would be a disaster. But if he had to make the choice . . .

He raked a hand through his hair worriedly. He didn't know. He'd never met anyone like her before. He was so smitten he didn't know what to think or how to act anymore. She'd turned his world upside down.

Still gazing down on her he wondered if he could be wrong about everything. She looked like Sleeping Beauty lying there, her hair tousled on the pillow, her sooty lashes sweeping her cheeks, her lovely lips waiting to be kissed.

He shook away the desire her innocence aroused in him. An actress she had said, she had wanted to be an actress. So was this the biggest performance of her life? Was she in as deep as Jessica Lambert and just as dangerous? He would know the truth when they arrived because no two women could fool the Webber brothers when they were together.

The thought spurred him into action. The crew might have walked out, but who needed them when he was an experienced yachtsman? If it was true and there was a bad weather warning he could handle it. The yacht practically piloted itself with all the latest technology on board, anyway.

Closing the door softly behind him he hurried along to the cockpit. He'd call Will on the ship to shore radio and tell him he was on his way.

Later Abby awoke. For a while she lay wondering where she was and what that noise was, a rumbling and shushing sound. She groaned and grasped her stomach. She shouldn't have drink all those rum punches because her insides were all over the place. She rolled across the bed and got to her feet and grasped at a bedside unit to steady herself.

It wasn't her insides rolling but the whole yacht. She remembered where she was, on board William Webber's dream machine, and Oliver had fired the crew!

Quickly Abby pulled on her jeans and shirt, fully alert now. The yacht was moving and it wasn't exactly cleaving it's way smoothly through the blue Caribbean sea. Good job she had good sea legs.

She swayed across to the porthole. Rain was lashing against it and storm clouds had darkened the sky. A huge wave came up and hit the window and Abby lurched back across the cabin. She had to find Oliver. He must be piloting the boat himself as there was no crew to do it.

Oh, God, if he was as good at steering this boat through choppy seas in a tropical storm as he was at driving a limo around London they were in trouble.

'Abby, go back below deck,' Oliver ordered as he turned when she came into the cockpit.

Abby stared in amazement at the instruments that twinkled in the small room. 'Is it a typhoon or a hurricane?' she asked, suddenly get a picture of them whirling around in ever decreasing circles and plopping into the Bermuda Triangle never to be seen again.

Oliver grinned at her and flicked a few switches and because of his look of confidence in what he was doing she felt quite relieved. Nothing to fear, apparently the yacht was sailing itself with all this computerized technology.

Oliver laughed. 'No, just a squall. Nothing to worry about. I'm switching off automatic to manual to get us around this reef coming up.'

'A reef?' Abby shouted over the throb of the engines.

'Just a little one. Don't worry. I know what I'm doing. I've sailed in the America's Cup.'

'Yes, but this . . .' She was about to protest that it was different and this wasn't that sort of yacht, this more a pleasure cruiser, but the words died on her lips. The America's Cup?

'I could murder a cup of coffee,' he told her without turning from the wheel.

Abby stepped back, or rather lurched back against an instrument panel. How could he think of a cup of coffee when he was battling against the tempestuous seas, heading for a coral reef with all the dangers that entailed?

She realized that he was enjoying himself and the realization came with a jolt. He wasn't worried at all that there was a raging storm outside. He appeared to know exactly what he was doing and for in inept chauffeur that was quite something.

Puzzled and yet relieved that she was in safe hands she teetered her way down below deck and found the galley kitchen. The America's Cup? Surely that was a sport for priviliged people? Abby shrugged it off as she concentrated on trying to find coffee. She knew so little about his life, perhaps William Webber was into all that sort of thing or perhaps Oliver had worked for someone before who loved yachting.

'All shipshape and Bristol fashion. No need to abandon ship,' he joked when she managed to get back to him with two mugs of coffee without spilling a drop.

She was relieved the yacht had settled and the skies were incredibly blue again. Out of the windows she could see there were several small islands dotted on the horizon, all tiny little pockets of paradise with white beaches and green swaying palms. It was a very comforting sight.

'Oh, it's lovely, Oliver,' she enthused. 'Which one is William Webber's?'

He nodded his head towards a tiny jewel ahead of them. 'We'll be there in a few minutes. Are you feeling better?' he asked and Abby grinned sheepishly.

'Sorry about that, flaking out. I drank too much and it's so hot.' She sipped her coffee and watched a school of dolphins racing the yacht through the aquamarine water. 'Oh, look, aren't they sweet? Weren't you going to tell me something before I went all dizzy?'

'It can wait, darling,' he murmured and Abby noticed he was frowning as he sipped his coffee. Then he smiled. 'Just remember one thing, I love you.'

Abby smiled and hugged her coffee mug. She knew there was nothing to worry about. Oliver had guided them through a storm – he was such a hero and so wonderful. Soon they would be with Jess and William Webber and then everything would be all right. Whatever this was about it was a mistake and WW would know that by now. Jess would have worked her charms on him, though what she was supposed to have done was still a mystery. But then Jess wasn't renowned for living an uncomplicated life and she had obviously done or said something to have aroused such drastic measures as this, gathering down in the Caribbean on some magical little island. Soon they would all be relaxing on the beach with champagne and laughing about it all.

Abby suddenly frowned. No, everything wasn't quite all right. Oliver still didn't know she was Jess's sister and she would rather it came from her than his boss and Jess. And, of course, he wouldn't have known from looking at her passport when booking their plane tickets because the passport was in her stage name Abby Summers. Oh, he'd surely think the deception was even worse than he'd imagined. Poor darling, Oliver had been through so much already and it wasn't fair to hide anything more from him.

'I have something to tell you too, Oliver,' she began seriously and because of her change in tone he turned quickly and his eyes hardened to a suspicious glare. 'I'm sorry,' she whispered, lowering her gaze away from his because she felt so guilty for not telling him before now. 'I should have told you before but, well, you rather took me aback with your accusations. I thought it best not to come clean with you at the time because I didn't want to spoil things for us and possibly make things worse for Jessica. She does crazy things sometimes, no one knows that better than I do, but . . . well she'll charm you when you meet her. She charms everyone. What I'm trying to say is, now we are getting closer to meeting up with everyone well . . .' she drew more breath and looked at him. 'I want to tell you the truth, Oliver. I haven't been completely honest with you and – '

Oliver's eyes had narrowed alarmingly now and a slight flush of colour had risen to his cheekbones.

'I don't want to hear this,' he grated suddenly and slammed his mug down beside him. With his jaw set rigidly he gave his attention back to steering the yacht alongside a jetty that jutted out into the sea where it was deep enough to moor.

'But you must hear it, Oliver,' she insisted, panicking now because they had arrived and she wanted to get it all out before they went ashore.

'It's important and I don't want you to hear it from Jessica or Mr Webber and – '

'Save it for the lawyers,' he said, tight-lipped.

'Look will you stop going on about lawyers – '

'Get your things together,' he ordered thickly without looking at her. 'Whatever confessions you have to make you make them in front of a lawyer because telling me won't save your skin now. Christ, I must have been out of my mind to let you fool me.'

There was more, under-breath mutterings about her and Jessica and the scam they thought they were going to get away with as he fiddled with dials and cut the engines.

White-lipped, Abby hurried away, back to the bridal bedroom to get her things. Her eyes were stinging with tears of frustration. He was impossible. He just wouldn't listen! And still he was insisting there was something going on. What, for pity's sake?

Abby saw her sister immediately she came up on deck. The engines were throbbing to a halt and the yacht slid perfectly into it's berth and Oliver leapt over the side to grapple with ropes and moorings. Abby rushed to the side and gripping the rail with one hand she waved excitedly with the other.

'Jess! Jess!' she called, blinking her eyes in the glare from the sun.

Jess was running along the jetty, barefoot, her wild hair blowing in the hot breeze, a gorgeous flame sarong flapping in her wake. Oh, it was so

good to see her, such a relief after all the misunderstandings.

Abby's heart nearly stopped as Jess got closer.
Jess wasn't looking as ecstatic to see Abby as she
was to seeing Jess. In fact she looked wild with
anger. And there was a man hurrying after her and
he was looking mad, too.

Abby narrowed her eyes and stared hard at the
man. He looked so familiar but she knew she
couldn't possibly have met him before. He wore
white shorts and a grey T-shirt and like Jess he
was barefoot. Though mad with fury Abby could
acknowledge he was strikingly good looking. He
caught Jess just as she reached the helm of the
yacht where Oliver was tying up. Abby had to lean
over the side to see what was going on.

The man had swung Jess around to face him, his
face was as black as thunder.

'Oh, no, you don't!' he shouted. 'There will be
no collusion between you two before the lawyers
get here.'

Jess lashed out at him but the man caught her
wrists smartly before any blow could make it's
mark.

'And I've had all I can take from you, buster!'
Jess screamed at him. 'You are mad, totally and
completely mad. Twenty-four hours on this island
of hell with you is enough for anyone and boy have
I had enough, cooking for you, jumping when you
shout, listening to your accusations. And if that
mad, naff, brother of yours has harmed one hair of

my Abby's head there *will* be need for lawyers because I'll kill you!'

Abby's hands came up to her face with shock. What was Jess saying, why was everyone so angry? Her eyes widened more as Jess tore herself from the man's grasp and swung round to face Oliver, who was watching the scene with wide-mouthed wonder.

'As for you, how dare you kidnap my sister, how dare you hold her hostage against her will!'

Wide-mouthed herself Abby watched as Jess pulled back her arm and . . . Oh, no, Abby couldn't believe this . . . she punched Oliver right on the jaw! The punch was delivered with such impact it caught him completely by surprise and he reeled backwards. The stranger with Jess, reached out to catch him, but it was too late. Oliver, caught off balance by the surprise blow, went right off the jetty and plunged into the sea.

Not satisfied, Jess turned furiously on the man who had chased her along the jetty. 'You too, buster!' Her fist came back again and repeated the action on his jaw and in shocked disbelief he went over the side, too.

Stunned into silence and shocked to her very depths Abby gaped at her sister, who had gone to the edge of the jetty to look down on the two floundering men who had surfaced and were treading water in total confusion.

'Let that be a lesson to you Webber brothers,' she screamed at the pair of them. 'No man, not bloody one, get's the better of the Lambert sisters, let alone two. You took on too much and now you know we are not to be tangled with. You want a bloody war, well you've got it!'

Then Jess looked up at Abby, who was gripping the rail of the yacht white-knuckled and white-faced, frozen to the spot. A wide triumphant grin spread across Jess's face and then suddenly she winced with pain and sucked at her knuckles. 'Hell, that hurt,' she cried. 'They make it look so easy on the movies.'

Abby burst into tears and it unlocked her whole body and she flew to the steps and before she knew it the sisters were in each other's arms and hugging each other tightly.

'Oh, Jess,' Abby sobbed, clinging to her. 'What have you done? And who is that man? And what an earth did you mean the Webber brothers? You shouldn't have hit Oliver, he's nothing to do with this. He's a chauffeur and he's been so good and – '

Jess held Abby away from her and gazed at her mystified. 'A chauffeur? What chauffeur? That bloke I've just decked along with William Webber is his brother and business partner, Oliver Webber.'

If Abby hadn't been supported by her sister she would have fainted away on the spot. Her head spun, her knees went weak and her stomach swanned up to her throat. No, it wasn't true. It couldn't be. She stared and stared at Jess and then she knew it was true because for all her faults Jess wasn't a liar.

Abby clamped an ice pack around her heart as her mind spun till all the wild thoughts settled in to place. Oliver . . . Webber. She could see it all now and what a blind fool she had been not to have seen it sooner. Oh, the rat! Oh, my God, how he had fooled and deceived her and how stupidly she had swallowed it all.

Once her heart had been filled with love but now anger and revenge burned. She stared back at her sister and tightened her heart and her lips determindely.

'Jess,' Abby said, tight-lipped, 'What was that about starting a war?'

CHAPTER 13

'And another fine mess you've got me into,' Abby fumed, pacing up and down the dirt floor. 'Oh, the indignity of being thrown over Oliver's shoulder and tossed in here like a sack of potatoes. What is it anyway, the chamber of horrors?'

'The generator room,' Jess told her mournfully, still sucking her bruised knuckles as she sat hunched on an old packing case by one of the narrow windows, too narrow to make an escape from, though. 'It's where you get shoved when you speak out of turn.'

'Well you did more than speak out of turn, Jess. Where did you learn to pack a punch like that?'

'I didn't train for it, I assure you. Everyone reaches a breaking point and that was mine. For all the good it did me,' Jess grinned ruefully. 'Oh, boy were they mad, hauling us across their shoulders and marching us up here. It's a wonder William didn't have a heart attack under my weight.'

'This isn't funny, Jess,' Abby reprimanded. 'How long will they keep us locked in here? I'm melting in these jeans and look, the sun's going down. I bet there's all sorts of ghastly creatures in here at night.'

'You heard William, just to keep us out of harm's way till they get showered and dressed, then it will be the Spanish Inquisition all over again.'

'Oh, Jess,' Abby moaned and sat across from her on another dusty packing case, 'What an earth is going on? I'm beginning to think this is a nightmare and I'll wake up at home and all will be right with the world, but it isn't, is it?'

'No, it isn't,' Jess said quietly. 'And it's all my fault, as usual. Tell me, Abby, was it awful, him holding you hostage at the flat? I didn't know, you know, how could I have done?' She got up and went to her sister to put her arm around her. She hugged her. 'I'm so sorry for putting you through all this. Was he beastly to you?'

Abby got up and stood by one of the narrow windows. The hum of the generator was giving her a headache and the heat was unbearable. Worse, though, was the dreadful ache in her heart at how Oliver had deceived her so. It was much worse than her little deception. He should have told her who he really was when she had made her confessions. She remembered he had tried to on several occasions but obviously his need to clear his conscience had been less than hers. She had confessed because of love, but his supposed caring for her hadn't bitten very deeply into his conscience.

'I've been a complete idiot, Jess,' Abby confessed mournfully. 'When I think about it now I can't believe I could have been so blind. I did everything as planned, the dinner and everything for William Webber. Then *he* turned up.'

Abby turned around and leaned against the wall and closed her eyes. 'He said he was the chauffeur and I had no reason to disbelieve him. He said Mr Webber couldn't make it and he apologized and brought flowers and chocolates and well . . . I felt a bit sorry for him and well . . .'

'Well what? Jess urged.

Abby took a big breath and opened her eyes to look at her sister in the growing dimness of the room. 'I . . . asked him to stay to dinner and . . . and one thing led to another and . . .'

'Oh, God, Abby!' Jess was on her feet suddenly. 'You haven't been having an affair with him?'

'Oh, don't, Jess, please don't condemn me,' Abby pleaded, starting to pace the dirt floor again. 'He was so nice and charming and we had such a lovely evening and then he offered to drive me to the airport to get my flight to Paris and it was a disaster because he didn't know where he was going and I missed my flight and then he was going to drive me to Le Shuttle and we got lost again and ended up in Kent, at William Webber's lovely mansion and then there was Melanie and the deaf, Spanish gardener and the sauna and the lovely romantic four-poster bed and – '

'Hold on! Slow down!' Jess interrupted. She

grasped her sister's shoulders and held her firmly. 'Right, Abby, cool it. Start from the very beginning. Take it easy and tell me everything.'

Abby shook her head, almost too ashamed to confess all to her sister. She had acted so out of character and Jess would think her such a fool and everything was so awful.

'Not till you tell me what all this is about, Jess,' she whispered. 'Oliver has made such dreadful accusations. I didn't understand what he was talking about most of the time. I know it's to do with that package you asked me to hand over – '

'Did you hand it over?'

'Of course. It was the point of all this.'

Jess groaned and slid down to perch on the edge of the packing case. 'Oh, the bastards. They have both copies now. What fools we have been, both of us playing into their hands.' Jess held her head in her own hands. 'They are liars and cheats, both of them. And they are going to pay, believe me they are going to pay!'

'W . . . what are you talking about, Jess? Please tell me. I don't understand any of this.'

Jess looked up at Abby. 'They have stolen my game, Abby,' Jess told her in a voice thick with emotion. 'You gave Oliver Webber one copy – '

'I didn't know he was a Webber,' Abby protested. 'He said he was William Webber's chauffeur and anyway that was the arrangement, to give him the package. To give William Webber the package so what difference did it make that I gave it to Oliver?'

'I'm not blaming you, Abby. I know that was the plan but what I didn't know was that he intended *stealing* the idea. William Webber ransacked my room in New York, *stole* my copy, actually *stole* it. He never had any intention of buying it from me. They are both thieves and – '

'Jess!' Abby interrupted with a splutter. She couldn't believe this. 'You've seen the wealth surrounding those two. Why on earth would they steal your idea? It just doesn't make sense.'

There was a long silence, so long Abby's heart started to race. There was more, as Oliver had indicated. Scams and deceptions and criminal acts, Jess a scheming bitch.

'Oh, Jess,' Abby husked. 'What exactly have you done?'

They both jumped as they heard the padlock being unlocked. Jess grabbed Abby quickly and held her shoulders urgently. 'Listen to me,' she whispered. 'Keep quiet in front of those two. Let me handle this and let me do all the talking. You're not going to understand what they will be accusing us of so just leave everything to me.'

And as the two Webber brothers stepped into the room to seize them by their upper arms to march them outside Abby was stricken with concern over what Jess was up to. How could she leave it all up to Jess? Look at the mess she had got them both in already.

'Got your stories together?' Will grated as he grasped Jess and thrust her along the path to the villa.

'Got yours together?' Jess bit back. She jerked herself free of him and strode on ahead. 'I know the way, you don't have to force me like your heavies forced that reporter off the plane.'

'How could you, Abby,' Oliver whispered to her, as he held her firmly as they followed the other two.

'Let go of me!' Abby snapped. 'There is nowhere I can run to and don't you dare make out your feelings are hurt. Yes, I'm Jessica Lambert's sister and you are William Webber's brother and that makes us quits!'

They reached the verandah of the wooden villa and Jess, knowing the way, took hold of Abby's arm and swung round to face the brothers. 'Don't think I'm cooking a meal either,' she told them tightly. 'It's quite obvious you two are spoilt brats and not used to looking after yourselves, well tough. And don't think you can starve the truth out of us. You can never be too rich or too thin and if we don't eat that's fine by us!'

'You speak for yourself,' Abby muttered under her breath, her stomach rumbling in protest as Jess led her along to the far end of the verandah. She'd taken one last dismal look at Oliver and took no solace from the fact he looked as miserable as she felt. She allowed a tiny thought to blossom, that Oliver wasn't a willing participant in all of this, but then it all came flooding back to her, his deception, his fooling her into believing he was a chauffeur, his cheating and lying. The Webber brothers were as bad as each other, a couple of thieving crooks.

Jess slid open glass patio doors at the end of the verandah and they both stepped inside. Abby's shoulders sagged wearily.

'What do you think then?' Jess asked cheerily.

'About what?' Abby asked gloomily.

'The accommodation, of course. Bliss or what?'

Abby looked around her. Her eyes travelled up to the high ceiling, criss-crossed with wooden beams, the fans whirring lazily overhead, the cool rattan chairs upholstered with white calico, the Persian rugs on the wooden floors. A colourful parrot sat on the back of the sofa and bounced up and down at the sight of her and Abby wanted to cry because this was all so bizarre and unreal.

'It's a cut above the torture room, but it's still a prison,' Abby told her, gulping back the tears because she didn't want to look wet in front of her sister.

Jess came to her and gave her a hug. 'Darling, we've been through hell and back, both of us, but we are going to come out of this on top. I've got plans – '

Abby groaned and pushed her away. 'Like the last plan and look where it has led us. This might look like paradise to you, Jess, but it isn't. Those two think we have committed some terrible crime and as far as I know you have. There are lawyers on their way here and there's no smoke without fire. Just what have you done, Jess? I might not be able to follow all this computer lark but you must have done something to arouse the fury of those two. You've told me nothing of how you came to meet this William Webber in New York. I was hanging around in Kent waiting for him to come back, not knowing you were together. Oliver thought I was you and I let him believe it and –

'Shiver my timbers!'

'Shut up, Pinky,' Jess hissed at the parrot.

Abby burst into tears again. 'I can't take anymore,' she wailed. 'You are all mad and I'm mad too and everything is so bloody, bloody!'

'Hey, now sis,' Jess soothed and hugged her. 'Don't lose hold of your spirit. You've done so well so far and you just have to be strong a little longer.'

'But I love him, Jess,' Abby wailed. 'That's the worst thing to cope with. I fell in love with Oliver and I thought he was in love with me and he said he wanted to protect me and he actually said he wanted to marry me and – '

'Oh, my God,' Jess breathed in her ear and hugged her tighter. 'Darling, it's going to be all right.' What a couple of conniving bastards those two were. Oh, they would pay for this. If it was the last thing she did on earth it would be to settle this score with them both. Oliver seducing her sister, William seducing her, all with intent and for gain, nothing to do with love and caring.

Abby pushed her sister away, angry now instead of tearful. 'Oliver always does that when he can't face the truth, hugs me and says it's going to be all right. Anyone would think I'm a baby, well I'm not.' She rubbed her nose with the back of her hand. 'I need the bathroom and I'm going to shower and then I'm going out there and tell that stupid chauffeur just what I think of him,' she stated determindly.

'Atta girl,' Jess breathed. 'Come on. You take a shower and I'll mix us a couple of stiff rum punches and we'll swap notes.' She sighed heavily. 'Oh, Abby, if it's any consolation to you, I'm in the same boat.'

Abby lifted her tear-streaked face. 'What do you mean?' she whispered.

Jess shrugged and lowered her lashes. 'What do you think?'

Abby couldn't think for a minute and then the truth dawned and it was so appalling she wanted to cry for Jess now, and not herself.

'You're . . . you're in love with . . . William Webber?' she croaked in astonishment and not without a surge of resounding sympathy. Jess had never given her heart to any man. No one had ever come up to scratch for her and now, now she had found someone and that someone was a thief and a kidnapper and certainly didn't feel the same way about her by the treatment he was dishing out. Shouting at her in a rage, locking her up in the generator room and goodness knows what else.

Jess lifted her chin bravely. '*Was* in love with him,' she said firmly. 'But not any more. He fooled me completely and no man gets away with that with me. I didn't know who he was, you see. He called himself Oliver, would you believe, took his own brother's name to fool me. You can't love a bastard like that, Abby, you just can't. But he will pay, that's for sure.'

Jess turned abruptly away. 'Come on, I'll show you the bathroom.'

Abby followed her sister across the room and knew that Jess was lying. She still loved the man. Abby knew because she unwillingly felt the same about Oliver. She, too, had loved a man who had deceived her, though she hadn't known that at the time, but the ache of love was still inside her. Jess might deny her love and plot her revenge but Abby knew how deeply hurt she was. Wanting revenge was the key. Wanting to hurt back showed how deep the feelings had been in the first place. She wanted revenge on Oliver too, perhaps to a lesser degree because she and Jess had different personalities, Jess being the tougher, more streetwise one, but Abby wanted revenge just the same.

But how was it possible to get back at two such strong, powerful characters? Money talked in their world. And they were both clever, look how they had fooled the sisters already. Here they were being held prisoners on some faraway paradise island with nothing between them and sanity and civilization but miles of blue water. And there were lawyers on the way and . . .

'I think you had better start telling me everything, Jess,' Abby said sensibly as she started to peel off her clothes in the white marble bathroom beside a twin-bedded bedroom.

'You too,' Jess agreed enthusiastically. 'And then we'll make some plans.'

Abby eyed her warily as she stepped under the shower. What plans and what was Jess hiding? There must be more than just the theft of a computer game.

'I'll get the drinks fixed and then we'll tell each other everything, right from the very beginning.' Jess scooped up her sister's clothes from the floor. 'I'll get you some fresh clothes. I've got masses. William bought me everything in New York. You'll die of envy when you see my Versaces.'

Abby stood under the shower and closed her eyes. Her sister was ever a source of amazement to her. How could she be thinking of designer clothes at a time like this? And then Abby thought very deeply about the situation. Here she was questioning her own sister when she should be supporting her unequivocally. Jess was her own dear sister, her own flesh and blood, and she knew her well enough to know that though scatty and whacky at times she was certainly no scheming bitch. Blood was thicker than water, her love for her sister must be greater than her love for Oliver so she shouldn't even be considering that Jess was

301

hiding something. If there were choices to be made she was with her sister all the way. Wasn't she?

Later the girls sat coiled on the rattan chairs, sipping their drinks, talking, interrupting each other, squealing with shock and amazement at what had happened to each other. They even had a good old weep for their lost loves.

It was very dark now and Jess had lit candles in large glass bowls. Pinky sat behind them on the back of the sofa as they talked and Jess occasionally tossed him a peanut which he responded to with a 'Thank you very much, how charming.'

Abby couldn't believe where they were, couldn't believe what she was hearing from Jess and what she was telling her in return. It was like some mad Mel Brooks movie with underlying tones of a Stephen King horror tale. But the main plot line Abby was still in confusion over.

'So from the start the Webber's meant to steal your computer game,' Abby queried.

'It seems that way. I go along with you on the point about why should they need to do such a thing, but you never know the background, do you? I mean the company could be in serious financial trouble and they need to steal ideas to get themselves out of it.'

'Come on, Jess, they are rolling in it,' Abby reasoned. 'You should have seen their mansion in Kent and this island and the yacht and the limo.'

'Means nothing. Everything could be leased and they could be in debt and all sorts. Anyway,' Jess shrugged, 'whatever the reason, they have done it, stolen my game.'

'What's this hacking business then?' Abby asked.

'Who mentioned hacking?' Jess asked in astonishment.

'Oliver did.' Abby ran the cool glass across her forehead trying to think of exactly what Oliver had said about it. Because she didn't understand it she couldn't remember exactly.

'Yes. William mentioned it too,' Jess admitted. She got up suddenly and started to pace up and down. 'William seemed to think that I had set everything up, tossing my cocktail all over him, manipulating him into bed, huh, as if, and then announcing to the press that we were to be married, all a conspiracy to get control of him, I suppose. It was then he hit the roof and started making these allegations. He wouldn't come out with it directly, what exactly he thought I had done, said we needed lawyers present and whisked me down here. Then when we got here he let it slip, more or less accused me of being a hacker.'

'So what does that mean?'

'You wouldn't understand,' Jess said dismissively. 'You haven't got a head for computers – you know you haven't.'

'Thanks,' Abby grumbled. 'Yet you've dragged me into all this.'

'I didn't mean to,' Jess sighed. She looked earnestly at her sister. 'I'll simplify it for you.

Hackers are computer buffs who hack into other people's highly confidential computer set ups. Some do it for fun, others do it to get information. Nasty ones are able to plant viruses into the system that can cause devastating damage to businesses. It's a sort of computer spy network, like bugging a phone.'

'And the Webbers think you have done that?' Abby looked aghast. 'But for what reason? I mean why should you do such a thing?'

'I haven't,' Jess insisted, 'but William, and Oliver, seem to think I have and that you're my accomplice.'

'But why steal your game in the first place?'

'How the hell should I know? But it seems they are linked somehow – I don't know.'

'Haven't you asked?' Abby couldn't believe that her sister hadn't. With such a strong personality Jess could usually get blood out of a stone. Her heart began to pulse tremulously. Had Jess done that hacking thing and was so scared now she wouldn't admit to it, or even discuss it? All those hours and days and weeks she and their father had spent playing with those machines. Jess was an expert. To have devised such a valuable computer game she had to be. The awful truth came to Abby, that Jess, with her knowledge and expertise, was very probably capable of doing such a thing.

Abby rubbed her forehead and watched her sister pacing up and down. She hadn't answered her question. Why hadn't she asked William Webber outright, what she was supposed to have done?

'Jess, are you being completely honest with me? Is there something you haven't told me?'

Jess stopped dead in her tracks. Pinky stopped bouncing up and down on the back of the sofa. There was silence except for the gentle throb of the fans overhead.

'You don't believe me, do you?' Jess breathed in disbelief. 'My very own sister, so bloody smitten by that damned wannabee chauffeur, doesn't want to believe that I am innocent! How could you, Abby, how could you be so disloyal?'

Abby shot to her feet and Pinky took off in fright and flew up into the rafters.

'And don't turn on me making accusations like that, Jess!' Abby cried. 'I'm just trying to get to the bottom of all this and – '

'Having a domestic, are we?' William Webber drawled from the patio doors.

The girls swung to face him, so involved in their argument neither had heard him slide open the doors.

'No, we are not having a domestic!' Jess cried, face flushed with embarrassment at being caught out. 'And we might be prisoners, but have the decency to knock before coming in here.'

'I don't knock on doors in my own property, Jessica. Dinner is served if you would like to join us.'

305

'Do we have a choice?' Jess snapped.

'You do. Eat or not, quite simple.'

'Not!'

'Come on, Jess,' Abby cut in. 'This is ridiculous. I'm starving, if you're not. Besides, over dinner we might be able to get to the bottom of all this.'

'Your sister has the sense you weren't born with, Jessica. Indeed we might get somewhere with her around. Take my arm, Abby,' William smiled and held up his elbow to her, seeing her as an ally rather than an enemy. 'Let me escort you to the table.'

'On your bike, William Webber,' Abby snapped as she walked right past him. 'You may have bewitched one sister but you're not going to make us into a matching pair.'

Jess followed her and grinned wickedly and triumphantly at William as she swept passed him too. 'Have you got a lot to learn, buster.'

Oliver was already seated at the table on the verandah outside the sitting-room. The table looked lovely set with crystal and silverware, all sparkling in the glow of the candles. It painfully reminded Abby of how all this had started, wining and dining William Webber in their lovely flat back in Kensington. They had travelled a continent since, and if Abby had to make a choice she would rather be sitting down to a meal at home.

Oliver stood up as she approached. 'Abby, we have to talk,' he whispered. 'Later, after dinner, when the others are in bed. I'll meet you on the beach, down by the jetty.'

He held her chair back for her and their fingers brushed and though the effect was electric on Abby's skin she fought the sensation with all her will-power. She couldn't forgive him for what he had done and was doing now, going along with his brother in this mad accusation. He could wait out on the beach till the cows came home but she wouldn't be there.

William and Jess were right behind her, William holding out Jess's chair for her till she was seated.

'I suppose introductions are first on the agenda,' William suggested.

'I think we all know who we are by now,' Jess said bitingly.

'Drop the attack at my every suggestion, Jessica,' William drawled wearily. 'We will get nowhere fast with your attitude.'

'Right, down to business then,' Jess said, helping herself to wine from an ice bucket standing between her and William. 'When do the lawyers arrive?'

William nodded to Oliver who stood up to go inside the villa. 'I've postponed them for the time being,' he told her, taking the wine bottle from her and filling Abby's glass.

Abby sat with her hands in her lap, not daring to drink any more. She might say something out of place and Jess had advised her to keep quiet and let her do the talking.

Oliver came back with a huge silver platter of shellfish which he placed in the middle of the round table. Abby eyed it in amazement. Had Oliver prepared it? He'd been such a goose in the kitchen in Kent. Another of his deceptions?

William went on, 'My brother and I have talked about this and decided the lawyers can wait for the time being. If you don't agree with our terms they will be summoned immediately, of course.'

'Huh, blackmail already,' Jess sniffed, waving her hand dismissively at the platter of food Oliver was dishing up.

'You used the word blackmail, Jessica, which is what all this is about, isn't it?' William suggested slyly.

Jess gave him a black look.

'Yes, blackmail,' Oliver reiterated. 'It's the only explanation we can come up with for the behaviour of both of you.'

'Blackmail!' Abby squawked, thinking she must have picked up some habits from the parrot! She reached for her drink after all.

'Be quiet, Abby,' Jess ordered. 'I said to leave this to me.' She leaned back in her seat and her eyes flicked from brother to brother. 'What am I supposed to be blackmailing you over?' she asked.

'You tell us. You are the one that started all this, faxing me and suggesting dinner to discuss your new project. You are the one that all this stems from. I would just like to say at this stage that I think your tactics in involving your sister in this scam of yours are just plain dirty. It's quite obvious from what Oliver tells me that she knows nothing about computers and appears to be an innocent and very vulnerable accomplice in all this.'

Abby felt a tiny glow that at least Oliver had stuck up for her in front of his formidable brother.

'My sister knew exactly what she was getting involved in,' Jess said and Abby gazed at her wide-eyed, wondering if she knew how condemning that sounded. 'She did everything for me with the best will in the world. Which is more than can be said for you two tricksters. You had no intention of trading for my game. You, William, accepted my faxed dinner invitation because the outline was enough for you to know I had devised something very valuable. You wanted it, for nothing. You sent your own brother, disguised as your chauffeur – '

'And damned uncomfortable the uniform was too,' Oliver said ruefully.

'Shut up, Oliver!' William ordered.

'How you knew I was in New York is a mystery though,' Jess went on, ignoring the interruption. 'But then nothing surprises me anymore. You tricked me, stole my evening bag, ransacked my room, stole my precious game. So now you have the two copies, both stolen because although Abby gave over her copy willingly – '

'Don't forget there's another one,' Oliver interrupted, while tearing the head and tail off a pink king-sized prawn.

'What other one?' William asked, glaring at his brother.

Oliver plunged his fingers into a finger bowl of iced water before going on. 'I told you about it, the one Abby was taking to Paris,' he reminded him.

'I was not!' Abby protested hotly. 'I was going to Paris for an interview for a job!'

Oliver glowered at her across the table. 'You said there were plenty more fish in the sea and you had to speculate to accumulate and you were going to offer the software in Europe.'

Abby flushed deeply. 'I only said that for Jess's sake, to help her and – '

'I offered to put the copy in the safe at Brooklands and you said not to bother – '

'There wasn't another copy!' she insisted. 'How could I have given you something I didn't have!'

'Oh, it's all coming out now!' Oliver blazed. 'Another of your little deceptions. So what else haven't you told me?'

'Girls, girls!' Jess interjected sarcastically. 'Let's not fight over something so bloody trivial.' She glared at Oliver. 'Don't accuse Abby of lies and deception when you aren't squeaky clean in all this.'

'Right that's enough!' William shouted, slamming his fist on the table to silence them all. 'This is getting ridiculous.'

'I agree,' Jess snapped. 'The whole thing is a farce. I thought I was dealing with the top computer software company in the world but it's obvious you two are Laurel and bloody Hardy reincarnated. I offered you my game in good faith because Webbers is the best and what do I find, trickery and deception. And you have the audacity to accuse us of the same.'

Jess stood up and threw her napkin down on the table. 'Enough is enough. Come on, Abby, leave these two to choke on their own inadequacies. I'm not listening to anymore.'

Abby gulped down a luscious mussel as if it were the last morsel she'd get the chance to eat. She went to get to her feet but William stretched out his hand to still her.

'Sit down the pair of you and stop acting like a couple of children,' he ordered thickly. 'So far, Jessica, you've done all the talking and a feeble tale it is too. Do I say, Jessica, sit down.'

Jess did. Flopped down on her chair and glared furiously at her one-time lover.

'More seafood?' Oliver offered.

Jess turned her burning gaze to him and Oliver sheepishly lowered the plate to the table.

'Right, let's get down to business,' William said authoritively. 'How much do you want?'

Jess gave him a smile of derision. 'Oh, you're willing to trade now, are you? You realize that you have no chance of getting away with this so you are doing an about turn. You've cancelled the lawyers because you know you haven't a leg to stand on and now you are willing to trade.' Jess leaned across the table to him, her green eyes wide with determination. 'Well, I've got a surprise for you, William Webber, no sale. I wouldn't sell you my idea now if – '

'You can't sell something that doesn't belong to you,' Oliver cut in darkly.

Jess turned her attention to him, Abby too. 'You might have stolen my software but the idea is still mine!' she blurted.

Oliver leaned back in his chair and the way he was looking at Jess now, coldly and with menace, made Abby's blood run cold.

'You, Jessica Lambert, are a cheat and a liar,' he said flatly.

'Oliver!' Abby bleated, shocked to her very roots that he could speak to her sister so damningly.

William reached out to her yet again and placed his hand over her wrist to calm her. 'Listen to this, Abby,' he said quietly. 'Go on, Oliver.'

Oliver leaned towards Jessica who had been numbed into silence by the cruel accusation.

'That game is not yours to trade with. You talk of us being the thieves but you are the one who is the thief,' he said steadily. 'I devised that game, Jessica. It belongs to Webber's because I devised it. I can prove it because it is already copyrighted. You stole the idea from our computer system.'

Suddenly Jess was on her feet, almost swaying with rage. 'You bastards,' she blurted angrily. 'You crooks, you hoods! I see it all now. No wonder you kidnapped us and are holding us here against our will. To keep us out of the way. Both of you have had copies in your possession for a while now. When did you copyright it, yesterday, the day before – '

'Six months ago,' William told her.

Abby clenched her fists in her lap. She wanted to die. If this was true and the silly, silly game was . . . But it couldn't be true. Jess couldn't have done such a thing.

'It's not in production yet,' William went on, 'but nevertheless it's our game.'

Abby's head was reeling with these allegations, but somehow she managed to find her voice. 'So . . . so why . . . why are you suddenly willing to trade?' Abby asked tremulously.

Suddenly all eyes were on her, as if she had said something completely unexpected.

'Yes,' Jessica added, gripping the edge of the table to steady herself. 'Why are you willing to trade if you believe this game to be yours?'

Abby stared up at her sister. Why wasn't she denying it all?

'To buy your silence,' William said quietly. 'Because, Jessica, there is more than just the game, isn't there?'

Jess almost fell back in her chair. She reached for the wine and no one stopped her. Abby watched as Jess poured the wine with a trembling hand. Jess knew something. She wasn't easily scared; in fact Abby couldn't think of one occasion when her sister wasn't on top of a situation, or thought she was, at least. True, she made enormous blunders in her life but always she came out determined it wasn't her doing, just rotten luck. William had said there was more than just the game and judging by Jess's nervous reaction it was true. Some extra secret that the Webbers knew about and Jess was quick to pick up on and Abby hadn't a clue about.

Abby couldn't take her eyes off her sister. Jess was definitely worried now. She turned the wine glass in her fingers before raising it to her lips, thoughtfully and nervously.

Eventually she spoke. 'I know what is going on now,' she said, surprisingly calmly. She lifted her dark lashes and looked William directly in the eye. 'OK, you can buy my silence. A million,' she stated firmly.

Abby reached for her wine and gulped it down furiously.

'Dollars or sterling?' Oliver asked.

'Sterling, you idiot!'

'Jess,' Abby moaned under her breath.

'Done,' William said sternly. 'And your silence is guaranteed.'

Jess simply nodded, her head bowed.

Abby looked at William because she couldn't bear to look at Oliver. She looked at William glaring at her sister after finalizing the deal and there was no satisfaction in the cold mood of his eyes. He was an extremely good-looking man, slightly more mature and stiff upper lipped than his brother. A devastatingly handsome man and Abby could well understand Jess falling for him. But there was something in the way he looked at Jess now that disturbed her deeply. He had made a deal, but there was no pleasure or even relief lighting his eyes or relieving the tension in his features. He looked bereft, as if the whole transaction had left a bad taste in his mouth. He looked like a man in love who had just discovered his lady's unfaithfulness.

Abby knew then that William did indeed love her sister. It was a shocking realization, but she was convinced she was right. When Jess had been telling her all about their affair in New York she had suspected that William couldn't be all bad, as Jess had defensively made out.

And Jess was hating him now and plotting revenge. Perhaps that was it, the revenge, take the million pounds and run. She sincerely hoped so and that there was nothing more sinister on her mind . . .

So all her sister's dreams were about to come true. Whatever she had done it had lined her pocket, but they were all suffering by it. All of them victims. Jess still loved William, he loved her. Abby knew she still loved Oliver and though he had deceived her so convincingly she knew in her heart he wasn't all bad either and perhaps he had truly loved her. He had done his best to protect her, but when it came down to it he had done what she would do for her own sister, stood by her kith and kin. Oliver was loyal to his brother, he couldn't help but be.

Abby shivered and got up from the table because Jess was already standing by it waiting for her. Nothing more needed to be said or done. Abby took one last look at Oliver, but his eyes didn't meet hers. She knew he wouldn't be down at the jetty waiting for her later.

Everything but everything had been finalized with a million-pound deal that Abby didn't understand.

CHAPTER 14

Jess waited till she was sure Abby was asleep. Nothing had been said when they got back to their room. Abby seemed to be pensive and quite exhausted by the day and had demanded her bed.

How could she sleep, Jess wondered as she gazed down at her in the bed across from hers, when their world was in tatters? But Abby didn't really understand what was going on and best it stay that way. Jess knew it all now, and it didn't sit well on her shoulders.

William had so willingly agreed to her outrageous demand and hadn't even quibbled over the amount. He wanted her out of his life so fast and furiously he would pay anything to be rid of her.

She didn't want the damned money, she thought angrily as she tied a colourful silk sarong around her. Not this way. If all was right she would much rather have traded for it honestly. Her game for a million, not a bad piece of trading. But of course it wasn't hers to trade. But the game was only the tip of the iceberg, the game that had given the game away! And now Jess knew what all this was about.

Jess quietly slid open the patio doors and stepped out onto the verandah. All was silent except for the tree frogs chirping away and the gentle shoosh of the surf on the beach. The Webber brothers would be asleep, at two in the morning the world was asleep.

Jess strolled slowly down to the shore, kicking her feet in the sand, wanting to clear her head, wanting to wish it all away because the more she thought about it the more guilty she felt.

But Abby must never know. No one must ever know. It was a secret she must keep to her dying day.

A cloud obliterated the moon as Jess wandered along the jetty. Webbers' Wonder bobbed gently on the water and Jess vaguely wondered if Abby, during one of her cruises, had mastered the technique of driving a boat. They could make their getaway in it, sail off into the sunset and leave the brothers to stew. It was all they deserved, to be marooned here for eternity in revenge for believing what they did about her and Abby.

The evidence was damning. Their tactics at getting at the truth were evil, though. Seduction. How could those brothers have made love to them, fooled them so completely? It had been wicked. Poor, darling Abby, suffering so, her loyalties torn between her sister and the man she loved. Abby would stick by her, though because that was the way their father had brought them up. Family ties were strongest, he had taught them after their mother had left. They had closed ranks. How she missed her father now, more than ever.

As for herself. How ironic she should at last have found the man of her dreams only to find his loyalty to his brother and his company meant more to him than she did. But his lovemaking, so deep and passionate, the sort of lovemaking that could only come from deep feeling, surely that hadn't been all deception?

She was suddenly swung around and a pair of powerful arms enfolded her and for a second her heart swelled with hope that William had called a halt to this awful charade and had decided he couldn't live without her.

But the lips on hers, so hot with desire, weren't her lover's lips.

'What the hell!'

She pulled back, reeled against the side of the yacht and quickly steadied herself. The moon lazily emerged from the cloud and she glared furiously at Oliver!

'Oh, I'm so terribly sorry!' Oliver too reeled back with shock. 'I . . . I thought you were – '

'My sister,' Jess blurted, all her hopes dashed that it was William. She rubbed at her mouth. 'And why would you think that unless of course you made some secret assignation with Abby? Well, let me tell you, you've been stood up. After all this, don't think she is going to fall into your arms as easily as she did the first time around.'

'It wasn't like that – '

'It was like that!' Jess insisted. 'You are as twisted as your brother. You both think you are God's gift to women.'

'I truly love Abby,' Oliver retaliated quickly. 'And if it wasn't for you I could have her. None of this was my intention, none of this scheming. It was all down to you and now you have ruined your sister's life. I'm sure she loves me too,' he added huskily.

Jess wasn't to be softened by a change of tone. 'So why didn't you tell her who you were from the start? Huh, you can't answer that, can you? Because it's true. You seduced her to get hold of the game and – '

'Oh, it's *the* game now, not *your* game!' Oliver suddenly rallied. 'By taking the million and running you have admitted your guilt. Why not take this a step further and admit the truth to Abby? If you have any decency in you at all, tell your sister the truth, because she doesn't know it. I was watching her pinched little face tonight during dinner. She knows nothing of what you have done. She's as innocent as the day is long.'

Jess glared at him furiously and then her eyes misted with tears. She lifted a hand and raked it through her tousled hair. How could she tell Abby the truth? It would devastate her. She'd been through enough already, any more would be too much to bear.

She lifted her face to William's brother. 'The truth wouldn't help you, Oliver,' she said softly, the anger draining out of her. 'You deceived Abby and she can't forgive you for that. I could accept that William has been a playboy in his past and probably will be for ever more because I've seen more of life than Abby. But you are cast in the same mould as your brother and that can mean nothing but heartache for Abby in the future. She is a trusting soul and you are not to be trusted, you've proved it. She's told me everything that happened between you two from the moment you met and I filled in the pieces that she, in her innocence, couldn't see. You have a Melanie back home, you have a life that is alien to Abby's. She fell in love with a chauffeur, not Oliver Webber, millionaire playboy. Your affair didn't have a chance from the off.'

He stared at her for a while and then Oliver narrowed his eyes at her in the bright moonlight. 'I'd give it all up for her,' he said thickly. 'That's how much I care for her. I'd drive a number sixteen bus up Oxford Street all day for her. But you wouldn't believe that possible, would you? You with your scheming devious mind, knowing who my brother was from the beginning, couldn't believe that love was possible without some monetary incentive behind it.'

'I *didn't* know who William was,' Jess insisted.

'Like you deceived Abby, your brother deceived me. I really didn't know I was making love to William Webber. But he knew exactly who I was, right from the very start, because I told him. This is where all your accusations fall apart. Why, in heaven's name, if I was out to cheat him, would I admit to my own name?'

'Probably because you thought you were smarter than him and anyway, why the million pound demand?' he asked scathingly.

'Why not?' Jess bit back. 'Why not take you for as much as I can? I've learnt one thing out of all this. Cut your losses and run like hell because anything I say or do would fall like summer snow on yours and your brother's ears.'

'Cutting and running is an admittance of guilt,' Jess heard from behind.

Jess swung round to see William standing in the moonlight, just a few feet from them both. How long he had been there in the shadows she didn't know.

'What are you two doing down here in the middle of the night? Trying to solve the world's problems?'

'You wouldn't go amiss if you talked more,' Oliver told his brother. 'If you overheard that conversation you would know how I feel about all this.'

'I know how you feel already, Oliver, it's as plain as the nose on your face. You've been bewitched and are besotted with the one decent female you've met. But remember one thing, if you let your heart rule your head over this you will be marrying the sister of this dangerous lady. If you can live with that, go ahead, but you won't have my blessing,' William told him gravely.

The brothers' eyes warred with each other and Jess wondered if Oliver had the strength to defy his brother. In the short while she had seen them together she knew the bond between them was deep, as deep as hers and Abby's, so she doubted he would.

If she could have one wish now it would be that at least Oliver and Abby would find happiness out of all this.

Oliver didn't say anything to his brother's warning. Shoulders hunched he turned away and walked back along the jetty to the shore.

As Jess was about to follow, disheartened and crushed by the whole business, William caught her arm and stopped her and his touch on her bare arm brought everything flooding back to her. The fun, the passion, the depth of emotion she had felt for him and believed he had felt for her. Now it was all pain and disillusionment. She pulled back her arm and rubbed at it as she waited to hear what he obviously had to say to her now that his brother had gone.

'Not content with trying to ruin our business you have successfully ruined my brother's life and your own sister's. You've seen the way they look at each other, you know what they've been to each other. How could you be so utterly heartless?'

Jess bravely lifted her chin and swallowed hard. She was well aware of what she had done and if he thought she wasn't suffering he knew nothing about anything.

'Your brother will survive, as for my sister I think she's had a narrow escape. And you can talk about being heartless, William,' she breathed menacingly. 'What about what you have done to me? You were the only one of us who knew it all from the start. You were the one who seduced me knowing who I was. And don't protest that I knew who you were, because hand on heart, I didn't.'

'You have no heart to swear on, Jessica,' he said darkly. 'In New York I wavered a bit and thought perhaps you did have some feelings for me but it was all part of your scheme. Tonight was the final straw that broke the camel's back. You knew the game was up and rather than bargain for more you settled for a measly million.'

'A measly million is a lot in my life!'

'It'll just about cover your overdraft,' he said knowingly.

'How do you know . . .' Oh, what did it matter that he knew about her debts. He'd probably ran checks on her from the start, knew everything about her and her life. But he didn't want to know about her future. 'And you agreed so damned quickly to that measly million that it's obvious you couldn't wait to get me out of your life,' she added venomously.

'Can you blame me?'

Her eyes were pained as she looked at him in the moonlight. She blamed him for everything. He shouldn't have loved her the way he had, making her believe she was someone special.

'That's what really hurts, William,' she said tremulously. 'Your treachery and pretending to love me, bedding me for gain. A man who does that deserves what is coming to him.'

He caught her arm as she turned away from him. 'And what do you mean by that?'

'Make of it what you will, *Will*.'

Again she tried to get away from him, again he swung her around but this time right into his arms. His breath was hotter than the tropical breeze on her face, his mouth treacherously close to hers. 'If you are planning the oldest trick in the book, forget it, Jessica. You might have turned me on when I had everything to lose, danger certainly adds something to the libido, but our bargain has been struck and it's all over and you couldn't arouse me now if you were the last woman on earth. I thought you might have got the message on the boat when you tried your little seduction ploy.'

Wasn't it just typical of a man to think of such a thing when all else failed? Sex. She had been just a sex object to him, nothing more. And how very wrong could he be. She'd bet that measly million that if she came onto him now he would succumb. The pressure was off now. The bargain sealed.

Neither had anything more to lose. There might not be any danger and risk to add to his libido anymore but so what? Yes, he would succumb because he was a man and it was the way they were.

'Ah, but I have the million now so there would be no point in me trying to seduce you, would there? I haven't exactly got it in my palm yet, but you won't welch on the deal because you have too much to lose if you tried. I want to make love to you as much as you want to make love to me, which is just about nilch!'

'So a kiss to seal the bargain and to prove we are both cold, calculating opportunists wouldn't come as a shock then.'

With that his mouth closed over hers in the promised kiss that was all-revealing despair to Jess. Even with this burning rage inside her he could arouse her, her heart floundered helplessly, every pulse point of her body hung suspended in time. His arms folded around her back, his hands spread across the naked skin above her sarong and he parted her lips and there was no fight left in her. If he guessed how she really felt she didn't care. She had no pride left because he had wiped the floor with it. To even fight him and show with the coldness of her lips under his how little she cared for him was impossible because she did care. Let him think and believe what he wanted, because it wouldn't change a thing. He despised her and this was his punishment, to show her what she would be missing for the rest of her life.

And yet his kiss wasn't all punishment Jess felt as it deepened. However cold and calculating he claimed to be she felt the rise in his passion. She felt his body harden against hers and knew. She knew she could still arouse him and there was no triumph in the knowing. It was but a reflex action with him.

He broke away at last and Jess stood waiting tremulously for the last cutting stab at her which she was sure he would use. She wasn't disappointed in her assumption, though her heart froze at the content of it.

'You *were* the best, past tense. But as your own sweet sister said, there are plenty more fish in the sea. I won't lose sleep over you, Jess. Goodnight.'

He walked away, stiff-shouldered, proud and probably forgetting her already. Jess stood watching him, the pain burning her eyes, the anger and bitterness welling inside her till it was almost a life-threatening urgency. She put aside all the deception, all the awful misunderstandings, all the dreadful things they had said and done to each other and what was left was a dreadful dragging sadness. They had had something special going for them. She wasn't wrong where her own heart was concerned and if she picked the bones of all that happened to them as lovers she wasn't wrong where his heart was concerned. He had cared and she had been the best for him but sometimes that wasn't enough. Their love hadn't been enough because so much else had encroached and it was all insurmountably impossible.

And she still wanted revenge for what he had put her through and what he had just said, that there were plenty more fish in the sea. He was obviously stronger than her, more determined to put all this behind him and to continue on with his playboy life. And she hated him and wanted revenge for his strength when she was sadly lacking in it, feeling so bereft and vulnerable now. Yes, she despised him for making her feel this way, totally inadequate.

The oldest trick in the book. Seduction. She was capable of doing it but it would be a punishment for her and perhaps she deserved such masochism. Look on it as a cleansing process. Let it be a lesson to her, the turning point in her life, the stabilizing force behind her future. After, she would have to get her life together or wither away and die. All her life she had fooled around, taking nothing seriously, not applying herself as sensibly as Abby did in her life. It would be different after this. One last night with William, for her and for him never to forget. For her the deep cleansing, for him, the sting in the tail from a dangerous lady.

Jess checked to make sure Abby was still sleeping soundly, which she was, and Jess's heart pulled for her. Maybe when this was all over she could do something to help her and Oliver. What, she couldn't imagine, because when she delivered the sting in the tale to William all hell would break lose in his and his brother's life. Perhaps she would go and live in America. With her knowledge and expertise it would be easy to get a good job. It was a shame she hadn't thought of it before all this started. Abby was such a good, loyal sister and had always stood by her when things got grim and Jess had done nothing to help, only nearly destroyed her love for Oliver.

Jess didn't like herself for that and she vowed that somehow she would make it better for Abby. Perhaps a confessional letter to the two brothers after, explaining why she had done what she had. By then they would know she wasn't the dangerous lady they thought, by then the furore would have died down, by then Oliver and Abby might be able to work something out together.

Because Oliver slept in a room at the end of the verandah, Jess held her breath as she crept quietly along towards her goal. William's room was at the back of the villa, through the sitting-room, overlooking the other side of the island. The patio doors of the sitting-room were wide open to take advantage of the breeze and Jess stepped through them and stood for a moment as her eyes became accustomed to the darkness. Her skin burned as she blinked. Extraordinary how her body reacted to just a thought. The thought of what she was going to do.

She bit her lip and purposely went forward,

across the room to the wide interior hallway, and from there across to William's bedroom. The door was open and she stepped inside. The moon shone in this room and she could clearly see him lying face down in the bed, naked, a sheet up to his waist. She stood for a while looking down on the back of his head. His hair was tousled, as if he'd raked his hands through it a million times with worry. It would be nice to think she was the main worry in his life, but she knew that not to be.

She wanted it all different. She wanted a life with him, to be able to gaze down on him like this every night and morning of her life. But life wasn't that accommodating, life was a bitch most of the time.

She loosened the knot of the sarong at her cleavage and let it soundlessly slide to the floor. She stood naked, skin burning more than ever, her need pulsing through her. Could she do it, make love to him and then deliver her blow? But think of all the blows he had dealt her.

Cautiously she slid under the covers next to him. His body burned too, though with the heat of the night. She touched him, ran her hands down over his hard body, savouring the feeling, wanting to remember how it was between them and not what it had turned into, a battle of the sexes.

He murmured softly as her soft, sensual caresses got through to his subconscious and aroused him. She breathed warm, tempting kisses across his shoulder blades, indulged him with small licks of the tip of her tongue around his ears, which always sent him wild.

He moaned then, a submissive moan, and then he turned and gathered her into his arms and it was then Jess wavered in her intention. This was wrong and she couldn't go through with it. It would be unbearable and . . .

And then his mouth was heatedly exploring hers and his arms snaked around her and pulled her with full force aganst his aroused body and . . . and there was no going back.

Why was it all so different? Jess wondered. There was a desperate intensity to his kisses, a desperation in her as she clung to him. And then she knew why, knew that he recognized it too. It was for the last time. But to think and dwell on it was impossible if she was to come out of this sane. She blocked her mind off, refused to think. Went to some secret place where nothing but sensuality and pleasure were all.

She arched against him as his hands moved over her curves, stroking her temptingly, rushing her mouth and throat with fevered kisses. Her fists bunched into his back as he moved his lips to her full breasts, suckling her, drawing deeply on her nipples till she was forced to bite her lips to stop herself crying out with ecstasy. Then her fingers dug deeply into his back as his mouth came back to her lips, parting them with passion and plunging her into a turmoil of desire.

As he kissed her she felt the tension of his hard

body, the thrusting movements against her groin, the delicious dampness of his skin against hers. She coiled her legs around him, heard his hopeless moan of submission and then he pushed her back and her heart seized, thinking he was rejecting her.

But there was no rejection, only more hapless submission as he ran his mouth over her breast again, working his way across the flat of her stomach, down and down to the soft springy hair between her thighs. Jess lay tense, her fists bunched above her head on the pillow, holding her breath as his tongue and lips probed till she thought she would die of pleasure. She couldn't move, she was powerless when he did this to her, weak and vulnerable under the tantalizing pressure.

And when his lips finally came back to hers she tasted herself on his mouth and she wanted to cry for all that was lost between them. She clung to him, feverish now, wanting to be under his skin, to be a part of him forever.

Soft strokes between her thighs now, heat on heat. His fingers stroked and probed, evermore tantalizing, more insistent, deeper and deeper. Desire filled her, moistened her till the strokes became more fluid. He was the best, no one like him. He was the most delicious of sensations, flooding her through and through, thrusting her arousal higher and higher till it was almost a torture.

Jess moaned his name and reached for him and

he was parting her legs and pressing into her and she bit hungrily and passionately on his mouth. Almost in a frenzy of hunger she arched against him and he responded with an equal frenzy, thrusting into her with long, even, rhythmic strokes of pure erotica. She snaked her tongue across his, clung to his hips, drew him deep inside her, as if to possess him so completely he would never be able to leave her.

She cried out when she could hold on no longer, when the heat was so tempestuous release was the only relief. She muffled her mouth against his as he rode her climax, rode her into ecstasy and pain and joy. She felt his own climax swell, rising with hers to be with her all the way and then the effusion of life exploding inside her, coupled, together, twinned in powerful, pumping life-giving source.

She clung to him as their bodies shuddered together, desperate not to let the tears flow from her in the aftermath of perfection. He must never know how truly and deeply she loved him. At last Jess rolled away from him and buried her face in his pillow, smelling his scent and knowing it was the last time it would arouse her senses.

Later she felt his hands on her body, turning her over onto her back. A candle burned in a glass bowl by the bed and she could see his face, shadowed, but it was light enough to highlight the coldness in his eyes.

'And what exactly was that all about?' he asked.

His tone and the mood of his gaze said it all about how he felt at the moment. Disgusted with himself for allowing it to happen. She shouldn't be surprised or even disappointed. For a wild impulsive second or two she had hoped he was rolling her over to say he loved her and wanted her in his life after all.

'I guess you know what it's about,' she murmured dully.

'I wouldn't ask if I knew.'

'No, men, never do,' she sighed wearily. 'According to some, you lot are supposed to be the more intelligent of the species.'

'I'm sure you don't include yourself amongst the some.'

She smiled thinly. 'Got it in one, I've just proved that the male *isn't* the dominant one.'

'You couldn't have done that without me,' he parried.

'Nor you without me but I guess that proves my point, that I could seduce you without you putting up a fight.'

'I'm not sure I see your point, but I wasn't going to look a gift horse in the mouth, was I?'

She glared up at him. He'd just confirmed it all for her. He didn't care for her or about her, not one bit. He'd just taken what was an offer and it was the final straw that broke *her* back.

Slowly and achingly she got off the bed and stood naked by it to look down on him.

'Remember when we first met you thought I

was a hooker? If I remember rightly I said you couldn't afford me and you said you didn't want me but if you did price wasn't a problem. I don't suppose in your wildest dreams you had ever considered paying a million for it. Well, you just did, William. You've been taken to the cleaners.'

She saw his eyes darken with anger and it pleased her that she could rile him out of the coldness that had gone before.

'I sure know how to give value for money, don't I? That was a bonus for you and here's another – '

'I don't want to hear any more!' William snapped and shot out of the bed to face her across it. 'I rue the day I ever got tangled with you. You are everything I suspected from the start. Scheming, greedy, manipulative and –

'And I metaphorically spit in your face too, William Webber!' Jess blazed. 'You never did think I was anything but what you've just said and I hate you for that.'

'The feeling is mutual, as I believe you have in writing,' he told her scornfully. 'Now get out of here, Jessica. Take your million and get out of my life.'

'Should be easy as I was never in it in the first place!'

'Too right. You mean as much to me as a banana daiquiri does and you know how I loathe them!'

'Huh, I should have thrown acid down you!' Jess screamed, clenching her fists beside her in case she lost control and gave him another punch on the jaw. 'Just one or two things before I go.' Furiously she reached down beside the bed and picked up her sarong and wrapped it tightly around her. She needed to be fully clothed before she delivered the final blow to him because she would have to run for her life when she did.

'Firstly, you can stuff your measly million. I don't want your blood money. I never did, as it happens. All I ever wanted was to trade my game but you well and truly took the wind out of my sails. I'm not going to belittle myself with a denial because it would be wasted on you but I'm going to tell you something that will really freak you out. I needn't tell you at all, but because you are the rat you are I want to see your face when I come out with it.'

His glare was one of pure vitriol as he waited for her to go on. Jess wondered if she had the nerve. But nerve was one of her strong points and she wasn't about to weaken now. He had treated her disgustingly and he deserved this.

'Everything you have accused me of I am guilty of! That's what you want to hear, isn't it? Well, you have it, my admission of guilt. I stole your brother's game, I hacked into your network. I know more about your company set up than you know yourself. And while I was snooping around in your computer world, in the comfort of my father's study, I thought about getting caught. So to fail safe my arrest and prosecution I left a calling card on the Internet – '

'Jesus Christ, no!' William suddenly roared.

This time Jess was quicker because she had anticipated his reaction. As he rushed around the bed, Jess sprinted across the room and picked up a rattan chair on the way to hold defensively in front of her as if she were warding of a raging lion, which she was in fact. She had never seen him so mad.

'You know exactly what I mean, don't you?' she taunted. 'I've planted a virus, a nasty virulent virus in Webber's computers. The E-mail message reads, "Call the ubiquitous Hooker" and not one of your staff will be able to resist downloading into that. Once in it will trash everything you hold dear to your heart. Just you wait till you get home and watch those figures and letters dropping off the screens like bloody confetti. You're ruined, William Webber. It will cost you more than a measly million to put it all back to rights! That's my parting gift to you!'

With that she flung the chair across the room and fled for her life. She didn't even know if William was behind her, she just ran blindly, skidding across the polished floor of the sitting-room and out onto the verandah.

She heard a strangled sob and wondered if it was her own and then she saw a figure cowering by the open patio doors. The sobbing was coming from the hunched figure.

'Oh, Jess,' Abby cried, holding her throat to try and control the cries of anguish in her throat. 'Oh, Jess, what have you done?'

Jess stopped dead and gazed at her distraught sister. She must have heard it all. Their rowing must have awoken her and she had crept out to see what was going on. Jess's heart plummeted to an all-time low. If she could go back and delete the terrible night she would.

'Oh, Abby,' Jess moaned and tried to gather her sister into her arms but Abby cowered back.

'Don't, Jess, don't touch me. I couldn't bear it. I heard it all, all you said to William,' she croaked in distress. 'Oh, Jess, why do such . . . such a terrible thing. There was no need. We would have managed. Oh, Daddy would be so shocked and – '

And on that, the plaintive reminder of their dear father, Jess burst into tears and fled along the verandah.

CHAPTER 15

Abby was in the kitchen the next morning, trying to find something to eat, when Oliver walked in. It was a gleaming white kitchen, with all the equipment, totally out of place on a small lush paradise island, but nothing surprised her anymore. She couldn't look at Oliver but she tensed at his presence. After his treatment of Jess at dinner did he think she would have gone to meet him on the jetty as he had requested?

'We usually have fruit for breakfast when we're here,' Oliver volunteered. 'Mangoes, paw paw, pineapple. You didn't come last night. I waited and waited and then Jess came along and I thought it was you and kissed her.'

'Bet she loved that,' Abby muttered as she attacked a huge pineapple with a sharp knife.

'Darling, we have to talk,' Oliver said wearily. 'I can't bear anymore of this . . . this torture and confusion!'

Abby bit her lip and sucked her finger which she'd caught on one of the spines of the fruit.

'Have you hurt yourself?' He was at her side immediately. He took her hand and lifted the sore finger to his lips and tenderly kissed it.

Abby snatched her finger back. 'I'm all right,' she told him. 'Here, you do it.'

She slammed the knife down and went outside and sat in one of the tall peacock chairs and stared out into the tropical gardens. She still felt numb after the dreadful night. She had awoken, hot and restless, and found Jess wasn't in her bed and had gone out to look for her and heard the row. After Jess had cried and cried, eventually falling asleep as the sun burst into the room.

Most of what Abby had heard last night she didn't understand. It was something bad and serious though. William Webber had roared like an enraged lion with toothache. She'd heard Jess's confession too and at the time she had been so shocked she hadn't been able to bear her sister touching her.

But with the dawn had come a different reasoning. Jess wasn't guilty, she couldn't be. Why sob all night if she were the schemer she had claimed to be? She was irresponsible at times but she wouldn't have done those things she said she had. To do that, steal and then destroy someone's livelihood? No, Jess wasn't capable of it.

Oliver stepped out onto the verandah with a tray holding a jug of fruit juice, glasses and bowls of pineapple cut into chunks so perfect they looked as if they'd come out of tins.

'Will's getting the yacht ready,' he told her as he sat down at the table. He handed her a bowl of fruit and a fork. 'We'll be leaving when everyone is ready.'

'Hardly seems worth coming in the first place,' Abby mumbled before biting into a piece of fruit.

'No, well none of us knew how things were going to work out.' He sighed deeply. 'I'd better tell you the latest developments – '

'No need,' Abby interrupted quickly and stiffly. 'I already know. Jess is a criminal. She's done awful things. She stole your game, hacked into your company's secrets, left a virus to trash your years of work. She ought to be locked up.'

'I thought you didn't know anything about computers.'

She looked at him then, scathingly for thinking that she was still a part of this. 'I don't. I'm just repeating what I overheard in the wee small hours of the morning. My sister confessing to all you suspected her of and a bit more and your brother going crazy with rage.'

'His anger is understandable.'

Abby slammed her bowl of fruit down on the glass-topped table. 'The only thing understandable about all this is that your brother drove her insane enough to make a confession that wasn't true!' she retorted

Oliver sighed and drank some juice and gazed out beyond the verandah to the gardens. He looked drained with exhaustion.

'It's natural to side with your sister, I suppose,' he muttered.

'Just as you are siding with your brother.'

He turned to her. 'I know my brother better than I know your sister.'

'And I know my sister better than I know William!'

'Well, this conversation is going a long way, isn't it?' he said sarcastically.

'The further away the better for me,' Abby grumbled. She snatched at her glass of juice and drank thirstily and then she said, 'You know, I feel like an outsider looking in on all this, a bit like a visitor to the zoo gawping at a tribe of chattering baboons and wandering how the world survives against such odds. I don't know anything about computers and yet I seem to be the only one with any common sense. You are all so wrapped up in your weird software world you can't see for looking, like the baboons searching for their bananas with a blank expression on their faces.'

Oliver's eyes widened in surprise. 'Baboons are very intelligent.'

'Which is more than you lot are then!'

'I don't see where this is leading. What are you talking about?'

Abby leaned towards him. 'Where is the evidence for all this? It looks to me like supposition all the way. Webber's *supposing* that Jess had committed all these felonies. To use a phrase I've picked up from Jess, where is your hard copy back up? Both of you *believe* Jess stole your game from your own computers. Isn't it possible that you both devised the same game and it's just a coincidence that you came up with the same formula? As for all this hacking, what proof have you that Jess knows anything about anything? Has she fed you back any vital piece of information that only you and Will know about? As for the trashy virus thingy, wouldn't you have known by now if she had planted it? She must have done it weeks ago, before her trip to New York, before all this kidnapping business and – '

'That's enough, Abby,' Jess ordered as she came up behind her chair. 'You don't know what you are talking about.'

Oliver and Abby were stunned into silence and watched Jess as she poured herself some juice from the jug. She sat down to sip it and Abby thought how desperately tired she looked. Even her normally glossy wild hair lacked lustre this morning. She was drained of all emotion. She couldn't have had a wink of sleep last night and just managed a few short hours at daybreak.

'That was what I was just saying to Oliver, I don't understand it all, but I'm looking at it from a different angle to you computer buffs. I might have heard your row last night, this morning,' she corrected, 'but I don't believe a word of it.'

'You did when you heard it,' Jess reminded her.

'But not now, because I've had time to think, which is what you lot ought to do some time instead of rushing around the world causing mayhem and scenes and all sorts of disruptions in our lives.'

'Thanks for your support, Abby,' Jess said quietly, 'but you're wrong, you see. I did do all those things. I planned it ages ago.'

'How could you?' Abby huffed. 'You couldn't plan a booze up in a brewery. You're so dizzy you didn't even know what time it was in New York and missed your flight back to the UK.'

'Purposely,' Jess uttered.

'No way!' Abby cried and got to her feet. Oliver stood up with her, Abby ignored him. 'You wouldn't have done that to me, Jess,' Abby said confidently. 'You wouldn't have put me through the stress of entertaining William Webber if there was no need – '

'I knew he was in New York so I wasn't putting you through any stress, was I?' Jess reasoned. 'Why do you think I switched hotels? Because I knew William was there.'

'Even I didn't know my brother was there,' Oliver suddenly intervened ruefully, wondering just who's side he was on at the moment.

'More fool you then,' Jess insulted, giving him daggers. 'Give me the Internet now and I'll tell you what the Queen is doing at this precise moment.'

'Court circulars don't go out on the Internet, surely?' Oliver queried.

'Shut up, Oliver,' the sisters said in unison.

Oliver huffed impatiently and took off down the

verandah steps, striding purposefully towards the gardens, no doubt to join his brother on the jetty to make sure they got off this island sooner rather than later.

Abby waited till he was out of sight before sitting down again and directing her attention to Jess.

'Why are you doing this, Jess?' she pleaded to know. 'You've done some pretty wild things in your time but taking the blame for all this is the wildest yet. No matter what you say I can't believe you did it.'

Jess gave her sister a steely eyed glare. 'Then you don't really know me at all, do you?'

'You're my own sister, I know you as well as I know myself, which is why I know you are incapable of such a thing.'

'You'll do and say anything if your back is against the wall,' Jess murmured.

'Are you talking about our monetary situation at the moment? If you are then it's a feeble excuse. I would have got that job in Paris. By now I would be cruising the Maldives and earning good money. We would have been all right. No, I think it's something else. I think you are so hurt by what William thinks of you that you would do anything, admit to anything and scare the living daylights out of him, just for revenge.'

Jess didn't say a word, not one in defence of herself. How could she? Let Abby believe whatever she liked, but she mustn't know the truth.

'Well, aren't you going to say anything?' Abby persisted. 'You're getting quite good at admissions lately. Go on, admit I've hit the nail on the head and this is what it's all about, revenge.'

Jess lifted her head and looked across at her sister. 'OK, yes, in a way you are right, but it doesn't change anything. I wouldn't have admitted my guilt if William hadn't been so beastly to me. I would have kept my mouth shut, but I still did it. The revenge took the form of telling him what he wanted to hear and hoping he feels rotten about it all.'

'That doesn't make sense, Jess.'

'No, I suppose it doesn't,' Jess breathed wearily, gazing out into space and wishing she was in it, floating off somewhere where nobody could find her. 'Shall we drop it now,' she murmured. 'I've had a helluva night.'

'And you're going to have a helluva life if you carry on this charade of yours. You'll be admitting to spying for Britain next.' Abby sighed and roughly pulled her hair away from her face. 'I'm going to pack. Apparently we're leaving. Bloody waste of time all this was.'

She left Jess to it, wondering what on earth was possessing her sister lately. She always had been wild and irresponsible, but her behaviour now was teetering on the perimeters of insanity.

'And who looks after you when the brothers aren't here?' Abby asked Pinky as he gazed down at her from the top of the wardrobe.

346

'Pieces of eight, pieces of eight.'

Abby smiled thinly. 'You're a corny old parrot. I bet Oliver taught you all that pirate jargon. It sounds like the sort of thing he would do.'

Suddenly her eyes filled with tears and she slumped down on the edge of the bed and covered her face with her hands. She didn't want to cry any more, it was too exhausting, but she couldn't stop. It was hopeless, everything was hopeless. Oliver, William, her own sister, all were hopeless and she was hopeless too, because she couldn't do anything about it.

Funny old world, everyone in love with each other and too hurt and angry to forgive and forget. Why wasn't life like this island, a lush, peaceful paradise?

Already she had forgiven Oliver. She'd turned everything over in her mind a thousand times and she was as much to blame, for being so blind. She should have known he wasn't a chauffeur, driving around, getting lost. She should have realized he wasn't that daft and he was doing it on purpose to delay her. Even Melanie she had come to terms with, and the gardener he hadn't wanted her to talk to in case he gave the game away on Oliver's identity. Yes, she understood why he had fooled her. He hadn't had a choice under the circumstances. But their love had been for real. Oliver looked distraught most of the time and she was sure that although he was worried about the company, there was more – her. Hadn't he said he wanted to protect her?

Yes, he cared, and Jess was in love with William and she guessed he was in love with her too, but his shirt was so stuffed with pride he couldn't admit it.

Abby rubbed her face and looked up at Pinky who was gazing down at her, his colourful pink head cocked to one side as he gazed back at her.

'So what can I do, oh wise one?' she murmured to him.

'He's a parrot, not an owl,' Jess clipped as she came into the room.

Abby watched her as she started to lazily pile all the lovely clothes William had bought her in New York into a bundle at the foot of the bed. The Diors, the Chanels, the Versaces. On top of the heap she piled the perfumes and the toiletries he had bought her too.

'Aren't you taking those with you?' Abby asked.

'I wouldn't be seen dead in them!'

Abby smiled through her tears. 'Now I know for sure you're not the scheming bitch everyone thinks you are. You'd have killed for those a month ago.'

'A month ago I was sane.'

'We all were,' Abby muttered profoundly.

Jess looked at her sister trying to put a brave face on and it really got to her. She sat across from her on the bed she had wanted to die in earlier this morning. She sighed deeply.

'Abby, there is no need for all this to affect your

life with Oliver, you know. He told me he really loves you and he'd give everything up for you if he had to.'

'Oh, yes, when did he tell you this, when you were snogging down on the jetty?'

Jess laughed and got up and plumped herself down next to her and put an arm around her. 'He got the shock of his life when he realized the mistake he had made. He's not a bad kisser, though.'

Laughing and crying Abby dug her in the ribs. 'Oh, Jess, you're wicked.'

'And you're not and I want you to be happy and you never will be without Oliver.' She gripped her firmly by the shoulders and looked at her earnestly. 'I want you to be happy, Abby. I want you to be with Oliver and you can be. William doesn't own him and – '

'Oh, don't, Jess, please don't go on. I could never be happy with Oliver with all this hanging over us. Every time I saw William I'd be thinking of how you two should be together as well. And then if we had children, Will would be the uncle and you would be the aunty and – '

'Bloody hell, Abby, you do go on.'

She didn't want to hear of such things, children and aunties and uncles. It hurt like hell. Jess got up and hauled her suitcase from the wardrobe. It was stuffed full of her own things, all she had taken to New York with her. How different things would have been if she hadn't decided to go there. But the world was full of ifs and buts she supposed.

'Where are you going?' she asked Abby as she got up from the bed.

'To find out when we are leaving. I didn't bring much, so packing won't take me a minute. I only had a few overnight things to take to Paris.' She sighed deeply, pulling herself together. 'Blimey, Jess, we nearly had it all, didn't we? A couple of gorgeous millionaires.'

'And a parrot,' Jess grinned ruefully, nodding towards Pinky, who had fluttered awkwardly down to one of the rattan headboards and was chewing a bit of loose cane. 'I'll miss *him* more than I'll miss William,' she added determindly.

'Looks a bit like him too.'

Abby ducked as Jess flung a crumpled Hermés scarf at her.

It was so like Jess to try and make light of it all, Abby mused as she followed the path through the gardens towards the beach. But she was hurting deeply, Abby could see the signs, the tension in her face and the slow movements as if she had lost her zest for life. And because Jess was hurting so Abby knew her sister was living a lie.

She reached the beach and lifted her hand to shield her eyes from the glare of the sun and the white sand and the pale crystal water. How could this be such a beautiful paradise with all this going on? It didn't seem right.

She saw the two brothers, William and Oliver,

obviously arguing on the deck of Webbers' Wonder because both their arms were flying in the air, and she held back. It had been her intention to talk to William on his own. Whatever she had to say to Oliver would depend on what she sorted out with his brother. She hadn't lied to Jess when she had told her she couldn't be happy with Oliver without Jess and William being happy too. She wouldn't be able to live like that.

She also realized she would be making the biggest sacrifice of her life by giving Oliver up for her sister, but there wasn't a choice if she couldn't speak to William and somehow sort something out . . .

So what else could she do to help resolve all this? She felt so useless. She was indeed the outsider looking in, because those three knew more than she did and the seriousness of what Jess had allegedly done. But surely Jess couldn't be ruining all their lives just out of spite for the way William had treated her? Why, oh why was she acting this way?

Abby ran a hand worriedly through her hair as the shore breeze tousled it. The brothers were still waving their arms irately at each other so her mission to talk to William was scuppered for the time being. Once they were all on board, setting off on the long journey home, she wouldn't get a chance to talk to him privately.

She held back in the shade of a leaning palm tree and watched them both leave the boat and walk along the jetty. She wasn't close enough to hear if they were still arguing but at least their arms were still now. Abby moved further back into the greenery so they wouldn't see her. A germ of an idea was forming in her head.

Yes, a shock was needed. Something to jolt them into sensibility.

Once the brothers had disappeared into the gardens which led to the villa Abby ran like the wind, across the beach to the jetty.

Once on the jetty she allowed a few precious seconds to peer behind her to see if she was being observed then, satisfied she wasn't, she started to undo the ropes that secured the yacht to the jetty. Her fingers were all thumbs, her heart raced nervously and perspiration was misting her vision. But she had to do this, she just had to.

'Where's Abby?' William asked, looking into the guest bedroom where Jess was tying her unruly hair up on the top of her head.

'How should I know? I'm not her keeper,' Jess replied sullenly. She looked at him through the mirror of the dressing table. His face was grave and tense and she had made him that way yet there was no triumph in the thought. She looked away, back to herself and didn't feel so good about her own looks either. Loving William Webber had taken its toll.

'Find her and both of you come down to the

jetty. We're leaving shortly. Leave your bags there and Oliver will pick them up.'

'How gentlemanly of him!' she couldn't resist saying tartly.

'Cut the sarcasm, Jess. It's childish. What the hell!'

Jess swung round to see what his worried exclamation was about but he had gone.

Then she heard it, the deep throb of the engines of the boat in the distance.

Hesitantly Jess went through to the verandah. She saw William and Oliver running across the gardens. So who was on board?

With a strangled cry of realization Jess started to run too, through the jasmine arbour to the beach. Her heart was thudding fearfully as she skidded to a flurried stop on the hot sands. William and Oliver were pelting towards the jetty but it was too late. Webbers' Wonder was heading out to sea. Jess started to run again.

'Abby, for God's sake, what are you doing?' Oliver was shouting to the boat.

'What's happening?' Jess cried as she reached the others.

William swung on her, eyes black with fury and concern. 'Does she know what she'd doing? Has she ever handled a boat like that before?' His hands came up to grip her shoulders fiercely as if to shake an answer from her. 'Does she know what she's doing?' he yelled again, when she made no response.

Confused, Jess shook her head. 'I don't know, I don't know,' she cried. 'She's used to ships, she's cruised them, all over the world.'

With relief William let her go.

Jess licked her dry lips. 'She . . . she does the entertainment on them, you know, bingo calling and – '

'Jesus Christ!'

William shouted at his brother who was on the edge of the jetty, jumping up and down and waving his arms erratically. 'She can't hear you, Oliver. Go back to the house and get the yacht's radio receiver, we'll contact her on that.'

Oliver was away like the wind, running as if his life depended on it. William stood anxiously on the jetty, a hand shading his eyes from the sun, his whole body stiff with whipcord tension.

Jess went to him and stood by him. 'What's happening?' she asked again.

'Your sister has gone crazy, that's what's happening,' he told her through tight lips. 'She's taken the yacht.' He jerked his head round to her. 'Did you put her up to this? Another of your crazy schemes to send us insane?' he accused.

'Don't be stupid!' Jess snapped irritably, not seeing the seriousness of the situation. 'What are you worried about anyway, got behind with the insurance premiums and sick at the thought of losing your precious boat?'

'My only concern is for Abby,' he growled. His

hand snaked out and grasped her chin and directed her face out to sea again. 'See that on the horizon? It's not scotch mist. It's one helluva a squall cloud approaching and your sister is heading for it and between her and that is a coral reef. If all three come together at the same time – '

He didn't finish because Jess's legs suddenly went from under her. William caught her before she crumbled to the wooden deck. He held her tightly to support her trembling body.

'It's all right, darling. We're going to get her back,' he said gruffly.

They both stood anxiously watching the yacht which was weaving through the water, further and further out to sea.

'Abby, darling. You can hear me I know. Press the red receiver button. Lift the receiver and press the button, to your right. Keep the other hand on the wheel,' Oliver shouted down the portable receiver as he ran along the jetty to join William and Jess.

They all heard a crackle and then Abby's voice, loud and clear. 'Hi kids. Hey, this is fun!'

'She's flipped,' William breathed, still hanging onto Jess, who was clinging to him for support.

'No, it isn't fun, Abby,' Oliver said seriously. 'Cut the engines. You obviously knew how to turn them on so cut them *now*.'

'No way,' Abby laughed. 'This really is fun. Oops, it's getting a bit choppy out here. Oops, I think there is a reef coming up, the water has gone a different colour, sort of pale and sort of shallow looking. Ooh, I can see lots of little fishes and – '

'Cut the engines!' Oliver screamed.

'Wheel to the left, ships ahoy,' Abby laughed. 'All with one hand too. Oh, Ollie, I love it.

'Don't call me, Ollie!'

'Sorry, darling,' Abby cooed.

'She's been drinking,' William growled.

They watched in horror as the yacht lurched horribly to the left and seemed to buck and bob in the water and then settled and ploughed on, heading towards the reef . . . and the storm clouds.

'Please, Abby, darling, cut the engines and – '

'Huh, if I do I'll hit something for sure. Over and out, darlings. I need to concentrate for this bit. Call me later.'

The line went dead.

Oliver pounded the receiver with the heel of one hand but nothing.

In grim silence they watched and waited. Jess was twisting William's shirt front in her fingers, hardly daring to watch. What an earth had possessed Abby? What was the point of all this? They had all driven her over the edge and she had indeed flipped.

'Why?' William breathed, his face white with anxiety as he watched the yacht drawing further and further away, getting closer and closer to the reef.

'Anything, I'll do and say anything to get Abby out of this,' Jess murmured feverishly.

'You've done and said enough already,' Oliver growled at her.

'Enough, Oliver,' William warned without taking his eyes off the yacht.

They all watched anxiously for what seemed like hours and then Oliver excitedly yelled out. 'Oh, good girl!' He leapt a foot off the ground and punched the air with his clenched fist. 'She's through! She took that deep channel and she's through the reef. I love that girl! I'm going to marry her. Oh, boy, am I going to make her happy!'

He spoke into the receiver. 'Abby, darling, you've done it, sweetheart, you've done it! Marry me, sweetheart, you're my sort of girl!'

'Quit it, will you!' William ordered, the tension draining from his body. 'Tell her to cut the engines and drop anchor.'

'Cut the engines and drop anchor, Abby.'

'What is he, a parrot?' Jess muttered, anxiety making her say it. William knew and hugged her tightly to him.

Jess wasn't able to fully realize that William was still holding her fast to him. She vaguely recalled that he had called her darling but anguish fuzzed the memory. Later perhaps, when Abby was safe and back with them she would think about it. Oh, Abby, why had she done such a risky thing and what was she going to do now?

There was a crackle from the receiver and then, 'Cutting engines, dropping anchor. Oh, this is so easy. There's a button for everything. After this I'll be able to surf the Internet with you guys.'

'She is crazy,' William murmured.

'I'm swimming out to you, Abby,' Oliver was saying, already kicking off his espadrilles and loosening his shirt with his free hand. 'Stay where you are, I'm coming to get you.'

'No, Oliver!'

All three stilled at the change of her tone. No more jesting, Abby was deadly serious now.

'Now listen, all three of you. I can see you all, dotted on the jetty. You can't see me though, just the boat. I'm staying out here, holding myself hostage, so to speak. I can see the storm clouds approaching but the sea is still calm. It won't be for long. I reckon you've got about half an hour to get your act together and – '

'Abby!' Oliver cried anxiously.

'No, Oliver, listen, you're not here to give me a hug and make it all go away. All of you listen. Consider this a hostage situation. Should be easy to you boys, you've had enough experience of it. These are my terms. Jess, are you listening?'

'Yes,' Jess shouted. 'I'm listening.'

'Right. We all want the truth from you, not all those lies you've been telling to get your own back. Tell William you made it all up because I know you did and they don't. Kiss and make up, or whatever you two do together. Oliver, I'm not going to marry you unless they make it up so you had better make sure they do. OK, you've got half an hour. Wave something white when it's all settled. If you don't . . .'

She said no more and they all looked bleakly at each other. Jess's eyes filled with tears as she gazed at William. This was all her fault. She had driven her sister to this, such desperate measures.

'Oh, William,' she moaned, dropping her head to his chest. 'What have I done?' she cried helplessly.

'What have *I* done?' he repeated and hugged her fiercely.

Oliver was stripped down to his white boxer shorts now and was about to plunge off the edge of the jetty to swim out to the moored yacht when William reached out and caught his arm to restrain him.

For a second Jess thought Oliver was going to punch his brother's jaw, but William spoke before he could do it. 'Tell her it's all over and everything is settled. Jess and I are going to be married. Bring her back safely, because if you don't I'll punch your jaw.'

Oliver suddenly grinned at his brother and then he turned and took a dive into the water and started to swim strongly out to sea.

Jess gazed up at William, tears streaming down her face. She could hardly find her voice it was so choked with emotion. 'You . . . you would do that to save my sister?' she eventually croaked.

'Of course,' William told her gravelly.

It was then it all hit her and Jess stepped back

from him. She lifted a hand and brushed the tears from her face and bravely took control of her emotions. She raised her chin and looked at him.

'But saying it to save Abby is one thing, actually doing it another.' She shook her head dismissively. 'You won't marry me, William,' she told him bravely. 'After what I've done, you wouldn't and couldn't.'

William took her by the shoulders, his hands soothing the burning heat of the sun from her bare skin. 'Abby wants the truth. Those were her terms, for us to make up and for you to come up with the truth. I will marry you, if you meet your sister's terms.'

Jess shook her head again. 'You don't understand – '

'I understand that you lied to me.'

'And knowing that you will marry me for Abby's sake? No, William, you will only marry me for your own sake or nothing. You don't have to keep your word on this. We'll get Abby back safely and I'll go along with it for the sake of those two, Abby and Oliver, for however long it takes to get them settled. But we will never be married, because you don't love me.'

'I fell in love with you the first moment you threw a yellow cocktail down me,' he told her tenderly.

Jess shook his hands from her shoulders then and in a turmoil of anguish she tried to turn way from him. He would do and say anything to smooth over the anxiety of the moment and save her sister. Oliver gave Abby reassuring hugs to get out of a tight situation, William used empty words.

William caught her wrists to stall her. 'I know you love me too, Jess. Whatever Abby tells Oliver it all gets back to me. Sisters tell each other everything and brothers tell each other everything. But I didn't need to be told anyway, it was only confirmation of what I knew already.'

Oh, how she wanted to believe it all. But it was impossible. This was all for Abby, not for her at all. 'How . . . how could you love someone who is a thief and a hacker and planter of viruses?'

'You never did plant a virus, Jessica. It was a lie. You said it in a rage, to hurt me and to get back at me. There is no virus.'

'There is! I did it all before I left for New York!'

'How could you have done? You couldn't have used the E-mail message you left to download before meeting me in person.'

Jess's mouth dropped open.

William smiled at her. '"Call the ubiquitous Hooker", you couldn't have anticipated that before leaving for New York, whatever your plans to seduce me were in the first place. You let yourself down there and I knew you were lying. It made me think of all the other deceptions you have laid claim to.'

Of course, what a slip up. She had been so hurt and mad with him she had named the virus with the first thing that had come into her head, something she couldn't have done before New York.

'But the game and the hacking?'

'I was giving you time to be honest with me and even if you still claim to have done those things I'm still going to marry you. I love you, you see, criminal or not, I can't change how I feel about you.'

Jess's eyes filled with tears and suddenly all the tension drained from her leaving her feeling extremely weak and dazed.

'I . . . I have to sit down,' she whispered and crumpled down on the edge of the jetty. She dangled her feet in the water while William sat down next to her. For a while they gazed out to the yacht bobbing in the water offshore. They watched Oliver reach the boat and climb aboard. Neither spoke. They watched and waited and then heard three short blasts on the yacht's siren.

Jess let out a long breath of relief and then she smiled and turned to William and looked at him adoringly.

'OK, buster,' she laughed. 'Yes, I'm going to marry you. But first I'm going to tell you everything and there are terms of course.'

He grinned ruefully as he slid his arm round her shoulder and drew her to him. He kissed her deeply and passionately before murmuring, 'Another measly million?'

Jess kissed the tip of his arrogant nose. 'Keep your money. But just give me a promise that you will never tell Abby what I'm going to tell you.'

'I don't make promises I can't keep,' he warned her with a tender smile.

'You once said you didn't do apologies either, but you made an exception.'

'It all depends on what you are going to tell me.'

'Yes, I suppose,' she sighed and ran the tip of her tongue over her lower lip as she gazed out to sea. The boat was still. Oliver was making no attempt to bring the yacht in yet. They would be in each other's arms, making it all right between themselves before returning to shore. Abby would be happy, deliriously so and perhaps her happiness would help her understand. It would be best if Abby did know. There had been enough lies and deception to keep them all going for a hundred years or more.

'OK, I won't hold you to that promise,' Jess resigned. 'No more secrets, no more deception, but I want it to come from me and no one else. When we get back to England I'll find a way of telling her.'

'I think you'd better start by telling me first,' William whispered into her hair as he nuzzled her earlobe. 'But make it quick, darling, I'm beginning to feel the effects of a certain dangerous lady and you know how risk affects my libido.'

Jess laughed, the tension easing. It was a beautiful day in paradise and the storm clouds on the horizon were breaking up and misting away to a haze and she was in a haze of happiness because everything was going to be all right.

And as they wandered back to the villa, arms tightly around each other, Jess started to tell him everything and as she talked and William listened she realized she had made a storm in a teacup out of a molehill, or was it a mountain out of a teacup in a storm? But whatever, it wouldn't have been half the fun if she had come clean from the start. A simple life without complications of her own doing were as improbable as the dawn not rising every morning. She would try harder in the future though, because all said and done she'd suffered some dreadful heartache with this man, William Webber.

But not altogether her own fault. Her adorable, cranky father, had a lot to answer for. He was up there now, probably surfing the heavenly Internet, and in his eccentric innocence wondering what all the fuss was about.

The door intercom buzzed.

'William and Oliver Webber for Jessica and Abby Lambert,' Will said over the intercom.

'Oh, help,' Abby cried in panic. 'They're here already. Did I remember to chill the champagne? I hope that pasta turns out OK, it looked all right to you, didn't it? How does the table look, Jess?'

Jess flicked the door release to let the brothers in downstairs and took a last look at herself in the hall mirror before the men got up to the flat. 'Apart from the naff candles, it looks just perfect. Now stop panicking. What is more important how do *I* look?' She flicked at a loose tendril of fiery hair and then shrugged hopelessly. 'Hey, where's that photo of us that's usually on this table?'

'Here.' Abby told her, pulling out the drawer and putting the silver framed photo of the sisters back in its rightful place.

'What's it doing there?'

'Does it matter?' Abby sighed, remembering how she had hidden it, not wanting Jess to see her making a fool of herself with William Webber, but Oliver had turned up instead. She gazed warmly at the picture. 'Daddy took that picture. Do you remember, down at Brighton before he was ill, you two playing those horrible video games till you both nearly had fits?'

Jess laughed. 'Our father was born out of his time. Those things fascinated him. He should be a young man now. He'd be running Webbers' software and Will and Oliver wouldn't get a look in.'

'He practically did run Webbers', naughty boy,' Abby grinned ruefully.

'Daddy never did it with malice, or any bad intentions, Abby,' Jess told her sister seriously. 'You do understand that now?'

'Of course I do,' Abby said with a laugh. 'You explained everything to me. He didn't have a dangerous bone in his body. Not like his dangerous daughters.'

'He just did it for fun,' Jess reminded her. 'He hacked into all sorts of systems. Judging by his notebook, he probably hacked into NASA too. He was just curious, that was all. He never used any of the information he found, just happily surfed away for fun. Of course, what he shouldn't have done was take notes on that game of Oliver's, when it was in the early stages. I had no idea, as I explained to William and to you. It wasn't complete and I just finished it off from Daddy's notes and devised the rest. It was a complete coincidence that I came up with an identical conclusion to Oliver's.'

'Oliver is so clever,' Abby said proudly.

'Yes, I suppose he must be as clever as me,' Jess laughed, taking some of the glory for herself.

Jess looked at her sister earnestly. 'Are you happy, Abby?'

'Sublimely. And you?'

'Ecstastically so. Will has promised me a designer wedding dress. I'll feel just like a film star. I'm the happiest girl in the world,' she giggled helplessly.

They were both still laughing when Jess opened the door and reeled back at the sight of an enormous bunch of white lilies and huge sunflower heads, that sent her into a paroxysm of sneezing.

Oliver behind the bouquet gathered her into his arms and kissed her full on the lips.

'Hey, cut that out!' Abby shrieked. '*I'm* the sister you are going to marry next week.'

'I know that, darling,' Oliver, hiding behind the bouquet, laughed. 'It wasn't a lover's kiss, just a brother-in-lawly one.'

Will pulled Jess into his arms and, before exploding a lover's kiss on her lips he murmured. 'Can you bear a double wedding, with *him* standing next to us?'

When Jess got her breath back she laughed and said. 'I'd marry you if Quasimodo was your brother.'

'I'm starving,' Oliver said as he finally let Abby go.

Abby looked at Jess and raised her eyes skywards and they both laughed.

'I cooked the meal,' Abby volunteered proudly.

This time Oliver's eyes went skyward.

'No, honestly, Oliver, it's all right. Jess has been giving me lessons. Not only is she the best hacker in the world but the best cook. She's teaching me everything. Come and look at the pasta in the kitchen, it's perfect.'

'Is the crate of Dom Perignon in the fridge?' Will asked Jess with a knowing gleam in his eyes as his brother and future sister-in-law disappeared into the kitchen to inspect their official engagement meal.

'Oh, Will,' Jess laughed, linking her arms around his neck and looking up at him adoringly. 'Can you imagine what would have happened if I hadn't missed my flight back from New York and I'd been waiting here for you as planned. None of *this* would have happened.'

'Oh, yes it would. We would have fallen in love over the champagne, instead of the dry Martinis and Abby and Oliver would have met anyway. It was just a temporary diversion, a bit like Oliver's driving skills. We all got there in the end.'

'I love you, William Webber,' Jess murmured happily, eyes glittering with happiness.

'I love you too, the ubiquitous dangerous lady,' he grinned.

'Dinner's up!' Abby called out.

'Probably will be later,' Jess muttered under her breath. 'It's no good Will, you are going to have to tell your brother that my sister will never make Cordon Bleu standards.'

'She won't have too. We have staff to do all that.'

Jess hugged him tightly before they went in to join the others. 'That's what I love about you, Will. You have style and a load of dosh too. You've made an out-of-work dangerous lady very happy.'

'And you've made a millionaire playboy very happy.'

And as they stood in the doorway of the dining room, arms around each other, watching Abby and Oliver kissing by the window, Jess thought she had never been happier.

'It's a funny old world, isn't it?' William whispered to her and Jess wiped a tear of happiness from her eye.

EPILOGUE

'That Venetian Crosspatch friend of yours was right,' Jess moaned plaintively to Will as she surveyed herself in the full length bedroom mirror. She was naked, turning this way and that, not quite believing what she was seeing. 'She said I'd turn to fat, sooner rather than later.'

Jess scooped her mass of fiery hair off her shoulders, into a pile on the top of her head, to see if it made any difference and she might, by a small miracle, have shed a stone or two by merely sweeping all her hair up. Not a bit of difference. She was still as huge as ever.

Will flung aside a computer magazine lay back against the pillows and grinned at his adorable wife who, to his eyes, had never looked lovelier. 'You're not fat, darling,' he reassured her tenderly, 'just incubating our baby, till it's time to hatch.'

Jess turned and playfully scowled at him. 'I'm not a bantam chicken, you know.'

'No, you're not that,' Will laughed teasingly. 'Bantams are a *small* variety of fowl.'

369

'Funny, ha, ha, Will,' Jess reprimanded lightly and gazed back into the mirror. She ran her hands over the huge mound in front of her and relished the tingles of excitement that rushed through her skin. It never ceased to amaze her, the way she just grew and grew like some marvellous, magical pumpkin. She sighed with deep contentment – well she couldn't grow anymore. She was full term her consultant had told her this very morning. The baby would be born any minute now. Then he had grinned at her and asked if it wasn't about time she came clean with her husband and told him the truth.

No way. Marriage to William "Mr fantastic Webber" hadn't changed her. She was still the impulsive, deceptive risk taker she always had been. Will would know her dark secret soon enough but, at the moment, he didn't know the half of it and that was the way she wanted it.

'Do you think it will happen tonight?' she sighed wistfully, peering at herself to see if there were any giveaway signs. Like her tummy button suddenly appearing up by her nose. It had happened to a friend of hers. All of a sudden the girl's waistline had popped up even higher, if that was possible, because the baby had moved . . . An hour later it had been born. Jess hoped her own labour was going to be as easy, not that it would make any difference if it wasn't. She'd vowed she wasn't going to be a martyr and suffer. She was going to have the works as far as a painless birth was concerned. Supporting the bump and exaggeratedly thrusting it forward, she waddled over to the bed to join Will, humming the "Jaws" theme as she progressed across the carpet.

Will couldn't stop laughing, as he rather clumsily gathered her into his arms when she flopped down beside him.

'I love you, Jess Webber,' he sighed, nuzzling her hair. 'You look as if you are carrying a baby elephant, instead of our tiny sprog but I love you all the same. And that elephant might come tonight, if we follow the midwife's advice and do what got you into this mess in the first place.' Jess linked her arms around his neck and laughed happily. 'How can you possibly still fancy me when I'm this size?' she teased.

'Easily,' he told her and proved it, by kissing her deeply and longingly. Then he drew back from her and gazed lovingly into her eyes. 'But perhaps a bit of restraint, seeing as you *are* so close, might be prudent,' he whispered regretfully.

'Spoilsport,' Jess giggled. 'Hey, what are you doing?'

Will had rolled away from her to pick up the bedside phone. 'Just calling Oliver, to see if he's all right.'

Jess snatched the phone from him, after he had punched out the number of his brother's and Abby's new mansion, which had just been completed, on the edge of the Brooklands estate. After the double wedding earlier in the year, the happy couples had inhabited their own wings at Brooklands, until Oliver and Abby had moved out two months ago.

'Blow Oliver,' Jess reproached. 'What about Abby? It's her having the baby, not Oliver.'

'Tell my brother that,' Will said reproachfully.

Jess grinned as she waited for someone to answer the phone. 'He has rather gone over the top with this fatherhood business,' she agreed. 'He's read all the books, done all the classes. I caught him practising panting with Abby this afternoon. Both of them sitting cross legged on that Turkish rug in the middle of the drawing-room, panting like a couple of labradors.'

'It wouldn't have done you any harm to join them, Jess. You've done nothing to prepare for the birth of our baby,' Will remonstrated, tenderly smoothing his hands over her bump.

'I sure have,' Jess protested. 'I've arranged the best medical care, with every pain killer known to man. No way am I going through any natural childbirth thingy like Abby. It's the works for me. The first twinge and I shall insist on being anaesthetized from the neck downwards and . . . There's no-one answering, Will,' Jess said worriedly. 'They must be on the way to the clinic. You don't think she's beaten me to it?'

Will took the phone from her. 'Of course not. They would have called before leaving but if they forgot in the heat of the moment, the answer phone would be on any-way. Oliver, there you are. Why so long answering? Is everything all right?' he asked worriedly.

Jess hauled herself up onto her knees, pulled a peach coloured silk peignoir around her shoulders and pressed her ear to the phone, next to Will's ear. She clearly heard a wearisome sigh from her brother-in-law.

'She's concocting some Bacchanalian feast at the moment. Some sort of vegetable melle, ratatouille, she calls it, though it looks more like ratsbane to me. Oh and tagliatelle – '

'Fettuccine!' Abby called out cheerily in the background.

Both Will and Jess clutched at their stomachs to held back the laughter.

Oliver sighed again and went on seriously. 'It's nearly time, Will. Dr Zabinski, you know, author of *Natural Childbirth for the Nineties*, says it's an early sign, wanting to eat and eat. It goes back to the cave dwellers, stoking up in case there is no food available after the birth and – '

'Yes, all right, Oliver,' Will interrupted with good humour, Jess clinging to him, still shaking with laughter. 'I don't want the potted history of man at this time of night. I just wanted to know if everything is OK.'

'Fine, just tickety boo with Abby. She's happy as a lark.' He lowered his voice. 'I'm feeling a bit queasy myself though, Will. Nerves I suppose. I've never done this before.'

Jess raised her eyes skywards and Will grinned at her in silent conspiracy.

'Just get her to the clinic in plenty of time and they will look after the both of you, Oliver,' he advised his brother.

'Any signs with Jess?' Oliver asked

Jess shook her head.

'No, nothing yet. We're in bed, which is where you should be. How you can eat at this time of night I don't know!'

'I doubt I *will* be eating,' Oliver whispered down the phone. 'Darling Abby's cooking skills haven't improved, Will, and she absolutely refuses to take on a cook. Thank God we're breast-feeding this baby. At least one of us is guaranteed a good meal in the future,' he said ruefully. 'I'll call you if anything happens.'

Jess clung to Will, giggling softly as he put down the receiver. 'Oh, Will, your brother makes me laugh so much. *We* are breast feeding the baby. He'll faint, you know, when the baby starts to come. The first squall from Abby and he'll pass out at her feet.'

Still laughing they snuggled down into the bed together, Will wrapping his arms protectively around her more than ample curves.

'Do you reckon there's anything in that eating business?' he mused as Jess dreamily closed her eyes against his shoulder. 'You know, it being an early sign that the baby is on the way?'

'Shouldn't think so,' she murmured lazily.

'Probably just an old wives' tale.'

'Aren't you just a teeny bit hungry?' Will enquired earnestly.

Jess smiled and manoeuvred a shapely leg across Will's. He couldn't wait to hold his first born in his arms. 'Actually, come to think of it, I might be able to manage a caviar sandwich. Brown bread, with a dollop of tomato ketchup.'

'Heathen,' he murmured, as he disentangled himself and swung his legs out of bed. 'Tomato ketchup indeed!'

Jess reached for him, caught his arm and pulled him back into bed. 'I was only joking,' she laughed. 'Do something really worthwhile and massage my back instead.' She lay on her side, because to lie on her front was impossible.

Tenderly, Will started to caress the base of her spine and then she felt his warm, loving lips on the back of her neck. 'You know what usually happens when one or other of us starts this massaging lark,' he murmured softly in her ear.

'Yeah, that was the idea behind the suggestion,' she giggled and then his mouth was hard on hers and suddenly they were wrapped in each others' arms and discovering yet another new position to exploit, in the pursuit of a sensual pleasure that carried them both dreamily into a heavy sleep.

'Honestly, Oliver, it isn't half bad,' Abby reasoned. 'Try some. I followed the recipe right through – '

375

'Yes, but did you have the book open on the right page?' Oliver queried, suspiciously prodding the pasta as they both leaned over the cooker, surveying her latest culinary effort

'Try it, darling,' Abby grinned, holding a forkful from the pan up to his lips. 'And don't squeeze your eyes tight like that,' she shrieked. '*I have* improved.'

'Hhm, it's not bad, not bad at all,' he uttered in relief and surprise.

'Sure you're not just saying that?'

'Hand-on-heart. Would I lie to you?'

'Huh, who would know with you!' Abby retorted.

Oliver gathered her into his arms before they dished up the meal, and held her as close as he could under the circumstances. 'Didn't we make a promise to each other on the island, before returning to the UK, no more deception and lies between us?'

Abby buried her face in the warm cashmere of the front of his sweater, so he wouldn't see her guilt. Oh, dear, nothing had changed since that paradise island. Here were she and Jess, carrying the Webber brothers' babies and living yet another deception. All Jess's idea of course. Somehow Jess had convinced Abby that it was a good idea. Another deception to keep the brothers on their toes. Funny, but several months ago, Abby, too, had thought the idea amusing, now guilt was thrumming through her. She wasn't very good at this, being secretive, Jess was brilliant at it.

She didn't suffer from pangs of guilt. She couldn't even see that the shock might be too much for Oliver and Will and it might put both their marriages into serious jeopardy. 'But they love us,' Jess had reasoned, 'and love conquers all.' So Abby had been persuaded and was going along with it, at times very reluctantly.

Now was one of those times. Oh, she so badly wanted to tell Oliver, now before it was too late. But it already was too late. These last few months had been a revelation to Abby. She had learned something new about Oliver. Well, not exactly new, because she already knew that he would do anything to protect her but this baby business had somehow quadrupled it all. He was obsessive about her, deliciously so, but, all the same, *obsessive*. He wouldn't let her do a thing for herself. He wanted the staff to do it all and it had taken Abby ages to convince him that being pregnant wasn't an illness but a condition, a condition she was happy to be in. She'd finally persuaded him not to make such a fuss, but she wanted to do it all right and then, when he had insisted on going through every stage with her, baby classes, relaxation, reading all the latest books on childbirth and parenting, taking out subscriptions to all those mother and baby mags, she realized he would be worse if he knew the truth. So for Oliver, ignorance was bliss for the moment.

Yes, Jess was right, the deception, this time, was right.

She eased back from him and looked up into his worried face. She lifted her hands and smoothed his face reassuringly. 'I love you, Oliver. Soon it will all be over and you can stop worrying.'

'I'm worried now,' Oliver said, white-faced and pale-lipped. 'I can't feel the baby moving.' He ran his hands over the bulge again.

Abby laughed, slapped his hands away and turned back to the pans and started scooping out the fettuccine. 'Babies don't move so much in the last stages. There's not enough room and besides – '

'They are conserving their strength for the actual birth,' Oliver finished for her, remembering and looking relieved.

'Yes, darling, if you say so,' Abby murmured as she dished up their supper.

They sat down to eat in the kitchen, a smaller replica of the Brooklands' kitchen. She had loved that kitchen so much, she had wanted one built on the same lines in their new home. Of course, their kitchen was smaller, because they didn't have a housekeeper, or so many staff as Will and Jess. Abby wouldn't have any staff at all, if she had her way but Oliver had insisted on a couple of dailies. Mim and Janet came up from the village every day and Abby always had the coffee pot on for them. Mim read tea leaves and the Tarot cards and they screamed with laughter as they sat at the kitchen table. If Oliver was at home he sometimes got cross with them all, but in a good natured way.

They didn't need a chauffeur of their own, though Eric, the brothers' personal driver, who had been with the Webbers for years (and was the same collar size as Oliver) still sufficed for the two brothers' business journeys. Abby drove herself around, in a fabulous white Mercedes with alloy wheels, and often over to Jess's where she would inevitably find her sister working in the super study Will had had converted for her, and equipped with all the latest computer equipment.

'Oh, I can't eat another mouthful,' Abby sighed, leaning back to stretch out her aching spine.

'I think this late stage of our pregnancy has definitely improved your cooking skills, sweetheart,' Oliver told her with a warm smile of contentment. 'We'll have to cancel our account down at the Chinese takeaway.'

Abby laughed. 'Don't you dare. When this is over,' she patted her tum, 'I'll be so rushed off my feet, I won't have time to cook.'

'I'll do it then. I'm determined to give every support.'

And, much as she loved her wonderful husband she knew she didn't exactly want him under her feet morning, noon and night, fussing around her. He really was taking this new man business too far. It made her feel better about her deception, less guilty. When he found out, he just might not find the idea of being on call every minute of the day quite so enrapturing.

Oliver stood up and came round the table to her.

He planted a kiss on her forehead. 'Now, you go up to bed and I'll clear away.'

'No, Oliver,' Abby insisted as she pulled herself up on to her feet and grinned happily at her husband, as he took her in his arms. 'We are going up, together, because we have staff coming in in the morning and you are always telling me to let them get on with their work.'

'Good idea,' Oliver grinned and planted another kiss on her nose. 'I'll follow you up when I've checked the alarms. Now take it easy up those stairs, or would you rather wait and let me carry you up?'

Abby playfully pushed him away. 'Not on your life. Even you haven't got the strength to throw me over your shoulder as you did that time you and Will threw us Lamberts into the generator room on fantasy island, as Jess calls it.'

'Ah, those were the days,' he uttered ruefully, as he went out of the kitchen door.

Once he had gone, Abby slumped down into the kitchen chair and bit her knuckles, just as Jess had done after punching the two brothers on the jaw that day. Oh, strewth, it hurt. The pain in her back throbbed hotly. She lifted her chin bravely though. No one had ever convinced her that it wasn't going to hurt, but she had done all the right things and it was going to be easy peasy. Oliver was the problem, though. She couldn't tell him yet that her labour had started. Must have been something she had added to the ratatouille. Two mouthfuls and the pain in her back had started to thrum. But it was far too early to tell Oliver. He would only panic and fuss and want to whisk her off to the clinic immediately. Labour took forever. She'd much rather be in the safety and warm elegant comfort of her own home for a few hours more.

Determinedly, she got up and waddled to the door, switching off the lights as she went. Soon the deception would be over. She felt a thrill of excitement at the thought of the Webber brothers' shock and amazement that the Lambert girls had fooled them once again.

Jess awoke in the early hours of the morning and knew that things had started to happen. It wasn't the pain she had expected, more a dull ache in the back. She lay next to a sleeping Will for a while and thought about all that was to come. Maybe she should have joined Abby in her relaxation classes, though she felt perfectly relaxed now, not panicking at all as she'd thought she might.

Perhaps it was a cop out to demand all those pain killers. Perhaps she ought to go for a natural birth, as Abby was doing. She'd wait and see how things went. Another few hours and she might be screaming for mercy and be grateful for an armful of morphine, or whatever they used these days.

She lay for a while, holding her huge bump, and thought about her darling father. Not sad thoughts, just nice soft warm thoughts, because, if it wasn't for him, she wouldn't be where she was now, about to give birth to the next generation of computer hackers and married to the most wonderful man in the world. Yes, nice warm thoughts, happy memories, tinged with just a tiny bit of sadness that he wasn't here to share her happiness.

'Darling, what are you doing? It's four o'clock in the morning.' Will asked sleepily, heaving himself up onto one elbow, as Jess rummaged through one of her wardrobes.

'I'm looking for that Chanel dress you bought me before I got fat. The one with the gilt buttons right down the front. I hope I can still get into it when it's time to leave the clinic. I suppose I might be pushing my luck a bit, but I might be able to squeeze into it. I could always – '

'Christ, Jess. The baby's coming, isn't it?' He leapt out of bed and nearly ricocheted off the bedside table.

Jess grinned at him widely and held her arms out to him, when he reached her. 'It's all right. Don't panic.' She slid her arms around his neck. 'Yes, darling the baby is coming. Now, listen. Don't phone Eric, not at this time of the night. *You* can drive us to the clinic. Phone Abby and Oliver. They'll be sleeping, but leave a message and – '

'Yes, yes, I know what to do,' Will growled and then his mouth widened into a grin. 'Oh, Jess, you are so wonderful. I was convinced you'd be screaming at the top of your voice at the first twinge.'

'Give me time,' Jess laughed.

She caught hold of his arm as he turned to the phone. 'Darling,' she said seriously, her eyes wide. 'You do love me, don't you?'

'Darling, I worship the ground you flatten beneath your feet.'

Jess laughed, but it hurt to laugh. 'Promise me you'll still love me when this is all over. Promise me you will forgive this last deception of mine.'

Will looked at her strangely. 'What do you mean?'

Jess lowered her lashes. Perhaps she had gone too far this time. Perhaps she should have told him. She looked at him then and her eyes sparkled mischievously. 'You'll find out soon enough,' she murmured and then the first serious contraction hit her and her face crumpled with pain and Will was holding her *and* supporting her and she clung to him, needing him more than she had ever needed anyone in her life before.

Two hours later Jess was writhing in agony in the delivery room of the private clinic Will had driven her too. She was desperately trying not to scream too loudly, for fear of upsetting Will. Will held her hand, smoothed her brow and whispered encouragement. He was such a tower of strength, Jess loved him even more if that were possible.

And then it was happening. The pain and the joy and the sheer bloody hard work. There were three midwives on hand and Jess's consultant, who strutted around the room getting in everyones' way and who tutt tutted throughout the delivery, and Will's personal physician who Jess had mysteriously insisted on being there.

And he was needed, for when William Webber's second daughter was born, three minutes after his first, he passed out at the foot of the bed!

'Don't be silly, Oliver. I won't hear of you calling Eric out to drive us to the clinic. The limo is in the garage, so you can drive us.'

Of course, as soon as she said it, Abby wondered if she was tempting fate. But she couldn't expect the chauffeur to come out at four o'clock in the morning. Anyway, she knew the route well enough and so did Oliver. He had always accompanied her for her check-ups. And on an important occasion such as this, he wouldn't dare get lost.

'Breath deeply, darling. In and out and in and out and – '

'Shut up, Oliver,' Abby laughed, partly to hide her pain from him. She had a ghastly feeling she had left it too long. The contractions were coming fast and furious now.

Oliver tucked her up in the back of the limo, fussing and placing a huge cashmere blanket round her knees. It was pouring with rain, so visiblity was limited and Abby closed her eyes and wished she had been sensible and told Oliver sooner.

She blinked open her eyes, after a few minutes

of driving. She remembered a short-cut to the clinic, from when there had been roadworks on the main road. They needed that short-cut, *like now.*

'Oliver!' Abby cried, squirming under the blanket. 'Take the next left, Oliver.'

'No, darling,' Oliver laughed over the intercom, not realizing her urgency. 'I know the way. Trust me. You're just a bit confused. Relax and do your breathing.'

'Oliver!' Abby screamed now. 'Do as I say! It's quicker. Oh, darling, please hurry!'

After a quick look in the rear view mirror Oliver got the message. He swung into the next left turning, foot hard down on the accelerator, face grave with worry. Sixty seconds later he brought the limo to a shooshing halt – in a dead end.

'Oh, hell,' Abby moaned, 'Wrong turning. I could have sworn . . . Oh, hurry, Oliver.'

Like a bat out of hell Oliver reversed back up the lane, cursing under his breath, in between instructing Abby to pant.

Panting was the last thing on Abby's mind. She wanted to scream not pant!

'Nearly there, sweetheart. Hold on darling, hold on. Oh, Lord, there's a police car behind us. I'm speeding. To hell with them!'

The limo swung into the the driveway of the clinic, with a siren blaring police car in hot pursuit. Oliver took one last glance at Abby, in the rear view mirror, as he screamed to a halt in front of the clinic and then he lent heavily on the horn to summon help from within, before leaping out into the pouring rain and wrenching open the rear door of the limo.

The two traffic police were out of their car too and trying to arrest Oliver, but he manhandled them aside and leapt into the spacious interior of the back of the car, just in time to deliver his first born, on the thick pile carpet of the plush Rolls Royce.

'Oh, darling,' Abby panted, lying back and trying to think of England. 'I've . . . I've some . . . something to tell you.'

'Not now, darling,' Oliver ground out, working feverishly, just as he had learned from the video. 'Just another small push, darling, nice and easy.'

'No, now!' Abby screamed and panted and panted for all her worth.

'Oh, darling, we have a baby girl,' Oliver shouted triumphantly, 'a beautiful baby girl.'

'No, darling,' Abby cried in anguish and pushed as hard as she could. 'Two, darling, there's two of them.'

'Bloody hell!' were the last two words Abby heard in unison from the two police officers, before everything went black and hazy.

'Congratulations you two,' the midwife grinned at William and Oliver Webber as they sat hunched in the waiting room, waiting while the rest of the medical team checked over their daughters and their wives. A bottle of champagne sat in an ice bucket, on the table in front of them, but both men were too shocked to pour it.

'Special congratulations to you,' she directed at Oliver, 'delivering both babies so expertly. And, Mr Webber, how are you feeling now?' she asked of William. 'You gave us all a fright passing out like that.'

Oliver turned a white face to his brother and a small smile lightened his face.

'You didn't?' he breathed in shocked amusement.

Will couldn't look at his younger brother. He waved a hand, dismissively.

'Don't worry,' the midwife reassured him, with a twinkle in her eye. 'You weren't the first father to faint and you won't be the last. Now, when you feel up to it, you can go in and see your wives and babies. They are quite adorable, the babies, I mean.' She sighed. 'You'll have your hands full with your wives, though. What a couple of schemers. They both swore us here at the clinic to secrecy. Did you honestly not know they were both expecting twins?'

William and Oliver didn't say a single word. Both stared at the champagne as if it held the secret of life.

'In your own good time then,' the midwife said as she breezed efficiently away, leaving them with their thoughts.

Will was the first to move. He reached for the

387

bottle and poured the wine into two flutes, then a wide grin spread across his face, as he handed his brother one of the glasses.

'Jess will pay for this, of course. I shall halve her dress allowance and cancel her credit cards. I'll dismiss the staff and ball and chain her to the kitchen sink for the rest of her life.'

Oliver grinned. 'You'll do nothing of the sort. She gets away with murder with you. You're tickled pink, if the truth be known.'

Will smiled wanly. 'I am, but I don't think I've ever been so shocked in my life.'

'Me too,' Oliver agreed. 'Twins. I'm the father of twin girls,' he uttered in disbelief.

'And the *uncle* of twin girls,' Will added ruefully.

'You too.'

Will nodded. 'To my reckoning, that makes six of those Lamberts to contend with for the rest of our lives. Six dangerous Lambert ladies.'

'Webbers,' Oliver corrected, warming to the champagne now.

'Yes, that's a point,' Will mused. 'They are all Webbers. Think of the collective brain power. We could take over the computer world!'

'We already have,' Oliver told him.

They both grinned and got to their feet.

'How are you feeling, brother?' Will asked Oliver.

Oliver proudly puffed his expansive chest out even further and held aloft his champagne glass.

'Just about on top of the world, Will. Here's to our dangerous ladies, bless their treacherous little hearts.'

They both drained their glasses, then Will gathered up the champagne bucket and glasses and they went along the corridor to the room where the girls were resting and waiting.

Abby and Jess were sitting up in their beds when the men opened the door. Both women grinning sheepishly and yet glowing with pride and loveliness. Their baby girls were tucked into their arms, all beautiful, dark-haired, tiny replicas of their handsome fathers.

'It was all Jess's idea,' Abby whispered to Oliver, as he gathered her and the babies into his arms. 'I went along with it, because I thought you might panic even more if you knew there were two coming. But, darling you wouldn't have panicked, would you? Oh, Oliver, you were so wonderful, such a wonderful hero. You handled everything so beautifully. I couldn't have done it without your strength. I do love you so. And I want millions more babies and I pray you don't get a speeding ticket.'

They clung to each other.

'I suppose this was all your idea?' Will breathed into Jess's hair as he clasped her and his lovely daughters to him. 'I don't know what I'm going to do with you. You're quite, quite, incorrigible.'

'But you adore me, nevertheless,' Jess murmured happily, knowing he did and knowing he would forgive her anything. But never again would she deceive him. She was a responsible mother now and she was determined to be a good one. She'd have the girls surfing the Internet before they could walk.

'Yes, I adore you,' Will breathed happily, 'But be warned, if ever you pull a stroke like that again – '

'You'll do what?' Jess tempted lightly, moving her hand up to secure his chin, so she could kiss him deeply on the mouth.

After she released him, he looked down into her lovely green eyes. 'I'll do what I always do when you wind me up,' he whispered lovingly. 'You'll be back in here this time next year.'

'And the next *and* the next *and* the next.' Jess laughed happily.

And then there was silence in the pink room, as all gazed down in wonderment at the new generation of tiny, perfect, Lambert-Webbers. Four more dangerous ladies to turn the world of the computer tycoons upside down! And the computer tycoons would love it!

THE EXCITING NEW NAME IN WOMEN'S FICTION!

PLEASE HELP ME TO HELP YOU!

Dear *Scarlet* Reader,

As Editor of *Scarlet* Books I want to make sure that the books I offer you every month are up to the high standards *Scarlet* readers expect. And to do that I need to know a little more about you and your reading likes and dislikes. So please spare a few minutes to fill in the short questionnaire on the following pages and send it to me. I'll send *you* a surprise gift as a thank you!

Looking forward to hearing from you,

Sally Cooper

Editor-in-Chief, *Scarlet*

QUESTIONNAIRE

Please tick the appropriate boxes to indicate your answers

1 Where did you get this Scarlet title?
Bought in Supermarket ☐
Bought at W H Smith or other High St bookshop ☐
Bought at book exchange or second-hand shop ☐
Borrowed from a friend ☐
Other _____

2 Did you enjoy reading it?
A lot ☐   A little ☐   Not at all ☐

3 What did you particularly like about this book?
Believable characters ☐   Easy to read ☐
Good value for money ☐   Enjoyable locations ☐
Interesting story ☐   Modern setting ☐
Other _____

4 What did you particularly dislike about this book?
_____

5 Would you buy another Scarlet book?
Yes ☐   No ☐

6 What other kinds of book do you enjoy reading?
Horror ☐   Puzzle books ☐   Historical fiction ☐
General fiction ☐   Crime/Detective ☐   Cookery ☐
Other _____

7 Which magazines do you enjoy most?
Bella ☐   Best ☐   Woman's Weekly ☐
Woman and Home ☐   Hello ☐   Cosmopolitan ☐
Good Housekeeping ☐
Other _____

cont.

And now a little about you –

8 How old are you?

Under 25 ☐   25–34 ☐   35–44 ☐
45–54 ☐   55–64 ☐   over 65 ☐

9 What is your marital status?

Single ☐   Married/living with partner ☐
Widowed ☐   Separated/divorced ☐

10 What is your current occupation?

Employed full-time ☐   Employed part-time ☐
Student ☐   Housewife full-time ☐
Unemployed ☐   Retired ☐

11 Do you have children? If so, how many and how old are they?

_____

_____

12 What is your annual household income?

under £10,000 ☐   £10–20,000 ☐   £20–30,000 ☐
£30–40,000 ☐   over £40,000 ☐

Miss/Mrs/Ms _____

Address _____

_____

_____

Thank you for completing this questionnaire. Now tear it out – put it in an envelope and send it before 31 December 1996, to:

Sally Cooper, Editor-in-Chief

SCARLET
FREEPOST LON 3335
LONDON W8 4BR
Please use block capitals for address.
No stamp is required!

DALAD/6/96

Scarlet titles coming next month:

MARRY ME STRANGER Kay Gregory
Being newly married is difficult enough, but when the couple concerned are strangers . . . difficult becomes impossible! At first, though, it seems that Brand and Isabelle will make their marriage work, until, that is, real life intervenes . . .

A QUESTION OF TRUST Margaret Callaghan
Billie is everything Travis Kent claims to despise in a women: she's an impetuous tomboy, who lives in a ramshackle cottage with a mischievous cat. Throw in Travis' suspicious fiancée and the outcome is anyone's guess. But one thing is certain . . . passion is the most important ingredient!

DECEPTION Sophie Weston
Ash believes that _all_ men should be treated as enemies, Jake has other ideas: he wants something from Ash . . . something she isn't prepared to give! Jake sets out to melt her resistance and, against her will, Ash begins to turn into the sensual woman she was always meant to be . . . until she remembers the saying 'Once bitten, twice shy!'

IT TAKES TWO Tina Leonard
No woman has ever dared to refuse Zach Rayez . . . particularly when he decides he wants something! So when Annie says 'no', Zach is determined to win his battle of the sexes with this feisty lady. Annie can't believe that a successful man like Zach is interested in a country mouse like her, but if he isn't, why does he keep finding reasons not to leave her?